# "I want to kiss you."

"That's a bad idea," Tasha said

"Why?" Matt asked.

"The signature on my paycheck. Besides, I'm not that kind of girl."

"The kind that kisses men?"

"The kind that randomly kisses men, while I'm working, in an engine room, covered in grease."

"So, are there any circumstances under which you'd agree to kiss me? Maybe if we left the engine room? Perhaps if you washed off the grease?"

"Nice try."

"I thought so."

"You're just not used to hearing the word no."

"You're right. It makes you even more attractive to me. Now I'm hoping against hope that you'll admit you're attracted to me."

A flush came up on her cheeks. "We both know you struck out."

"Maybe. But this is only the first inning. In fact, let's call it batting practice."

\* \* \*

**Twelve Nights of Temptation**
is part of the Whiskey Bay Brides series:
Three friends find love on the shores of Whiskey Bay.

# TWELVE NIGHTS OF TEMPTATION

BY
BARBARA DUNLOP

First Published in Great Britain 2017
By Mills & Boon, an imprint of HarperCollins*Publishers*
1 London Bridge Street, London, SE1 9GF

© 2017 Barbara Dunlop

ISBN: 978-0-263-92844-0

51-1117

Our policy is to use papers that are natural, renewable and recyclable products and made from wood grown in sustainable forests. The logging and manufacturing processes conform to the legal environmental regulations of the country of origin.

Printed and bound in Spain
by CPI, Barcelona

*New York Times* and *USA TODAY* bestselling author **Barbara Dunlop** has written more than forty novels for Mills & Boon, including the acclaimed Chicago Sons series for Mills & Boon Desire. Her sexy, lighthearted stories regularly hit bestseller lists. Barbara is a three-time finalist for the Romance Writers of America's RITA® Award.

# For Jane Porter

# One

A banging on Tasha Lowell's bedroom door jarred her awake. It was midnight in the Whiskey Bay Marina staff quarters, and she'd been asleep for less than an hour.

"Tasha?" Marina owner Matt Emerson's voice was a further jolt to her system, since she'd been dreaming about him.

"What is it?" she called out, then realized he'd never hear her sleep-croaky voice. "What?" she called louder as she forced herself from beneath the covers.

It might be unseasonably warm on the Pacific Northwest coast, but it was still December, the holiday season, and the eight-unit staff quarters building had been around since the '70s.

"*Orca's Run* broke down off Tyree, Oregon."

"What happened?" she asked reflexively as she crossed the cold wooden floor on her bare feet. Even as she said the words, she knew it was a foolish question. Wealthy, urbane Matt Emerson wouldn't know an injector pump from an alternator.

She swung the door open, coming face-to-face with the object of what she suddenly remembered had been a very R-rated dream.

"The engine quit. Captain Johansson says they're anchored in the bay."

This was very bad news. Tasha had been chief mechanic at Whiskey Bay Marina for less than two weeks, and she knew Matt had hesitated in giving her the promotion. He'd be right to hold her responsible for not noticing a problem with *Orca's Run*'s engine or not anticipating some kind of wear and tear.

"I serviced it right before they left." She knew how important this particular charter was to the company.

*Orca's Run* was a ninety-foot yacht, the second largest in the fleet. It had been chartered by Hans Reinstead, an influential businessman out of Munich. Matt had recently spent considerable effort and money getting a toehold in the European market, and Hans was one of his first major clients. The last thing Whiskey Bay Marina needed was for the Reinstead family to have a disappointing trip.

Tasha grabbed the red plaid button-down shirt she'd discarded on a chair and put it on over her T-shirt. Then she stepped into a pair of heavy cargo pants, zipping them over her flannel shorts.

Matt watched her progress as she popped a cap on top of her braided hair. Socks and work boots took her about thirty seconds, and she was ready.

"That's it?" he asked.

"What?" She didn't understand the question.

"You're ready to go?"

She glanced down at herself, then looked back into the dim bedroom. "I'm ready." The necessities that most women carried in a purse were in the zipped pockets of her pants.

For some reason, he gave a crooked smile. "Then let's go."

"What's funny?" she asked as she fell into step beside him.

"Nothing."

They started down the wooden walkway that led to the Whiskey Bay Marina pier.

"You're laughing," she said.

"I'm not."

"You're laughing at me." Did she look that bad rolling straight out of bed? She rubbed her eyes, lifted her cap to smooth her hair and tried to shake some more sense into her brain.

"I'm smiling. It's not the same thing."

"I've amused you." Tasha hated to be amusing. She

wanted people, especially men, *especially* her employer, to take her seriously.

"You impressed me."

"By getting dressed?"

"By being efficient."

She didn't know what to say to that. It wasn't quite sexist…maybe…

She let it drop.

They went single file down the ramp with him in the lead.

"What are we taking?" she asked.

*"Monty's Pride."*

The answer surprised her. *Monty's Pride* was the biggest yacht in the fleet, a 115-footer, refurbished last year to an impeccably high standard. It was obvious what Matt intended to do.

"Do you think we'll need to replace *Orca's Run*?" She'd prefer to be optimistic and take the repair boat instead. *Monty's Pride* would burn an enormous amount of fuel getting to Tyree. "There's a good chance I can fix whatever's gone wrong."

"And if you can't?"

"What did the captain say happened?" She wasn't ready to admit defeat before they'd even left the marina.

"That it quit."

It was a pathetic amount of information.

"Did it stop all of a sudden?" she asked. "Did it slow? Was there any particular sound, a smell? Was there smoke?"

"I didn't ask."

"You should have asked."

Matt shot her a look of impatience, and she realized she'd stepped over the line. He was her boss after all.

"I'm just thinking that taking *Monty's Pride* is a whole lot of fuel to waste," she elaborated on her thinking. "We can save the money if I can do a quick repair."

"We're not even going to try a quick repair. I'll move the

passengers and crew over to *Monty's Pride* while you fix whatever's gone wrong."

Tasha hated that her possible negligence would cost the company so much money. "Maybe if I talk to the captain on the radio."

"I don't want to mess around, Tasha." Matt punched in the combination for the pier's chain-link gate and swung it open.

"I'm not asking you to mess around. I'm suggesting we explore our options. *Monty's Pride* burns a hundred gallons an hour."

"My priority is customer service."

"This is expensive customer service."

"Yes, it is."

His tone was flat, and she couldn't tell if he was angry or not.

She wished she was back in her dream. Matt had been so nice in her dream. They'd been warm, cocooned together, and he'd been joking, stroking her hair, kissing her mouth.

*Wait. No.* That was bad. That wasn't what she wanted at all.

"I want Hans Reinstead to go back to Germany a happy man," Matt continued. "I want him to rave to his friends and business associates about the over-the-top service he received, even when there was a problem. Whether we fix it in five minutes or five hours is irrelevant. They had a breakdown, and we upgraded them. People love an upgrade. So much so, that they're generally willing to gloss over the reason for getting it."

Tasha had to admit it was logical. It was expensive, but it was also logical.

Matt might be willing to take the financial hit in the name of customer service, but if it turned out to be something she'd missed, it would be a black mark against her.

They approached the slip where *Monty's Pride* was moored. A crew member was on deck while another was on the wharf, ready to cast off.

"Fuel?" Matt asked the young man on deck.

"Three thousand gallons."

"That'll do," Matt said as he crossed the gangway to the stern of the main deck.

Tasha followed. *Monty's Pride*'s twin diesel engines rumbled beneath them.

"Is my toolbox on board?" she asked.

"We put it in storage."

"Thanks." While they crossed the deck, she reviewed *Orca's Run*'s engine service in her mind. Had she missed something, a belt or a hose? She thought she'd checked them all. But nobody's memory was infallible.

"It could be as simple as a belt," she said to Matt.

"That will be good news." He made his way to the bridge, and she followed close behind.

She had to give it one last shot, so as soon as they were inside, she went for the radio, dialing in the company frequency. "*Orca's Run*, this is *Monty's Pride*. Captain, are you there?"

While she did that, he slid open the side window and called out to the hand to cast off.

She keyed the mike again. "Come in, *Orca's Run*."

Matt brought up the revs and pulled away from the pier.

Matt knew he had taken a gamble by using *Monty's Pride* instead of the repair boat, but so far it looked like it had been the right call. Two hours into the trip down the coast, even Tasha had been forced to admit a quick fix wasn't likely. She'd had Captain Johansson walk her through a second-by-second rehash of the engine failure over the radio, asking him about sounds, smells and warning lights. Then she had him send a deckhand back and forth from the engine room for a visual inspection and to relay details.

He'd been impressed by her thorough, methodical approach. But in the end, she concluded that she needed to check the engine herself. There was nothing to do for the next three hours but make their way to Tyree.

It was obvious she was ready to blame herself.

But even if the breakdown turned out to be her fault, it wasn't the end of the world. And they didn't even know what had happened. It was way too early to start pointing fingers.

"You should lie down for a while," he told her.

She looked tired, and there was no point in both of them staying up all night.

"I'm fine." She lifted her chin, gazing out the windshield into the starry night.

There were clusters of lights along the shore, only a few other ships in the distance, and his GPS and charts were top-notch. It was an easy chore to pilot the boat single-handed.

"You don't have to keep me company."

"And you don't have to coddle me."

"You have absolutely nothing to prove, Tasha." He knew she took pride in her work, and he knew she was determined to do a good job after her promotion. But sleep deprivation wasn't a job requirement.

"I'm not trying to prove anything. Did you get any sleep at all? Do you want to lie down?"

"I'm fine." He knew she was perfectly capable of piloting the boat, but he'd feel guilty leaving all the work to her.

"No need for us both to stay awake," she said.

"My date ended early. I slept a little."

Since his divorce had been finalized, Matt and his friend TJ Bauer had hit the Olympia social circuit. They were pushing each other to get out and meet new people. They met a few women, most were nice, but he hadn't felt a spark with any of them, including the one he'd taken out tonight. He'd come home early, done a little Christmas shopping online for his nieces and nephews and dozed off on the sofa.

"You don't need to tell me about your dates," Tasha said.

"There's nothing to tell."

"Well, that's too bad." Her tone was lighter. It sounded like she was joking. "It might help pass the time."

"Sorry," he said lightly in return. "I wish I could be more entertaining. What about you?" he asked.

As he voiced the question, he found himself curious about Tasha's love life. Did she have a boyfriend? Did she date? She was always such a no-nonsense fixture at the marina, he didn't think of her beyond being a valued employee.

"What about me?" she asked.

"Do you ever go out?"

"Out where?"

"Out, out. On-a-date out. Dinner, dancing..."

She scoffed out a laugh.

"Is that a no?"

"That's a no."

"Why not?" Now he was really curious. She might dress in plain T-shirts and cargo pants, but underneath what struck him now as a disguise, she was a lovely woman. "Don't you like to dress up? Do you ever dress up?"

He tried to remember if he'd ever seen her in anything stylish. He couldn't, and he was pretty sure he'd remember.

She shifted on the swivel chair, angling toward him. "Why the third degree?"

"Since stories of my dates won't distract us, I thought maybe yours could." He found himself scrutinizing her face from an objective point of view.

She had startling green eyes, the vivid color of emeralds or a glacial, deep-water pond. They were framed in thick lashes. Her cheekbones were high. Her chin was the perfect angle. Her nose was narrow, almost delicate. And her lips were deep coral, the bottom slightly fuller than the top.

He wanted to kiss them.

"Nothing to tell," she said. Her voice jolted him back to reality, and he turned to the windshield, rewinding the conversation.

"You must dress up sometimes."

"I prefer to focus on work."

"Why?"

"Because it's satisfying." Her answer didn't ring true.

He owned the company, and he still found time for a social life. "I dress up. I date. I still find time to work."

She made a motion with her hand, indicating up and down his body. "Of course you date. A guy like you is definitely going to date."

He had no idea what she meant. "A guy like me?"

"Good-looking. Rich. Eligible."

"Good-looking?" He was surprised that she thought so, even more surprised that she'd said so.

She rolled her eyes. "It's not me, Matt. The world thinks you're good-looking. Don't pretend you've never noticed."

He'd never given it much thought. Looks were so much a matter of taste. He was fairly average. He'd never thought there was anything wrong with being average.

"I'm eligible now," he said.

The rich part was also debatable. He hadn't had enough money to satisfy his ex-wife. And now that they'd divorced, he had even less. He'd borrowed money to pay her out, and he was going to have to work hard over the next year or two to get back to a comfortable financial position.

"And so are you," he said to Tasha. "You're intelligent, hardworking and pretty. You should definitely be out there dating."

He couldn't help but compare her with the women he'd met lately. The truth was, they couldn't hold a candle to her. There was so much about her that was compelling. Funny that he'd never noticed before.

"Dazzle them with your intelligence and hard work."

"Can we not do this?" she asked.

"Make conversation?"

"I'm a licensed marine mechanic. And I want people to take me seriously as that."

"You can't do both?"

"Not in my experience." She slipped down from the high white leather chair.

"What are you doing?" he asked. He didn't want her to leave.

"I'm going to take your advice."

"What advice is that?"

"I'm going to lie down and rest." She glanced at her watch. "You think two hours?"

"I didn't mean to chase you away."

"You didn't."

"We don't have to talk about dating." But then he took in her pursed lips and realized he still wanted to kiss them. Where was this impulse coming from?

"I have work to do when we get there."

He realized he'd be selfish to stop her. "You're right. You should get some sleep."

As she walked away, he considered the implications of being attracted to an employee. He couldn't act on it. He shouldn't act on it.

Then he laughed at himself. It wasn't like she'd given him any encouragement. Well, other than saying he was good-looking.

She thought he was good-looking.

As he piloted his way along the dark coastline, he couldn't help but smile.

Tasha's problem wasn't dating in general. Her problem was the thought of dating Matt. He wasn't her type. There was no way he was her type. She knew that for an absolute fact.

She'd dated guys like him before—capable, confident, secure in the knowledge that the world rolled itself out at their feet. She knew all that. Still, she couldn't seem to stop herself from dreaming about him.

They'd arrived off Tyree and boarded *Orca's Run* shortly

after dawn. Tall and confident, he'd greeted the clients like he owned the place—which he did, of course.

Tasha had kept to the background, making sure her toolbox was moved discreetly on board, while Matt had charmed the family, apologizing for the delay in the trip, offering *Monty's Pride* as a replacement, explaining that the larger, faster yacht would easily make up the time they'd lost overnight.

It was obvious the client was delighted with the solution, and Tasha had turned her attention to the diesel engine. It took her over an hour to discover the water separator was the problem. In an unlikely coincidence, the water-in-fuel indicator light bulb had also broken. Otherwise, it would have alerted her to the fact that the water separator was full, starving the engine of fuel.

The two things happening together were surprising. They were more than surprising. They were downright strange.

From their anchorage in Tyree, Matt had taken the launch and run for parts in the small town. And by noon, she'd replaced the water separator. While she'd worked, she'd cataloged who'd had access to *Orca's Run*. Virtually all the staff of Whiskey Bay Marina had access. But most of them didn't know anything about engines.

There were a couple of contract mechanics who did repairs from time to time. And there were countless customers who had been on the property. She found her brain going in fantastical directions, imagining someone might have purposely damaged the engine.

But who? And why? And was she being ridiculously paranoid?

She had no idea.

While she'd worked, diesel fuel had sprayed her clothes and soaked into her hair, so she'd used the staff shower to clean up and commandeered a steward's uniform from the supply closet.

After cleaning up, her mind still pinging from possibility to possibility, she made her way up the stairs to the main cabin. There she was surprised to realize the yacht wasn't yet under way.

"Did something else go wrong?" she asked Matt, immediately worried they had another problem.

He was in the galley instead of piloting the yacht. The deckhand had stayed with *Monty's Pride*, since the bigger ship needed an extra crew member. Matt and Tasha were fully capable of returning *Orca's Run* to Whiskey Bay.

"It's all good," Matt said.

"We're not under power?" Her hair was still damp, and she tucked it behind her ears as she approached the countertop that separated the galley from the main living area.

"Are you hungry?" he asked, placing a pan on the stove.

She was starving. "Sure. But I can eat something on the way."

"Coffee?"

"Sure."

He extracted two cups from a cupboard and poured. "*Monty's Pride* is headed south. Everyone seems happy."

"You were right," she admitted as she rounded the counter. "Bringing *Monty's Pride* was a good idea. I can cook if you want to get going."

He gave a thoughtful nod. "This charter matters."

"Because it's a German client?"

"It's the first significant booking out of the fall trade show. He's a prominent businessman with loads of connections."

"I'm sorry I argued with you." She realized her stance had been about her pride, not about the good of the company.

"You should always say what you think."

"I should listen, too."

"You don't listen?"

"Sometimes I get fixated on my own ideas." She couldn't help but revisit her theory about someone tampering with the engine.

Matt gave a smile. "You have conviction. That's not a bad thing. Besides, it keeps the conversation interesting."

He handed her a cup of coffee.

She took a sip, welcoming the hit of caffeine.

He seemed to ponder her for a moment. "You definitely keep things interesting."

She didn't know how to respond.

His blue eyes were dark but soft, and he had an incredibly handsome face. His chin was square, unshaven and slightly shadowed, but that only made him look more rugged. His nose was straight, his jaw angular and his lips were full, dark pink, completely kissable.

Warm waves of energy seemed to stream from him to cradle her. It was disconcerting, and she shifted to put some more space between them. "The engine was interesting."

Mug to his lips, he lifted his brow.

"The odds of the water separator filling and the indicator light going at the same time are very low."

His brow furrowed then, and he lowered the mug. "And?"

"Recognizing that this is my first idea, and that I can sometimes get fixated on those, it seems wrong to me. I mean, it seems odd to me."

"Are you saying someone broke something on purpose?"

"No, I'm not saying that." Out loud, it sounded even less plausible than it had inside her head. "I'm saying it was a bizarre coincidence, and I must be having a run of bad luck."

"You fixed it, so that's good luck."

"Glass half-full?"

"You did a good job, Tasha."

"It wasn't that complicated."

A teasing glint came into his eyes. "You mean, you're that skilled?"

"The cause was peculiar." She could have sworn she'd just serviced the water separator. "The repair was easy."

Their gazes held, and they fell silent again. Raindrops clattered against the window, while the temperature seemed to inch up around her. Her dream came back once again, Matt cradling her, kissing her. Heat rose in her cheeks.

She forced herself back to the present, trying to keep her mind on an even keel. "It could have been excess water in the fuel, maybe a loose cap. I did check it. At least I think I checked it. I always check it." She paused. "I hope I checked it."

He set down his mug. "Don't."

She didn't understand.

He took a step forward. "Don't second-guess yourself."

"Okay." It seemed like the easiest answer, since she was losing track of the conversation.

He took another step, and then another.

Inside her head, she shouted for him to stop. But she didn't make a sound.

She didn't want him to stop. She could almost feel his arms around her.

He was right there.

Thunder suddenly cracked through the sky above them. A wave surged beneath them, and she grabbed for the counter. She missed, stumbling into his chest.

In a split second, his arms were around her, steadying her.

She fought the desire that fogged her brain. "Sorry."

"Weather's coming up," he said, his deep voice rumbling in her ear and vibrating her chest, which was pressed tight against his.

"We won't be—" Words failed her as she looked into his blue eyes, so close, so compelling.

He stilled, the sapphire of his eyes softening to summer sky.

"Tasha." Her name was barely a breath on his lips.

She softened against him.

He lowered his lips, closer and closer. They brushed lightly against hers, then they firmed, then they parted, and the kiss sent bolts of pleasure ricocheting through her.

She gripped his shoulders to steady herself. A rational part of her brain told her to stop. But she was beyond stopping.

She was beyond caring about anything but the cataclysmic kiss between them.

It was Matt who finally pulled back.

He looked as dazed as she felt, and he blew out a breath. "I'm…" He gave his head a little shake. "I don't know what to say."

She forced herself to step back. "Don't." She had no idea what to say either. "Don't try. It was just…something…that happened."

"It was something," he said.

"It was a mistake."

He raked a hand through his short hair. "It sure wasn't on purpose."

"We should get going," she said, anxious to focus on something else.

The last thing she wanted to do was dissect their kiss. The last thing she wanted to do was admit how it impacted her. The last thing she wanted her boss to know was that she saw him as a man, more than a boss.

She couldn't do that. She had to stop doing it. In this relationship, she was a mechanic, not a woman.

"We're not going anywhere." He looked pointedly out the window where the rain was driving down.

Tasha took note of the pitching floor beneath her.

It was Matt who reached for the marine radio and turned the dial to get a weather report.

"We might as well grab something to eat," he said. "This could last awhile."

# Two

Waiting out the storm, Matt had fallen asleep in the living area. He awoke four hours later to find Tasha gone, and he went looking.

The yacht was rocking up and down on six-foot swells, and rain clattered against the windows. He couldn't find her on the upper decks, so he took the narrow staircase, making his way to the engine and mechanical rooms. Sure enough, he found her there. She'd removed the front panel of the generator and was elbow deep in the mechanics.

"What are you doing?" he asked.

She tensed at the sound of his voice. She was obviously remembering their kiss. Well, he remembered it, too, and it sure made him tense up. Partly because he was her boss and he felt guilty for letting things get out of hand. But partly because it had been such an amazing kiss and he desperately wanted to do it again.

"Maintenance," she answered him without turning.

He settled his shoulder against the doorjamb. "Can you elaborate?"

"I inspected the electric and serviced the batteries. Some of the battery connections needed cleaning. Hoses and belts all look good in here. But it was worth changing the oil filter."

"I thought you would sleep."

This was above and beyond the call of duty for anyone. He'd known Tasha was a dedicated employee, but this trip was teaching him she was one in a million.

She finally turned to face him. "I did sleep. Then I woke up."

She'd found a pair of coveralls somewhere. They were miles too big, but she'd rolled up the sleeves and the pant legs. A woman shouldn't look sexy with a wrench in her hand, a smudge of oil on her cheek, swimming in a shapeless steel gray sack.

But this one did. And he wanted to do a whole lot more than kiss her. He mentally shook away the feelings.

"If it was me—" he tried to lighten the mood and put her at ease "—I think I might have inspected the liquor cabinet."

She smiled for the briefest of seconds. "Lucky your employees aren't like you."

The smile warmed him. It turned him on, but it also made him happy.

"True enough," he said. "But there is a nice cognac in there. Perfect to have on a rainy afternoon." He could picture them doing just that.

Instead of answering, she returned to work.

He watched for a few minutes, struggling with his feelings, knowing he had to put their relationship back on an even keel.

Work—he needed to say something about work instead of sharing a cozy drink.

"Are you trying to impress me?" he asked.

She didn't pause. "Yes."

"I'm impressed."

"Good."

"You should stop working."

"I'm not finished."

"You're making me feel guilty."

She looked his way and rolled her eyes. "I'm not trying to make you feel guilty."

"Then what?"

"The maintenance needed doing. I was here. There was an opportunity."

He fought an urge to close the space between them. "Are you always like this?"

"Like what?"

"I don't know, überindustrious?"

"You say that like it's a bad thing."

He did move closer. He shouldn't, couldn't, *wouldn't* bring up their kiss. But he desperately wanted to bring it up, discuss it, dissect it, relive it. How did she feel about it now? Was she angry? Was there a chance in the world she wanted to do it again?

"It's an unnerving thing," he said.

"Then, you're very easily unnerved."

He couldn't help but smile at her comeback. "I'm trying to figure you out."

"Well, that's a waste of time."

"I realize I don't know you well."

"You don't need to know me well. Just sign my paycheck."

Well, that was a crystal clear signal. He was her boss, nothing more. He swallowed his disappointment.

Then again, if he was her boss, he was her boss. He reached forward to take the wrench from her hand. "It's after five and it's a Saturday and you're done."

Their fingers touched. Stupid mistake. He felt a current run up the center of his arm.

Her grip tightened on the wrench as she tried to tug it from his grasp. "Let it go."

"It's time to clock out."

"Seriously, Matt. I'm not done yet."

His hand wrapped around hers, and his feet took him closer still.

"Matt." There was a warning in her voice, but then their gazes caught and held.

Her eyes turned moss green, deep and yielding. She was feeling something. She had to be feeling something.

She used her free hand to grasp his arm. Her grip was strong, stronger than he'd imagined. He liked that.

"We can't do this, Matt."

"I know."

She swallowed, and her voice seemed strained. "So let go."

"I want to kiss you again."

"It's a bad idea."

"You're right." His disappointment was acute. "It is."

She didn't step back, and her lips parted as she drew in a breath. "We need to keep it simple, straightforward."

"Why?"

"The signature on my paycheck."

"Is that the only reason?" It was valid. But he was curious. He was intensely curious.

"I'm not that kind of girl."

He knew she didn't mean to be funny, but he couldn't help but joke. "The kind that kisses men?"

"The kind that randomly kisses my boss—or any co-worker for that matter—while I'm working, in an engine room, covered in grease."

"That's fair."

"You bet, it's fair. Not that I need your approval. Now, let go of my hand."

He glanced down, realizing they were still touching. The last thing he wanted to do was let her go. But he had no choice.

She set down the wrench, replacing it with a screwdriver. Then she lifted the generator panel and put it in place.

He moved away and braced a hand on a crossbeam above his head. "The storm's letting up."

"Good." The word sounded final. Matt didn't want it to be final.

He was her boss, sure. He understood that was a complication. But did it have to be a deal breaker? But he wanted to get to know her. He'd barely scratched the surface, and he liked her a lot.

They'd brought *Orca's Run* back to the marina, arriving late in the evening.

Tasha had spent the night and half of today attempting to purge Matt's kiss from her mind. It wasn't working. She kept reliving the pleasure, then asking herself what it all meant.

She didn't even know how she felt, never mind how Matt felt. He was a smooth-talking, great-looking man who, from everything she'd seen, could have any woman in the world. What could possibly be his interest in her?

Okay, maybe if she'd taken her mother's advice, maybe if she'd acted like a woman, dressed like a woman and got a different job, maybe then it would make sense for Matt to be interested. Matt reminded her so much of the guys she'd known in Boston, the ones who'd dated her sisters and attended all the parties.

They'd all wanted women who were super feminine. They'd been amused by Tasha. She wasn't a buddy and she wasn't, in their minds, a woman worth pursuing. She hadn't fit in anywhere. It was the reason she'd left. And now Matt was confusing her. She hated being confused.

So, right now, this afternoon, she had a new focus.

Since she'd been promoted, she had to replace herself. Matt employed several general dock laborers who also worked as mechanical assistants, and they pulled in mechanical specialists when necessary. But one staff mechanic couldn't keep up with the workload at Whiskey Bay. Matt owned twenty-four boats in all, ranging from *Monty's Pride* right down to a seventeen-foot runabout they used in the bay. Some were workboats, but most were pleasure craft available for rental.

Cash flow was a definite issue, especially after Matt's divorce. It was more important than ever that the yachts stay in good working order to maximize rentals.

Tasha was using a vacant office in the main marina building at the edge of the company pier. The place was a sprawling, utilitarian building, first constructed in 1970, with major additions built in 2000 and 2010. Its clay-colored steel siding protected against the wind and salt water.

Inside, the client area was nicely decorated, as were Matt's and the sales manager's offices. But down the hall, where the offices connected to the utility areas and eventually to the boat garage and the small dry dock, the finishing was more Spartan. Even still, she felt pretentious sitting behind a wooden desk with a guest chair in front.

She'd been through four applicants so far. One and two were nonstarters. They were handymen rather than certified marine mechanics. The third one had his certification, but something about him made Tasha cautious. He was a little too eager to list his accomplishments. He was beyond self-confident, bordering on arrogant. She didn't see him fitting in at Whiskey Bay.

The fourth applicant had been five minutes late. Not a promising start.

But then a woman appeared in the doorway. "My apologies," she said in a rush as she entered.

Tasha stood. "Alex Dumont?"

"Yes." The woman smiled broadly as she moved forward, holding out her hand.

Tasha shook it, laughing at herself for having made the assumption that Alex was a man.

"Alexandria," the woman elaborated, her eyes sparkling with humor.

"Of all people, I shouldn't make gender assumptions."

"It happens so often, I don't even think about it."

"I hear you," Tasha said. "Please, sit down."

"At least with the name Tasha nobody makes that mistake." Alex settled into the chair. "Though I have to imagine you've been written off a few times before they even met you."

"I'm not sure which is worse," Tasha said.

"I prefer the surprise value. That's why I shortened my name. I have to say this is the first time I've been interviewed by a woman."

Alex was tall, probably about five foot eight. She had wispy, wheat-blond hair, a few freckles and a pretty smile. If Tasha hadn't seen her résumé, she would have guessed she was younger than twenty-five.

"You're moving from Chicago?" Tasha asked, flipping through the three pages of Alex's résumé.

"I've already moved, three weeks ago."

"Any particular reason?" Tasha was hoping for someone who would stay in Whiskey Bay for the long term.

"I've always loved the West Coast. But mostly, it was time to make a break from the family."

Tasha could relate to that. "They didn't support your career choice?" she guessed.

"No." Alex gave a little laugh. "Quite the opposite. My father and two brothers are mechanics. They wouldn't leave me alone."

"Did you work with them?"

"At first. Then I got a job with another company. It didn't help. They still interrogated me every night and gave me advice on whatever repair I was undertaking."

"You lived with them?"

"Not anymore."

Tasha couldn't help contrasting their experiences. "I grew up in Boston. My parents wanted me to find a nice doctor or lawyer and become a wife instead of a mechanic. Though they probably would have settled for me being a landscape painter or a dancer."

"Any brothers and sisters?"

"Two sisters. Both married to lawyers." Tasha didn't like to dwell on her family. It had been a long time since she'd spoken to them. She stopped herself now, and went back to Alex's résumé. "At Schneider Marine, you worked on both gas and diesel engines?"

"Yes. Gas, anywhere from 120-horse outboards and up, and diesel, up to 550."

"Any experience on Broadmores?"

"Oh, yeah. Finicky buggers, those."

"We have two of them."

"Well, I've got their number."

Tasha couldn't help but smile. This was the kind of confidence she liked. "And you went to Riverside Tech?"

"I did. I finished my apprenticeship four years ago. I can get you a copy of my transcript if you need it."

Tasha shook her head. "I'm more interested in your recent experience. How much time on gasoline engines versus diesel?"

"More diesel, maybe seventy-five/twenty-five. Lots of service, plenty of rebuilds."

"Diagnostics?"

"I was their youngest mechanic, so I wasn't afraid of the new scan tools."

"You dive right in?" Tasha was liking Alex more and more as the interview went on.

"I dive right in."

"When can you start?"

Alex grinned. "Can you give me a few days to unpack?"

"Absolutely."

Both women came to their feet.

"Then, I'm in," Alex said.

Tasha shook her hand, excited at the prospect of another female mechanic in the company. "Welcome aboard."

Alex left, but a few minutes later, Tasha was still smiling when Matt came through the door.

"What?" he asked.

"What?" she returned, forcibly dampening her exhilaration at the sight of him.

She couldn't do this. She *wouldn't* do this. They had an employer-employee relationship, not a man-woman relationship.

"You're smiling," he said.

"I'm happy."

"About what?"

"I love my job."

"Is that all?"

"You don't think I love my job?" She did love it. And she had a feeling she'd love it even more with Alex around.

"I was hoping you were happy to see me."

"Matt." She put a warning in her voice.

"Are we going to just ignore it?"

She quickly closed the door to make sure nobody could overhear. "Yes, we're going to ignore it."

"By *it*, I mean our kiss."

She folded her arms over her chest and gave him a glare. "I know what you mean."

"Just checking," he said, looking dejected.

"Stop." She wasn't going to be emotionally manipulated.

"I'm not going to pretend. I miss you."

"There's nothing to miss. I'm right here."

"Prepared to talk work and only work."

"Yes."

He was silent for a moment. "Fine. Okay. I'll take it."

"Good." She knew with absolute certainty that it was for the best.

He squared his shoulders. "Who was that leaving?"

"That was Alex Dumont. She's our new mechanic."

Matt's brows went up. "We have a new mechanic?"

"You knew I was hiring one."

"But…"

Tasha couldn't help an inward sigh. She'd seen this reaction before. "But…she's a woman."

"That's not what I was going to say. I was surprised, is all."

"That she was light on testosterone?"

"You keep putting words in my mouth."

"Well, you keep putting expressions in your eyes."

He opened his mouth, but then he seemed to think better of whatever he'd planned to say.

"What?" she asked before she could stop herself.

"Nothing." He took a backward step. "I'm backing off. This is me backing off."

"From who I hire?"

Matt focused in on her eyes. His eyes smoldered, and she felt desire arc between them.

"I can feel it from here," he said, as if he was reading her mind.

Her brain stumbled. "There's…uh… I'm…"

"You can't quite spit out the lie, can you?"

She couldn't. Lying wouldn't help. "We have to ignore it."

"Why?"

"We do. We do, Matt."

There was a long beat of silence.

"I have a date Saturday night," he said.

A pain crossed her chest, but she steeled herself. "No kidding."

"I don't date that much."

"I don't pay any attention."

It was a lie. From the staff quarters, she'd seen him leave his house on the hill on many occasions, dressed to the nines. She'd often wondered where he'd gone, whom he'd been with, how late he'd come home.

And she'd watched him bring women to his house. They often dined on the deck. Caterers would set up candles and white linens, and then Matt and his date would chat and laugh the evening away.

She'd paid attention all right. But wild horses wouldn't drag the admission out of her.

So Saturday night, Matt had picked up the tall, willowy, expensively coiffed Emilie and brought her home for arctic char and risotto, catered by a local chef. They were dining in his glass-walled living room to candlelight and a full moon. The wine was from the Napa Valley, and the chocolate truffles were handcrafted with Belgian chocolate.

It should have been perfect. Emilie was a real estate company manager, intelligent, gracious, even a little bit funny. She was friendly and flirtatious, and made no secret of the fact that she expected a very romantic conclusion to the evening.

But Matt's gaze kept straying to the pier below, to the yachts, the office building and the repair shop. Finally, Tasha appeared. She strode briskly beneath the overhead lights, through the security gate and up the stairway that led to the staff quarters. Some of his staff members had families and houses in town. The younger, single crew members, especially those who had moved to Whiskey Bay to work at the marina, seemed to appreciate the free rent, even if the staff units were small and basic. He was happy at the moment that Tasha was one of them.

He reflexively glanced at his watch. It was nearly ten o'clock. Even for Tasha, this was late.

"Matt?" Emilie said.

"Yes?" He quickly returned his attention to her.

She gave a very pretty smile. "I asked if they were all yours?"

"All what?"

"The boats. Do you really own that many boats?"

"I do," he said. He'd told this story a hundred times. "I started with three about a decade ago. Business was good, so I gradually added to the fleet."

He glanced back to the pier, but Tasha had disappeared from view. He told himself not to be disappointed. He'd see her again soon. It had been a few days now since they'd run into each other. He'd tried not to miss her, but he did. He'd find a reason to talk to her tomorrow.

Emilie pointed toward the window. "That one is *huge*."

"*Monty's Pride* is our largest vessel."

"Could I see the inside?" she asked, eyes alight. "Would you give me a tour?"

Before Matt could answer, there was a pounding on his door.

"Expecting someone?" she asked, looking a little bit frustrated by the interruption.

His friends and neighbors, Caleb Watford and TJ Bauer, were the only people who routinely dropped by. But neither of them would knock. At most, they'd call out from the entryway if they thought they might walk in on something.

Matt rose. "I'll be right back."

"Sure." Emilie helped herself to another truffle. "I'll wait here."

The date had been going pretty well so far. But Matt couldn't say he was thrilled with the touch of sarcasm he'd just heard in Emilie's voice.

The knock came again as he got to the front entry. He swung open the door.

Tasha stood on his porch, her work jacket wrinkled, a blue baseball cap snug on her head and her work boots sturdy against the cool weather.

His immediate reaction was delight. He wanted to drag her inside and make her stay for a while.

"What's up?" he asked instead, remembering the promise he'd made, holding himself firmly at a respectful distance.

"Something's going on," she said.

"Between us?" he asked before he could stop himself, resisting the urge to glance back and be sure Emilie was still out of sight.

Tasha frowned. "*No.* With *Pacific Wind.*" She named the single-engine twenty-eight-footer. "It's just a feeling. But I'm worried."

He stepped back and gestured for her to come inside.

She glanced down at her boots.

"Don't worry about it," he said. "I have a cleaning service."

"A cable broke on the steering system," she said.

"Is that a major problem?"

He didn't particularly care why she'd decided to come up and tell him in person. He was just glad she had.

It was the first time she'd been inside his house. He couldn't help but wonder if she liked the modern styling, the way it jutted out from the hillside, the clean lines, glass walls and unobstructed view. He really wanted to find out. He hadn't been interested in Emilie's opinion, but he was curious about Tasha's.

"It's not a big problem," she said. "I fixed it. It's fixed."

"That's good." He dared to hope all over again that this was a personal visit disguised as business.

"Matt?" came Emilie's voice.

He realized he'd forgotten all about her.

"I'll just be a minute," he called back to her.

"You're busy," Tasha said, looking instantly regretful. "Of course you're busy. I didn't think." She glanced at her watch. "This is Saturday, isn't it?"

"You forgot the day of the week?"

"Matt, honey." Emilie came up behind him.

*Honey?* Seriously? After a single date?

Not even a single date, really. The date hadn't concluded yet.

"Who's this?" Emilie asked.

There was a dismissive edge to her voice and judgment in her expression as she gave Tasha the once-over, clearly finding her lacking.

The superior attitude annoyed Matt. "This is Tasha."

"I'm the mechanic," Tasha said, not seeming remotely bothered by Emilie's condescension.

"Hmph," Emilie said, wrinkling her perfect nose. She wrapped her arm possessively through Matt's. "Is this an emergency?"

Tasha took a step back, opening her mouth to speak.

"Yes," Matt said. "It's an emergency. I'm afraid I'm going to have to cut our date short."

He wasn't sure who looked more surprised by his words, Emilie or Tasha.

"I'll call you a ride." He took out his phone.

It took Emilie a moment to find her voice. "What *kind* of emergency?"

"The mechanical kind," he said flatly, suddenly tired of her company.

He typed in the request. He definitely didn't want Tasha to leave.

"But—" Emilie began.

"The ride will be here in three minutes," he said. "I'll get your coat."

He did a quick check of Tasha's expression, steeling himself for the possibility that she'd speak up and out him as a liar.

She didn't.

He quickly retrieved Emilie's coat and purse.

"I don't mind waiting," Emilie said, a plaintive whine in her voice.

"I couldn't ask you to do that." He held up the coat.

"How long do you think—"

"Could be a long time. It could be a very long time. It's complicated."

"Matt, I can—" Tasha began.

"No. Nope." He gave a definitive shake to his head. "It's business. It's important." It might not be critical, but Tasha had never sought him out after hours before, so there had to be something going on.

"You're a *mechanic*?" Emilie asked Tasha.

"A marine mechanic."

"So you get all greasy and stuff?"

"Sometimes."

"That must be awful." Emilie gave a little shudder.

"Emilie." Matt put a warning tone in his voice.

She crooked her head back to look at him. "What? It's weird."

"It's not weird."

"It's unusual," Tasha said. "But women are up to nearly fifteen percent in the mechanical trades, higher when you look at statistics for those of us under thirty-five."

Emilie didn't seem to know what to say in response.

Matt's phone pinged.

"Your ride's here," he told Emilie, ushering her toward the door.

Tasha stood to one side, and he watched until Emilie got into the car.

"You didn't have to do that," Tasha said as he closed the door.

"It wasn't going well."

"In that case, I'm happy to be your wingman."

Matt zeroed in on her expression to see if she was joking. She looked serious, and he didn't like the sound of that.

"I don't need a wingman."

"Tell me what's going on." He gestured through the archway to the living room.

She crouched down to untie her boots.

"You don't have to—"

"Your carpet is white," she said.

"I suppose."

Most of the women he brought home wore delicate shoes, stiletto heels and such.

Tasha peeled off her boots, revealing thick wool socks. For some reason, the sight made him smile.

She rose, looking all business.

"Care for a drink?" he asked, gesturing her forward.

She moved, shooting him an expression of disbelief on the way past. "No, I don't want a drink."

"I opened a great bottle of pinot noir. I'm not going to finish it myself."

"This isn't a social visit," she said, glancing around the room at the pale white leather furniture and long, narrow gas fireplace.

She was obviously hesitant to sit down in her work clothes.

"Here," he suggested, pointing to the formal dining room. The chairs were dark oak, likely less intimidating if she was worried about leaving dirt on anything.

While she sat down, he retrieved the pinot from the glass porch and brought two fresh glasses.

He sat down cornerwise to her and set down the wine.

She gave him an exaggerated sigh. "I'm not drinking while I work."

"It's ten o'clock on a Saturday night."

"Your point?"

"My point is you're officially off the clock."

"So, you're not paying me?"

"I'll pay you anything you want." He poured them each some of the rich, dark wine. "Aren't you on salary?"

"I am."

"You work an awful lot of overtime."

"A good deal for you."

"I'm giving you a raise." He held one of the glasses out for her.

"Ha ha," she mocked.

"Take it," he said.

She did, but set it down on the table in front of her.

"Twenty percent," he told her.

"You can't do that."

"I absolutely can." He raised his glass. "Let's toast your raise."

"I came here to tell you I might have made a big mistake."

# Three

Tasha reluctantly took a sip of the wine, noting right away that it was a fantastic vintage. She looked at the bottle, recognizing the Palmer Valley label as one of her parents' favorites, and the Crispin Pinot Noir as one of their higher-end brands.

"You have good taste in wine," she said.

"I'm glad you like it."

His smile was warm, and she felt an unwelcome glow in the pit of her stomach.

To distract herself, she tipped the bottle to check the year.

"You know the label?" he asked, sounding surprised.

"Mechanics can't appreciate fine wine?"

He paused to take in her expression. "Clearly, they can."

It was annoying how his deep voice strummed along her nervous system. She seemed to have no defenses against him.

She set down her glass and straightened in her chair, reminding herself this was business.

"What did I say?" he asked.

"I came here to tell you—"

"I just said something wrong," he persisted. "What was it?"

"You didn't say anything wrong." It was her problem, not his. "*Pacific Wind* broke down near Granite Point."

"Another breakdown?"

"Like I said, a cable was broken."

"But you fixed it." He slid the wineglass a little closer to her. "Good job. Well done, you."

"It shouldn't have happened. I serviced it just last week. I must have missed a weak point."

His lips tightened in what looked like frustration. "Why

are you so quick to blame yourself? It obviously broke *after* you did your work."

"The sequence of events isn't logical. It shouldn't have broken all of a sudden. Wear and tear should have been obvious when I was working on it." She'd been mulling over the possibilities for hours now. "It could have been a faulty part, weak material in the cable maybe, something that wasn't visible that would leave it prone to breaking."

"There you go."

"Or…" She hesitated to even voice her speculation.

"Or?" he prompted.

"Somebody wanted it to break. It's far-fetched. I get that. And on the surface, it seems like I'm making excuses for my own incompetence—coming up with some grand scheme of sabotage to explain it all away. But the thing is, I checked with the fuel supply company right after we got back from Tyree. We were the only customer that had a water problem. And none of our other yachts were affected, only *Orca's Run*. How does that work? How does water only get into one fuel system?" She gave in and took another drink of the wine.

"Tasha?" Matt asked.

"Yeah?" She set down her glass, oddly relieved at having said it out loud. Now they could discuss it and dismiss it.

"Can you parse that out a little more for me?"

She nodded, happy to delve into her theory and find the flaws. "It's far from definitive. It's only possible. It's possible that someone put water in the fuel and damaged the pump. And it's possible someone partially cut the cable."

"The question is, why?"

She agreed. "Do you have any enemies?"

"None that I know about."

"A competitor, maybe?"

He sat back in his chair. "Wow."

"*Wow* that somebody could be secretly working against you?"

"No. I was just thinking that after-dinner conversation with you is *so* much more interesting than with Emilie."

"So you think my theory is too far-fetched." She was inclined to agree.

"That's not what I said at all. I'm thinking you could be right. And we should investigate. And that's kind of exciting."

"You think it's exciting? That someone might be damaging your boats and undermining your company's reputation?"

He topped up both of their glasses. "I think it could be exciting to investigate. It's not like anything was seriously or permanently damaged. It seems like more mischief than anything. And haven't you ever wanted to be an amateur sleuth?"

"No." She could honestly say it had never crossed her mind.

"Come on. You investigate, diagnose and fix problems all the time."

"There are no bad guys lurking inside engines."

"The bad guy only adds a new dimension to the problem."

She couldn't understand his jovial attitude. There wasn't a positive side to this. "There's something wrong with you, Matt."

"Will you help me?" he asked, his eyes alight in a way that trapped and held her gaze. His eyes were vivid blue right now, the color of the bay at a summer sunrise.

"It's my job." She fought an inappropriate thrill at the prospect of working closely with him. She should be staying away from him. That's what she should be doing.

"We need to start with a list of suspects. Who has access to the engines and steering systems?"

"I do, and the contract mechanics from Dean's Repairs and Corner Service. And Alex now. But she wasn't even here when we had the *Orca's Run* problem."

"Was she in Whiskey Bay?"

"Yes but… You're not suggesting she's a mole."

"I'm not suggesting anything yet. I'm only laying out the facts."

Tasha didn't want to suspect Alex, but she couldn't disagree with Matt's approach. They had to start with everyone who had access, especially those with mechanical skills. Whoever did this understood boats and engines well enough to at least attempt to cover their tracks.

"At least we can rule you out," Matt said with a smirk.

"And you," she returned.

"And me. What about the rest of the staff? Who can we rule out?"

"Can we get a list of everyone's hours for the past couple of weeks?"

"Easily."

"What about your competitors?" It seemed to Tasha that Matt's competitors would have motive to see him fail.

"They'd have a financial motive, I suppose. But I know most of the ones in the area, and I can't imagine any of them doing something underhanded."

"Maybe they didn't," she said, realizing the enormity of her accusations. Never mind the enormity, what about the likelihood that somebody was out to harm Matt's business?

She was reevaluating this whole thing. "Maybe it was just my making a mistake."

He paused and seemed to consider. "Do you believe that's what happened?"

"Nobody's perfect." She knew her negligence could account for the cable.

Then again, the water in the fuel of *Orca's Run* was something else. It was a lot less likely she'd been responsible for that.

He watched her closely, his gaze penetrating. "Tasha, I can tell by your expression you know it wasn't you."

"I can't be one hundred percent certain."

He took her hand in both of his. "I am."

Their gazes met and held, and the air temperature in the room seemed to rise. Subtle sounds magnified: the wind, the surf, the hiss of the fireplace. Heat rushed up her arm, blooming into desire in her chest.

Like the first rumblings of an earthquake, she could feel it starting all over again.

"I have to go." She jumped to her feet.

He stood with her, still holding her hand. His gaze moved to her lips.

They tingled.

She knew she should move. She needed to move *right now*.

She did move. But it was to step forward, not backward.

She brought her free hand up to his. He interlaced their fingers.

"Tasha," he whispered.

She should run. Leave. But instead she let her eyes drift closed. She leaned in, crossing the last few inches between them. She tipped her chin, tilted her head. She might not have a lot of experience with romance, but she knew she was asking for his kiss.

He didn't disappoint.

With a swift, indrawn breath, he brought his lips to hers.

The kiss was tender, soft and tentative. But it sent waves through her body, heat and energy. It was she who pressed harder, she who parted her lips and she who disentangled her hands to wrap her arms around his neck.

He gave a small groan, and he embraced her, his solid forearms against her back, pressing her curves against the length of his body, thigh to thigh, chest to chest. Her nipples peaked at his touch, the heat of his skin. She desperately wanted to feel his skin against hers. But she'd retained just enough sanity to stop herself.

The kiss was as far as it could go.

She reluctantly drew back. She wished she could look away and pretend it hadn't happened. But she didn't. She wouldn't. She faced him head-on.

His eyes were opaque, and there was a ghost of a smile on his face.

"You're amazing," he said.

"We can't do that." Regret was pouring in, along with a healthy dose of self-recrimination.

"But, we do."

"You know what I mean."

"You mean *shouldn't*." His closeness was still clouding her mind.

"Yes, shouldn't. No, can't. You have to help me here, Matt." She stepped away, putting some space between them.

He gave an exaggerated sigh. "You're asking a lot."

She wanted to be honest, and she wanted both of them to be realistic. "I like it here."

He glanced around his living room that jutted out from the cliff, affording incredible views of the bay. He was clearly proud of the design, proud of his home. "I'm glad to hear that."

"Not the house," she quickly corrected him.

"You don't like my house?"

"That's not what I mean. I do like your house." The house was stunningly gorgeous; anyone would love it. "I mean I like working at Whiskey Bay. I don't want to have to quit."

His expression turned to incredulity. "You're making some pretty huge leaps in logic."

She knew that was true, and she backpedaled. "I'm not assuming you want a fling."

"That's not what I—"

"It's hard for a woman to be taken seriously as a mechanic."

"So you've said."

"I want to keep my personal life and my professional life separate."

"Everybody does. Until something happens that makes them want something else."

Now she just wanted out of this conversation. "I'm afraid I've given you the wrong idea."

"The only idea you've given me is that you're attracted to me."

She wanted to protest, but she wasn't going to lie.

He continued. "That and the fact that you believe my company is the target of sabotage."

She quickly latched onto the alternative subject. "I do. At least, it's a possibility that we should consider."

"And I trust your judgment, so we're going to investigate."

Tasha drew a breath of relief. They were back on solid ground. All work with Matt, no play. That was her mission going forward.

Matt couldn't concentrate on work. He kept reliving his kiss with Tasha over and over again.

He was with TJ and Caleb on the top deck of his marina building, standing around the propane fireplace as the sun sank into the Pacific. The other men's voices were more a drone of noise than a conversation.

"Why would anyone sabotage your engines?" TJ broke through Matt's daydreaming.

"What?" he asked, shaking himself back to the present.

"Why would they do it?"

"Competition is my guess." Matt hadn't been able to come up with another reason.

Caleb levered into one of the padded deck chairs. It was a cool evening, but the men still sipped on chilled beers.

"What about your surveillance cameras?" Caleb asked.

"Not enough of them to provide full coverage. They're pretty easy to avoid if that's your intention."

"You should get more."

"I've ordered more." It was one of the first moves Matt had made. He took a chair himself.

"Did you call the police?" TJ asked, sitting down.

"Not yet. I can't imagine it would be a priority for them. And I want to make sure we're right before I waste anybody's time."

"So, Tasha is wrong?"

Matt found himself bristling at what was only the slightest of criticisms of Tasha. "No, she's not wrong."

"I'm just asking," TJ said, obviously catching the tone in Matt's voice.

"And I'm just answering. She's not one hundred percent convinced yet either. So, we'll wait."

"Until it happens again?" Caleb asked. "What if it's more serious this time? What if whoever it is targets more than the marina?"

"Are you worried about the Crab Shack?" Matt hadn't thought about the other businesses in the area, including the Crab Shack restaurant run by Caleb's new wife, Jules, who was five months pregnant with twins.

"Not yet." Caleb seemed to further contemplate the question. "I might ask Noah to spend a little more time over there."

"Nobody's going to mess with Noah," TJ said.

"He's scrappy," Caleb agreed.

Caleb's sister-in-law's boyfriend had spent a short time in jail after a fistfight in self-defense. He was tough and no-nonsense, and he'd protect Jules and her sister, Melissa, against anything and anyone.

"What about your security cameras at the Crab Shack?" TJ asked Caleb. "Would any of them reach this far?"

"I'll check," Caleb said. "But I doubt the resolution is high enough to be of any help."

"I'd appreciate that," Matt said to Caleb.

It hadn't occurred to him to worry about Tasha's or anyone else's safety. But maybe Caleb was onto something. Maybe Matt should take a few precautions. So far, the incidents had been minor, and nobody had come close to being hurt. But that wasn't to say it couldn't happen. The incidents could escalate.

"Matt?" It was Tasha's voice coming from the pier below, and he felt the timbre radiate through his chest.

He swiftly rose and crossed to the rail, where he could see her. "Are you okay?"

She seemed puzzled by his concern. "I'm fine."

"Good."

"*Never Fear* and *Crystal Zone* are both ready to go in the morning. I'm heading into town for a few hours."

"What for?" The question was out of Matt's mouth before he realized it was none of his business. It was after five, and Tasha was free to do anything she wanted.

"Meeting some guys."

*Guys?* What did she mean *guys*? He wanted to ask if it was one particular guy, or if it was a group of guys. Were they all just friends?

"Hey, Tasha." TJ appeared at the rail beside him.

"Hi, TJ." Her greeting was casual, and her attention went back to Matt. "Alex will fill the fuel tanks first thing. The clients are expected at ten."

"Got it," Matt said, wishing he could ask more questions about her evening. Or better still, invite her to join them, where they could talk and laugh together.

Not that they were in the habit of friendly conversation. Mostly, they debated. But he'd be happy to engage her in a rollicking debate about pretty much any subject.

As she walked away, TJ spoke up. "I may just take another shot."

"Another shot at what?" Matt asked.

"At your mechanic."

*"What?"* Matt turned.

"I like her."

"What do you mean *another* shot?" Matt was surprised by the level of his anger. "You took a shot at her already?"

TJ was obviously taken aback by Matt's reaction. "I asked you back in the summer. You told me to go for it."

"That was months ago."

"That's when I asked her out. I suggested dinner and dancing. That might have been my mistake."

Matt took a drink of his beer to keep himself from saying anything more. He didn't like the thought of Tasha with any guy, never mind TJ. TJ was the epitome of rich, good-looking and eligible. Matt had seen the way a lot of women reacted to him. Not that Tasha was an ordinary woman. Still, she was a woman.

TJ kept talking, half to himself. "Maybe a monster truck rally? She is a mechanic."

Caleb joined them at the rail.

TJ tried again. "Maybe an auto show. There's one coming up in Seattle."

"You can't ask her out," Matt said.

The protest caught Caleb's attention. "Why can't he ask her out?"

"Because she's already turned him down."

"I could be persistent," TJ said.

"I really don't think dinner and dancing or persistence was the problem," Matt said.

"How would you know that?" TJ asked.

Caleb's expression took a speculative turn. "You have a problem with TJ asking Tasha out?"

"No," Matt responded to Caleb. Then he reconsidered his answer. "Yes."

TJ leaned an elbow on the rail, a grin forming on his face. "Oh, this is interesting."

"It's not interesting," Matt said.

"Is something going on between you two?" Caleb asked.

"No. Nothing is going on."

"But you like her." TJ's grin was full-on now.

"I kissed her. She kissed me. We kissed." Matt wasn't proud that it sounded like he was bragging. "She's a nice woman. And I like her. But nothing has happened."

"Are you telling me to back off?" TJ asked.

"That's pretty loud and clear," Caleb said.

TJ held up his hands in mock surrender. "Backing off."

"She said she was meeting a guy tonight?" Caleb raised a brow.

Matt narrowed his gaze. "She said *guys*, plural. They're probably just friends of hers."

"Probably," said TJ with exaggerated skepticism, still clearly amused at Matt's expense.

"It took you long enough," Caleb said.

"There is no *it*," Matt responded. It had taken him too long to notice her. He'd own that.

"Have you asked her out?"

"We're a little busy at the moment. You know, distracted by criminal activity."

"That's a no," TJ said. "At least I took the plunge."

"You got shot down," Caleb reminded TJ.

"No risk, no reward."

"She's gun-shy," Matt said. He didn't know what made her that way, but it was obvious she was wary of dating.

"So, what are you going to do?" Caleb asked.

"Nothing."

"That's a mistake."

"I'm not going to force anything." The last thing Matt wanted to do was make Tasha feel uncomfortable working at the marina.

He wanted her to stay. For all kinds of different reasons, both personal and professional, but he definitely wanted her to stay.

The Edge Bar and Grill in the town of Whiskey Bay was a popular hangout for the marina staff. It also drew in the working class from the local service and supply businesses. The artsy crowd preferred the Blue Badger on Third Avenue. While those who were looking for something high-end and refined could choose the Ocean View Lounge across the highway. While the Crab Shack was becoming popular, drawing people from the surrounding towns and even as far away as Olympia.

Tasha liked the Edge. The decor was particularly attractive tonight, decked out for the season with a tree, lights and miles of evergreen garlands. A huge wreath over the bar was covered in gold balls and poinsettia flowers.

As was usual, the music had a rock-and-country flare. The menu was unpretentious. They had good beer on tap, and soda refills were free. She was driving her and Alex home tonight, so she'd gone with cola.

"Have you heard of anybody having any unexpected engine problems lately?" she asked Henry Schneider, who was sitting across the table.

Henry was a marine mechanic at Shutters Corner ten miles down the highway near the public wharf.

"Unexpected how?" he asked.

"We had some water in the fuel with no apparent cause."

"Loose cap?"

"Checked that, along with the fuel source. The water separator was full."

"There's your problem."

"I swapped it out, but I couldn't figure out how it got that way."

Henry gave a shrug. "It happens."

Alex returned from the small dance floor with another mechanic, James Hamilton, in tow.

"So, no reports of anything strange?" Tasha asked Henry.

"Strange?" James asked, helping Alex onto the high stool.

"Unexplained mechanical failures in the area."

"There's always an explanation," James said. "Sometimes you just have to keep looking."

"You want to dance?" Alex asked Henry.

"Who says I was through dancing?" James asked her.

"Dance with Tasha." Alex motioned for Henry to come with her.

He swallowed the remainder of his beer and rose from his chair.

James held out his hand to Tasha.

She gave up talking shop and accepted the invitation.

James was younger than Henry, likely in his late twenties. He was from Idaho and had a fresh-faced openness about him that Tasha liked. He was tall and lanky. His hair was red, and his complexion was fair. She didn't think she'd ever seen him in a bad mood.

It wasn't the first time they'd ever danced together, and he was good at it. He'd once told her barn dancing was a popular pastime in the small town where he'd grown up. She knew he'd left his high school sweetheart behind, and she got the feeling he'd one day return to her, even if he did prefer the West Coast to rural Idaho.

As the song ended, a figure appeared behind James. It took only a split second for Tasha to recognize Matt.

"What are you doing here?" she asked him, her guard immediately going up. She assumed this was too simple, too low-key to be his kind of place. "Is something wrong?"

"Dance?" he asked instead of answering.

James backed away. "Catch you later."

Matt stepped in front of her as a Bruce Springsteen song came up.

He took her hand.

"Did something happen?" she asked. "Was there another breakdown?"

"Nothing happened. Can't a guy go out for the evening?"

She struggled to ignore his light touch on her back and the heat where his hand joined hers. It was a lost cause. "This isn't your typical hangout."

"Sure it is."

"I can tell when you're lying."

He hesitated. "I was worried about you."

"Why?"

"There's a criminal out there."

She almost laughed. "If there is, he's focused on your company. It has nothing to do with me."

"We don't know that."

"We do."

He drew her closer as they danced, even though she knew getting more intimate with Matt was a big mistake.

But the words didn't come. Instead of speaking, she followed his lead. It was the path of least resistance, since their bodies moved seamlessly together. He was tall and solid and a smooth, skilled dancer.

She told herself she could handle it. They were in public after all. It's not like they would get carried away.

"I know you like to be independent," he said.

"I am independent."

"The truth is, people are less likely to harass you if you're with me."

His words were confusing.

"Nobody's been harassing me. Nobody's going to harass me."

Matt glanced around the room with apparent skepticism, as if he was expecting a gang of criminals to be lurking next to the dance floor.

"See that guy in the red shirt?" She pointed. "He worked at Shutters Corner. And the guy talking to Alex? He's Henry's coworker. They're local guys, Matt. They're mechanics. There are a lot of local mechanics here. And I'm talking to them all."

Matt's hold on her tightened. "Are you dancing with them all?"

She tipped her chin to look up at him, seeing his lips were thin and his jaw was tight.

He looked jealous. The last thing she wanted him to be was jealous. But her heart involuntarily lifted at the idea.

"No." The sharp retort was as much for her as it was for him. "I'm here asking questions. I'm gathering evidence, if you must know."

"Oh," he drawled with immediate understanding.

"Yes, *oh.* If anybody's having the same problems as us, these guys are going to know about it."

"That's a really good idea."

She put a note of sarcasm into her tone. "Why, thank you."

"I'm not crazy about the dancing part."

"*You* asked *me*," she pointed out.

"What? No, not with me." He canted his head. "With them."

She wanted to point out that he was dating other women. But she quickly stopped herself. Matt's romantic life was none of her business. And hers was none of his. The more women he dated, the better.

His voice lowered. "You can dance with me all you want."

"We're not going there, Matt."

"Okay." His agreement was easy, but his hold still felt intimate.

"You say okay, but we're still dancing." She knew she could pull away herself. She knew she should do exactly that, but he felt so good in her arms, she wanted to hang on just a little bit longer.

"The song will be over soon." He went silent for a moment. "How are you getting home?"

"Driving."

"You came alone?"

"I drove with Alex. Matt, I've been going out at night on my own for the past six years."

"Not while my boats were being sabotaged all around you."

"We don't know that they are being sabotaged. Honestly, I'm beginning to regret sharing my suspicions with you." The last thing she'd expected was for him to go all bodyguard on her.

"We don't know that they're not. And don't you dare hold anything back."

She stopped dancing. "Matt."

His hand contracted around her shoulder. "I didn't mean for that to sound like an order."

"Is there something you're not telling me?"

Had there been some development? Was there a danger she didn't know about?

"I heard TJ ask you out."

The statement took her completely by surprise. "That was a long time ago. You can't possibly suspect TJ."

Sure, she'd turned TJ down. But he and Matt were good friends. He wouldn't take out his anger with her by harming Matt. Plus, he hadn't even seemed to care that much. He was still friendly to her.

"I *don't* suspect TJ."

The song changed to a Christmas tune. It wasn't the best dance music in the world, but Matt kept leading, so she followed.

"Then why are we talking about him?"

Matt seemed to be reviewing their conversation so far. "It was Caleb."

"You suspect Caleb?" That was even more outlandish than suspecting TJ.

"Caleb's the one who got me worried about the sabotage. He's worried about Jules, which got me to thinking about you. And then TJ mentioned that he'd asked you out."

"Caleb worries too much. And TJ was months ago."

"So, you're not interested in him?"

Tasha was more than confused here. "Did he ask you to ask me?"

One minute, she thought Matt was romancing her, and she braced herself to shut him down. And then he seemed to be TJ's wingman. Their kisses notwithstanding, maybe she was reading his interest all wrong.

Before Matt could respond, she jumped back in. "TJ's not my type."

Alex appeared beside Tasha on the dance floor.

She took Tasha's arm and leaned into her ear. "James offered me a ride home."

Tasha pulled back to look at her friend. "Is that a good thing?"

Alex's eyes were alight. "You bet."

Since Alex had a done a whole lot more dancing than drinking, Tasha wasn't worried about her. And Tasha had known James for months. He seemed like a very upstanding guy.

"Do you mind if I bail on you?" Alex asked.

"Not at all. I'll see you later."

Alex grinned. "Thanks." Her walk was light as she moved away.

"So, you're driving home alone," Matt said. "I'll follow you."

Tasha rolled her eyes at him.

"I'm serious."

"Thanks for the dance," she said and pulled back from his arms.

She was going to have another drink. She was going to chat with Henry and the other mechanics. She didn't need a bodyguard.

# Four

Matt hung back as Tasha approached her compact car in the Edge's parking lot. It was in a dark corner, and he moved out of the building's lights so his eyes could adjust.

It was obvious she knew he was there, knew he'd waited for her to leave for home. She'd shot him a look of frustration as she'd headed for the front door and he'd risen from his seat at the bar.

Now, she shook her head with exaggerated resignation and gave him a mocking wave as she slipped into the driver's seat.

He didn't really care how she felt. Caleb had him worried about safety. He headed for his own car at the opposite side of the parking lot. The bar was only half-full at ten o'clock. But even on a weeknight, the crowd here would keep going until midnight, when the place shut down.

Tasha's engine cranked. Then it cranked again. But it didn't catch and start. A third crank was followed by silence.

Matt turned back.

She was out of the car and opening the hood.

"Need some help?" he asked as he approached.

She laughed. "You *have* read my résumé, right?"

"I'm not questioning your technical skills. And it's obviously a dead battery."

Her annoyance seemed to fade. "That's exactly what it is."

As they gazed at the cold engine, a thought struck him. "Could this be sabotage?"

"No." Her answer was definitive.

"How can you be sure?"

"Because it's related to my having an old battery. I've been limping it along for a while now. Do you have cables?"

"In my BMW?"

"BMWs run the same way as any other car."

"My battery's under warranty. And I have roadside assistance. You don't have cables?"

Tasha was a be-prepared kind of woman. Jumper cables seemed like the kind of thing she would carry.

She looked embarrassed. "I do. Usually. I took them out of my trunk to help Alex move her stuff."

"Come on," he said, motioning to his car.

"I'll call a tow truck and get a jump."

"There's no need." He wasn't about to leave her standing in a dark parking lot waiting for a tow truck. "I'll bring you back tomorrow with your jumper cables."

"I can take care of it."

His frustration mounted. "Why are you arguing?"

She squared her shoulders and lifted her chin but didn't answer.

"Well?" he prompted.

"I don't know."

He couldn't help but grin. "Pride?"

"Maybe. I don't like to be rescued."

"But you'll accept help from a random tow truck driver."

She dropped the hood down, and the sound echoed. "He's paid to help me. But you're right. I'm wrong. I'd appreciate the ride home."

"Did you just say I was right?"

She locked the driver's door and started walking. "I did."

He fell into step beside her. "It's fun being right."

"Calm down. It's not that exciting."

He hit the remote to unlock the doors. "You're positive somebody wasn't messing with your battery?"

"I'm positive. It's unrelated. And if we try to link it in, we'll set ourselves off in the wrong direction."

Matt thought about her logic for a moment. "Okay. Now you're the one who's right."

She cracked a smile. "Thank goodness I'm evening things up."

He opened the driver's door while she did the same on the passenger side.

"But I'm not wrong," he pointed out.

"Maybe a little bit."

"Maybe not at all. I just asked a question. Postulating something is not the same as being incorrect about it."

"You're right," she said and plunked into the seat.

He leaned down to look through his open door. "That's two for me."

She was smiling as she buckled her seat belt.

He started the engine, turned down the music and pulled out of the parking lot.

The temperature was in the fifties, but the interior heated up quickly, and Tasha unzipped her fitted gray leather jacket. She wore a purple tank top beneath it over a boxy pair of faded blue jeans and brown Western-style boots. Her hair was pulled into a high ponytail. It was mostly brunette, but it flashed with amber highlights as they drove.

She looked casual and comfortable, sexy at the same time. He liked it. He liked it a lot.

"Nobody I talked to knew anything," she said. "Nothing weird going on out there in the broader Whiskey Bay mechanical world."

"So the marina is the target."

"That would be my guess. Or it's a couple of coincidences. It could still be that."

He didn't disagree. He hoped it was a couple of coincidences. "I'm going to check out my competition."

"How?"

"'Tis the season. There are a lot of gatherings and parties coming up. The business community likes to celebrate together."

"I remember."

"Were you here last year?"

She'd been working at the marina only since March.

"I was talking about the business community anywhere. It was the same while I was growing up."

"You went to corporate Christmas parties?" He tried to picture it.

"I read about them," she continued, quickly. "They sounded...posh and snooty and boring."

He laughed at how she wrinkled her nose. "They're not bad. They are fancy. But some of the people are interesting."

She gave a derisive scoff.

"Hey, I'm one of those people. Am I that bad?"

"In some ways, yes."

"What ways?" He tried not to let her opinion get to him.

"The way you dress. The way you talk."

"What's wrong with the way I talk?"

She seemed to think about that. "It's clear and precise, with very little slang. You have a wide vocabulary."

"I'm not seeing the problem."

"It sounds posh."

"What about you?"

She was easily as articulate as him.

"I'm perfectly ordinary."

She wasn't. But he wasn't going to get into that argument right now.

"And so are the people at the corporate parties. You shouldn't be biased against them." He slowed the car and turned from the highway down his long driveway that wound through the woods.

"I can't stand those frilly, frothy dresses, those pretentious caviar and foie gras canapés, and the ceaseless conversation about who's making partner and the who's marrying who."

He wasn't about to admit she'd nailed it—at least when it came to some of the guests at those parties.

"You shouldn't knock it until you've tried it," he said instead.

"You're right."

He chuckled. "And I've hit the trifecta."

Then the headlights caught his house. He blinked to check his vision on what he thought he saw there. His stomach curled. It couldn't be.

"Who's that?" Tasha asked as the car came to a stop.

Matt shut off the engine. "My ex-wife."

Tasha gazed through the windshield. "So that's her."

"I take it you haven't met her?"

"I only saw her from a distance. She didn't seem to be around much."

Those last few months, his ex had used any excuse to travel.

"She liked France," he said. "She still likes France. There's a man there."

"Oh," Tasha said with obvious understanding.

"Yeah." Matt released his seat belt. "I can't even imagine what she's doing back here."

He and Tasha both stepped out of the car.

"Hello, Dianne," he said as he approached the lit porch.

Her dark hair was pulled back from her face with some kind of headband, the ends of her hair brushing her shoulders. She wore a black wool jacket with leather trim, a pair of black slacks and very high heels. Her makeup was perfect, as always. Her mouth was tight. Her eyes narrowed.

"Where have you been?" she asked. Then her gaze swept Tasha.

"This is Tasha." He didn't like the dismissive expression on Dianne's face. "She and I have been dancing."

He felt Tasha's look of surprise but ignored it.

"What are you doing here?" he asked Dianne.

"I need to speak with you."

Her nostrils flared with an indrawn breath. "It's a private matter."

"Well, I'm not about to end my evening early to listen to you."

Whatever Dianne had to say to him—and he couldn't imagine what that might be—it could wait until morning.

"You can call me tomorrow, Dianne." He started for the door, gesturing for Tasha to go ahead of him.

"It's about François," Dianne blurted out.

Matt kept walking.

Whatever was going on between Dianne and her new husband was completely their business. Matt couldn't stay far enough away.

"He left me."

Matt paused. "I'm sorry, Dianne. It's none of my business."

"He stole my money."

"Matt?" Tasha said with a little tug against his hand.

"*All* of my money," Dianne said.

"It'll still wait until morning." Matt punched in the key code to his front door. "Do you need me to call you a ride?"

"*Matt,*" Dianne practically wailed.

"We're divorced, Dianne. As I recall, your settlement was more than generous."

Matt had only wanted it to be over. Although his lawyer had argued with him, he'd given her everything she'd asked for. It had meant significant refinancing of the marina, but if he worked hard, he'd be back on solid footing within two or three years.

He retrieved his phone and pulled up his ride app, requesting a car. "Call me tomorrow. I assume you still have my number?"

"I'm in trouble, Matt," Dianne said. "Deep trouble."

"Then I suggest you call a lawyer."

Her voice rose. "I didn't commit a crime."

"I'm glad to hear that. Your car will be here in a couple of minutes."

He opened the door and Tasha went inside.

"How can you be so cruel?" Dianne called out from behind him.

He turned. "How can you have the nerve to ask me to drop everything and deal with your problems? You cheated

on me, left me and put my business at risk through your un-
bridled greed."

A pair of headlights flashed through the trees.

"Your ride is here, Dianne." He stepped through the open
door, closing it to then face Tasha.

Matt leaned back against his front door as if he expected
his ex-wife to try to break it down.

"Sorry about that," he said.

Tasha wasn't sure how she should feel about the exchange.
She knew divorces could be acrimonious, and Matt was
within his rights to stay at arm's length from his ex-wife,
but Dianne had seemed genuinely upset.

"It sounds like she could use a friend," Tasha said.

"Truthfully, it's hard to know for sure. She's a drama
queen. Her reaction to a fire or a flood is the same as her reaction to a broken fingernail."

Tasha tried not to smile. It didn't seem like there was anything funny in the situation.

Matt pushed away from the door. "She was supposed to
be in France. She was supposed to stay in France. I'd really
hoped she'd stay in France forever. I need a drink. Do you
want a drink?"

He started down the short staircase to the glass-walled
living room. On the way, he seemed to absently hit a wall
switch, and the long fireplace came to life. Fed by gas, it was
glassed in on all sides and stretched the length of the living
room, separating a kitchen area from a lounge area where
white leather armchairs faced a pair of matching sofas.

Tasha knew she should head home. But she found herself
curious about Matt, about Dianne, and she'd been sipping on
sodas all night long. A real drink sounded appealing.

"I'm thinking tequila," Matt said as he passed one end of
the fireplace into the kitchen.

Tasha threw caution to the wind. "I love margaritas."

"Margaritas it is." He opened a double-doored stainless steel refrigerator. "We have limes." He held them up. "Glasses are above the long counter. Pick whatever looks good."

Feeling happier than she had any right to feel about sharing a drink with Matt, Tasha moved to the opposite end of the kitchen. Near the glass wraparound wall, she opened an upper cupboard, finding a selection of crystal glasses. She chose a pair with deep bowls and sturdy-looking bases.

"Frozen or on the rocks?" he asked.

"Frozen."

He was cutting limes on an acrylic board. "There should be some coarse salt in the pantry. Through that door." He pointed with the tip of his knife.

Tasha crossed behind him to the back of the kitchen.

The walk-in pantry was impressive. It was large and lined with shelves of staples and exotic treats.

"Do you like to cook?" she called out to him.

"It's a hobby."

She located the coarse salt and reemerged. "I wouldn't have guessed that."

"Why?" He seemed puzzled.

"Good question."

"Thanks."

"You seem—" she struggled to put it into words "—like the kind of guy who would have a housekeeper."

"I do."

"Aha!"

"She's not a cook. I decided a long time ago that I couldn't do everything around here and run a business, too, so I chose to do the things I like the best and give up the things I didn't enjoy."

"What is it you like best?" Tasha helped herself to one of the limes. She'd spotted some small glass bowls in the cupboard and retrieved one for the salt.

"Cooking, working, the gym."

"Dating?" she asked.

"That's recent."

"But you like it. You do it quite a lot now."

"I do, and I do." He stilled then and seemed to think more about his answer.

"What?" she prompted.

"Nothing. That about sums it up."

"What about friends?"

"Caleb and TJ? Sure. I hang with them whenever I can. With them being so close, we don't really plan anything, we just drop by. It's kind of like background noise."

"Like family," Tasha mused as she cut the lime in half.

She'd observed the relationship between the three men. It was as if they were brothers. She'd like to have close relationships like that. But she had absolutely nothing in common with her two sisters.

"Like family," Matt agreed. "They're going to flip when they find out Dianne's back."

"Do you expect her to stick around?"

It was none of Tasha's business. And she wasn't entitled to have an opinion one way or the other. But she liked that Matt was single. After all, a fantasy was fun only if it had an outside chance of coming true.

The knife slipped, and she cut her finger.

"Ouch!"

"What happened?" He was by her side in an instant.

"I wasn't paying attention."

"Is it bad?" He gently took her hand. "You're bleeding."

"Just a little. Don't let me ruin the drinks."

He seemed amused by her priority as he reached for a tissue from a box on the counter. "Let's get you a bandage."

"I bet it'll stop on its own." She pressed the tissue against the cut.

"This way." He took her elbow. "We can't have you bleeding into the salt."

He led her up the steps toward the entry hall, but then veered right, taking her down a long hallway with plush silver-gray carpet. Some of the doors were open, and she saw an office and what looked like a comfortable sunroom.

"This is nice," she said.

They entered one room, and it took her only a second to realize it had to be the master bedroom. She hesitated and stumbled.

"Careful," he said.

"This is…"

He paused and glanced around at the king-size bed with taupe accents, two leather and polished metal easy chairs, twin white bedside tables and a polished oak floor with geometric-patterned throw rugs. Here, too, there were walls of windows looking across the bay and over the forest.

"What?" he prompted.

*"Big."* She settled on the word. She wanted to say *intimidating*, maybe even *arousing*. She was inside Matt's bedroom. How had that happened?

"I know there are bandages in here." He gestured toward the open door to an en suite.

She struggled to even her breathing as she entered the bathroom. "This is big, too."

"I like my space. And I didn't need too many bedrooms, so it was easy to go for something big for the master."

She moved with him to the sink.

"Do you want kids?" She had no idea where that question came from.

He shrugged. "Dianne didn't want them. I'm easy. I could go either way." Then he gave a chuckle as he opened the upper cabinet.

Tasha averted her eyes. Seeing what was in his medicine cabinet seemed far too personal.

"I figure once I meet Caleb's twins," Matt continued, "it'll either make me want some of my own, or cure me of that idea forever."

He set a small bandage on the counter, shut the cabinet and gently removed the tissue from her cut finger.

"I can do this myself," she said, feeling the effects of his closeness.

She liked his smell. She liked his voice. His touch was gentle.

"Two hands are better than one." He turned on the water, waited a moment then tested the temperature.

Tasha could feel her heart tap against her rib cage. Her gaze was caught on his face. He looked inordinately sexy, and amazingly handsome.

"What about you?" he asked, his attention on her finger as he held it under the warm flow of water.

"Huh?" She gave herself a mental shake and shifted her gaze.

"Do you want kids?"

"Sure. I suppose so. Maybe."

"You haven't thought about it?"

She really hadn't. Her focus had been on her career and making it to the top of her profession. "I guess I'm not in any rush."

"Fair enough." He wrapped the small bandage around the end of her finger and secured it in place. "Good as new."

"Thank you." She made the mistake of looking into his eyes.

His twinkled, and he smiled at her.

For a moment, she thought he was going to kiss her. But instead, he brushed a playful finger across the tip of her nose and stepped back.

"Our ice is melting," he said. "We better blend those drinks."

Sitting across from Dianne at a window table in the Crab Shack, Matt had asked for a water. Now he wished he'd ordered something stronger.

He hadn't wanted to meet her at his house. He was steadily working to move forward with his life; he didn't want to go backward.

"You gave him control of your *entire* portfolio?" Matt couldn't believe what he was hearing.

"He had a mansion," Dianne said, a whine in her tone. "He had a yacht and a jet and memberships at these exclusive clubs. He didn't even want a prenup. Why wouldn't I trust him?"

"Because he was a con artist?"

She gave a pout. "How was I supposed to know that?"

"You weren't," Matt acknowledged. "What you were supposed to do was keep control of your own assets." He was appalled that she would be so blindly trusting of anyone.

"It was all in French," she said. "I couldn't understand it. It only made sense for him to take over the details."

It sounded like the man had taken over a whole lot more than just the details of her assets. He'd obviously taken complete charge of her money. But Matt wasn't about to lengthen the debate. He'd agreed to meet Dianne today, but he had no intention of stepping back into her life, no matter what kind of mess she'd made of it. And by the sounds of it, she'd made a pretty big mess.

Her exotic French husband had taken her money and disappeared, leaving a trail of debts and charges of fraud behind him.

"So, what are you going to do?" he asked her.

She opened her eyes wide, and let her lower lip go soft. "I miss you, Matt."

"Oh, no you don't." He wasn't going there. He so wasn't going there. "What are you going to do, Dianne? *You*, not me. You alone."

Her eyes narrowed, and he stared straight back at her.

Then what looked like fear came over her expression. "I don't know *what* to do."

"Get a job?" he suggested.

The Crab Shack waitress arrived with their lunches, lobster salad for Dianne, a platter of hand-cut halibut and fries for Matt. He had developed a serious fondness for the Crab Shack's signature sauces.

Dianne waited for the waitress to leave. Then she leaned forward, her tone a hiss. "You want me to work? I don't know how to work."

"I don't *want* you to do anything."

"I can't do it, Matt," she said with conviction.

"I'm not going to solve this for you, Dianne." He popped a crispy fry into his mouth.

"You've got loads of money."

"No, I don't. I had to refinance everything to pay your settlement. And even if I did have money, you have no call on it."

"That's my home." She gazed out the window at the cliff side where his house jutted out over the ocean.

"It *was* your home. Temporarily. I paid for the house. Then I paid you half its value in the divorce. Then you sucked out every nickel of my business profits."

"But—"

"Enjoy your lunch, Dianne. Because it's the last thing I'll ever buy for you."

Her mouth worked, but no sounds came out.

"Matt?" Caleb's wife, Jules, arrived to greet him, her tone tentative. She'd obviously caught the expression on his face and Dianne's and knew something was wrong.

He neutralized his own expression. "Jules. How are you?"

Her stomach was well rounded from the twins she was carrying.

"Doing great." She rested a hand on her belly. Then she turned to Dianne, obviously waiting for an introduction.

"Jules, this is my ex-wife, Dianne."

Jules's eyes widened. "Oh."

"She's in town for a short visit."

"I see." It was pretty clear Jules didn't see. As far as Caleb or anybody else knew—including Matt—Dianne had planned to spend the rest of her life in France. "It's nice to meet you, Dianne. Welcome to the Crab Shack."

Dianne didn't respond, her face still tight with obvious anger.

"Are you coming to the chamber of commerce gala?" Matt asked Jules, ignoring Dianne's angry silence.

Jules was coming up on six months pregnant, and her doctor had advised her to keep her feet up as much as possible.

"I'll definitely be there. I'm good for a couple of hours between rests."

"You look fantastic."

Dianne shifted restlessly in her seat, drawing Jules's brief glance.

"You'll be there?" Jules asked Matt.

"I agreed to speak."

"Oh, good. You'll be so much more entertaining than the mayor, and that Neil Himmelsbach they had on Labor Day. I should let you two finish lunch."

Matt rose to give her a quick hug and a kiss on the cheek. "Nice to see you, Jules."

She patted his shoulder. "Better go." Her attention moved to the front entrance, where a customer had just entered the restaurant.

Matt did a double take when he saw it was Tasha. He paused, watching, wondering what she was doing at the Crab Shack.

"Sit *down*," Dianne said to him.

Matt didn't want to sit down. He was waiting to see if Tasha would notice him and react in some way, maybe a wave, maybe a hello, maybe to come over and talk to him.

But she didn't.

"I'll be right back," he said to Dianne, taking matters into his own hands.

"But you—"

He didn't hear the rest.

"Hey, Tasha," he said as he came up to her.

She looked at him in obvious surprise.

"Lunch break?" he asked.

He couldn't help but notice she was dressed in clean jeans and wearing a silky top and her leather jacket. She didn't dress like that for work.

"I started early this morning." It was obviously an explanation for her boss.

"You don't need to punch a time clock with me. Take as long a lunch as you want."

"I'm having lunch with Jules."

"Really?" The revelation surprised Matt. He hadn't realized she and Jules were getting to know each other.

"She invited me," Tasha said.

"That's nice. That's good."

Tasha's gaze strayed past him, and he could tell the moment she spotted Dianne.

"This is going to sound weird," he said, moving in closer and lowering his voice.

"That would be a first."

"Can I kiss you on the cheek? Maybe give you a hug? Just a little one."

Tasha stared up at him. "Are you drunk?"

"No. It's Dianne. It would help me if she thought you and I were... You know..."

"I take it she wants to rekindle something?"

"She wants money above anything else. If she believes I'm with you, it'll stop her from thinking romancing me to get it is an option."

Tasha glanced around the crowded restaurant. It was clear she was checking to see if they knew anyone else here.

"Jules will understand the score," he assured her, assuming she didn't want anyone to get the wrong impression. "I'm sure Caleb's told her all about Dianne."

"I'm not worried about Jules."

"Then what?"

Something was making her hesitate. He dared to hope she

was remembering those brief moments in his bathroom when he'd felt a connection to her. Could she be worried about developing feelings for him?

But then her answer was brisk. "Nothing. I'm not worried about anything. Kiss on the cheek. Quick hug. No problem."

Though he was disappointed, Matt smiled his appreciation. "You're the best."

"You gave me a twenty percent raise. It's the least I can do."

So much for his musings about her feelings for him.

"This is above and beyond," he whispered as he moved in for the cheek kiss.

She smelled amazing. She tasted fantastic. It was brutal for him to have to pull back.

"You know it is," she said with a thread of laughter.

He gave her an equally quick hug. "I owe you."

He squeezed her hands, wishing with all his heart the crowd would disappear from around them and he could be alone with her.

Then he turned away, heading back across the restaurant to where Dianne was glaring at him.

# Five

As always, Tasha was impressed with the Crab Shack. During lunch, it was bright and airy, with wooden tables, a casual ambiance and sweeping views of the ocean and cliffs. Then for dinner, they set out white tablecloths, candles and linen, bringing up the outdoor lighting, making it both elegant and cozy. It was no surprise that its popularity was growing fast.

Back in Boston, expensive restaurants had been the norm for her on weekends. She'd been forced to stop whatever it was she was doing far too early in the afternoon, clean up, dress up and go on parade to impress her parents' associates with their three perfect daughters.

She had wasted so much valuable time primping and engaging in inconsequential conversation. To top it off, the food had been absurdly fancy, not at all filling. There were many nights that she'd gone home and made herself a sandwich after dining at a five-star restaurant.

But the Crab Shack wasn't like that. The food was good and the atmosphere comfortable. It was refreshing to be in a place that was high quality without the pretention.

"It's this way," Jules told her, leading a weaving pattern through the tables.

Tasha gave in to temptation and took a final glance at Matt's handsome profile before following.

Jules led her into an office next to the kitchen. "It's a bit crowded in here," she apologized.

"Not a problem."

The square room held a desk with a computer and stacks of papers, a small meeting table with three chairs, and a couple of filing cabinets. It wasn't as bright as the restaurant, but there was a window that faced toward the marina and Caleb's partially built Neo restaurant.

Jules gestured to the table. "I hope you don't mind, I ordered us a bunch of appetizers."

"That sounds great." Tasha wasn't fussy.

"I do better with small things." Jules gave a self-conscious laugh. "That sounds silly. What I mean, is I tend to graze my way through the day rather than attempting a big meal."

"I can imagine your stomach is a bit crowded in there."

Jules was glowing with pregnancy.

"Between the three of us, we do fight for space," Jules said.

Tasha smiled.

Jules opened a laptop on the table. "We have security video files going back three weeks."

"I really appreciate this," Tasha said.

"Caleb has ordered more security cameras, better security cameras with higher resolution. The ones we have now don't show a lot of detail at a distance."

"Anything will help."

Jules moved the mouse and opened the first file.

To say it was boring was an understatement. They set it on a fast speed and sat back to watch.

"Matt's not normally an affectionate guy," Jules mentioned in an overly casual tone.

The observation took Tasha by surprise. It also put her on edge.

"He hugged you," Jules continued, turning her attention from the screen to Tasha. "And he kissed you."

"On the cheek," Tasha said, keeping her own attention on the view of the marina.

The camera angle showed the gate, part of the path and the first thirty feet of the pier. The yachts rocked in fast motion, while people zipped back and forth along the pier and the sun moved toward the horizon.

"It's still odd for him."

"It was for Dianne's benefit," Tasha said. "He wants her to think we're dating."

"They're divorced."

Tasha gave a shrug. "It could be ego, I suppose."

"That doesn't sound like Matt."

Tasha agreed. "Dianne seems to need money. Matt's worried she'll try to latch back onto him."

"Now, *that* sounds like the Dianne I've heard about."

On the video, the lights came up as the sun sank away.

That had been Tasha's impression, as well. "I only met her briefly last night, but—"

"Last night?" The interest in Jules's tone perked up.

"We were coming back from the Edge, and she was waiting for him."

"A date?"

"No." Tasha was careful not to protest too strongly. "A coincidence. I was there talking to the mechanics in the area. I wanted to know if anyone else was having weird engine failures."

"That's a good idea."

"I thought so. Wait, what's that?" Tasha pointed at the screen. The picture was dark and shadowy, but it looked like someone was scaling the fence. She checked the date and time stamp. "That's the night before *Orca's Run* went out."

"So, it was sabotage."

"Maybe."

They watched the figure move along the pier. It went out of the frame before coming to the slip for *Orca's Run*.

"That has to be it," Jules said.

Tasha wasn't as ready to draw a concrete conclusion. "It didn't look like he was carrying anything, no fuel, no water."

"But he broke in. Whoever it was, was up to no good."

"It's evidence of that," Tasha agreed. She'd hate to assume something and potentially be led in the wrong direction. "We should watch the rest of the video. I can do it myself if you're busy."

"No way. This is the most interesting thing I've done lately. And I'm supposed to sit down every couple of hours." Jules made a show of putting her feet up on the third chair.

There was a light rap on the door, and a waitress pushed it open, arriving with a tray of appetizers and two icy soft drinks.

"I hope you're hungry," Jules said as the server set everything down on the table.

"I'm starving."

"Make sure you try the crab puffs. They're my secret recipe."

"I'm in." Tasha spread a napkin in her lap and helped herself to a crab puff.

"I've been going nuts over smoked salmon," Jules said, going for a decorative morsel on a flat pastry shell. "I don't know why, but my taste buds are big into salt."

Tasha took a bite of the crab puff. It was heavenly. "Mmm," she said around the bite.

Jules's eyes lit up. "See what I mean?"

"You're a genius."

"They're the most popular item on the menu. Caleb wants to steal them for Neo, but I won't let him."

"Stick to your guns," Tasha said before popping the second half of the crab puff into her mouth.

"Oh, I will. We're each half owner of the other's restaurant now, but it's still a competition."

"I hope you're winning. Wait. Take a look." Tasha drew Jules's attention to the laptop screen.

The figure returned to the gate and seemed to toss something over the fence beside it. The two women watched as he climbed the fence, then appeared to look for the object. But then something seemed to startle him, and he ducked away, out of camera range.

"He was up to something," Jules said.

"That was definitely odd," Tasha said. "It could have been tools. I wish we had a better view."

The video got boring again, nothing but yachts bobbing on the midnight tide. Jules took a drink and went for another crab puff.

The office door opened and Caleb appeared.

"How's it going in here?" he asked.

Jules stretched her back as she spoke. "We saw a guy climb over the fence onto the pier and sneak back out again."

Caleb moved past Tasha. He stood behind Jules's chair and began rubbing her shoulders.

"What did he do?" Caleb asked.

"He threw something over the fence," Jules said. "Tasha thinks it might have been tools."

"We couldn't tell for sure," Tasha put in, not wanting to jump to conclusions. "And the frame's not wide enough to see what he did while he was on the pier. It could have been nothing."

The door opened again, and Matt joined them.

"I'll bet it was something," Jules said.

"You'll bet what was something?" Matt asked, glancing around at all three of them.

Tasha couldn't stop herself from reacting to his presence. She imagined his hands on her shoulders, the way Caleb was rubbing Jules's.

"There was a guy," Jules said.

"It might have been something," Tasha jumped in, shaking off the fantasy. "A guy climbing the fence and leaving again. But we couldn't see enough to be sure. There's a lot more video to watch."

"Dianne gone?" Jules asked Matt.

"Hopefully."

"What happened?" Caleb asked. "I didn't expect to see her back in Whiskey Bay...well, ever."

"Neither did I," Matt said. "It turns out her French finance tycoon wasn't all he claimed to be."

"Uh-oh," Caleb said.

"All that money she got in the divorce..."

"No way," Caleb said.

Tasha kept her attention fixed on the screen and away from Matt.

"All gone," he said.

"How is that possible?" Jules asked. "You gave her a fortune."

"The court gave her a fortune," Matt said.

"You didn't fight it."

"I wanted my freedom."

"And she's back anyway," Caleb said. "That didn't work out so well."

"You're not giving her any more money," Jules said.

Tasha wanted to echo the advice, but she didn't feel that it was her business to jump in. Matt and Caleb had been good friends for years. She knew Matt thought of him as a brother.

"I told her to get a job."

"Good advice."

"Let's see if she takes it." Matt didn't sound convinced she would.

Then his hand did come down on Tasha's shoulder. The warmth of his palm surged into her, leaving a tingle behind.

"Anything else going on?"

It was daylight on the video now and people were moving back and forth along the pier: crew, customers, delivery companies and Matt. She watched Matt stride confidently through the frame, and her chest tightened.

She had to struggle to find her voice. "Nothing out of the ordinary. It would be nice to have a wider view."

"You've looked through your own footage?" Caleb asked Matt.

"We have," Matt answered. "But the camera showing the main part of the pier had malfunctioned."

"Malfunctioned?" The skepticism was clear in Caleb's tone.

"We had a technician look at it. The case was cracked.

Salt spray got in and caused corrosion. It might be wear and tear, but it could have been pried open on purpose."

"Who would do that?" Caleb asked. "Why would they do that?"

"I wish I knew," Matt said. "I hate to suspect staff, but there are a couple of new hires on the dock. We're checking into their histories."

"Why would staff have to climb the fence?" Caleb asked.

"Not everyone has the combination," Tasha answered. "Not everyone needs it."

"I don't hand it out to the new hires," Matt said.

Tasha knew the footage narrowed the list of suspects—at least of possible staff members as suspects.

"A little to the left," Jules said on a moan.

Caleb smiled down at his wife.

Matt's hand tightened around Tasha's shoulder.

Arousal washed through her with the force of a riptide.

She ordered herself to concentrate. She refocused on the screen, desperately hoping something would happen on the pier to distract her from his touch.

Matt was happy to speak at the chamber of commerce's annual Christmas gala. He knew the chamber did important work. He'd benefited from its programs in the past. Without its loan guarantees, he never could have purchased Whiskey Bay Marina, never mind grown it to the size it was today, or recovered from the financial hit of his divorce for that matter.

He'd started life out in South Boston. There, his father ran a small residential construction company, while his mother did home care for the elderly. His parents had raised six children. Matt was the youngest and easily the most ambitious. His older siblings all still lived in the South Boston area, most working for his father, all raising families of their own.

They seemed content with barbecues and baseball games. But Matt had wanted more. He'd always wanted more out of life. He'd worked construction long enough to put himself through college and set aside a nest egg. Then he'd bought a few fixer-upper houses, sold them for a profit and finally ended up on the West Coast taking what was probably a ridiculous risk on the Whiskey Bay Marina. But it had turned out well.

It seemed people found it an inspiring story.

Finished with his cuff links and his bow tie, he shrugged into his tux jacket. It was custom fitted and made him feel good, confident, like he'd arrived. It was a self-indulgent moment, dressing in an expensive suit for a fine dinner. And he'd admit to enjoying it.

Tonight he had an additional mission. The owners of the three other marinas in the area would be at the gala. A competitor would have a motive for sabotage. Matt had never trusted Stuart Moorlag. He seemed secretive, and Matt had heard stories of him cutting corners on maintenance and overbilling clients. He could have financial troubles.

There was a knock on the front door, and Matt made his way past the living room to the entry hall. He'd ordered a car for the evening to keep from having to drive home after the party.

But it wasn't the driver standing on his porch. It was Tasha.

"We have a problem," she said without preamble, walking into the entry hall.

"Okay."

Then she stopped and looked him up and down. "Wow."

"It's the gala tonight," he said.

"Still. Wow."

"Is *wow* a good thing?"

"You look pretentious."

"So, not good." He told himself he wasn't disappointed. He'd have been surprised if she had liked him in a tux. He wished she did. But wishing didn't seem to help him when it came to Tasha.

"Good if pretentious was your goal."

"Well, that was a dig."

"I'm sorry. I didn't mean it to sound like that. What I meant was, you'll impress all the people at what I'm guessing is a very fancy event tonight."

"Thanks. I think." It wasn't quite an insult anymore, but it wasn't quite a compliment either. He decided to move on.

He gave a glance to his watch. He had a few minutes, but not long. "What's the problem?"

"The sabotage is escalating."

That got his instant and full attention. Tasha definitely wasn't one to exaggerate.

"How?" he asked.

"I found a peeled wire in the electric system of *Salty Sea*. It seemed suspicious, so I checked further and found a fuel leak."

He didn't understand the significance. "And?"

"Together, they would likely have started a fire."

"Are you *kidding* me?" He couldn't believe what he was hearing.

"I wish I was."

"People could have been *hurt*?"

A fire on a boat was incredibly serious, especially in December. If they had to jump into the water, hypothermia was the likely result.

"Badly," she said.

He didn't want to leave her to attend the gala. He wanted to explore what she'd found, talk this out. He wanted to plan their next move.

"I have to go to the gala," he said, thinking maybe they could meet later. "I'm speaking at it. And the other marina owners will be there. I was going to use it as an excuse to feel them out."

She didn't hesitate. "I want to come."

The statement took him completely by surprise. He couldn't help but take in her outfit of cargo pants, jersey top and a work jacket.

"Not like this," she said, frowning at him.

"Do you have something to wear?"

Her hands went to her hips, shoulders squaring. "You don't think I can clean up, right?"

Registering the determination in her expression—although he had his doubts—he wasn't about to argue that particular point. He looked at his watch again. "I don't have a lot of time. My car will be here in a few minutes."

Her lips pursed in obvious thought. "I don't have a ball gown in my room. But did Dianne leave anything behind? A dress or something?"

"You want to wear my ex-wife's clothes?" Matt was no expert, but that didn't sound like something an ordinary woman would volunteer to do.

"What've you got?"

"You're serious?"

"You don't think I look serious?" she asked.

"You look very serious."

"So?"

He gave up, even though he had major reservations about how this was going to turn out. "There are some things left in the basement. This way." He led her around the corner to the basement stairs.

He flipped the switch as they started down. "She was a shopaholic. Didn't even bother to take all of it with her. Some of the stuff has probably never been worn."

They went past the pool table and entered a cluttered storage room. The dresses were in plastic film, hanging on a rack, jackets and slacks beside them, shoes in boxes beneath. "I hadn't had the time to get rid of it yet."

"I'll be quick," Tasha said, marching up to the rack and searching her way through.

After a few minutes, she chose something red with sparkles.

"Wow," he said.

"You don't think I can pull off red?"

"It's very bold."

"Trust me. I want them to notice." She hunted through the shoe boxes. "I don't suppose you know what size shoe your ex wore?"

"I have no idea."

Tasha held up a black pump, turning it to various angles. Then she straightened, stripped off her boot and fuzzy sock and wiggled her foot into it.

"It'll do," she said.

"Seriously? Just like that?" He'd seen Dianne spend two hours choosing an outfit.

"You said you were in a hurry." Tasha brushed by him.

"Yes, but…"

"Then, let's do this."

He followed behind, shutting off the lights as they went. "You're a strange woman."

"If by *strange*, you mean *efficient*, then thank you."

By *strange*, he meant *unique*. She was like nobody he'd ever met. Not that it was a bad thing. It was a good thing. At the very least, it was an entertaining thing.

"Yes," he said. "I meant efficient."

"Can I borrow your bathroom?"

"Be my guest."

There was another knock on the front door. This time it was sure to be the driver.

"I have to speak at eight," he called to Tasha's back as she scooted down the hall, clothes bundled in her arms, wearing one work boot and one bare foot.

She waved away his warning, and he turned to answer the door.

Ten minutes later, or maybe it was only five, she emerged from the hallway looking ravishing.

Matt blinked, thinking it had to be an optical illusion. No woman could go from regular Tasha to this screaming ten of a bombshell in five minutes. It wasn't possible.

Her hair was swooped in a wispy updo. The straps of the

dress clung to her slim, creamy shoulders. It sparkled with rhinestones as she walked, the full red skirt swishing above her knees. Her green eyes sparkled, the dark lashes framing their beauty. Her lips were deep red, her cheeks flushed, and her limbs were long, toned and graceful.

He couldn't speak.

"Will I do?" she asked, giving him a graceful twirl. Her tone was softer than normal, her words slower and more measured.

He opened his mouth. "Uh…"

"Don't get all fussy on me, Matt. It was a rush job."

"You look terrific."

She glanced down at herself. "Good enough."

"No, not just good enough. Jaw dropping. How did you do that?" How had this gorgeous, feminine creature stayed hidden beneath the baggy clothes and grease all this time?

"I took off my other clothes and put these ones on."

There was more to it than that. "Your hair?"

"Takes about thirty seconds. Are you ready?"

"I'm ready." He was more than ready. He was *so* ready to go on a date with Tasha.

Okay, so they were investigating more than they were dating. And the new information she'd just brought him was unsettling. They'd have to talk more about that in the car.

But she was more ravishingly beautiful than he could have possibly imagined, and she was his partner for the gala. He felt fantastic, far better than he had merely putting on the fine tux, maybe better than he'd felt in his whole life.

At the ballroom in downtown Olympia, Tasha felt like she was stepping into her own past. She'd been to this party dozens of times, the chamber orchestra, the high-end hors d'oeuvres, the glittering women and stiffly dressed men. And, in this case, the rich Christmas decorations, floral arrangements, garlands of holly and evergreen, thousands of white lights, swirls of spun-glass snow and a huge Christmas tree on the back wall, covered in oversize blue and white ornaments and twinkling lights.

"You going to be okay in all this?" Matt asked as they walked through the grand entry.

"I'll be fine." She could do this in her sleep.

"We'll have to sit down near the front. They want me close by for my presentation."

"No problem." She was used to her parents being VIPs at events in Boston. From the time she was seven or eight, she'd learned to sit still through interminable speeches and to respond politely to small talk from her parents' friends and business connections. "Shall we mingle our way down?"

He looked surprised by the suggestion. "Sure."

"Can you point out the other marina owners?"

They began walking as Matt gazed around the room.

"Hello there, Matt." A fiftysomething man approached, clasping Matt's hand in a hearty shake.

"Hugh," Matt responded. "Good to see you again." He immediately turned to Tasha. "This is Tasha Lowell. Tasha, Hugh Mercer owns Mercer Manufacturing, headquartered here in Olympia."

Tasha offered her hand and gave Hugh Mercer a warm smile. "It's a pleasure to meet you, sir." She quickly moved her attention on to the woman standing next to Hugh.

Hugh cleared his throat. "This is my wife, Rebecca."

"Hello, Rebecca," Tasha said, moving close to the woman, half turning away from Hugh and Matt. If she'd learned anything over the years, it was to keep her attention firmly off any man, no matter his age, who had a date by his side. "I *love* that necklace," she said to Rebecca. "A Nischelle?"

Rebecca returned Tasha's smile. "Why, yes. A gift from Hugh for our anniversary."

"How many years?" Tasha asked.

"Twenty-five."

"Congratulations on that. Was it a winter wedding?"

"Spring," Rebecca said. "We were married in New York. My parents lived there at the time."

"I love New York in the spring." Tasha put some enthusiasm in her voice. "Tell me it was a grand affair."

"We held it at Blair Club in the Hamptons."

"Were the cherry blossoms out?" Tasha had been to the Blair Club on a number of occasions. Their gardens were legendary.

"They were."

"It sounds like a dream." Tasha looped her arm through Matt's, taking advantage of a brief lull in the men's conversation. "Darling, I'm really looking forward to some champagne."

He covered her hand. "Of course. Nice to see you, Hugh. Rebecca, you look fantastic."

"Enjoy the party," Hugh said.

Tasha gave a cheery little wave as they moved away.

"*What* was that?" Matt whispered in her ear. "Cherry blossoms? You made it sound like you'd been there."

She didn't want to reveal her past to Matt. She wanted it kept firmly there—in the past.

"Cherry blossoms seemed like a safe bet in the spring. You don't mind my pulling us away from the Mercers, do you? They're not our target."

Too late, it occurred to her that Matt might have some kind of reason for chatting Hugh up. She hoped she hadn't spoiled his plans.

"You were right. They're not our targets." He put a hand on the small of her back. "There. Two o'clock. The man with the burgundy patterned tie."

Ignoring the distraction of Matt's touch, Tasha looked in that direction. "Tall, short brown hair, long nose?"

"Yes. That's Ralph Moretti. He owns Waterside Charters. They're smaller than Whiskey Bay, but they're closest to us geographically."

"Is he married?"

Matt's hand flexed against her waist. "Why?"

"So I know how to play this."

"Play this?"

"If he's up to something, he'll be a lot more likely to give information away based on my giggling, ingenuous questions than if you start grilling him. But if he has a wife who's likely to show up halfway through the conversation, it going to throw us off the game."

"You're going to flirt with him?" Matt did not sound pleased.

"I wouldn't call it flirting."

"What would you call it?"

"Disarming." She sized up Ralph Moretti as they drew closer.

"There's a distinction?" Matt asked.

"Absolutely."

They'd run out of room. Ralph was right there in front of them.

"Moretti," Matt greeted with a handshake.

"Emerson," Ralph responded.

Ralph's guarded tone immediately piqued Tasha's interest. It took about half a second for his gaze to move to her and stop.

"Tasha Lowell." She offered him her hand.

"Call me Ralph," he told her, lightly shaking. He was gentlemanly enough not to squeeze.

"Ralph," she said with a bright smile. "Matt tells me you have a marina."

"I do indeed."

"I have a thing for boats."

The pressure of Matt's hand increased against her back.

"Really?" Ralph asked, with the barest of gazes at Matt. "What do you like about them?"

"Everything," she said. "The lines of the craft, the motion of the waves, the way they can take you on adventures."

"A woman of good taste," he said.

"How far do you go?" she asked.

Matt coughed.

"Excuse me?" Ralph asked.

Tasha leaned in just a little bit. "Your charters. Oregon? California? Do you go up to Canada?"

"Washington and Oregon mostly," he said.

"Are you looking to expand?"

Ralph's gaze flicked to Matt. Was it a look of guilt?

"Maybe in the future," Ralph said, bringing his attention back to Tasha.

"What about markets?" she asked.

His expression turned confused, maybe slightly suspicious.

"Do you get a lot of women clients?" She breezed past the topic she'd intended to broach. "Party boats. Me and my friends like to have fun."

"Ah," he said, obviously relaxing again. "Yes. Waterside can party it up with the best of them."

"Whiskey Bay—" she touched Matt lightly on the arm "—seems to go for an older crowd."

He stiffened beside her.

She ignored the reaction and carried on. "I don't know if I've seen your advertising. Do you have a website?"

"We're upgrading it," Ralph said.

"Expanding your reach? There is a Midwest full of clients right next door. Spring break would be an awesome time to get their attention."

"Do you have a job?" Ralph asked her.

She laughed. "Are you offering?"

"You'd make one heck of an ambassador."

She held up her palms. "*That's* what I keep telling Matt."

"You're missing the boat on this, Matt." There was an edge of humor to Ralph's tone, but he kept his gaze on Tasha this time.

Matt spoke up. "She can have any job she wants at Whiskey Bay for as long as she wants it."

Ralph quickly glanced up. Whatever he saw on Matt's expression caused him to take a step back.

"It was nice to meet you, Tasha," Ralph said.

"Moretti," Matt said by way of goodbye. Then he steered Tasha away.

"Well, that was interesting," Tasha said.

"Is *that* what you call it?"

"Yes. He wants to expand his business. And something about you put him on edge."

"Because he was trying to steal my date."

"Nah." She didn't buy that. "He reacted when I asked if he was expanding. And he's revamping his website. He's looking to make a move on your customers."

"He's looking to make a move on you."

"Don't be so paranoid."

A wave of mottled mauve silk moved in front of them.

"Hello, Matt."

Tasha was astonished to come face-to-face with Dianne.

"Dianne," Matt said evenly. "What are you doing here?"

"Enjoying the season." She eyed Tasha up and down, a delicate sneer coming over her face as she looked down her nose.

Tasha had seen that expression a thousand times, from women and girls who were certain they were a cut above a plain-looking mechanic and not the least bit hesitant to try to put Tasha in her place.

Still, Tasha felt like she should muster up some sympathy. Dianne was in a tough spot.

"Merry Christmas," she said to Dianne in her most polite voice.

"I see you got out of those oily rags," Dianne returned. "Is that last year's frock?"

"I like to think Bareese is timeless," Tasha said with an air of indifference.

Dianne wrinkled her nose.

Tasha took in Dianne's opulent gown. "Your Moreau must

be worth a fortune." She blinked her eyes in mock innocence. "You could auction it after the party. For the funds, I mean."

Matt stifled a laugh.

Dianne's complexion went a shade darker. "Why, you little—"

"Time for us to take our seats," Matt said, taking Tasha's hand. "What is up with you?" he asked as they moved away.

Tasha winced. "I'm sorry. I shouldn't have said that."

"That's not what I meant."

"It was really rude."

The lights blinked, and the MC made his way onto the stage.

"Dianne was the one who was rude. And I'm grateful," Matt continued, picking up the pace. "You keep it up, and she's going to leave town in a hurry. Besides, she deserves a little of her own medicine for once."

Matt's odd compliment warmed Tasha. She wasn't particularly proud of going mean-girl debutante on Dianne. But Matt's life would be better if Dianne left. And Tasha found she wanted that, too.

# Six

Matt's speech had gone well. People had laughed in the right spots and clapped in the right spots. He was happy to have been entertaining. But he was happier still to watch Tasha's face in the front row. Every time she'd smiled, he'd felt a physical jolt.

He couldn't believe how feminine, how beautiful, how downright elegant she'd looked surrounded by the splendor of the ballroom. And now, swaying in his arms, she was graceful and light. The transformation was astonishing. Cinderella had nothing on Tasha.

"You've done this before," he guessed as he guided her into a slow spin.

"Danced? Yes, I have."

"Been the belle of a ball."

She smiled at that as she came back into his arms. "I'm far from the belle of any ball."

The dance floor was nicely filled. The music was superb, and beautiful women floated past on the arms of their partners. None could hold a candle to Tasha.

"You are to me," he said.

"You're flirting?"

"No. I'm disarming."

She gave a short laugh. "It's not going to work."

He supposed not. "You have definitely done this before."

"I've been to a few balls in my time."

"I never would have guessed. I mean before tonight I never would have guessed. You sure don't let on that there's an elegant lifestyle in your past."

"I don't spend much time dwelling on it."

"You're very good at this." He'd been stunned at her ability to make small talk, to get the other marina owners to relax and be chatty. They hadn't come up with any solid leads or suspects, but they'd learned Waterside Charters was expanding and Rose and Company was taking delivery of a new seventy-five-foot yacht in the spring. Both would be competing head-to-head with Whiskey Bay Marina.

"You don't have to like something to be good at it."

"Do you like dancing?" he asked, wanting to hear that she did, hoping to hear that she liked dancing with him.

"Yes. But not necessarily in these shoes."

He glanced down. "Do they hurt?"

"You've never worn high heels before, have you?"

"That would be a no."

"Yes, they hurt. They don't fit all that well."

"Should we stop?"

"I'll survive."

He debated finding them a place to sit down. But he liked having her in his arms. So he settled for slowing the pace, inching even closer to her. It was a good decision.

"So where did you attend these formative balls?"

"Boston, mostly. Some in New York. Once in DC when I was around seventeen."

"You're a fellow Bostonian?" He was surprised by the idea.

She drew back to look at him. "You, too?"

"Southie."

"And you left?" She seemed to be the one surprised now.

"I did. The rest of my family stayed in the neighborhood, though."

The song ended, and another started. He danced them right through the change.

"Brothers and sisters?" she asked.

"Three brothers, two sisters. I'm the youngest. What about you?"

"Wow. Six kids?"

"Yep."

"Your parents must have been busy."

"It was busy and crowded. I had absolutely no desire to live like that. Where did you grow up?"

Since she'd talked about balls and flying off to New York and Washington for parties, he was guessing she wasn't a Southie.

It took her a minute to answer. "Beacon Hill."

So, she had lived posh.

"It's nice up there," he said.

"It's snooty up there. At least the people I knew, and especially my parents' friends and associates. I couldn't wait to get away from their judgment."

"Spread your wings?" he asked.

"Something like that. Yes, very much like that."

He found the insight quite fascinating. "Does your family still live there?" For some reason, learning she was from Boston made their connection seem stronger.

"Absolutely."

"Brothers and sisters?" he asked when she didn't offer details.

"Two sisters. Youngest here, too," she said with an almost guilty smile.

"Makes it easy to get away with things," he said.

"Made it easy to slip town."

"Are you close to them?"

He'd never heard her talk about her family. Then again, they hadn't had a whole lot of in-depth conversations about either of their backgrounds. Mostly he liked to leave his alone.

"We don't have a lot in common." There was something in her tone, not regret exactly, but acceptance of some kind.

"I hear you," he said, recognizing the emotion.

He and his family seemed to operate in different dimensions. He saw value in financial success. He'd worked hard to get here, and he had no problem enjoying it. The rest of his family held financial success in suspicion. He'd tried to get his mind around it, but at the end of the day he just couldn't agree.

Dianne had understood. It was one of the things that first drew him to her. She liked the finer things, and was unapologetic about her ambition. That trait might have turned on her now. But the theory was still sound. He was still going after success.

"My family…" he began, wondering how to frame it. "They're content to pay the bills, throw potlucks on Sundays, take their kids to community center dance lessons and cheer for the Red Sox at tailgate parties."

"Oh, the horror," she mocked.

"I want more," he said.

"Why?"

"Why not?" He looked around the ballroom. "This is nice. This is great. And who wouldn't want the freedom to take any trip, eat at any restaurant, accept any party invitation."

"Are you free, Matt? Really?"

"I'm pretty damn free."

His choice of lifestyle had allowed him to work hard, to focus on his business, to succeed in a way that was satisfying to him. If he'd strapped on a tool belt in Southie, met a nice woman and had a few kids, it would have meant being dishonest about himself.

It was Tasha's turn to look around the room. "This all doesn't feel like a straitjacket to you?"

"Not at all." He didn't understand her attitude. She seemed to be having a good time. "And I'm here by choice."

"These people don't seem disingenuous to you?"

"Maybe the ones that are sabotaging my boats. But we're not even sure they're here. It's just as likely they're at the Edge."

"What's wrong with the Edge?"

"Nothing. Did I say there was something wrong with the Edge?"

"You used it as a negative comparator to this party."

"It's a whole lot different than this party. Like Beacon Hill and Southie. Do you honestly think people prefer Southie?"

"They might."

Matt wasn't buying the argument. "Sure. People from Southie are proud. I get that. Believe me, I've lived that. But you give them a real and serious choice, they'd be in Beacon Hill in a heartbeat."

Tasha's steps slowed. "It's kind of sad that you believe that."

"It's not sad. And I don't just believe that. It's true."

She stopped. "Thanks for the dance, Matt."

"You can't honestly be annoyed with me." It wasn't reasonable.

"I'm going to rest my feet."

"I'll take you—"

"No." She put her hand on his chest and moved back. "Go mingle. I'll see you later on."

"Tasha." He couldn't believe she was walking away.

Tasha wasn't angry with Matt. She felt more sad than anything.

Sure, he'd made some money in his life. But up to now he'd struck her as being mostly down-to-earth. She'd thought the money was incidental to him, running a business that he loved. It was disappointing to discover that his goal had been wealth.

Seeing him tonight, she realized her initial instincts were right. He was exactly the kind of man she'd left behind. Ironically, he was the kind of man her parents would love.

If this were a Boston party, her parents would be throwing her into his arms. The Lowells were an old Bostonian family, but her parents wouldn't hold Matt's Southie roots against him, not like her grandparents or great-grandparents would have.

In this day and age, money was money. Her father in particular respected men who pulled themselves up from nothing. It was a darn good thing they weren't back in Boston right now.

She crossed the relative quiet of the foyer, following the signs to the ladies' room. She needed to freshen up. Then she really was going to find a place to sit down and rest her feet. The shoes might be slightly large, but they were also slightly narrow for her feet, and she had developed stinging blisters on both of her baby toes.

As she passed an alcove, she caught sight of Dianne's unmistakable mauve dress. Dianne was sitting on a small bench, gazing out a bay window at the city lights. Her shoulders were hunched, and they were shaking.

Tasha felt like a heel. One of the reasons she avoided these upper-crust events was that they brought out the worst in her. She seemed too easily influenced by the snobbery and spitefulness.

The last thing in the world she wanted to do was comfort Matt's ex-wife. But it was partly her fault that Dianne was upset. She'd been insufferably rude in suggesting she auction off her dress.

Tasha took a turn and crossed the alcove, coming up beside Dianne.

Dianne looked up in what appeared to be horror. She quickly swiped her hand beneath her eyes. But the action did nothing to hide the red puffiness.

"Are you okay?" Tasha asked.

"I'm fine." Dianne gave a jerky nod. "Fine."

It was patently obvious it was a lie.

Tasha gave an inward sigh and sat down on the other end of the padded French provincial bench. "You don't look fine."

"I got something in my eyes. Or maybe it was the perfume. Allergies, you know."

Tasha told herself to accept the explanation and walk away. She didn't know Dianne. Given the circumstances, fake though her relationship with Matt was, she was likely the last person Dianne wanted to talk to. But it would be heartless to simply leave her there.

"You're obviously upset," Tasha said.

"Aren't *you* the observant one."

"Don't."

"Why? What do you want? To rub my nose in it? Again?"

"No. I want to apologize. I was nasty to you earlier. I'm really sorry about that. I thought you were..." Tasha struggled for the right words. "Stronger. I thought you were tough. I didn't mean to upset you."

Dianne's tone changed. "It's not you. It's..." She closed her eyes for a long second. A couple of more tears leaked out. "I can't," she said.

Tasha moved closer. She put a hand on Dianne's arm. "Will talking to me make it any worse?"

Dianne drew in a shuddering breath. She opened her eyes and gazed at Tasha for a long time.

"I've made such a mess of it," she finally said.

"You mean losing the money?"

Dianne nodded. "François was charming, attentive, affectionate. Matt was working all the time. He never wanted to travel with me. I thought... I thought our life together would be different. But it wasn't any fun. It was all work, work, work. And then I met François. It wasn't on purpose. I'm not a bad person."

"I don't think you're a bad person." Tasha was being honest about that.

Dianne might not be the right person for Matt, and maybe she had a selfish streak, but right now she just seemed sad and defeated. Tasha would have to be made of stone not to feel sympathy.

Dianne gave a brittle laugh. "I thought François not wanting a prenup was the perfect sign, the proof that he loved me for me. He seemed to have so much more money than I did. And he'd invested so successfully, that I thought I couldn't lose...but I did lose. And I'd hoped Matt..."

"What exactly do you want from Matt?" Tasha might be sympathetic, but she knew sympathy alone wouldn't help Dianne.

Dianne shrugged. "At first... At first I thought there might still be a chance for us. I was the one who left him, not the other way around. I thought he might still..." She shook her head. "But then I met you, and I realized he'd moved on."

A part of Tasha wanted to confess. But she knew Matt wouldn't consider a reconciliation with Dianne. And telling Dianne she and Matt weren't dating would be a betrayal of him. She couldn't do it.

"So, now what?" Tasha asked.

"I don't know." Dianne's tears welled up again. "I honestly don't know."

"You need to know," Tasha said as gently as she could. "You need a plan. You need to take care of yourself."

"I can't."

"You can. Everyone can. It's a matter of finding your strengths."

"My strength is marrying rich men."

"That's not true. It's not your only strength. And even if it was your only strength, it's a bad strength, not one you want to depend on. Look what happened last time."

"I have no money," Dianne said, looking truly terrified. "I've nearly maxed out my credit cards. I've missed payments. They're going to cancel them. I really will be selling my clothes on the street corner."

"Okay, now you're being melodramatic."

"I'm not," she moaned.

"What about your family? Could you stay with family?"

Dianne gave a choppy shake of her head. "There's no one."

"No one at all?"

"My dad died. My stepmother sent me to boarding school. She couldn't wait to get me out of the house."

"Are they in Washington State?"

"Boston."

Tasha was surprised. "You, too?"

Dianne stilled. "You're from Boston?"

"I am."

Dianne searched Tasha's face. "You're a Lowell. *The* Lowells?"

Tasha was embarrassed. "I don't know if there are any 'the' Lowells."

"The Vincent Lowell Library?"

"My grandfather," Tasha admitted.

"Does Matt know?" Before Tasha could respond, Dianne continued on a slightly shrill laugh. "Of course he knows. Why didn't I see that before? You're his dream match."

Tasha was confident Matt didn't know. And there wasn't much to know anyway. The Lowells might be an old Boston family. But there were plenty of those around. It wasn't all that noteworthy.

"Do you want to go back to Boston?" Tasha asked, turning the subject back to Dianne.

"No. Never. That's not in the cards."

"Do you want to stay here?" Tasha was trying to find a starting point, any starting point for Dianne.

Dianne lifted her head and looked around. "There's nothing left for me here either." Her voice cracked again. "Not without Matt."

"You really need to think about a job. You're young. Get started on a career. Did you go to college?"

"Only for a year. I took fine arts. I didn't pass much."

"What would you like to do? What are you good at?"

Dianne looked Tasha in the eyes. "Why are you doing this?"

"I want to help," Tasha answered honestly.

"Why? I'm nothing to you."

"You're a fellow human being, a fellow Bostonian, part of the sisterhood."

Dianne gave a hollow laugh. "There's no sisterhood. Are you a do-gooder? Am I a charitable thing for you?"

"No." Tasha gave it some thought. "I don't know, really." It was as honest as she could be.

"I gave parties," Dianne said in a tired, self-mocking voice. "I can make small talk and order hors d'oeuvres."

The germ of an idea came to Tasha.

Caleb had fancy restaurants all over the country. Perhaps Jules, Tasha knew her better than she did Caleb, might be willing to help Dianne.

"I'm going to ask around," Tasha said.

"Matt won't like that."

"Doesn't matter." Tasha wasn't sure if Matt would care or not. But surely he'd be in favor of anything that put Dianne back on her feet, helped her to take care of herself.

She didn't have to make a big deal with Jules. And if Matt did find out, he'd see the logic and reason, she assured herself. He was a very reasonable man.

On the drive home, Tasha seemed lost in thought. Either that, or she was still annoyed with Matt for appreciating financial security. He'd wanted to talk about it some more, maybe help her understand his motivations. But he didn't want to rekindle their argument. He liked it better when they were on the same side of something.

"Could we really have had a fire?" he asked her.

She turned from where she'd been gazing out the window into the darkness. "What?"

"On *Salty Sea*. Would there have been a fire?"

"Yes. Almost certainly. The fuel from the fuel line leak would have sprayed across the spark from the electric short, and *bam*, it would have ignited."

"It looks odd," he said. "You talking about the inner workings of an engine while you're dressed like that."

"That's why I don't dress like this."

"You look terrific."

"I feel like a fraud. I can't wait to get out of this getup." She reached down and peeled off the black pumps.

The action was sexy, very sexy. He immediately imagined her shrugging down the straps of the dress. He shifted in his seat.

"Feet sore?" he asked.

"And how. Steel-toed boots might be clunky, but they're built for wearing, not for show."

"They wouldn't go with the dress."

"Ha ha."

"And it would be hard to dance in them."

Tasha curled her legs up on the seat, a hand going to one foot to rub it. "I'd be willing to give it a shot."

Matt curled his hands to keep them still. "The new cameras are being installed tomorrow."

"We need them. I'm doubling up on my inspections. Alex and I are going to check every boat the morning before it leaves port."

"Won't that be a lot of work?"

"I couldn't do everything I'd like, not without hiring three more mechanics. But we can cover the basics."

"Do you need to hire someone else?"

She switched her self-massage to the other foot. "I'll call in all the contract mechanics. But I have to believe this is temporary. The next time that guy tries something, we're going to catch him on camera and have him arrested."

Matt gave in to temptation and reached across the back seat for one of her feet.

"Don't." She jumped at his touch.

He looked meaningfully at the driver. "It's just a foot."

"That's not a good idea."

He ignored her, settling her foot in his lap and pressing his thumb into the arch.

She gave a small moan.

"Those blisters look awful," he said.

Her baby toes and the backs of her heels were swollen and red.

"They'll heal."

"Why didn't you say something?"

"I did."

"You didn't tell me how bad it was." He massaged carefully around the swollen skin.

"That feels good," she said.

"Do you need to take the day off tomorrow?"

"You're funny."

"I'm serious. It's Sunday. Don't work."

"And let Alex do it all?"

He didn't have a comeback for that. He had to admire Tasha's work ethic. Still, he couldn't let her burn herself out. And her feet were going to be painful tomorrow.

"As long as I don't put on the same shoes," she said. "I'll use bandages and wear thick socks. I'll be fine."

"You're a trouper," he said with honest admiration.

The driver slowed as Matt's driveway came up on the right.

"You're easily impressed," she said.

"Not really."

They were silent as the car cruised through the trees to the house. While they did, Matt continued his massage. His image of her strong and sturdy on the job faded to how she was now…soft, smooth, almost delicate.

When the car came to a stop, he reached to the floor and collected her shoes.

"What are you doing?" she asked.

"Wait right there." He exited from his side and tipped the driver.

Then he went around to her, opening the door and reaching in to lift her from the seat.

"Oh, no you don't," she protested.

"Oh, yes I do. You can't put these shoes back on. You'll burst the blisters and bleed all over the place."

"Then I'll walk barefoot."

"Over the rocks and through the mud? Hang on."

"Put me down."

But even as she protested, he hoisted her easily into the air, and her arms went around his shoulders. He pushed the sedan door shut with his shoulder and started to the stairs that led to the staff quarters.

"This is ridiculous," she said. "Nobody better see us."

"It's dark."

"There are lights on the porch."

"It's after midnight. Everyone will be asleep."

"They better be."

He couldn't help but smile to himself. He'd learned by now that Tasha hated anything that made her look remotely weak.

"Blisters are nothing to be ashamed of," he said.

"I'm not ashamed of having blisters." She paused. "I'm ashamed of having some Neanderthal carry my apparently feeble self to my room."

"I'm wearing a tux."

"So?"

"I'm just saying, your average Neanderthal probably didn't wear a tux."

The joke got him a bop in the shoulder.

"Not much of a comeback," he said.

"We're here. You can put me down now."

"Not yet." He mounted the stairs for the second floor.

She squirmed in his arms. "I can walk on wooden stairs in my bare feet."

"Splinters."

"I'm not going to get splinters."

"We're here. Where's your key?"

"You can put me down on the mat."

"I like holding you." He did. He was in absolutely no hurry to put her down. "You're light. You're soft. Your hair smells like vanilla."

"It's not locked," she said.

"Are you kidding me?" he barked. "With all that's been going on?" He couldn't believe she would be so cavalier about her own safety.

He reached for the doorknob and opened the door. He set her down on the floor inside and immediately turned on the light switch, checking all the corners of the room, the small sitting area, the kitchenette, the double bed. Then he crossed to the bathroom and opened up the door.

"Matt, this is silly."

He was annoyed with her. No, he was downright angry. Somebody was targeting them for unknown reasons, and so far it had more to do with her than with anybody else at Whiskey Bay, and she was leaving her door unlocked?

He turned back. "Please tell me you lock it at night."

She looked decidedly guilty. "I can start."

He took the paces that brought him in front of her. "You bet your life you're going to start. You're going to start tonight, now, right away."

"You don't need to get upset," she said.

"You're scaring me." His gaze fell on her gorgeous green eyes. "I'm afraid for you." He took in her flushed cheeks. "I want to protect you. I…"

Their gazes meshed, and the sound of the surf filled the silence. She just stood there in the shadows looking like his fondest dream come true.

She looked delicate and enticing. Her hair was mussed. One strap had fallen down, leaving her shoulder bare. He wanted to kiss her shoulder. He wanted to taste that shoulder more than he'd ever wanted anything in his life.

He gave in.

He leaned forward, gently wrapping his hands around her upper arms. He placed a light kiss on her shoulder. Then he tasted her skin with the tip of his tongue. He kissed her again, made his way to her neck.

She tipped her head sideways, giving him better access.

He brushed her hair back, kissing his way to her ear, her temple, her closed eyes and finally her mouth.

She kissed him back, and he spread his fingers into her hair.

She stepped into his arms, an enchanting, elegant, utterly feminine woman pressing against his hard, heated body.

He reached out and pushed the door shut behind her.

He deepened their kiss.

He began to unzip her dress, paused, running his hands over the smooth skin of her back.

"Don't stop," she gasped. "Don't, don't stop."

# Seven

Everything flooded from Tasha's mind, everything except the taste of Matt's lips, the feel of his hands and the sound of his voice. His heart beat against her chest where they pressed together. She wanted this. No, she needed this. Whatever it was that had been building between them for days on end was bursting out, and there was no stopping it.

She pushed off his tux jacket, and he tossed it on the chair. She tugged his bow tie loose, and it dangled around his neck. She kissed his square chin, struggled with the buttons of his shirt, while his hands roamed her back.

His hands were warm, the fingertips calloused. As she peeled away his tuxedo, the urbane facade seemed to melt away along with it. He was tough underneath, muscular and masculine. A small scar marred his chest, another across his shoulder.

She kissed the shoulder and traced a fingertip along his chest. "What happened?"

"Working," he answered, his breathing deep. "Winch handle and a rogue wave."

"You should be more careful."

"I will."

She couldn't help but smile at his easy capitulation.

His hands went to her dress straps. He eased them down, baring her breasts in the cool air.

"Gorgeous," he said stopping to stare.

It had been a long time since a man had seen her naked, never if you didn't count an eighteen-year-old freshman. She was glad it was Matt, glad he seemed pleased, happy to bask in the heat of his gaze.

He slowly reached out, brushing his thumb across her

nipple. She sucked in a breath, a shudder running through to her core. She closed her eyes, waiting for him to do it again.

"Oh, Tasha," he whispered, his hand closing over her breasts.

She tipped her head for his kiss, and her dress slithered to the floor.

His palms slipped to her rear, covering her satin panties. His lips found hers again, his kiss deep and delicious. His shirt separated, and they were skin to skin.

"You're so soft." His hand continued its exploration of her breast.

Rockets of sensation streamed from her hard nipples to the apex of her thighs.

Impatient, she reached for his belt, looping it free, popping the button of his pants and dragging down the zipper.

He groaned as her knuckles grazed him.

Then he scooped her back into his arms and carried her to the double bed, stripping back the blankets to lay her on the cool sheets. He was beside her in a moment, shucking his pants.

He came to his knees, hooking his thumbs in the waist of her panties, drawing them slowly down, to her thighs, to her knees and over her ankles.

He kissed her ankle, then her knee, then her thigh and her hip bone, making his way to her breasts, kissing them both, making her heartbeat echo all through her.

She raked her fingers into his hair. A buzzing started within her, making her twitch with need.

"You have a condom?" she asked breathlessly. She was woefully unprepared.

"I've got it," he said. "Don't worry."

He rose up and kissed her mouth. Then his hands went on a glorious exploration, touching her everywhere, discovering secrets, making her writhe with impatience and need.

"Please, Matt," she finally whimpered.

"Oh, yes," he said, levering above her, stroking her thighs. She watched him closely as he pressed slowly, steadily inside.

She rocked her hips upward, closing her legs around him.

He moved, pulling out, pushing in, grasping her to him as he kissed her deeper and deeper. She met his tongue thrust for thrust, and her hands gripped his back. She needed an anchor as gravity gave way.

The room grew hotter. The waves sounded louder on the rocks below. Matt's body moved faster, and she arched to meet him, the rhythm increasing.

Fulfillment started as a deep glow, burning hotter, moving outward, taking over her belly, then her breasts, then her legs and her arms. It tingled in her toes and in the roots of her hair. She cried out as sensation lifted her. Then she flew and then floated.

"Tasha," Matt cried, his body shuddering against her.

She absorbed every tremor, his body slick, his heartbeat steady. Her waves of pleasure were unending, until she finally fell still, exhausted, unable to move beneath his comfortable weight on top of her.

She didn't know what she'd done.

Okay, she knew what she'd done. She knew exactly what she'd done. She also knew she shouldn't have done it.

"Stop," he muttered in her ear.

"Stop what?"

He rose up on an elbow. "I can feel you second-guessing yourself."

"We can't undo that," she said.

"Who wants to undo it?"

"We do. We should. That wasn't part of the plan."

"There was a plan?"

"Quit laughing at me."

He enveloped her in a warm hug.

It shouldn't have felt so great. It couldn't feel this great.

"Oh, Tasha. We made love. People do it all the time. The world will keep spinning, I promise."

"Maybe *you* do it all the time."

"I didn't mean that the way it sounded." He eased back to look at her again. He smoothed the hair from her eyes. "I don't do it all the time. My marriage was on the rocks for quite a while. And since then… Well, I've only just started dating again."

Tasha shouldn't have cared whom Matt had been with before her. But she found herself glad that he hadn't had an active sex life. She didn't want it to matter, but it did.

"I'm—" She stopped short, realizing she was going to sound hopelessly unsophisticated.

His eyes widened, and he drew sharply back. "You weren't…"

"A virgin? No. I would have said something."

"Thank goodness."

"I did have a boyfriend," she said. "Right after high school."

"One?" Matt asked. "Singular?"

"I couldn't date anyone in trade school. There were three women in a class of thirty-six. We were way too smart to get involved with anyone. It could have killed our chances of being treated as peers."

"I suppose," Matt said. Then he touched a finger to the bottom of her chin. "So, you're saying one then? Just the one guy?"

"Just the one," she admitted, feeling a bit foolish. She should have kept her mouth shut.

"Tasha Lowell." His kissed her tenderly on the mouth. "I am honored."

"Oh, that didn't sound outmoded at all."

He grinned. "You could be honored back at me."

"Okay," she said, fighting a smile. "Matt Emerson, I am honored. And I'm embarrassed. And I'm certainly soon to be regretful."

"But not yet?" he asked on an exaggerated note of hopefulness.

"I can feel it coming."

"You have nothing to regret."

She wriggled to relieve the pressure on her hip, and he eased off to one side.

"You said that about our kiss," she said, sitting up and pulling a sheet over her breasts.

"Did you?" He traced a line along her knuckles.

"I don't know." Things had changed so fundamentally between them. Was that single kiss to blame?

She didn't want to talk about it right now. She didn't want to dissect this.

"I could stay," he offered in a soft voice.

She jumped an inch off the bed and her voice rose an octave. "What?"

"I don't have to rush off."

"Yes, you do." She looked around for her clothes, realizing she needed to get out of the bed right now. "You can't stay here. It's the staff quarters. You need to get out while it's still dark, before anybody starts work."

He didn't look happy. But he also seemed to understand. "I know. This isn't exactly discreet. But I don't want to leave you." He reached for her.

She evaded his grasp. "If you don't. If somebody sees you, then it's trade school all over again. Only this time I had a one-night stand with the teacher."

His brow went up. "How am I the teacher?"

"You know what I mean. You're in a position of authority. It's worse than sleeping with a peer. I lose any and all credibility. Everybody's reminded that I'm not one of the guys."

"They respect you, Tasha. And who says this is a one-night stand?"

"Who says it's not? So far that's exactly what it is."

"But—"

"But nothing, Matt. The mathematical odds that this leads to something, I mean something besides a fling based on chemistry alone, are, I don't know, maybe five, six percent.

The mathematical odds of this leading to the dismantling of my credibility and reputation are around ninety. What would you do if you were me?"

"Where did you come up with five or six percent?"

"I did a quick calculation in my head."

"That's insane." He reached for her again, and she backed to an ever safer distance.

She didn't want him to leave. But he had to leave. He had to leave now before she weakened.

"Please, Matt," she said.

He hardened his jaw. "Of course." He threw back the covers and came to his feet.

She didn't want to watch him walk naked across the room. But she couldn't help herself. He was magnificent, and the sight of him brought back instant memories of their lovemaking.

Her skin flushed. Then goose bumps formed. But she had to be strong. She would force herself to let him leave.

With Noah Glover's electric expertise to guide them, Matt, Caleb and TJ had spent the day installing the new security cameras. Now as a thank-you, Matt was hosting dinner for Caleb and Jules, TJ and Jules's sister, Melissa, along with Noah.

Watching Caleb with Jules, and Noah with Melissa, Matt couldn't help thinking about Tasha. She'd made herself scarce all day, while he'd spent most of it watching for her. He couldn't stop thinking about her. He'd lain awake half the night thinking about her, wishing he could have slept with her. After their mind-blowing lovemaking, his arms felt completely empty without her.

"I hope the extra cameras do the trick," TJ said as he joined Matt by the dining table.

Matt was setting out plates and glasses, since Jules had all but kicked him out of the kitchen.

"I don't care what it takes," Matt responded. "I'm catching this guy and throwing him in jail. His last stunt could have caused a fire. People could have been seriously hurt, or worse."

"Your competition?" TJ asked, gazing through the glass wall to the marina below.

"I talked to all of them at the gala last night. Waterside Charters is expanding, and Rose and Company bought a new seventy-five-footer. Both would be happy to steal business from me. But I don't see them doing it this way."

"Then what?" TJ asked.

"If I have my way, we'll find out soon." Matt took in the overview of the marina, his gaze settling on the staff quarters. Tasha was there.

Giving up fighting with himself, he extracted his cell phone. "I'll just be a minute," he said to TJ, then moved down the hall.

He typed into his phone: Dinner with Caleb and Jules at my place. Talking about the new cameras. Can you come?

He hit Send and waited. It was a stretch of an excuse, but he didn't care. He wanted her here with him.

Jules and Melissa were laughing in the kitchen. TJ's voice blended with Caleb's and Noah's. Everybody sounded happy. It had been a good day's work. It was a good night with friends. Matt should have felt terrific.

His phone pinged with Tasha's response. Just leaving. Meeting some people for drinks.

Disappointment thudded hard in his stomach. He wanted to ask who. He wanted to ask where. Mostly, he wanted to ask why she'd choose them over him.

"Hey, Matt?" Noah appeared and moved down the hall toward him.

"Hi. Thanks again for your help today."

"Sure." Noah looked nervous.

"What's up?" Matt asked.

Noah glanced down the hall behind him. "You mind if I hijack dessert tonight?"

"You brought dessert?"

"No, no. I brought a bottle of champagne."

Matt waited for the explanation.

"And this," Noah said, producing a small velvet box.

There was no mistaking the shape of the box.

"Are you serious?" Matt asked, surprised.

Noah flipped it open to reveal a diamond solitaire. "Dead serious."

"Are you sure?" Matt lowered his voice. "I mean, not are you sure you want to propose, Melissa is amazing. Are you sure you want to do it in front of us?"

Noah gave a self-conscious grin. "You've all been fantastic. You're all family. I really think she'd want to share the moment."

"That's a bold move. But you know her better than the rest of us. Well, maybe not better than Jules. Does Jules know?"

"Nobody knows."

"Okay." Matt couldn't help but grin. He had to admire Noah for this one. "Dessert's all yours."

Noah snapped the ring box shut and tucked it back in his pocket.

Matt slapped him on the shoulder as they turned for the living room. "I thought you looked a little overdressed tonight."

It was rare for Noah to wear a pressed shirt, jacket and slacks. He was more a blue jeans kind of guy.

"Everything's ready," Jules called out from the kitchen.

"Let's get this show on the road," Melissa added.

Matt and TJ took the ends of the rectangular table, with Caleb and Jules along the glass wall, and Noah and Melissa facing the view.

Matt lit the candles and Caleb poured the wine. Caleb had the best-stocked cellar, and he always brought along a few bottles. Matt had long since given up trying to compete.

"Why haven't you decorated for the holidays?" Jules asked Matt, gazing around the room. "No tinsel? No tree?"

Caleb gave a grin as he held the baked salmon platter for Jules. "Our place looks like Rockefeller Square attacked the North Pole."

"You don't even have a string of lights," Melissa said, helping herself to a roll.

"There's not a lot of point." Matt wasn't about to put up the decorations he'd shared with Dianne. And he didn't care enough to go shopping for more.

"Is it depressing?" Jules asked him, looking worried. "Being here on your own for Christmas?"

Depressed was the last thing Matt was feeling. Relieved was more like it. The last Christmas with Dianne had been painful.

"I'm fine," he told Jules. "I'm just not feeling it this year."

"Well, I can't stand it," Melissa said. "We need to do something. You do have decorations, right?"

"Whoa," Noah said. "That's up to Matt."

"No big deal," Matt was quick to put in. The last thing he wanted was for Noah and Melissa to get into an argument tonight.

"He needs new stuff," TJ said. "That's what I did. Well, I waited one Christmas." He sobered as he added some salad to his plate.

The table went silent, remembering the loss of TJ's wife.

He looked up at the quiet table. "Oh, no you don't. It's been two years. I'm all right, and I'm looking forward to Christmas this year."

"You'll come to our place," Jules said. "You'll *all* come to our place."

"We can figure it out closer to the day." Matt didn't want to hold her to the impulsive invitation.

It was her first Christmas with Caleb. And Noah and

Melissa would be engaged. The two sisters were working through a rocky, although improving, relationship with their father. They might not need a big crowd around them.

Matt's thoughts went back to Tasha. He wondered to what she'd done last year for Christmas. Had she gone home for a few days? Had she celebrated here with friends? He didn't know. He was definitely going to ask.

Conversation went on, and it was easy for him to coast. He laughed in the right places, made the odd comment, but his mind wasn't there. It was with Tasha, where she'd gone, what she was doing, whom she was doing it with.

As they finished eating, Matt cleared away the plates while Jules cut into the chocolate hazelnut layer cake. He couldn't take any credit for it. A local bakery, Persichetti, had delivered it earlier in the day.

"I love Persichetti cake," Melissa said with a grin. "Do you have whipped cream?" she asked Matt.

"Coming up." He had it ready.

"A man after my own heart."

Matt couldn't help but glance at Noah. But Noah just grinned and rolled his eyes. He was clearly confident in his relationship. Matt couldn't help but feel a stab of jealousy. He couldn't remember ever being that content.

When Matt sat down, Noah rose.

"Before we start," Noah said.

"No." Melissa gave a mock whine.

"Hold tight," he said to her, giving her a squeeze on the shoulder.

Then he went to the refrigerator and produced the bottle of champagne he'd squirreled away.

"We need the right beverage for this." Noah presented the bottle.

"Oh, my favorite," Melissa said, clearly mollified by the offer of champagne.

Matt quickly moved to get six flutes from his cupboard.

"Nice," Caleb said. "What's the occasion?"

"Good friends," Noah said as he popped the cork. "Good family." He filled the flutes and Matt passed them around.

Then Matt sat down again.

Noah took Melissa's hand. He raised it and gave it a gentle kiss.

Something in his expression made her go still, and everyone went quiet along with her.

"You accepted me from minute one," he said to her. "All of you." He looked around at the group. "Every one of you welcomed me in, without judging, without suspicion."

"I judged a little," Caleb said.

Jules reached out to squeeze her husband's hand.

"You were protecting Jules," Noah said. "And you were protecting Melissa. And you were smart to do that with my history."

"You proved me wrong," Caleb said.

"I did. And now, I think, I hope…" Noah drew a deep breath. "Melissa, darling." His hand went to his pocket and extracted the ring box.

When she saw it, Melissa's eyes went round, and a flush came up on her cheeks.

Matt quickly reached for his phone, hitting the camera button.

Noah popped open the box. "Marry me?"

Melissa gasped. Jules squealed. And Matt got a fantastic picture of the moment.

Melissa's gaze went to the ring, and she leaned closer in. "It is absolutely gorgeous."

"Not as gorgeous as you."

She looked back to Noah. "Yes," she said. "Yes, yes, yes!"

His grin nearly split his face. Everyone cheered.

Her hand trembled as he slipped the ring on her finger. Then he drew her to her feet and kissed her, enveloping her in a sheltering hug. He looked like he'd never let her go.

Matt took one more shot, finding his chest tight, his

thoughts going back to Tasha. He'd held her that tight and more last night. And, in the moment, he'd never wanted to let her go.

Tasha had to get away from Matt for a while. She needed to do something ordinary and find some perspective. Their lovemaking last night had tilted her universe, and she was desperate to get it back on an even keel.

She and Alex had taken a cab to the Edge tonight. They'd started with a couple of tequila shots and danced with a bunch of different guys. Then James Hamilton showed up and commandeered Alex for several dances in a row.

Tasha moved from partner to partner, and by the time she and Alex reconnected at the table, she was sweaty and on a second margarita. The drinks were bringing back memories of Matt, but she'd stopped caring.

James was talking to a couple of his friends across the room, leaving Alex alone with Tasha.

"So, are the two of you an item?" she asked Alex.

Alex shrugged. "I don't know. I like him. He seems to want to hang out a lot. Why?"

"Does it worry you?" Tasha asked. "Dating a mechanic. Do you think you'll lose your credibility? I always worried about dating someone in the business."

"It's a risk," Alex agreed, sipping some ice water through a straw. "But so far all we're doing is dancing."

"Oh." Tasha was surprised by that.

"You thought I was sleeping with James?"

"You left together the other night."

Alex laughed. "I wonder if that's what everybody thinks. And if it is…" She waggled her brows. "What's holding me back?"

Tasha felt terrible for making the assumption, worse for saying it out loud. "I didn't mean to judge, or to push you in any particular direction."

"You're not. You won't. You need to stop worrying so much. We're here to have fun."

"That's right. We are." Tasha lifted her drink in a toast.

As she clinked glasses with Alex, a man at the front door caught her attention. It was Matt. He walked in, and his gaze zeroed in on her with laser precision.

"No," she whispered under her breath.

"What?" Alex asked, leaning in to scrutinize her expression.

"Nothing. Do you mind if I dance with James?"

"Why would I mind? Go for it. I can use the rest."

Tasha slipped from the high stool at their compact round table. As Matt made his way toward her, she went off on an opposite tangent, heading straight for James.

"Dance?" she asked him brightly.

He looked a little surprised, but recovered quickly. "You bet." He took her hand.

The dance floor was crowded and vibrating, and she quickly lost sight of Matt, throwing herself into the beat of the music.

The song ended too soon, and Matt cut in. James happily gave way.

"No," Tasha said to Matt as he tried to take her hand.

"No, what?"

"No, I don't want to do this."

The music was coming up, and she had to dance or look conspicuous out on the floor. She started to move, but kept a distance between them.

He closed the gap, enunciating above the music. "We're going to have to talk sometime."

She raised her voice to be heard. "What's the rush?"

"You'd rather let things build?"

"I was hoping they'd fade."

"My feelings aren't fading."

She glanced around, worried that people might overhear. The crowd was close, so she headed for the edge of the floor.

Matt followed.

When they got to a quieter corner, she spoke again. "Give it some time. We both need some space."

"Can you honestly say your feelings are fading?"

Her feelings weren't fading. They were intensifying.

"If nothing else, we work together," he said. "We have to interact to get our jobs done. And besides, beyond anything else, I'm worried about you."

"There's nothing to worry about." She paused. "Okay, but that thing is *you*."

"Very funny. I'm watching for anything unusual."

"So am I." She'd been working on the sabotage problem all night.

"What I'm seeing is a guy."

Her interest perked up. "At the pier?"

"Not there. Don't look right away, but he's over by the bar. He's been staring at you. And it looks odd. I mean, suspicious."

"What's that got to do with your yachts?"

"I don't know. Maybe nothing."

"Probably nothing. Almost certainly nothing."

"Turn slowly, pretend you're looking at the bottle display behind the bar, maybe picking out a brand. Then glance at the guy in the blue shirt with the black baseball cap. He's slouched at the second seat from the end."

"That sounds needlessly elaborate." She felt like she was in a spy movie.

"I want you to know what he looks like. In case he shows up somewhere else."

"This is silly."

"Humor me."

"Fine." She did as Matt suggested, focusing on the bottles, then doing a quick sweep of the guy Matt had described.

He looked like a perfectly normal fiftysomething, probably a little shy and nerdy sitting alone having a drink. He wasn't staring. He was likely people watching and just happened on Tasha when Matt walked in.

She turned back to Matt. "Okay, I saw him."

"Good. You need a drink?"

"I have a drink."

Matt looked at her hands.

The truth was Tasha didn't normally leave her drinks alone. She'd done it now because Matt had thrown her when he walked in. She hadn't been expecting him, and she'd taken the first opportunity to get out of his way. She might be in a low-risk environment, but it wasn't a risk she normally took.

"I'll get myself a new drink." She started for the bar, hoping he'd stay behind. She'd come here to clear her head, avoid the memories of Matt's lovemaking. She had to focus, wanting to figure out whether the marina was in trouble...or maybe Matt was? The last thing she needed was to be distracted by his quick smile, broad chest and shoulders, his handsome face...

A tune blasted from the turntable, while voices of the crowd ebbed and flowed, laughter all around them under the festive lights. He fell into step beside her.

"I thought you were having dinner with Caleb and Jules," she said.

"Dinner ended early. Noah and Melissa got engaged."

Tasha was getting to know Melissa, and she'd met Noah a few times. "Noah proposed in front of everyone?"

"It was a daring move on Noah's part." Matt's gaze swept the room, obviously checking on the guy at the end of the bar. "I expect it left everybody feeling romantic, so they wanted to head home. Bit of a bummer for TJ. He fights it, but he's lonely. He liked being married."

"How did his wife die?" Tasha liked TJ. Her heart went out to him over the loss.

"Breast cancer."

"That's really sad."

"Yeah." Matt's voice was gruff. "It's been a tough haul. Let me get you that drink."

"I'm going to take off." She wanted to stay, but she needed to go. Clearing her head with Matt in front of her was impossible.

"We need to talk eventually."

"Later."

"I don't want you to be upset."

"I'm not. Actually, I'm not sure what I am."

He hesitated. "Okay. Fine. I don't want to push."

Relieved, she texted for a cab and let Alex know she was leaving. She knew it was the right thing to do, but she couldn't shake a hollow feeling as she headed for the parking lot.

# Eight

When Tasha left the bar, the stranger left, too.

Matt followed him as far as the door, watching to be sure he didn't harass her in the parking lot. But she got immediately into a cab and left.

The stranger drove off a few minutes later in the opposite direction.

Back inside, Matt returned to the table to where Alex was now sitting.

"Hey, boss," she greeted with a smile.

"Having a good time?" he asked.

"You bet. Have you met James Hamilton?"

Matt shook the man's hand. "Good to meet you, James."

James nodded. "You, too."

Matt returned his attention to Alex. "Did you happen to notice if anyone was paying particular attention to Tasha tonight?"

Alex looked puzzled, but then shook her head. "She was dancing with lots of guys, but nobody in particular. A lot of them she knows from the area."

"Do you mean the old dude in the black cap?" James asked.

"Yes," Matt answered. "He was watching her the whole time I was here."

"Yeah. I noticed it most of the night. I don't know what his deal was. He never talked to her."

Alex looked to James. "Somebody was watching Tasha?"

"She's pretty hot," James said. "I just thought it was a bit of a creep factor. You know, because the guy was old. But he seemed harmless enough."

"He left when she left," Matt said.

James's gaze flicked to the door. "Did he give her any trouble?"

"No. I watched her get into a cab."

James gave a thoughtful nod.

"With everything that's going on at the marina…" Matt ventured.

"I know what you mean," Alex said. "It's happening more and more."

"What do you mean more and more?" Matt asked.

"Little things," Alex said. "Stupid things."

"Was there something besides the fuel leak and the electric short?"

"None worth getting excited about on their own. And we've checked the cameras. Nobody climbed the fence again."

"So a staff member? While you were open during the day?"

"It's possible. But I hear you've done at least ten background checks and didn't find anything."

Matt knew that was true.

"What's weird to me," Alex continued, "is that they're always on jobs done by Tasha."

Matt felt a prickle along his spine. "Are you sure about that?"

"Positive. We fix them. It doesn't take long."

"Why hasn't she said anything to me?" He'd hate to think the change in their personal relationship had made her reluctant to share information.

"She's starting to question her own memory. Any of them could have been mistakes. But any of them could have been on purpose, too."

"There's nothing wrong with her memory."

Tasha was smart, capable and thorough.

"I'm still wondering if it could be an inside job. I don't want to think that about any of my employees, but… As you're new to the team, has anyone struck you as suspicious?" A hand clapped down on Matt's shoulder.

He turned quickly, ready for anything. But it was TJ.

"Didn't know you were headed out, too," TJ said.

"I didn't know you hung out here," Matt responded, surprised to see his friend.

"I spotted your car in the lot. I was too restless to sleep. Hey, Alex." Then TJ turned his attention to James, holding out a hand. "TJ Bauer."

"I know who you are," James said.

"Really?"

"My mom's on the hospital auxiliary. I hear all about your generous donations."

Matt looked to TJ. He knew TJ's financial company made a number of charitable contributions. He hadn't realized they were noteworthy.

TJ waved the statement away. "It's a corporate thing. Most companies have a charitable arm."

"They were very excited to get the new CT scanner. So on behalf of my mom and the hospital, thank you."

"I better buy you a drink," Matt said to TJ.

"You'd better," TJ returned. "So, what's going on?"

"Some guy was watching Tasha all night long."

"Tasha's here?" TJ gazed around.

Matt couldn't seem to forget that TJ had been attracted to Tasha. Sure, it was mostly from afar, and sure, he'd promised to back off. Still, Matt couldn't help but be jealous.

"She left," he said.

"Too bad." Then TJ gave an unabashed grin and jostled Matt with his elbow.

Alex watched the exchange with obvious interest.

Matt braced himself, wishing he could shut TJ up.

But TJ was done. He drummed his hands against the wooden tabletop. "Is there a waiter or waitress around here?"

"I can go to the bar," James quickly offered.

"I'll come with," Alex said, sliding off the high stool.

"Whatever they have on tap," TJ said.

"Same for me," Matt said, sliding James a fifty. "Get yourselves something, too."

"Best boss in the world." Alex grinned.

"You know how to keep employees happy," TJ said as the pair walked away.

"I wish I knew how to keep one particular employee safe."

"You've got the new cameras now."

"Alex just told me there've been a couple of other minor incidents that looked like tampering. Tasha didn't say anything to me about them." Matt was definitely going to bring that up with her. He wished he could do it now. He didn't want to wait until morning.

"She probably didn't want you going all white knight on her."

"I don't do that."

"You like her, bro."

Matt wasn't about to deny it.

"And you worry about her. And she strikes me as the self-sufficient type."

"She is that," Matt agreed. "But she knows we're all looking to find this guy. Why would she withhold information?"

"Ask her."

"I will. The other thing Alex said was the weird things only happened after Tasha had done a repair, not when it was Alex or anyone else. And this guy watching her tonight? That makes me even more curious." Matt hated to think Tasha might be some kind of target in all this.

"It seems unlikely tonight's guy is related to the sabotage," TJ said.

"He followed her out."

"Probably working up his nerve to ask her on a date."

Matt scoffed at that. "He was twice her age."

"Some guys still think they have a shot. And he doesn't know he'd have to go through you to get to her."

Matt didn't respond. He didn't usually keep things from

his friend, but he had no intention of telling TJ how far things had gone with Tasha. "I'm worried about her."

"Worry away. Just don't do anything outrageous."

Like sleeping with her? "Like what?"

"Like locking her up in a tower."

Despite his worry, Matt couldn't help but smile at that. "My place does have a great security system."

TJ chuckled. "Now *that* would be an example of what not to do."

"I won't." But there were a dozen reasons why Matt would love to lock her away in his house and keep her all to himself.

As the sun rose in the early morning, Tasha made her way up from the compact engine room into the bridge and living quarters of the yacht *Crystal Zone*. Between reliving her lovemaking with Matt and worrying about the sabotage, she'd barely been able to sleep. After tossing and turning most of the night, an early start had seemed like the most productive solution.

Now, she came to the top of the stairs in the yacht's main living area, and a sixth sense made her scalp tingle. She froze. She looked around, but nothing seemed out of place. She listened, hearing only the lapping of the waves and the creak of the ship against the pier.

Still, she couldn't shake the unsettling feeling. She wrinkled her nose and realized it was a scent. There was an odd scent in the room. It seemed familiar, yet out of place. She tried to make herself move, but she couldn't get her legs to cooperate.

She ordered herself to quit freaking out. Everything was fine with the engine. It was in better shape than ever, since she kept fussing with it. The door to the rear deck was closed. Dawn had broken, and she could see through the window that nobody was outside.

Nobody was watching her.

She forced herself to take a step forward, walking on the

cardboard stripping that covered the polished floor to protect it from grease and oil. *Crystal Zone* was going out today on a six-day run.

Then she heard a sound.

She stopped dead.

It came again.

Somebody was on the forward deck. The outer door creaked open. She grabbed for the biggest wrench in her tool belt, sliding it out. If this was someone up to no good, they were going to have a fight on their hands.

She gripped the wrench tightly, moving stealthily forward.

"Matt?" a man's voice called out.

It was Caleb.

Her knees nearly gave way with relief. Nobody had broken in. Caleb had the gate code and was obviously looking for Matt.

She swallowed, reclaiming her voice. "It's Tasha. I'm in here."

"Tasha?" Caleb appeared on the bridge. "Is Matt with you?"

"He's not here."

"I saw the light was on. Why are you starting so early?" Caleb glanced at his watch.

"Couldn't sleep," she said, her stomach relaxing. She slid the wrench back into the loop.

"Way too much going on," he said with understanding.

"I heard Melissa and Noah got engaged."

"They did. It was pretty great." Caleb moved farther into the living area. "Did Matt tell you Melissa and Jules are determined to decorate his place for the holidays?"

"I'm sure he appreciates it."

Caleb chuckled. "I'm sure he doesn't. Dianne was big on decorating."

"Oh."

"I heard you met her." Caleb seemed to be fishing for something.

"I did."

"How did it go?"

Tasha couldn't help remembering her last conversation with Dianne. "I'm not sure. She seems...sad."

The answer obviously surprised Caleb. "Sad? Dianne?"

Tasha weighed the wisdom of taking this chance to ask Caleb directly about a job. She didn't want to put him on the spot.

Then again, she didn't know him very well, so he could easily turn her down without hurting her feelings.

"Can I ask you something?" she asked.

He looked curious. "Fire away."

"I know you have Neo restaurant locations all over the country."

"We have a few."

"Dianne is in pretty dire straits. She's lost everything."

Caleb's expression hardened a shade, but Tasha forced herself to go on.

"She has no money. And she needs a job. I think she's pretty desperate."

"She snowed you," Caleb said, tone flat.

"That doesn't seem true. She didn't know I was there. And she was pretty obviously distraught. Also, she doesn't strike me as somebody whose first plan of attack would be to seek employment."

"You've got that right. She likely hasn't worked a day in her life."

"She admits she doesn't have a lot of marketable skills. But she said she can host parties. She's attractive, articulate, refined."

"What are you getting at?"

"Maybe a hostess position or special events planner somewhere...not here, maybe on the eastern seaboard?"

"Ah." A look of comprehension came over Caleb's face. "Get her out of Matt's hair."

"Well, that, and give her a chance at building a life. If she's telling the truth, and she definitely seemed sincere, she has absolutely nothing left and nowhere to turn."

"It's her own fault," Caleb said.

"No argument from me. But everybody makes mistakes."

He paused, seeming to consider the point. "I know I've made enough of them." He seemed to be speaking half to himself.

"Will you think about it?" Tasha dared to press.

"I'll see what I can do. I suppose it's the season to do the right thing."

"It is."

Light rain drizzled down from the gray clouds above, the temperature hovering in the fifties. It hadn't snowed this year. Snow was always a rare event in this pocket of the coast, and the last white Christmas had been ten years back.

"If you come across Matt, will you tell him I'm looking for him?" Caleb was probably regretting his decision to check inside *Crystal Zone*.

"Anything I can help you with?" she asked.

"Nope. I just want to warn him that Jules and Melissa are going shopping today for holiday decorations. He better brace himself to look festive."

Tasha couldn't stop a smile. "I'll tell him."

"Thanks."

"No, thank you. Seriously, Caleb, thank you for helping Dianne."

"I haven't done anything yet."

"But you're going to try."

He turned to leave, but then braced a hand on the stairway, turning back. "You do know this isn't your problem."

"I know. But it's hard when you don't have a family. People to support you."

He hesitated. "You don't have a family?"

"Estranged. It's lonely at times."

"Same with me," he said. "But my wife, Jules, Melissa,

Noah, TJ, they're good people, I've found a family here. I bet you have, too."

"Soon you'll have two more members in your new family."

Caleb broke into a wide smile. "You got that right. See you, Tasha."

"Goodbye, Caleb."

The sun was now up, and Tasha's feeling of uneasiness had completely faded. She was glad she'd asked Caleb about the job directly. It was better than dragging Jules into the middle of it.

Tasha gathered up the rest of her tools, turned off the lights and secured the doors. She'd head to the main building and get cleaned up before she started on the next job. Alex would probably be in by now, and they could plan the details of their day.

Out on the pier, she shifted the toolbox to her right hand and started to make her way to shore. Almost immediately she saw Matt coming the other way.

His shoulders were square, his stride determined and his chin was held high. She wondered if he'd found some information on the saboteur.

"Morning," she called out as she grew closer.

He didn't smile.

"Did something happen?" She reflexively checked out the remaining row of yachts. She didn't see anything out of place.

"I just talked to Caleb."

"Oh, good. He was looking for you." She struggled to figure out why Matt was frowning.

"You asked him about Dianne." The anger in Matt's tone was clear.

"I…" She'd known it was a risk. She shouldn't be surprised by his anger. "I only asked if he could help."

"Without even *telling* me, you asked my best friend to give my ex-wife a job?"

When he put it that way, it didn't sound very good.

"Only if he didn't mind," she said.

"You don't think that was unfair to him? What if he doesn't want to hire her? Heck, I'm not sure I'd want to hire her."

"Then he can say no. It was a question. He has a choice."

"You put him in an impossible situation."

"Matt, I know it was a bad divorce. Dianne might not be the greatest person in the world. But she is a person. And she is in trouble."

"She got herself into it."

"She made a mistake. She knows that."

Tasha set down the toolbox. It was growing heavy. "You can give her a break, Matt. Everybody deserves a break at some point."

"There's such a thing as justice."

"It seems she's experienced justice and then some."

"You don't know her."

"She can't be all bad. You married her. You must have loved her at some point, right?"

The question seemed to give him pause. The wind whipped his short hair, and the salt spray misted over them.

"I'm not sure I ever did," he finally said.

"What?" Tasha couldn't imagine marrying anyone she didn't love. She would never marry someone she didn't love.

"I didn't see her clearly at first. It seemed like we wanted the same things out of life."

The admission shouldn't have taken her by surprise. Matt had never made a secret of the fact that he wanted wealth, status and luxury.

"Don't be like them," she said.

He looked confused. "Like Dianne? I'm not like Dianne. I've worked hard for everything I've earned, and I appreciate it and don't take it for granted."

"I know." She did. "What I mean is, don't turn into one of those callous elites, forgetting about the day-to-day struggles of ordinary people."

"Except that Dianne is calculating."

"She needs a job."

"She does. But all she's ever aspired to is a free ride."

"Desperation is a powerful motivator. And Caleb can always fire her."

Matt clamped his jaw. "You shouldn't have interfered."

"Maybe not." She couldn't entirely disagree. "I felt sorry for her."

"Because you're too trusting."

Tasha didn't think that was true, but she wasn't going to argue anymore. She'd done what she'd done, and he had every right to be upset. "I have to meet Alex now."

"Right." He looked like he wanted to say more. "I'll catch you later."

"Sure." At this point, she had her doubts that he'd try.

Matt entered the Crab Shack after the lunch rush to find Caleb at the bar talking with his sister-in-law, Melissa.

He knew he couldn't let this morning's argument sit. He had to address it right away.

He stopped in front of Caleb, bracing himself. "I didn't mean to jump down your throat this morning."

"Not a problem," Caleb easily replied.

From behind the bar, Melissa poured them each an ice water and excused herself.

"I was shocked is all," Matt said. "Tasha put you in an awkward situation. I should have made it clear right then that I didn't want you to do it."

"It's already done."

"What?"

Caleb stirred the ice water with the straw. "Dianne has a job at the Phoenix Neo and a plane ticket to get there."

"You didn't. Why would you do that? We didn't even finish our conversation."

"I didn't do it for you, Matt. I did it for Dianne. I did it for everyone."

"She probably won't work out."

"Maybe, maybe not."

"She needs to face the results of her own actions. It's not up to you to rescue her."

"I didn't rescue her. I gave her a shot. She's lost her fortune. She's lost you. She's lost that guy she thought was going to be her Prince Charming. It's not up to me, you're right. It's up to her. She'll make it at Neo or she won't, just like any other employee we've ever hired."

Matt hated to admit it, but Caleb was making good points. Dianne was on her own now. And she'd have to work if she wanted to succeed. There was justice in that.

"And she's in Phoenix," Caleb finished. "She's not here."

"I suppose I should thank you for that," Matt said. He took a big swallow of the water. Not having to see Dianne, frankly, was a huge relief.

"You bet you should thank me for that. And that's what friends do, by the way."

"There's a fire!" Melissa suddenly cried from the opposite side of the restaurant. "Oh, Matt, it looks like one of your boats!"

Matt dropped his glass on the bar and rushed across the room. Smoke billowed up from the far end of the pier. He couldn't tell which yacht was on fire, but all he could think of was Tasha. Where was Tasha?

"Call 911," he yelled to Melissa as he sprinted for the door.

He jumped into his car. Caleb clambered in beside him. Caleb barely got the door shut, and Matt was peeling from the parking lot.

"Can you tell what's on fire?" he asked Caleb as they sped along the spit of land that housed the Crab Shack.

"It has to be a boat. *Orca's Run* is blocking the view. But I don't think it's the one on fire."

"How the hell did he do it?" Matt gripped the steering wheel, sliding around the corner at the shoreline, heading for the pier. "If it's a stranger, how did he get to another one? Everyone's been on the lookout."

"I can see flames," Caleb said. "It's bad."

"Can you see people? Tasha?"

"There are people running down the pier. I can't tell who is who."

It felt like an eternity before Matt hit the parking lot. He slammed on the brakes, but it was still a run to get to the pier. The gate was open, and he sprinted through. "Grab the hoses," he called to the deckhands and maintenance crews. Could it be one of them? Was it possible that someone on the inside had actually set a boat on fire? "Start the pumps!"

The staff drilled for fires. At full deployment, their equipment could pump over a hundred gallons a minute from the ocean.

It was the fifty-foot *Crystal Zone* that was on fire. The entire cabin was engulfed in flames, and they were threatening the smaller craft, *Never Fear*, that was moored directly behind on a floater jutting out from the pier.

He looked behind him to see three crew members lugging lengths of fire hose. Caleb was helping them. But Matt didn't see Tasha. Where was Tasha?

And then he saw her. She was climbing onto the deck of *Salty Sea*, which was in the berth next to *Crystal Zone*. It was barely ten feet away from the flames. There were clients on that boat, two families due to leave port in a couple of hours. The smoke was thick, and she quickly disappeared into it.

Matt increased his speed, running up the gangway to the deck of *Salty Sea*.

"Tasha!" His lungs filled with smoke, and he quickly ducked to breathe cleaner air.

And then he saw her. She was shepherding a mother and two children toward the gangway.

"Five more," she called out harshly as she passed him.

He wanted to grab her. He wanted to hug her. He wanted to reassure himself that she was okay. But he knew it would have to wait. The passengers needed his help.

Eyes watering, he pressed on toward the cabin.

There he met one of the dads, the other mother and the remaining two children.

"Follow me," he rasped, picking up the smallest child.

They made it quickly to the gangway, where the air was clear.

"We're missing one," Tasha said, starting back.

"Stay here!" he told her.

She ignored him, pushing back into the smoke.

Together, they found the last man. He was on the top deck, and Matt guided him to a ladder. They quickly got him to the gangway, and he made his way down.

Matt took a second to survey the disastrous scene.

Neither he nor Tasha said a word.

Caleb and the workers were connecting the lengths of hose.

Alex was preparing the pump.

His gaze went to *Crystal Zone*. She was a complete loss, and *Never Fear* was next. It was too far away from the pier. The spray wouldn't reach it.

Then Matt heard it or smelled it or felt it.

"Get down!" he shouted, grabbing Tasha and throwing her to the deck, covering her body with his and closing his eyes tight.

*Never Fear*'s gasoline tanks exploded. The boom echoing in his ears, the shock wave and heat rushed over him. People on the dock roared in fear.

While debris rained down on him and Tasha, and his ears rang from the boom, Matt gave a frantic look to the people on the pier.

Some had been knocked down, but *Crystal Zone* had blocked most of the blast. He and Tasha had taken the brunt.

"We're good," Caleb called out to him, rushing from person to person. "We're all good."

Matt watched a moment longer before looking to Tasha beneath him.

"Are you hurt?" he asked her.

She shook her head. Then she coughed. When she spoke, her voice was strangled. "I'm fine." She paused. "Oh, Matt."

"I know," he said.

"I don't understand. Who would do this? People could have been killed."

"Yeah," he agreed, coughing himself. He eased off her. "Can you move?"

"Yes." She came to her knees.

He did the same.

She looked around. "You've lost two boats."

"Maybe three." *Salty Sea* was also damaged, its windows blown out from the blast.

Sirens sounded in the distance as the fire department made its way down the cliff road.

Matt took Tasha's hand. "We need to get off here. It's going to catch, too."

She came shakily to her feet.

Caleb met them at the bottom of the gangway.

Alex had the pumps running, and the crew was spraying water on the flames.

The fire engine stopped in the parking lot, and the firefighters geared up, heading down the pier on foot.

Matt turned Tasha to face him, taking in every inch of her. "Are you sure you're all right?"

"You're hurt," she said, pointing to his shoulder.

"You're bleeding," Caleb told him.

"It feels fine." Matt didn't feel a thing.

"You'll need stitches," she said.

"There'll be a medic here in a few minutes. They can bandage me up."

Looking around, it seemed Matt's was the only injury. He'd have plenty of attention. And his shoulder didn't hurt yet.

"Thank you." Tasha's low voice was shaking.

He wrapped an arm around her shoulders. "You probably

saved their lives." If she hadn't got everyone out of the cabin, they would have been caught in the blast.

"You, too."

He drew a deep breath and coughed some more.

"The media is here," Caleb said.

Matt realized publicity was inevitable. "I'll talk to them in a minute."

"Are you going to tell them about the sabotage?" Tasha asked.

"No. It's better that we keep that quiet for now."

"I checked *Crystal Zone* this morning. There was no reason in the world for it to catch fire." A funny expression came over her face.

"What is it?"

Her eyes narrowed.

"Tasha?"

"You're going to think I'm nuts."

"Whatever it is, tell me."

"When I came up from the engine room, I got this creepy feeling, a sixth-sense thing. It felt like somebody was watching me. But then Caleb showed up, and I thought he was the reason."

Fear flashed through Matt. "Somebody else was on the boat with you? Did you see who?"

"I didn't. I mean, besides Caleb. But now…"

"Mr. Emerson?" A reporter shoved a microphone in front of him.

Someone else snapped a picture.

He nudged Tasha to leave. She didn't need to face this.

He'd get it over with, answer their questions, get the fire out and then sit down and figure out what on earth was going on.

# Nine

For the first time, Tasha wished her room in the staff quarters had a bathtub. She was usually content with a quick shower. Getting clean was her objective, not soaking in foamy or scented water.

But tonight, she'd have given a lot for the huge soaker tub from her old bathroom in Boston. She shampooed her hair a second time, trying to remove the smoke smell. She scrubbed her skin, finding bumps and bruises. And when she started to shake, she reminded herself that she was fine, Matt was fine, everybody was thankfully fine.

The police were getting involved now, so surely they'd get to the bottom of the inexplicable sabotage. Matt had said, and she agreed, this went far beyond what any of his competitors would do to gain a business advantage. So unless something had gone catastrophically wrong in an unplanned way today, they were looking for a much more sinister motive.

The firefighters had said the blaze had started in the engine room, identifying it as the source of the fire. They expected to know more specifics in the next few days.

She shut off the taps, wrapped a towel around her hair, dried her skin and shrugged into her terry-cloth robe. It was only eight in the evening, but she was going to bed. Maybe she'd read a while to calm her mind. But she was exhausted. And tomorrow was going to be another overwhelming day.

A knock sounded on her door, startling her. Adrenaline rushed her system, and her heart thudded in her chest. It was silly to be frightened. She was not going to be frightened.

"Tasha?" It was Matt.

"Yes?"

He waited a moment. "Can you open the door?"

She almost said she wasn't dressed. But the man had already seen her naked. The bathrobe, by comparison, was overdressed. She tightened the sash and unlocked the door, pulling it open.

"Hey," he said, his blue eyes gentle.

She fought an urge to walk into his arms. "Hi."

"How are you feeling?"

"I'll be fine."

"I didn't ask what you'd be. I asked how you are." He looked solid and strong, like a hug from him would be exactly the reassurance she needed right now.

But she had to be strong herself. "Sore." It was a truthful answer without going into her state of mind. "You?"

"Yeah. Pretty sore." He gestured into the room.

She stepped aside. It felt reassuring to have him here. It was good to have his company.

He closed the door and leaned back against it. "I don't think you're safe."

She was jumpy. But she knew it was a natural reaction to being so close to an explosion. She'd be fine after a good night's sleep.

"I'm okay," she said.

He eased a little closer. "We agree this wasn't a competitor. And if it's not Whiskey Bay Marina—and it's likely *not* Whiskey Bay Marina—then the next logical guess is you."

"That doesn't make sense." She couldn't wrap her mind around someone, *anyone*, targeting her.

"I'm afraid for you, Tasha."

"We don't know—"

He moved closer still. "I don't care what we know and don't know."

"Matt."

He took her hands in his. "Listen to me."

"This is wild speculation."

She tried to ignore his touch. But it felt good. It felt right. It felt more comforting than made sense. She prided herself on her independence, and here she was wishing she could lean on Matt.

"Somebody's targeted you," he said. "Somebody who's willing to commit arson and harm people."

"Why would they do that to me? Who would do that to me?"

"I don't know. All I do know is that it's happening, and you need protection. I want to do that, Tasha. I want to protect you." He squeezed her hands. "I couldn't live with myself if anything happened to you."

"You're blowing this out of proportion, Matt."

He crossed the last inches between them, and his arms brushed hers. "They set a boat on fire."

She didn't have a response for that.

"I want you to stay at the main house."

"You mean your house." That was a dangerous idea. It was a frightening idea. Just standing so close to him now, her emotions were swinging off-kilter.

"I have an alarm system. I have good locks on my doors. And I'm there. I'm *there* if anything goes wrong."

"It's nice of you to offer," she said, her logical self at odds with the roller coaster of her emotions.

She couldn't stay under the same roof as Matt, not with her feelings about him so confused, not with her attraction to him so strong, and certainly not right out there in front of the entire staff and crew of the marina.

"I am your boss, and as a condition of your employment, you need to stay safe, Tasha."

"You *know* what people will think." She grasped at a perfectly logical argument. No way, no how was she going to admit she didn't trust herself with him.

"I couldn't care less what people will think."

"I do. I care."

"Do you want a chaperone? Should we ask someone to come stay there with us?"

"That would make it look even worse."

He drew back a little and gently let her hands go, seeming to give her some space.

"I have a guest room. This is about security and nothing more. Everybody here knows you. If you don't make a big deal about the arrangement, neither will they. The police are involved. There's a serious criminal out there, and it has something to do with you."

She closed her eyes for a long second, steeling herself, telling herself she could handle it. She had control of her emotions.

He was right, and she needed to make the best of it. She'd go stay behind his locks and his alarm system. She'd be practical. She could keep her distance. And she'd keep it light.

"Do you have a soaker tub?" she joked, wincing at her sore muscles.

He gave a ghost of a smile. "Yes, I do. Get your things."

She moved to the closet where she had a gym bag, feeling every muscle involved. "I feel like I've been in a bar fight."

"Have you been in many bar fights?"

"Have you?" she countered.

"A couple. And, yeah, this is pretty much what it feels like."

Having accepted the inevitable, Tasha tossed some necessities into her gym bag, changed in the bathroom and was ready in a few minutes.

"You're frighteningly fast at that," Matt noted as they stepped onto the porch.

"I'm leaving my ball gowns behind."

"Are you going to lock it?" he asked, looking pointedly at the door.

"There's not much inside."

"With all that's going on?" He raised his brow.

"Fine. You're right. It's the smart thing to do." She dug into the pocket of her pants, found the key and turned it in the lock.

He lifted her bag from her hand. She would have protested, but it seemed like too much trouble. It was only a five-minute climb to the front door of his house. She couldn't bring herself to worry about which one of them carried her bag.

Inside Matt's house, boxes and bags littered the entryway. There were more of them in the living room, stacked on the coffee table and on the sofa and chairs.

"You did a little shopping?" she asked, relieved to have something to be amused about.

"Jules and Melissa. They were going to decorate tonight. But, well…maybe tomorrow."

"Maybe," Tasha echoed.

It was less than two weeks until Christmas, but she couldn't imagine Matt was feeling very much like celebrating the season.

He set her bag down at the end of the hall. "Thirsty?"

"Yes." She found a vacant spot on the sofa and sat down.

If Matt wanted to bring her a drink, she wasn't about to argue. He went into the kitchen, opening cupboards and sliding drawers.

Curious, she leaned forward to look inside one of the shopping bags. Wrapped in tissue paper were three porcelain snowmen with smiling faces, checkerboard scarves and top hats. They were adorable.

She spied a long, narrow white shelf suspended above the fireplace. It was sparsely decorated, so she set the snowmen up at one end.

"There's no way to stop this, is there?" Matt gazed in resignation at the snowmen.

"You don't like them?" She was disappointed.

"No. They're cute. They're different. Different is good." He had a glass of amber liquid in each hand. It was obvious from their balloon shape that he'd poured some kind of brandy.

"This is your first Christmas since the divorce." It wasn't a question. It was an observation.

"It is." He handed her one of the glasses. "Caleb gave Dianne a job in Phoenix thanks to you."

Tasha wasn't sure how to respond. She couldn't tell from Matt's tone if he was still angry. "We aren't going to fight again, are we?"

"No. I hope not. Too much else has happened."

She returned to the sofa and took a sip of the brandy.

"This is delicious," she said.

He took the only vacant armchair. "A gift from Caleb. He's more of a connoisseur than I am."

"He has good taste."

Matt raised his glass. "To Caleb's good taste."

She lifted her own. "Thank you, Caleb."

Matt sighed, leaned back in the soft chair and closed his eyes.

Tasha felt self-conscious, as if she'd intruded on his life.

She gazed at his handsome face for a few more minutes. Then her attention drifted to the glass walls, to the extraordinary view of the bay and the marina. The Neo restaurant was well under way. The job site was lit at night, a few people still working. She could see the flash of a welder and the outline of a crane against the steel frame of the building.

The yachts bobbed on the tides, a gaping black hole where the fire had burned. *Crystal Zone* hadn't been the finest in the fleet, but it was a favorite of Tasha's. She was going to miss working on it.

"You're going to have to help me," Matt said.

"Help you with what?"

He opened his eyes. "Buy a new boat. Make that two new boats."

"You'll be able to repair *Salty Sea*?"

"I think so. We'll have to strip it down, but it's not a total write-off. *Never Fear* is mostly debris at the bottom of the bay."

"Ironic that," she said.

"In what way?"

"We should have feared her."

Matt smiled. Then he took another sip of his brandy.

She set down her glass and looked into another of the shopping bags. This one contained cylindrical glass containers, stubby candles, glass beads and a bag of cranberries.

"I know exactly what to do with these," she said.

"Here we go." He sat up straighter.

She opened the bag of glass beads, slowly pouring a layer into each of the two containers. "Do you mind if I put this together?"

"Please do."

She set the candles inside, positioning them straight. Then she poured a layer of cranberries around them, finishing off with more glass beads.

While she worked, Matt rose and removed the bags from the coffee table, the sofa and elsewhere, and gathered them off to the side of the room. He positioned her finished creations in the center of the table and retrieved a long butane lighter from above the fireplace.

"You're not going to save them for Christmas?"

"I'm sure we can get more candles." He touched the lighter's flame to each wick. Lastly, he dimmed the lights. "This is nice."

When he moved past her, his shoulder touching hers, her nerve endings came to attention. He paused, and the warmth of his body seemed to permeate her skin.

She drew a deep breath, inhaling his scent. A part of her acknowledged that this was exactly what she'd feared and reminded herself she needed to fight it. Another part of her wanted the moment to go on forever.

"I'm glad you're here," he said in a soft tone.

It took a second to find her voice. She forced herself to keep it light. "Because you need help decorating?"

He didn't answer right away. When he did, he sounded disappointed. "Right. That's the reason."

She gave herself an extra couple of seconds, and then she eased away.

He seemed to take the hint and moved back to his chair.

She shook her emotions back to some semblance of normal. "So that's it?" She looked pointedly at the rest of the bags. "We're giving up on the decorating?"

"We're resting." He sounded normal again. "It's been a long day."

"Well, I'm curious now." It felt like there were unopened presents just waiting for her to dig in.

He gave a helpless shrug and a smile. "Go for it."

Tasha dug into a few more bags. She put silver stylized trees on the end tables, a basket of pinecones and red balls next to the candles. She hung two silver and snowflake-printed stockings above the fire, and wrestled a bent willow reindeer out of its box to set it up on the floor beside the fireplace.

When she discovered the components of an artificial tree, Matt gave up watching and rose to help.

"I knew you'd cave," she told him with a teasing smile.

"It says on the box that it's ten feet high. You'll never get it up by yourself."

"Oh, ye of little faith."

"Oh, ye of little height."

She laughed, amazed that she could do that at the end of such a trying day.

Together, they read the directions and fit the various pieces together, eventually ending up with a ten-foot balsam fir standing majestically in the center of the front window.

They both stood back to admire their work.

"Is that enough for tonight?" he asked.

"It's enough for tonight."

She felt an overwhelming urge to hug him. She wanted to thank him for helping with the tree. She wanted to thank him for saving her from the explosion.

More than that, she wanted to kiss him and make love to

him and spend the night in his arms. Her feelings were dangerous. She had to control them.

Steeling herself, she stepped away. "Okay to finish my brandy in the tub?"

His gaze sizzled on her for a moment.

"Alone," she said.

"I know."

She forced her feet to move.

Matt shouldn't have been surprised to find Tasha gone when he went into the kitchen for breakfast. She'd probably left early, hoping nobody would notice she hadn't slept in the staff quarters.

He wanted to text her to make sure she was all right. But he settled for staring out the window as he sipped his coffee, waiting until he spotted her on the pier with Alex. Only then did he pop a bagel in the toaster and check the news.

As expected, the fire was front and center in the local and state news. But he was surprised to see the article displayed prominently on a national site. He supposed the combination of fire, high-end yachts and an explosion, especially when there were pictures, was pretty hard to resist. They showed a shot of him and Tasha coming off *Salty Sea* after the explosion, side by side with a still photo of the crews fighting the flames.

He had planned to work at home this morning, as he normally did. But he was going down to the office instead. He wanted to be close to Tasha in case anything more happened.

Before he could leave, Jules and Melissa came by, calling out from the entryway.

"In the kitchen," he called back.

Jules spoke up. "We came to see how you were doing." She paused before coming down the four steps into the main living area. "And to see how you liked the decorations." She continued into the living room and gestured around. "Hey, you really got into the spirit."

"I did."

"Nice work." Melissa gazed around approvingly.

He knew he should credit Tasha. And he knew it wouldn't stay secret that she was sleeping here. But he wasn't in a rush to share the information. There was enough going on today.

"The insurance adjustors will be here at noon," he said instead.

"That's fast."

"I need to get things under way." If he was going to replace the boats before the spring season, he had no time to lose.

"Good thing it's the off-season," Melissa said, obviously following his train of thought.

"If there's anything to be grateful for, that's it. And that nobody got hurt." He was grateful for both things, but he wasn't going to relax until the perpetrator was caught and put in jail.

TJ was next through the door.

"How're you doing?" he asked Matt, giving Jules and Melissa each a nod.

"Fine." Matt thought about his conversation with Tasha last night, and he couldn't help but smile. "A bit like I've been in a bar fight."

TJ grinned back. "My guess is that two of the yachts are write-offs?"

"I'll confirm that today. But, I can't see how we save either of them."

"If you need interim financing, just let me know."

It was on the tip of Matt's tongue to refuse. He hated to take advantage of his friends. And he was already one favor down because of Caleb hiring Dianne.

But he had to be practical. TJ had access to almost unlimited funds. Matt would cover any interest payments. And having TJ write a check, instead of explaining the situation to a banker, would definitely speed things up.

"I might," he said to TJ. "I'm going to track down replacements just as soon as I can make some appointments."

"New yachts," Melissa said with a grin. "Now, *that's* what I call a Christmas gift."

"You can help me test them out," Matt offered.

"I'm your girl," she said.

Matt retrieved his cup and took the final swallow of his coffee. "Thanks for checking on me, guys. But I have to get to work."

"We'll get out of your way," Jules said.

"Nice job with the decorating," Melissa said as they turned to leave.

"I thought we were going to have to do it all," Jules said to her sister as they headed through the foyer.

As the door closed behind Jules and Melissa, TJ looked pointedly around the room. "What is with all this?"

"Tasha helped," Matt said.

"Last night?" TJ asked, his interest obviously perking up.

"I wanted her safely surrounded by an alarm system."

"So, it wasn't…"

"She slept in the guest room."

"Too bad."

"Seriously? She was nearly blown up yesterday. So were we."

"And you couldn't find it in your heart to comfort her?"

Matt knew it was a joke. TJ was absolutely not the kind of guy who would take advantage of a woman's emotional state.

"Is she staying again tonight?" TJ asked.

"Until we catch the jerk that did this. Yes, she's staying right here. I wish I hadn't committed to the mayor's party this evening."

"I could hang out with her."

Since TJ had once asked Tasha on a date, Matt wasn't crazy about that idea.

TJ put on an affronted expression. "You honestly think I'd make a move on her?"

"Of course not."

"Take her with you," TJ suggested.

"She hates those kinds of parties." It was too bad. Matt would happily keep her by his side.

"Everybody hates those kinds of parties."

"I don't."

"Then there's something wrong with you."

Matt didn't think there was anything wrong with him. There were a lot of positives to his hard work, and socializing was one of them. He employed nearly fifty people. He brought economic activity to Whiskey Bay, a town he loved.

And he liked the people of Whiskey Bay. He liked discussing issues with them. He liked strategizing with the other business owners, and he sure didn't mind doing it in a gracious setting.

"The food's good. The drinks are good. I like the music, and the company is usually pleasant. Plus tonight. Tonight everyone will want to talk about the fire. And I can use that as a way to pump them all for information. You never know what people might have seen or heard around town."

"Tell that to Tasha," TJ said.

Matt paused to think about that. He had to admit it was a good idea. "She was willing to come along last time when it was part of the investigation."

"Keeps her with you."

"She's a pretty skilled interrogator. You know, for somebody who hates those kinds of parties, she handles them beautifully. Did you know she grew up in Boston? Beacon Hill. She can hobnob with the best of them. And she's totally disarming. She's pretty, smart and funny. Easy to talk to. Trustworthy. People will tell her anything. It's perfect."

Matt stopped talking to find TJ staring quizzically at him.

"You do get what's going on here, right?" TJ asked.

"No." Did TJ know something about the saboteur? "Did you hear something? Did you see something? Why didn't you *say* something?"

"You're falling in love with Tasha."

Matt shook his head to get the astonishment out. "I thought you were talking about the fire."

"Mark my words."

"You're about a thousand steps ahead of yourself."

Being attracted to a woman didn't equate to happily-ever-after. Sure, he was incredibly attracted to Tasha. And he'd admit to himself that it wasn't simply physical. Although mostly what they did was argue. And they'd slept together exactly *one* time. TJ didn't even know about that.

Matt was miles away from thinking about love.

"I can read the signs," TJ said.

"Well, you're getting a false reading. And I'm going to work now." Matt started for his front door.

TJ trailed behind. "Better brace yourself, buddy. Because I *can* read the signs."

Officially, Tasha agreed to attend the mayor's party because she could talk to people, see if anybody knew anything. If the price for that was dancing with Matt, so be it.

Anticipation brought a smile to her face as she got ready for the evening.

Tasha quickly found a dress she liked in Matt's basement. Sleeveless, with a short, full skirt, it was made of shimmering champagne tulle. The outer dress was trimmed and decorated with hand-stitched lace, and the underdress was soft satin. Altogether, it was made for dancing.

A pair of shoes and the small clutch purse in a box below had obviously been bought to match the dress. The shoes were definitely not made for dancing, but Tasha was going to wear them anyway. Her more practical side protested the frivolous decision. But she wanted to look beautiful tonight.

She wanted to look beautiful for Matt.

She paused for a moment to let the thought sink in.

She had at first chosen a basic black dress from the rack. There was nothing wrong with it. It was understated but perfectly acceptable. Black wasn't exactly her color. But it was a safe choice.

"Tasha?" Matt called from the hallway.

"Yes?" she called back.

"We've got about twenty minutes, and then we should get going."

"No problem." But then she'd spotted a champagne-colored gown and it had held her attention. She'd left with both dresses, and she glanced from one to the other now. Letting out a deep breath, she plucked the champagne-colored one from the hanger. She couldn't help feeling like one of her sisters, primping for a fancy party in the hopes of impressing a rich man.

She'd never understood it before, and she didn't want to understand it now. But she did. She couldn't help herself. She wanted Matt to see her as beautiful.

She set the dress on the bed and shoes on the floor. The guest bathroom was spacious and opulent. Her few toiletries took up only a tiny corner of the vanity.

She stripped off her clothes, noting small bruises on her elbow and her shoulder. She was feeling a lot better than yesterday, but she was still sore. Her gaze strayed to the huge soaker tub next to the walk-in shower. She promised herself she'd take advantage of it later.

For now, she twisted her hair into a braided updo, brushed her teeth, put on some makeup and shimmied into the dress. She didn't have much in the way of jewelry, but she did have a little pair of emerald-and-diamond studs that her parents had given her for her eighteenth birthday.

The last thing she put on was the shoes. They weren't a perfect fit, but they did look terrific. She popped her phone and a credit card into the purse, and headed out to meet Matt.

His bedroom door was open, and the room was empty, as was the living room. Then she heard movement at the front door. Feeling guilty for having kept him waiting, she headed that way.

When she rounded the corner, he stopped still and his eyes went wide.

"What?" She glanced down at herself. Had she missed removing a tag?

"You look fantastic."

She relaxed and couldn't help but smile. The compliment warmed her straight through.

He moved closer. "I shouldn't be so shocked when you dress up like this."

He took her hands. "Seriously, Tasha. You're a knockout. It's a crying shame that you hide under baseball caps and boxy clothes."

His compliment warmed her, and she didn't know how to respond. She knew how she should respond—with annoyance at him for being shallow and disappointment in herself for succumbing to vanity. But that wasn't what she was feeling. She was feeling happy, excited, aroused. She'd dressed up for him, and he liked it.

"You're not so bad yourself," she said, her voice coming out husky.

He wore a tux better than anyone in the world.

"I don't want to share you," he said, drawing her closer.

"You think I'm yours to share?" She put a teasing lilt in her voice.

"You should be. You should be mine. Why aren't you mine, Tasha?" He searched her expression for a split second, and then his mouth came down on hers.

She knew there were all kinds of reasons that this was a bad idea. But she didn't have it in her. She wanted it as much as he did, maybe more. She wrapped her arms around his neck and returned his kiss.

She pressed her body against his. The arm at her waist held her tight. His free hand moved across her cheek, into her hair, cradling her face as he deepened the kiss. His leg nudged between hers, sending tendrils of desire along her inner thighs. Her nipples hardened against him, and a small pulse throbbed at her core.

He kissed her neck, nibbled her ear, his palm stroked up her spine, coming to the bare skin at the top of her back, slipping under the dress to caress her shoulder.

"Forget this," he muttered.

Then he scooped her into his arms and carried her farther into the house, down the hallway to his bedroom.

He dropped to the bed, bringing her with him, stretching her out in his arms, never stopping the path of his kisses.

"Matt?" she gasped, even as she inhaled his scent, gripped tight to his strong shoulders and marveled at how the world was spinning in a whole new direction. "The party."

Her body was on fire. Her skin craved his touch. Her lips couldn't get enough of his taste.

"Forget the party," he growled. "I need you, Tasha. I've imagined you in my bed so many, many times."

"I need you, too," she answered honestly.

It might have been the emotion of the past two days. Maybe it was the way he'd saved her. Maybe it was the intimacy of decorating for Christmas. Or maybe it was just hormones, chemistry. Matt wasn't like anyone she'd ever met.

He stripped off her dress and tossed his tux aside piece by piece.

When they were naked, they rolled together, wrapped in each other's arms.

She ended up on top. And she sat up, straddling him, smiling down.

"I have dreamed of this," he whispered, stroking his hands up her sides, moving to settle on her breasts.

"This might be a dream." She'd dreamed of him too, too many times to count. If this was another, she didn't want to wake up.

"You might be a dream," he said. "But this isn't a dream. This is so real."

"It feels real to me." Unwilling to wait, she guided him

inside, gasping as sensations threatened to overwhelm her. "Very, very, very real."

"Oh, Tasha," he groaned and pulled her close to kiss her. She moved her hips, pleasure spiraling through her.

"Don't stop," he said, matching her motion.

"No way," she answered against his mouth.

She wanted to say more, but words failed her. Her brain had shut down. All she could do was kiss and caress him, drink in every touch and motion he made.

The world contracted to his room, to his bed, to Matt, beautiful, wonderful Matt.

She sat up to gaze at his gorgeous face. His eyes were opaque. His lips were dark red. His jaw was clenched tight. She captured his hand, lifted it to her face and drew one of his fingers into her mouth. Even his hands tasted amazing.

His other hand clasped her hips. He thrust harder, arching off the bed, creating sparks that turned to colors that turned to sounds. Lights flashed in her brain and a roar came up in her ears. Matt called her name over and over as she catapulted into an abyss.

Then she melted forward, and his strong arms went around her, holding her close, rocking her in his arms.

"That was…" he whispered in her ear.

"Unbelievable," she finished on a gasping voice.

"How did we do that? What's your magic?"

She smiled. "I thought it was yours."

"It's ours," he said.

Moments slipped by while they both caught their breaths.

"Are we still going to the party?" she asked.

"I'm not willing to share." He trailed his fingertips along her bare back.

She knew she should call him out for those words. But she was too happy, too content. She wasn't going to do anything to break the spell.

# Ten

Matt resented real life. He wanted to lock himself away with Tasha and never come out. He'd held her in his arms all night long, waking to her smile, laughing with her over breakfast.

But she had insisted on going to work, and now he had a fire investigator sitting across from him in his office.

"Who was the last person to work on the engine before the fire?" Clayton Ludlow asked.

"My chief mechanic, Tasha Lowell. She's on her way here, but I can guarantee you she didn't make a mistake."

"I'm not suggesting she did. But I need to establish who had access to the engine room."

"After Tasha, I have no idea."

"You have security cameras?"

"I do."

"You reviewed the footage?" Clayton made some notes on a small pad of paper.

"Of course."

"Did anyone else board *Crystal Zone* the rest of the day?"

"Not that we could see. But Tasha thought…" Matt hesitated.

"Thought what?"

"She had a feeling someone was on board at the same time as her."

"Did she see someone?"

"No. It was just a feeling." And at this point, it was worrying Matt more than ever.

"There's nothing I can do with the *feeling* of another potential suspect."

"Tasha's not a suspect." Matt wanted the investigator to be clear on that.

Clayton's tone became brisk. "Are there blind spots left by the security cameras?"

"No."

Clayton's arched expression told Matt he was jumping to conclusions about Tasha.

"You know we've suspected sabotage," Matt said.

"I know. And we also know what started the fire."

Matt's interest ramped up. "How did he do it?"

"He *or she* left some oily rags in a pile. They ignited."

There was a knock on the door and Tasha pushed it open.

Matt waved her inside, and she took the vinyl guest chair next to Clayton.

Matt got straight to the point. "There were some oily rags left in the engine room. Any chance they were yours?"

He didn't believe for a minute they were, but he didn't want Clayton to think he was covering for Tasha. Not that he would need to. There was absolutely no way she was the saboteur.

"No," she said. "Never. Not a chance."

Matt looked to Clayton.

"How many boats do you work on in an average day?"

"One to six."

"So, you're busy."

"I'm busy," she said. "But I didn't forget something like that."

"How many boats did you work on the day of the fire?"

"Three." She paused. "No, four."

"This is a waste of time," Matt said.

Clayton ignored him. "The other problems Whiskey Bay has been having. I understand you were the last person to work on each of the engines."

"I was also the one to discover the wire short and the fuel leak that prevented the last fire." She slid a glance to Matt. It was obvious her patience was wearing.

Clayton made some more notes.

"Are you planning to charge me with something?" Tasha asked.

Her voice had gone higher, and her posture had grown stiff in the chair. Matt would have given anything to spirit her back to his house.

"Are you expecting to be charged with something?"

"No." She was emphatic.

Clayton didn't answer. He just nodded.

"We're wasting time," Matt said. "The real criminal is out there, and we're wasting time."

"Let me do my job," Clayton said.

"That's all we want." Matt nodded.

"It wasn't me," Tasha said.

"Noted. And now I have to finish my report." Clayton came to his feet.

Tasha stood, as well. "And I have engines to inspect. Think what you want about me," she said to Clayton. "But whoever is trying to hurt Matt's business is still trying to hurt Matt's business. If you don't want another disaster on your hands, help us find them."

She turned and left the office.

"Is she always so emotional?" Clayton asked.

"She's never emotional. And she's not emotional now. But I'm getting there." Matt rose. "Fill out your report. But if you pursue Tasha as a suspect or accomplice, you'll only be wasting valuable time."

Tasha paced her way down the pier, past the burned boats to *Monty's Pride*, which, thankfully, hadn't been damaged at all. She knew the inspector was only doing his job. But it was frustrating to have them spend so much time on her instead of looking for the real culprit. She had no doubt she'd be exonerated, no matter what people might believe right now. But she hated to think about the damage that could potentially be done in the meantime.

She heard the echoing sound of an open boat moving toward her. From the sound, she figured it was a small cartopper with a 150-horse outboard. Alex had chased a couple of reporters and a dozen lookie-loos away from the docks already this morning.

The red open boat was piloted by a man in a steel gray hoodie. He wasn't even wearing a life jacket.

"Jerk," she muttered under her breath, climbing down to the floater where it was obvious he was planning to dock.

"This is private property," she called out to him, waving him away.

He kept coming.

He didn't have a camera out yet; at least that was something.

She moved to the edge of the floater. "I said, this is private property."

He put a hand up to cup his ear.

He looked to be in his late fifties. He could be hard of hearing. Or it could simply be the noise of the outboard motor.

It was odd that he was wearing a hoodie. She associated them with teenagers, not older adults.

The boat touched broadside on the tire bumpers.

Tasha crouched to grasp the gunwale. "Is there something I can help you with?"

The man seemed oddly familiar.

"Have we met?" she asked, puzzled.

Maybe she'd been too quick to try to send him away. His business could be legitimate.

He shifted in his seat, coming closer to her.

And then she smelled it, the cologne or aftershave that she'd smelled the morning of the *Crystal Zone* fire.

"Only once," he said, raising an arm.

She jerked back, but she was too late.

Her world went dark.

* * *

It could have been minutes or hours later when she pushed her way to consciousness. She felt disoriented, and pain pulsed at her temples. Her first thought was to reach for Matt. She'd fallen asleep in his arms last night, and she wanted to wake up the same way.

She reached out, but instead of finding Matt, her hand hit a wall. No, it wasn't a wall. It was fabric. It was springy. It felt like the back of a sofa, and it had a musty smell.

She forced her eyes open, blinking in dim light.

The light was from a window up high in the room.

Her head throbbed harder, and she reached up to find a lump at her temple.

Then it all came back to her, the boat, the man, the smell. He'd hit her on the head. He'd knocked her out.

She sat up straight, pain ricocheting through her skull.

"You should have come home, Tasha." The voice was low and gravelly.

She looked rapidly around, trying to locate the source.

"Your mother misses you," he said.

She squinted at a shadowy figure in a kitchen chair across the room. "Who are you? Where am I? What do you want?"

"You're safe," he said.

She gave a hollow laugh. "I have a hard time believing that."

She gazed around the big room. It was more like a shed or a garage. She could make out a workbench of some kind. There were yard tools stacked against one wall, some sheers and a weed trimmer hanging on hooks.

"Where am I?" She put her feet on the floor, finding it was concrete.

The garage wasn't heated, and she was chilly.

"It's not important." He waved a dismissive hand. "We won't be here long."

"Where are we going?" Her mind was scrambling.

He'd pulled down his hoodie, but her vision was poor in

the dim light. She'd thought she recognized him, but she couldn't place him. And she found herself wondering if she'd been mistaken.

But the cologne smell was familiar. It was... It was...
*Her father's!*

"Where's my dad?" she asked, sitting forward, debating her odds of overpowering the man.

He was older, but she was woozy, and her pounding headache was making her dizzy.

"He's in Boston. As always. Why would he be anywhere else?"

She wasn't going to give away that she'd made the cologne connection. It might give her some kind of advantage.

"No reason."

The man rose to his feet. "Tasha, Tasha, Tasha. You have proved so difficult."

She wished she knew how long she'd been here. Would Matt have noticed her missing yet? There'd be no tracks, nothing on the security cameras. The man had used a boat. That's how he'd got onto *Crystal Zone* without being seen yesterday morning. He'd come by water.

"You were the one who lit the oily rags," she said.

She couldn't tell for sure, but it looked as if he'd smiled.

"Used a candle as a wick," he said with a certain amount of pride in his voice, taking a few paces in front of her. "The wax just disappears." He fluttered his fingers. "For all anyone knows, they spontaneously combusted. Didn't anyone teach you the dangers of oily rags?"

"Of course they did. Nobody's going to believe I'd make a mistake like that."

"Well, it wouldn't have come to that—" now he sounded angry "—if you hadn't spent so much time cozying up to Matt Emerson. Otherwise you would have been fired days ago. I didn't see that one coming."

Tasha was speechless. Who was this man? How long had he been watching her? And what had he seen between her and Matt? As quickly as the thought formed, she realized that some stranger knowing she'd slept with Matt was the least of her worries.

She was in serious trouble here. She had no idea what this man intended to do with her.

Cold fear gripped the pit of her stomach.

"Have you seen Tasha?" Matt had found Alex on the pier next to *Orca's Run*, moving a wheeled toolbox.

"Not since this morning. Didn't she talk to the investigator?"

"That was three hours ago." Matt was starting to worry.

"Maybe she took a long lunch."

"Without saying anything?"

Alex gave him an odd look, and he realized his relationship with Tasha was far different from what everyone believed.

"Have you tried the Crab Shack?" Alex asked.

"That's a good idea."

Tasha had been getting to know Jules and Melissa recently. Matt liked that. He liked that she fit in with his circle of friends.

"Thanks," he said to Alex, waving as he strode down the pier. At the same time, he called Jules's cell phone, too impatient to wait until he got there.

"I don't know," Jules said when he asked the question. "I'm at home, feet up. They're really swollen today."

"Sorry to hear that."

"It's the price you pay." She sounded cheerful.

"Is Melissa at the restaurant?"

"I expect so. Is something wrong, Matt? You sound worried."

"I'm looking for Tasha."

Jules's tone changed. "Did something happen?"

"I don't know. She's not around. I can't find her on the

pier or in the main building. I checked the staff quarters and nothing."

"Maybe she went into town?"

"Not without telling me."

There was a silent pause. "Because of the fire?"

It was on the tip of his tongue to tell Jules he thought Tasha was the target. He might not have any proof, but his instincts were telling him somebody was out to discredit her. Heck, they already had the fire department thinking she was the culprit. But he didn't want to upset Jules. Her focus needed to be on her and the babies. She needed to stay relaxed.

"It's probably nothing." He forced a note of cheer into his voice. "I'll walk over to the Crab Shack myself. Or maybe she did go into town. She might have needed parts."

"I'll let you know if I hear from her," Jules said.

"Thanks. You relax. Take care of those babies."

Matt signed off.

He'd been walking fast, and he headed down the stairs to the parking lot.

"Matt!" It was Caleb, exiting his own car.

Matt trotted the rest of the way, hoping Caleb had news about Tasha.

Caleb was accompanied by an older woman.

"What is it?" he asked Caleb between deep breaths.

Caleb gestured to the fiftysomething woman. "This is Annette Lowell. She came to the Crab Shack looking for Tasha. She says she's her mother."

Matt didn't know how to react. Could Annette's appearance have something to do with Tasha being gone? "Hello."

The woman flashed a friendly smile. "You must be Matt Emerson."

"I am." Matt glanced at Caleb. He was beyond confused.

"Annette came to visit Tasha," Caleb said, his subtle shrug and the twist to his expression telling Matt he had no more information than that.

"Was Tasha expecting you?" Matt asked, still trying to pull the two events together. Was Tasha avoiding her mother? Matt knew they were estranged.

"No. I haven't spoken to Tasha in over a year."

"Not at all?"

"No."

Matt didn't really want to tell the woman her daughter was missing. He wasn't even sure if Tasha was missing. There could still be a logical explanation of why he couldn't find her.

"I saw the coverage of that terrible fire," Annette said to Matt. "I hope you'll be able to replace the yachts."

"We will."

"Good, good. I'm *so* looking forward to getting to know you." Her smile was expectant now. "I had no idea my daughter was dating such an accomplished man."

Dating? Where had Annette got the idea they were dating?

Then he remembered the picture in the national news, his arm around Tasha's shoulder, the expression of concern captured by the camera. Annette must have seen it and concluded that he and Tasha were together. It was clear she was happy about it.

"I'm a little busy right now." He looked to Caleb for assistance.

It wasn't fair to dump this on Caleb, but Matt had to concentrate on Tasha. He had to find her and assure himself she was safe. He was trying his house next. There was an outside chance she'd gone up there for a rest and turned off her phone. It was a long shot. But he didn't know what else to do.

Caleb stepped up. "Would you like to meet my wife?" he asked Annette. "She's pregnant and resting at the house right now, just up there on the hill. We're having twins."

Annette looked uncertain. It was clear she'd rather stay with Matt.

"Great idea," Matt chimed in. "I'll finish up here, and maybe we can talk later."

"With Tasha?" she asked.

"Of course."

The answer seemed to appease her, and she went willingly with Caleb.

Once again, Matt owed his friend big-time.

Without wasting another second, he called Melissa and discovered Tasha hadn't been to the Crab Shack in a couple of days. He checked his house but found nothing. So he asked the crew and dockworkers to check every inch of every boat.

They came up empty, and Matt called the police.

They told him he couldn't file a missing persons report for twenty-four hours. Then they had the gall to suggest Tasha might have disappeared of her own accord—because she knew she'd been caught committing arson.

It took every ounce of self-control he had not to ream the officer out over the phone.

His next stop was the security tapes from this morning. While he was reviewing them in the office, Caleb came back.

"What was *that* all about?" Caleb asked Matt without preamble.

"I have no idea. But I have bigger problems."

Caleb sobered. "What's going on?"

"It's Tasha. I can't find her."

"Was she supposed to be somewhere?"

"Here. She's supposed to be here!"

Caleb drew back.

"Sorry," Matt said. "I'm on edge. She's been missing for hours. The police won't listen."

"The *police*?"

"The fire department thinks she's an arsonist."

"Wait. Slow down."

"She was the last person known to be on board *Crystal Zone*. They concluded some oily rags combusted in the engine room, and they blame her for leaving them there—possibly on purpose."

"That's ridiculous," Caleb said.

"It's something else. It's someone else." Matt kept his attention on the security footage. "There she is."

Caleb came around the desk to watch with him.

Tasha walked down the pier. By the time clock, he knew it was right after she'd talked to the fire investigator. She'd disappeared behind *Monty's Pride*.

Matt waited. He watched and he waited.

"Where did she go?" Caleb asked.

"There's nothing back there." Matt clicked Fast-Forward, and they continued to watch.

"That's an hour," Caleb said. "Would she be working on *Monty's Pride*?"

"We checked. She's not there. And she couldn't have boarded from the far side."

"I hate to say it," Caleb ventured. "Is there any chance she fell in?"

Matt shot him a look of disbelief. "Really? Plus the tide's incoming." He had to steel himself to even say it out loud. "She wouldn't have washed out to sea."

"I'm stretching," Caleb said.

"Wait a minute." The answer came to Matt in a lightning bolt. "A boat. If she left the pier without coming back around, it had to have been in a boat."

"The Crab Shack camera has a different angle."

Matt grabbed his coat. "Let's go."

Tasha's head was still throbbing, but at least her dizziness had subsided. She was thirsty, but she didn't want to say or do anything that might upset the man who held her captive. When he turned, she could see a bulge in the waistband of his pants.

It could be a gun. It was probably a gun. But at least he wasn't pointing it at her.

If she could get back to full strength, and if he came close enough, she might be able to overpower him. She knew instinctively that she'd get only one chance. If she tried and failed, he might go for the gun or knock her out again or tie her hands.

He'd been pacing the far side of the garage for a long time.

"You need something else to wear," he said. His tone was matter-of-fact. He didn't seem angry.

"Why?" she dared ask.

"Because you look terrible, all tatty and ratty. Your mother wouldn't like that at all."

"You know my mother?"

His grin was somewhat sickly. "Do I know your mother? I know her better than she knows herself."

Struggling to keep her growing fear at bay, Tasha racked her brain trying to place the man. Had they met back in Boston? Why was he wearing her father's favorite cologne?

"Why did you want me to get fired?" she dared to ask.

"Isn't it obvious? Your mother misses you. You need to come home."

*Come home.* It sounded like home for him, too. *He must live in Boston.*

"You thought if Matt fired me, I'd move back to Boston?"

"Ah, Matt. The handsome Matt. You wore a nice dress that night."

Tasha turned cold again.

"You must have liked it. You looked like you liked it, all red and sparkly. You looked like your sister Madison."

"Where's Madison?" Tasha's voice came out on a rasp. Had this man done something to the rest of her family?

"What's with all the questions?" he chided. "If you want to see Madison, simply come home."

"Okay," she agreed, trying another tactic. "I'll come home. How soon can we leave?"

He stared at her with open suspicion. "I'm not falling for that."

"Falling for what? I miss Madison. And I miss Shelby. I'd like to see them. A visit would be nice."

"No, no, no." He shook his head. "That was too quick. I'm not stupid."

"I simply hadn't thought about it for a while," she tried.

"You're trying to trick me. Well, it won't work."

"I don't want to trick you." She gave up. "I honestly want to give you what you want. You've gone to a lot of trouble here. You must want it very badly."

"First, you need to change."

Her heart leaped in anticipation. Maybe he'd leave the garage. Maybe he'd go shopping for some clothes. If he left her alone, especially if he didn't tie her hands, she could escape. There had to be a way out of this place.

"It's in the car."

"What's in the car?"

"The red dress."

She was back to being frightened again. "How did you get the red dress?"

He looked at her like she was being dense. "It was in your room. I took it from your room. I'm disappointed you didn't notice. You should take more care with such an expensive gown. I had it cleaned."

Tasha's creep factor jumped right back up again. At the same time, she realized she hadn't even noticed the dress was gone. When she'd thought back on that night, making love with Matt had been foremost on her mind. The dress had faded to insignificance.

The security cameras covered the marina but the staff quarters were farther back, out of range. He'd obviously slipped in at some point.

"I'll get it," the man said, heading for the door.

"I'm not changing in front of you," she shouted out.

He stopped and pivoted. "I wouldn't expect you to, dear. Whatever you think of me, I am a gentleman."

"What's your name?" She braved the question, then held her breath while she waited for him to answer or get angry.

"Giles."

"And you're from Boston?"

"The West End, born and raised." He seemed to expect her to be impressed.

"That's very nice."

"I'll get your dress. We need to go now."

"Where are we going?"

He turned again, this time his eyes narrowed in annoyance, and she braced herself. "Pay attention, Tasha. We're going to Boston."

She shuddered at his icy expression. He couldn't get her all the way to Boston as his prisoner. He'd have to drive. They couldn't board a plane.

It would be all but impossible to watch her every second. She'd escape. She'd definitely find a way to escape.

But what if he caught her? What would he do then?

# Eleven

The Crab Shack security footage confirmed Matt's worst fears. The picture was grainy, but it showed Tasha being hauled into a boat and taken away.

"It's red," Caleb said, "but that's about as much detail as I'm getting."

"Probably a twenty-footer," Matt said. "There's no way they're leaving the inlet. That's something at least."

TJ arrived at the Crab Shack's office. "What's going on? Melissa said you were looking for Tasha."

"Somebody grabbed her," Matt said.

His instinct was to rush to his car and drive, but he didn't know where he was going. He should call the police, but he feared that would slow him down. He had to find her. He absolutely had to find her.

"What do you mean grabbed her?" TJ asked, his expression equal parts confusion and concern.

When Matt didn't answer, TJ looked to Caleb.

"Show him the clip," Caleb said.

Matt replayed it.

TJ swore under his breath.

"Matt thinks they won't leave the inlet," Caleb said. "It's a red twenty-footer. He might have pulled it onto a trailer, but maybe not. Maybe it's still tied up somewhere on the inlet."

"There are a lot of red cartoppers out there," TJ said, but he was taking out his phone as he said it.

Matt came to his feet. "We should start with the public dock." He was glad to have a course of action.

"What about the police?" Caleb asked.

"Herb?" TJ said into the phone. "Can you get me a helicopter?"

Matt turned to TJ in surprise.

"Now," TJ said and paused. "That'll do." He ended the call and pointed to the screen. "Can someone copy that for me?"

"Melissa?" Caleb called out.

She immediately popped her head through the doorway.

"Can you help TJ print out what's on the screen?"

"I'm going to the public dock," Matt said. "You'll call me?" he asked TJ.

"With anything we find," TJ said.

Under normal circumstances, Matt would have protested TJ's actions. But these weren't normal circumstances. He didn't care what resources it took. He was finding Tasha.

"I'll talk to the police," Caleb said. "What about Tasha's mother?"

Both TJ and Melissa stared at Caleb in surprise. "She's up with Jules. She suddenly dropped by for a visit."

"Yes," Matt said. "Talk to her. It's really strange that she's here. She might know something."

Matt sprinted to his car and roared out of the parking lot, zooming up the hill to the highway and turning right for the public dock. He dropped his phone on the seat beside him, ready to grab it if anyone called.

The sun was setting, and it was going to be dark soon. He could only imagine how terrified Tasha must be feeling. She had to be okay. She *had* to be okay.

It took him thirty minutes to get to the public dock. He leaped over the turnstile, not caring who might come after him.

He scanned the extensive docking system, row upon row of boats. He counted ten, no, twelve small red boats.

"Sir?" The attendant came up behind him. "If you don't have a pass card, I'll have to charge you five dollars."

Matt handed the kid a twenty. "Keep the change."

"Sure. Okay. Thanks, man."

Matt jogged to the dock with the biggest concentration of red twenty-footers.

He marched out on the dock, stopping to stare down at the first one. He realized he didn't know what he was looking for. Blood on the seat? He raked a hand through his hair. *Please, no, not that.*

Even if he found the boat, what would that tell him? He wouldn't know which way they went. Did the kidnapper have a car? Maybe the attendant was his best bet. Maybe the kid had seen something.

His phone rang. It was TJ, and Matt put it to his ear. "Yeah?"

"We see a red boat. It's a possible match."

"Where?"

"Ten minutes south of you. Take Ring Loop Road, third right you come to."

"TJ." Matt wanted him to be right. He so wanted him to be right. "I'm looking at a dozen red twenty-footers here."

"He hit her on the head," TJ reminded him. "I don't think he'd risk carrying her unconscious through the public dock. And if she was awake, she might call out. This place is secluded. And the boat is only tied off at the bow. The stern line is trailing in the water, like somebody was in a hurry."

"Yeah. Okay." Matt bought into TJ's logic. "It's worth a shot."

"We'll keep going farther."

"Thanks." Matt headed back to his car.

He impatiently followed TJ's directions, finally arriving at the turnoff. He followed the narrow road toward the beach, shutting off his engine to silently coast down the final hill.

He could see a red boat at the dock. The tide was high, pushing it up against the rocky shore. There was an old building visible through the trees.

He crept around to the front of the building and saw a car with the trunk standing open. He moved closer, silent on his feet, listening carefully.

The building door swung open, and he ducked behind a tree.

Tasha appeared. Her mouth was taped. Her hands were behind her back. And she was wearing the red party dress. A man had her grasped tight by one arm.

She spotted the open trunk. Her eyes went wide with fear, as she tried to wrench herself away.

"Let her go!" Matt surged forward.

The man turned. He pulled a gun and pointed it at Matt. Matt froze.

Tasha's eyes were wide with fear.

"You don't want to do this," Matt said, regretting his impulsive actions. How could he have been so stupid as to barge up on the kidnapper with no plan?

"I know exactly what I want to do," the man returned in a cold voice.

"Let her go," Matt said.

"How about *you* get out of my way."

"You're not going to shoot her," Matt said, operating in desperation and on the fly. He could not let the guy leave with Tasha. "You went to too much trouble to get her here."

"Who said anything about shooting *her*?" The man sneered.

Matt heard sirens in the distance, and he nearly staggered with relief. "The police are on their way."

"Move!" the man yelled to Matt.

"No. You're not taking her anywhere."

The man fired off a round. It went wide.

"Every neighbor for ten miles heard that," Matt said. "You'll never get away. If you kill me, that's cold-blooded murder. If you let her go, maybe it was a misunderstanding. Maybe you drive away. Maybe, you let her go, and I step aside, and you drive off anywhere you want."

To Matt's surprise, the man seemed to consider the offer.

Matt took a step forward. "The one thing that's not happening here is you leaving with Tasha."

The sirens grew louder.

"Last chance," Matt said, taking another step.

The man's eyes grew wild, darting around in obvious indecision.

Then he shoved Tasha to the side.

She fell, and Matt rushed toward her and covered her with his body.

The kidnapper jumped into the car and zoomed off, spraying them with dust and stones.

As the debris settled, Matt pressed the number for TJ. Then he gently peeled the tape from Tasha's mouth. "Are you hurt?"

"He's getting away," she gasped.

"He won't." Matt put the phone to his ear.

TJ had a bird's-eye view, and he was obviously in touch with both Caleb and the police.

The call connected.

"Yeah?" TJ said.

"He's running, red car," Matt said to TJ. "I've got Tasha."

"We see him."

The helicopter whirled overhead.

"There's only one road out," Matt said to Tasha. "And TJ can see him from the air. There's no way for him to escape. Now, please tell me you're all right."

"I'm fine. Frightened. I think that man is crazy."

"Did he tell you what he wanted? Why are you dressed up? Never mind. Don't say anything. Just…" Matt removed his jacket and wrapped it around her shoulders. "Rest. Just rest."

He wrapped his arms around her, cradling her against his chest. All he wanted to do was hold her. Everything else could wait.

The small police station was a hive of activity. Matt hadn't left Tasha's side since he'd found her, and everything beyond him and the detective interviewing her was a blur of motion, muted colors and indistinct sounds.

"You said you might have recognized Giles Malahide?" the detective asked her for what she thought was about the tenth time.

"Why do you keep asking?" Matt interjected.

The detective gave him a sharp look. "I'm trying to get a full picture." He turned his attention to Tasha again. "You said he seemed familiar."

"His smell seemed familiar. He was wearing the same brand of cologne as my father. And he talked about my mother."

"What did he say about your mother?"

"That she missed me."

"Tasha, darling." It was her mother's voice.

Tasha gave her head a swift shake. She was in worse shape than she'd thought. She tightened her grip on Matt's hands, waiting for the auditory hallucination to subside.

"I *need* to see her." Her mother's voice came again. "I'm her *mother*."

Tasha's eyes focused on a figure across the room. It was her mother and she was attempting to get past two female officers.

"Matt?" Tasha managed in a shaky voice.

She looked to him. He didn't seem surprised. Her mother was here? Her mother was actually in the room?

"You called my mother?" she asked. "Why would you call my mother?"

"I didn't call her. She showed up asking for you."

"You said Giles Malahide talked about your mother?" the detective asked.

"Is that his full name?" Tasha asked. Not that it mattered. She really didn't care who he was, as long as he stayed in jail and got some help.

"What is *he* doing here?" Tasha's mother demanded.

Tasha looked up to see Giles Malahide being marched past in handcuffs.

Matt quickly put his arms around Tasha and pulled her against his shoulder.

"Annette," Giles called out. "Annette, I found her. I found her."

"Bring that woman here," the detective barked.

"Can we go somewhere private?" Matt asked the detective.

"Yes," he said. "This way."

They rose, and Matt steered Tasha away from the commotion, down a short hallway to an interview room, helping her sit in a molded plastic chair.

"What is going on?" Tasha managed.

"We're going to find out," the detective said. Then his tone became less brisk, more soothing. "I know you've gone through this already. But can you start from the beginning? From the first instance of what you believed to be sabotage?"

Tasha was tired.

"Is that necessary?" Matt asked. His tone hadn't moderated at all.

She put a hand on his forearm. "I can do it."

"Are you sure?"

"I'm sure."

She reiterated the entire story, from the water found in the fuel in *Orca's Run*, to her eerie feeling on board *Crystal Zone* before the fire, to her terror at the prospect of being thrown in the trunk of Giles's car.

As she came to the end, there was a soft knock on the door. It opened, and a patrolwoman leaned her head into the room. "Detective?" she asked.

"Come in, Elliott."

"We have a statement from Giles Malahide. It's delusional, but it corroborates everything Annette Lowell is saying."

"My *mother* knew about this?" Tasha couldn't accept that.

"No, no," Officer Elliott was quick to say. "Malahide acted on his own." She glanced to the detective, obviously unsure of how much to reveal.

"Go on," he said.

"Giles worked on the Lowell estate as a handyman."

"Estate?" the detective asked and looked to Tasha.

Officer Elliott continued, "They're the Vincent Lowell family, libraries, university buildings, the charity.

"Giles claims he's in love with Annette," Officer Elliott said. "And he believed her fondest wish was to have her daughter Tasha back in Boston in the family fold. He tracked Tasha down. He thought if she got fired from the Whiskey Bay Marina, she'd come home. When that didn't work, he took a more direct approach."

Tasha felt like she'd fallen through the looking glass. The officer's summary was entirely plausible, but it didn't explain how her mother had turned up in the middle of it all.

"Why is my mother here?" she asked.

"She saw your photo in the newspaper. The one taken at the fire. The story talked about Matt Emerson and his business and, well…" Officer Elliott looked almost apologetic. "She said she wanted to meet your boyfriend."

Tasha nearly laughed. She quickly covered her mouth and tipped her head forward to stifle the inappropriate emotion.

"Are you all right?" Matt's tone was worried.

"I'm fine. I'm…" She looked back up, shaking her head and heaving a sigh. "It's my mother." She looked at Matt. "She thinks you're a catch. She thinks I've found myself a worthy mate who will turn me into a responsible married woman." Tasha looked to Officer Elliott. "Her fondest wish isn't to have me back in Boston. Her fondest wish is to see me settled down, not rattling around engine parts and boat motors."

"Do we have a full confession?" the detective asked Officer Elliott.

"He's denied nothing. We have plenty to hold him on."

The detective closed his notebook. "Then we're done here. You're free to go, Ms. Lowell."

"Are you ready to see your mother?" Matt asked as they rose.

With all that had happened today, facing her mother seemed like the easiest thing she'd ever been asked to do. "As ready as I'll ever be."

"You're sure?"

"It's fine." Tasha had been standing up to her mother for years. She could do it again.

They made their way back to the crowded waiting room. Melissa, Noah, Jules, Caleb and Alex were all there. Tasha found herself glad to see them. It felt like she had a family after all, especially with Matt by her side.

Jules gave her a hug. "Anything you need," she said. "All you have to do is ask."

"I'm just glad it's over," Tasha said. "It would have been nice to have a less dramatic ending."

The people within hearing distance laughed.

"But at least we know what was going on," Jules said. "Everything can get back to normal now."

"Tasha." Her mother made her way through the small cluster of people. She pulled Tasha into a hug. "I was so worried about you."

"Hello, Mom."

Tasha swiftly ended the hug. They weren't a hugging family. She could only assume her mother had been inspired by Jules to offer that kind of affection.

"You look lovely," her mother said, taking in the dress.

"Thank you."

"Are you all right? I had no idea Giles would do something like that. Your father fired him months ago."

"It wasn't your fault," Tasha said.

Matt stepped in. "It's time to take Tasha home."

"Of course. Of course," Annette said. "We can talk later, darling."

If her mother had truly come looking for a reformed daughter with an urbane, wealthy boyfriend, she was going to be sadly disappointed.

While Tasha slept, Matt had installed Annette in another of his guest rooms. Then Caleb, the best friend a man could ever ask for, invited Annette to join him and Jules for dinner at the Crab Shack. Matt was now staring at the clutter of Christmas decorations, wondering if Tasha would feel up to finishing the job in the next few days, or if he should simply cart them all down to the basement for next year.

He heard a noise, and looked to find her standing at the end of the hall.

"You're up," he said, coming to his feet. Then he noticed she was carrying her gym bag. "What are you doing?"

"Back to the staff quarters," she said.

"Why?" He knew she had to go eventually. But it didn't have to be right away.

"Thanks for letting me stay here," she said, walking toward the front door.

"Wait. Whoa. You don't have to rush off. You're fine here. It's good."

The last thing he wanted was for her to leave. He'd hoped... Okay, so he wasn't exactly sure what he'd hoped. But he knew for certain this wasn't it.

"No, it's not good. The danger has passed, and things can go back to normal."

"Just like that?" He snapped his fingers.

"Just like nothing. Matt, what's got into you?"

He followed her to the entry hall. "Your mother's here, for one thing."

Tasha dropped the bag at her feet. "I know she's here. And I'll call her tomorrow. We can do lunch at her hotel or something. I'll explain everything. She'll be disappointed.

But I'm used to that. She'll get over it. She has two other perfectly good daughters."

"I mean she's here, here," Matt said, pointing to the floor. "I invited her to stay in my other guest room."

Tasha's expression turned to utter astonishment. "Why would you do that?"

"Because she's your mother. And I thought you were staying here. It seemed to make sense." He knew they weren't on the best of terms, but Annette had come all the way across the country to see Tasha. Surely, they could be civil for a couple of days.

"That was a bad idea," Tasha said.

"She told me you hadn't seen her in years."

"It's not a secret."

"Don't you think this is a good chance?"

Tasha crossed her arms over her chest. "You know why she's here, right?"

"To see you."

"To see *you*. She thinks I found a good man. She thinks I've come to my senses, and I'm going to start planning my wedding to you any minute now."

"I think she misses you," Matt said honestly. He hadn't spent a lot of time with Annette, but her concern for Tasha seemed genuine.

"She came out here because of the picture in the paper."

"The picture that told her where to find you," he argued.

"The picture that she thought told her a wealthy man was in my life."

"Stay and talk to her." What Matt really meant was stay and talk with him. But he couldn't say that out loud. He hated the thought of her going back to that dim little room where she'd be alone, and then he'd be alone, too.

"I'll see her tomorrow," Tasha said.

He couldn't let her slip away like this. "What about us?"

She looked tired, and a little sad. "There isn't an us."

"There was last night."

"Last night was…last night. Our emotions were high."

He didn't buy it. "Our emotions are still high."

"The danger is over. I don't need to be here. And I don't need you taking my mother's side."

"I'm not taking her side."

She put her hand on the doorknob. "I appreciate your hospitality, and what you've done for my mom. But my life is my own. I can't let her change it, and I can't let you change it either."

"Staying in my guest room isn't changing your life."

"No? I already miss your bathtub."

He couldn't tell if she was joking. "That's another reason to stay."

"No, that's another reason to go. I'm tough, Matt. I'm sturdy and hardworking. I don't need bubbles and bath salts and endless gallons of hot water."

"There's no shame in liking bath salts."

"This Cinderella is leaving the castle and going back home."

"That's not how the story ends."

"It's how this story ends, Matt."

"Give us a chance."

"I have to be strong."

"Why does being strong mean walking away?"

"Not tonight, Matt. Please, not tonight."

And then she was gone. And he was alone. He wanted to go after her, but it was obvious she needed some time.

Through the night, Tasha's mind had whirled a million miles an hour. It had pinged from the kidnapping to her mother to Matt and back again. She'd been tempted to stay and spend the night with him, and the feeling scared her.

She'd been tempted by Matt, by everything about his lifestyle, the soaker tub the pillow-top bed. She'd even wanted to decorate his Christmas tree.

She was attracted to his strength, his support and intelligence, his concern and kindness. She'd wanted to throw every scrap of her hard-won independence out the window and jump headlong into the opulent life he'd built.

She couldn't let herself do that.

"Tasha?" Her mother interrupted her thoughts from across the table at the Crab Shack.

"Yes?" Tasha brought herself back to the present.

"I said you've changed."

"I'm older." Her mother looked older, too. Tasha hadn't expected that.

"You're calm, more serene. And that was a lovely dress you had on yesterday."

Tasha tried not to sigh. "It was borrowed."

"That's too bad. You should buy some nice things for yourself. Just because you have a dirty day job, doesn't mean you can't dress up and look pretty."

"I don't want to dress up and look pretty." Even as she said the words, she acknowledged they were a lie. She'd wanted to dress up for Matt. She still wanted to look nice for him. As hard as she tried, she couldn't banish the feeling.

"I don't want to argue, honey."

"Neither do I." Tasha realized she didn't. "But I'm a mechanic, Mom. And it's not just a day job that I leave behind. I like being strong, independent, relaxed and casual."

"I can accept that."

The answer surprised Tasha. "You can?"

Her mother reached out and covered her hand. "I'm not trying to change you."

Tasha blinked.

"But how does Matt feel about that?"

"Everything's not about a man, Mom."

"I know. But there's nothing like a good man to focus a woman's priorities."

Tasha was nervous enough about Matt's impact on her priorities. "You mean mess with a woman's priorities."

"What a thing to say. When I met your father, I was planning to move to New York City. Well, he changed that plan right away."

"You exchanged a mansion in the Hamptons for a mansion in Beacon Hill?"

"What do you have against big houses?" Annette asked.

"It's not the house. It's the lifestyle. Would you have married a mechanic and moved to the suburbs?"

The question seemed to stump her mother.

"I'd do that in a heartbeat. It would suit me just fine. But I can't be someone's wife who spends all her time dressing up, attending parties, buying new yachts and decorating Christmas trees."

"It's not the same thing. I'd be moving down the ladder. You'd be moving up."

Tasha retrieved her hand. "I'm on a different ladder."

Her mother's eyes narrowed in puzzlement. "Not needing to work is a blessing. When you don't need to work, you can do whatever you want."

"I do need to work."

"Not if you and Matt—"

"Mom, there is no me and Matt. He's my boss, full stop."

Her mother gave a knowing smile. "I've seen the way he looks at you. And I can't help but hear wedding bells. And it has nothing to do with wishful thinking."

"Oh, Mom. Matt doesn't want to marry me."

Matt wanted to sleep with her, sure. And she wanted to sleep with him. But he was her boss not her boyfriend.

"Well, not yet," Annette said. "That's not the way it works, darling. If only you hadn't left home so soon. There's so much I could have taught you."

"Mom, I left home because I didn't want to play those games."

"They're the only games worth playing."

"Oh, Mom."

It was an argument they'd had dozens of times. But

strangely, it didn't upset Tasha as much as it normally did. She realized, deep down, her mother meant well.

"I want you to keep in touch, honey. Okay?" Annette said.

"Okay." Tasha agreed with a nod, knowing it was time to move to a different relationship with her family. She wasn't caving to their wishes by any stretch, but her mother seemed a lot more willing to see her side of things. "I will."

Her mother's expression brightened. "Maybe even come for Christmas? You could bring Matt with you. He can meet your father and, well, you can see what happens from there."

Baby steps, Tasha told herself. "You're getting way ahead of yourself, Mom."

"Perhaps. But a mother can hope."

# Twelve

Matt sat sprawled on a deck chair in front of his open fireplace. He normally loved the view from the marina building's rooftop deck. Tonight, the ocean looked bland. The sky was a weak pink as the sun disappeared, and dark clouds were moving in from the west. They'd hit the Coast Mountains soon and rain all over him.

He should care. He should go inside. He couldn't bring himself to do either.

Tasha had asked him to back off, and he'd backed off. And it was killing him to stay away from her.

Footsteps sounded on the outdoor staircase a few seconds before Caleb appeared.

"What's going on?" he asked Matt.

"Nothin'." Matt took another half-hearted drink of his beer.

Caleb helped himself to a bottle of beer from the compact fridge. "Where's Tasha?"

Matt shrugged. "I dunno."

Caleb twisted off his cap and took a chair. "I thought you two were a thing."

"We're not a thing." Matt wanted to be a thing. But what Matt wanted and what he got seemed to be completely different.

"I thought she stayed with you last night."

"That was the night before. When she was in danger. Last night, she went home."

"Oh."

"Yeah. Oh."

Caleb fell silent, and the fire hissed against the backdrop of the lackluster tide.

"You practically saved her life," he said.

"I guess that wasn't enough."

"What the heck happened?"

TJ appeared at the top of the stairs. "What happened to who?"

"To Matt," Caleb said. "He's all lonesome and pitiful."

"Where's Tasha?" TJ asked. Like Caleb, he helped himself to a beer.

"I'm not doing that all over again," Matt said.

"What?" TJ asked, looking from Matt to Caleb and back again.

"Trouble in paradise," Caleb said.

"It wasn't paradise," Matt said. Okay, maybe it had been paradise. But only for a fleeting moment in time, and now he felt awful.

"You were her white knight," TJ said as he sat down. "I saw it from the air."

Matt raised his bottle to punctuate TJ's very valid point. "That jerk shot at me. There was actual gunfire involved."

"So what went wrong?" TJ asked.

"That's what I asked," Caleb said.

"I asked her to say. She wanted to leave."

"Her mom really likes you," Caleb said.

"That's half the problem."

"Did you tell her how you feel?" TJ asked.

"Yes," Matt answered.

"You told her you were in love with her?"

"Wait, what?" Caleb asked. "Did I miss something?"

"That's your wild theory," Matt told TJ.

He didn't even know why TJ was so convinced it was true.

Sure, okay, maybe someday. If he was honest, Matt could see it happening. He could picture Tasha in his life for the long term.

"You moved heaven and earth to rescue her," Caleb said.

"She was my responsibility. She's my employee. She was kidnapped while she was at work."

"I've never seen you panic like that," TJ said.

He pulled his chair a little closer to the fire. The world was disappearing into darkness around them, and a chill was coming up in the air.

"A crazed maniac hit Tasha over the head and dragged her off in a boat." How exactly was Matt supposed to have reacted? "You were the one who hired a chopper," he said to TJ.

"It seemed like the most expeditious way to cover a lot of ground."

"That doesn't make you in love with Tasha." Matt frowned. He didn't even like saying the words that connected Tasha with TJ.

"What would you do if I asked her out again?" TJ asked.

Matt didn't hesitate. "I'd respectfully ask you not to do that."

Caleb snorted.

"See what I mean?" TJ said to Caleb.

"That doesn't prove anything." Although Matt had to admit he was exaggerating only a little bit.

And it went for any other guy, as well. He didn't know what he might do if he saw her with someone else. She was *his*. She had to be his.

"I can see the light coming on." Caleb was watching Matt but speaking to TJ.

"Any minute now…" TJ said. "Picture her in a wedding dress."

An image immediately popped up in Matt's mind. She looked beautiful, truly gorgeous. She was smiling, surrounded by flowers and sunshine. And he knew in that instant he'd do anything to keep her.

"And how do you feel?" Caleb asked. The laughter was gone from his voice.

"Like the luckiest guy on the planet."

"Bingo," TJ said, raising his beer in a toast.

"You need to tell her," Caleb said.

"Oh, no." Matt wasn't ready to go that far.

"She needs to know how you feel," TJ said.

"So she can turn me down again? She doesn't want a romance. She wants her career and her independence. She wants everyone to think of her as one of the guys."

"She told you that?" Caleb asked.

"She did."

"Exactly that?" TJ asked.

"She said her life was her own, and I wasn't going to change it. She said this was how our story ended."

Caleb and TJ exchanged a look.

"Yeah," Matt said. "Not going to be a happily-ever-after." He downed the rest of his beer.

"Wuss," TJ said.

"Coward," Caleb said.

Matt was insulted. "A guy shot at me."

"Didn't even wing you," TJ said.

"That's nothing," Caleb said.

"It was something," Matt said.

TJ leaned forward, bracing his hands on his knees. "You still have to tell her how you feel."

"I don't *have* to do anything."

"Haven't we always had your back?" Caleb asked.

"I asked her to stay," Matt repeated. "She decided to go."

"You asked her to stay the night." TJ's tone made the words an accusation.

"I meant more than that."

"Then tell her more than that."

Caleb came to his feet. "Ask her to stay for the rest of your life."

"That's…" Matt could picture it. He could honestly picture it.

"Exactly what you want to do," TJ said.

Matt stared at his friends.

TJ was right. They were both right. He was in love with Tasha, and he had to tell her. Maybe she'd reject him, maybe she wouldn't. But he wasn't going down without one heck of a fight.

"You'll want to get a ring," TJ said.

"It always works better with a ring," Caleb said.

"It worked for Noah," Matt agreed. "Do you think I should ask her in front of everyone?"

"No!" TJ and Caleb barked out in unison.

"Noah was sure of the answer," TJ said.

"You guys think she's going to turn me down." That was depressing.

"We don't," Caleb said.

"Maybe," TJ said. "It would probably help to get a really great ring. You need a loan?"

"I don't need a loan."

Matt might not be able to purchase two new yachts on short notice. But he could afford an engagement ring. He could afford a dazzling engagement ring—the kind of ring no woman, not even Tasha, would turn down.


Tasha had found the solution to her problem. She hated it, but she knew it was right. What she needed to do was glaringly obvious. She wrote Matt's name on the envelope and propped her resignation letter against the empty brown teapot on the round kitchen table in her staff quarters unit.

Somebody would find it there tomorrow.

She shrugged into her warmest jacket, pulling up the zipper. Her big suitcase was packed and standing in the middle of the room. She'd stuffed as much as she could into her gym bag. Everything else was in the three cardboard boxes she'd found in the marina's small warehouse.

She should hand him the letter herself. She knew that. A better woman would say goodbye and explain her decision. But she was afraid of what would happen if she confronted him, afraid she might cry. Or worse, afraid she'd change her mind.

She'd dreamed of Matt for the past three nights, spectacular, sexy dreams where he held her tight and made her feel cherished and safe. She loved them while she slept, but it was excruciatingly painful to wake up. She'd spent the days working hard, focusing on the challenges in front of her, trying desperately to wear out both her body and her mind.

It hadn't worked. And it wasn't going to work.

She gazed around the empty room, steeling herself. Maybe she'd go to Oregon, perhaps as far as California. It was warm there. Even in December, it was warm in California.

She looped her gym bag over her shoulder and extended the handle on her wheeled suitcase. But before she could move, there was a soft knock on her door.

Her stomach tightened with anxiety.

Her first thought was Matt. But it didn't sound like his knock. He wasn't tentative.

It came again.

"Hello?" she called out.

"It's Jules," came the reply.

Tasha hesitated. But she set down the gym bag and made her way to the door. She opened it partway, mustering up a smile. "Hi."

"How are you doing?"

"I'm fine."

"I thought you might come to the Crab Shack to talk."

"I've been busy." Tasha realized she was going to miss Jules, as well. And she'd miss Melissa. Not to mention Caleb and TJ. She barely knew Noah, but what she knew of him she liked. It would have been nice to get to know him better.

"Are you sure everything's okay?" Jules asked, the concern in her eyes reflected in her tone.

"Good. It's all good." Tasha gave a rapid nod.

"Yeah? Because I thought you might…" Jules cocked her head. "Do you mind if I come in?"

Tasha glanced back at her suitcase. It wasn't going to stay a secret for long. But she wasn't proud of the fact that she was sneaking off in the dark.

Jules waited, and Tasha couldn't think of a plausible excuse to refuse.

"Sure," she said, stepping back out of the way.

Jules entered. She glanced around the room and frowned. "What are you doing?"

"Leaving," Tasha said.

"Are you going home for Christmas?"

"No."

Jules was clearly astonished. "You're *leaving*, leaving?"

"Yes."

"You quit your job?"

Tasha's gaze flicked to the letter sitting on the table. "Yes."

Jules seemed to be at a loss for words. "I don't get it. What happened?"

"Nothing happened." Tasha picked up her gym bag again. "I really need to get going."

"Matt knows?" Jules asked.

Tasha wished she could lie. "He will."

Jules spotted the letter. "You wrote him a Dear John?"

"It's a letter of resignation." Tasha made a move for the door.

"You can't," Jules said, standing in her way.

"Jules, don't do this."

"You're making a mistake."

Jules took out her phone.

"What are you—"

Jules raised the phone to her ear. A second passed, maybe two, before she said, "She's leaving."

Tasha grabbed her suitcase, making to go around Jules.

But Jules backed into the door, leaning against it. "Tasha, that's who."

"Don't be ridiculous," Tasha said to Jules.

"Right *now*," Jules said. "Her suitcase is packed and everything."

"Seriously?" Tasha shook her head. This was getting out of hand.

Jules's eyes narrowed on Tasha. "I don't know how long I can do that."

"Jules, *please*." Tasha was growing desperate. She didn't trust herself with Matt. There was a reason she'd quit by letter.

"Hurry," Jules said into the phone. Then she ended the call and flattened herself against the door.

Tasha glanced around for an escape. She could jump out the window, but it was quite a drop on that side. And her big suitcase wouldn't fit through. She'd probably sprain an ankle, and Matt would find her in a heap on the pathway.

"What have you done?"

"You'll thank me," Jules said, but she didn't look completely confident.

"This is a disaster. We made *love*."

"You did?"

Tasha gave a jerky nod. "Do you know how embarrassing this is going to be?"

"I promise it won't be."

"It will." Tasha was growing frantic. "We have chemistry. We have *so* much chemistry. He practically saved my life. Do you know what that does to a woman's hormones? I'll never be able to resist him."

Now Jules looked baffled.

"Why resist him?"

"Because I'm not going to be *that* woman."

"What woman is that?"

"The woman who had a fling with her boss, who lost all credibility. I'd have to quit eventually. I might as well do it now while I still have my dignity. It's important to me."

"But at what cost to your future? Don't you want to be happy, Tasha?"

Someone banged on the door.

"Open up," Matt shouted from the other side.

Tasha took a step backward, nearly tripping on the suitcase. The gym bag slipped from her shoulder.

Jules moved to the side, and Matt pushed open the door.

He took in the suitcase and the empty room, and then zeroed in on Tasha.

"*What* are you doing?" His expression was part worry, part confusion.

"I'm resigning."

"Why?"

"You know why."

His eyes flashed with what looked like desperation. "I have no idea why."

"We can't go on like this, Matt."

"On like what? I did what you asked. I backed off."

"Yes, well…" She knew that was true, and she didn't dare admit that it hadn't helped. She still wanted him. She missed him. She…

Oh, no.

Not that.

She would *not* love Matt.

His expression turned to concern. "Tasha?" He closed the space between them. "You just turned white as a sheet."

"Go away," she rasped.

"I'm not going away." His hands closed gently around her arms.

Caleb appeared in the open doorway. "What's going on?"

"Shh," Jules hissed at him.

"Tasha." Matt's voice softened, and he stroked his palms along her arms. "Do you need to sit down?"

"No." She needed to leave, that's what she needed.

But she didn't want to leave. She wanted to fall into his arms. She wanted him to hold her tight. But she couldn't do it. It would only make things worse.

She loved him, and her heart was breaking in two.

He took her hands. "Tasha."

She gazed at their joined hands, feeling tears gather behind her eyes. Her throat went raw and her voice broke. "Please let me go."

"I can't do that."

TJ's voice sounded. "What did I—"

"Shh," Jules and Caleb said in unison.

Matt glanced over his shoulder. Then he looked into Tasha's eyes.

"They told me not to do it like this," he said. He lifted her hands, kissing her knuckles. "I'm not sure of your answer, and it would definitely work better with a ring."

Tasha squinted at him, trying to make sense of his words.

"But I love you, Tasha. I want you forever. I want you to marry me."

A roaring came up so fast in her ears, she was sure she couldn't have heard right.

She glanced past Matt to find Jules, Caleb and TJ all grinning.

"Wh-what?" she asked Matt.

"I love you," he repeated.

"I hate dresses." She found herself saying the first thing that came to her mind.

"Marry me in cargo pants," he said. "I don't care."

But she knew there was more to it than that. "You want someone to go yacht shopping with you, to take to fancy balls, to decorate your stupid Christmas tree."

He laughed softly and drew her into his arms.

"I'll go yacht shopping with him," Caleb offered.

"I'll go, too," TJ said. "After all, I'm the guy fronting the money."

"Let her speak," Jules said to both of them.

"You haven't thought this through," Tasha said.

"This is why you don't do it in front of people," Caleb whispered.

Jules elbowed him in the ribs.

"I've thought it through completely," Matt said.

She could see he was serious, and hope rose in her heart. She wanted to dream. She wanted to believe. Her voice went softer. "What if you change your mind?"

He arched a skeptical brow. "Change my mind about loving you?"

"About marrying a woman in cargo pants."

He drew back and cradled her face between his palms. "Tasha, I love you *exactly* the way you are."

Her heart thudded hard and deep inside her chest. She loved him, and she felt sunshine light up her world.

"I can't imagine my life without you and your cargo pants," he said.

Her heart lifted and lightened, and her lips curved into a gratified smile. "I suppose I could wear one more dress." She paused. "For the wedding."

His grin widened. "Is that a yes?"

She nodded, and he instantly wrapped her in a tight hug.

A cheer went up behind him.

"Yes," she whispered in his ear.

He kissed her then, deeply and passionately.

"Congratulations," TJ called out.

Matt laughed in clear delight as he broke the kiss. He kept one arm around Tasha, turning to his friends. "You could have given me some privacy."

"Are you kidding?" Caleb asked. "We were dying to see how this turned out."

"It turned out great," Matt said, giving Tasha a squeeze.

Jules moved forward. "Congratulations." She commandeered Tasha for a hug.

"You were right," Tasha said to her.

"Right about what?"

"I do thank you."

Jules smiled. "I knew it! I'm so happy for you, for both of you."

"I can't believe this has happened," Tasha managed, still feeling awestruck.

"I can't believe she didn't say it," Caleb put in.

"She did," Matt said. He pointed to his friends. "You all saw her nod. That's good enough for me. I have witnesses."

"The I-love-you part," Caleb said.

Matt looked to Tasha, showing surprise on his face. "You did. Didn't you?"

"I don't remember." She made a show of stalling.

"You don't remember if you love me?"

She teased. "I don't remember if I said it." She felt it with all her heart, and she couldn't wait to say it out loud. "I do love you, Matt. I love you so very much."

He scooped her up into his arms. "Good thing you're already packed." He started for the door.

"I've got the bags," TJ said.

Tasha couldn't help but laugh. She wrapped her arms around Matt's neck and rested her head against his shoulder. She was done fighting. They were going home.

It was late Christmas Eve, and Tasha stepped back to admire her handiwork on the tree.

Returning from the kitchen, two mugs of peppermint hot chocolate in his hands, Matt paused. He'd never seen a more amazing sight—his beloved fiancée making his house feel like the perfect home.

"We finally got it decorated," she said, turning her head to smile at him. "Yum. Whipped cream."

"Only the best," he said.

She was dressed in low-waisted black sweatpants, a bulky purple sweater and a pair of gray knit socks. Her hair was up in a ponytail, and she couldn't have looked more beautiful.

He moved forward, handing her one of the mugs. "It tastes fantastic."

"Thanks." She took a sip through the froth of whipped cream.

"And so do you." He kissed her sweet mouth.

"And not a ball gown in sight."

"This is better than any old ball."

"Music to my ears." She moved around the coffee table to sit on the sofa.

It was the moment he'd been waiting for. "Look at the time."

She glanced to the wall clock. "It's midnight."

"Christmas Day," he said.

She smiled serenely up at him. "Merry Christmas."

He set his mug down on the table and reached under the tree. "That means you can open a present."

Her smile faded. "We're not going to wait until morning?"

"Just one," he said, retrieving it.

He moved to sit beside her, handing over a small mint-green satin pouch. It was embossed in gold and tied with a matching gold ribbon.

"This is beautiful." She admired the package for a moment. Then she grinned like a little kid, untying the ribbon and pulling open the pouch.

His chest tightened with joy and anticipation.

She peeked inside. "What?" Then she held out her palm and turned the little bag over.

A ring dropped out—a two-carat diamond surrounded by tiny deep green emeralds that matched her irises.

"Oh, Matt." Her eyes shimmered as she stared at it. "It's incredible."

He lifted it from her palm. "You're what's incredible."

He took her left hand. "Tasha Lowell. I love you so much." He slipped the ring onto her finger. "I cannot wait to marry you."

"Neither can I." She held out her hand, admiring the sparkle. "This is perfect."

"You're perfect."

"Stop doing that."

"What?"

"One-upping my ring compliments."

"The ring can't hold a candle to you." He drew her into his arms and gave her a long, satisfying kiss.

By the time they drew apart, they were both breathless.

"So, what now?" she asked, gazing again at the glittery ring.

"Now we plan a wedding. You want big and showy? Or small with just our friends? We can elope if you want." Matt didn't care how it got done, just so long as it got done.

"My mom would die for a big wedding."

He smoothed her hair from her forehead. "You called her back, didn't you?" He hadn't wanted to ask, not knowing how Tasha was feeling about her mother's renewed interest in her life.

"This afternoon."

"Did it go okay?"

Tasha shrugged. "She hasn't changed. But I get it, and I can cope. She's completely thrilled about you, remember? I imagine she'll be taking out an ad in the *Boston Globe* in time for New Year's."

"Do you mind?"

He'd support whatever Tasha wanted to do about her relationship with her mother.

"It feels good to make peace." She paused. "I suppose it wouldn't hurt to make them happy."

He searched her expression. "Are you actually talking about a formal wedding?"

A mischievous smile came across her face. "We could let Mom go to town."

Matt put a hand on Tasha's forehead, pretending to check for a fever.

"I could dress up," she said. "I could do the glitz-and-glamour thing for one night. As long as I end up married to you when it's over."

"You would look stupendous." He couldn't help but picture her in a fitted white gown, lots of lace, shimmering silk or satin.

"You'd like it, wouldn't you?"

"I would not complain."

"Then let's do it."

He wrapped her in another tight hug. "When I picture our future, it just gets better and better."

"Next thing you know, we'll be having babies."

"With you," he said. "I definitely want babies." He pictured a little girl in front of the Christmas tree looking just like Tasha.

Maybe it was Jules's being pregnant, but he suddenly found himself impatient. He put a gentle hand on Tasha's stomach, loving the soft warmth. "How soon do you think we might have them?"

"I don't know." She reached out and popped the top button on his shirt. Then she opened another and another. "Let's go find out."

\* \* \* \* \*

*If you loved this story, look for these other great reads from* New York Times *and* USA TODAY *bestselling author Barbara Dunlop!*

*ONE BABY, TWO SECRETS*
*THE MISSING HEIR*
*SEX, LIES AND THE CEO*
*SEDUCED BY THE CEO*

*And don't miss the first*
*WHISKEY BAY BRIDES story,*
*FROM TEMPTATION TO TWINS*

*Available now from Mills & Boon Desire!*

# "I'll walk you to your door."

"That isn't necessary," Libby said. "My cabin's right over there."

"Yes, but sometimes the coyotes come down from the hills at this hour," Matt insisted.

"But they wouldn't approach me, would they?"

"They might. I've heard they're partial to blondes in short skirts and fancy boots."

She broke into a smile. "I can fend them off. I'm tougher than I look."

"That's good. Because you look like a sugar cookie dipped in silver sprinkles."

"You don't like sugar cookies?"

"I never said I didn't like them. I can eat dozens of them." His amber eyes turned hungry. "I could even devour one whole."

Libby fidgeted in her seat. "You're making me nervous, Matt."

He dropped his gaze to her mouth. "I've been thinking about kissing you."

"You probably shouldn't be telling me this."

"I'm not taking it back, either. I admitted how I feel, and it's done and over now."

\* \* \*

**Wrangling the Rich Rancher**
is part of the Sons of Country series:
Three heirs to country-music royalty face
the music with three very special women...

# WRANGLING THE RICH RANCHER

**BY**
**SHERI WHITEFEATHER**

First Published in Great Britain 2017
By Mills & Boon, an imprint of HarperCollins*Publishers*
1 London Bridge Street, London, SE1 9GF

© 2017 Sheree Henry-Whitefeather

ISBN: 978-0-263-92844-0

51-1117

Our policy is to use papers that are natural, renewable and recyclable products and made from wood grown in sustainable forests. The logging and manufacturing processes conform to the legal environmental regulations of the country of origin.

Printed and bound in Spain
by CPI, Barcelona

**Sheri WhiteFeather** is an award-winning, bestselling author. She writes a variety of romance novels for Mills & Boon and is known for incorporating Native American elements into her stories. She has two grown children, who are tribally enrolled members of the Muscogee Creek Nation. She lives in California and enjoys shopping in vintage stores and visiting art galleries and museums. Sheri loves to hear from her readers at www.sheriwhitefeather.com.

thought, a chameleon, his moods shifting with the summer wind.

Her observations were hasty at best, and influenced, no doubt, by what his father had already told her about him. Matt was Kirby Talbot's illegitimate son. The half-Cherokee boy the famous country singer had done wrong. Kirby had even written a yet-unpublished song about it.

Libby knew all sorts of personal details about Kirby. He'd hired her to write his biography. He'd handpicked her himself, based on a series of articles she'd crafted for *Rolling Stone*. For her, the book was a dream come true. Kirby was her idol, his rough-and-ready music complementing her willful personality and determined life.

Still studying Matt from across the room, she smoothed the front of her boho-inspired blouse, the silky fringe attached to it fluttering around her hips. The salesclerk at the store where she'd bought it called it cowgirl chic; it was bold, beautiful and sweetly feminine. Whatever the style, the blouse made her feel pretty. Libby was small in stature, with long, pale, wavy blond hair and a wholesome face. Sometimes she made cat eyes with her eyeliner just to doll herself up, giving her wide blue eyes a dramatic transformation.

Eager to learn more about Matt, she headed in his direction. Some of her research on him had come from his father and the rest from public records and the web. So far, she knew that he was thirty-one years old and had lived in the Hill Country his entire life. He appeared to be an unpretentious man, but his net worth was staggering, going far beyond the trust fund his father had set up for him.

As a youth, he'd excelled in junior rodeos. These days, he was divorced. His ex was a local girl, a widow when he'd married her, with two small children. That interested Libby, of course. But everything about him did.

He was Kirby's secret son. No one except the family and a handful of lawyers knew about him. After her book was released, everyone would know. Kirby wanted to come clean, to acknowledge Matt's paternity in a public way.

Initially, he'd kept Matt under wraps because he was married at the time and didn't want his wife or other kids to find out. Eventually they learned the truth. But that hadn't changed the dynamics of Matt and Kirby's relationship. He saw Matt sporadically when he was growing up, visiting between road tours. At some point, he stopped seeing him at all, and now Kirby wanted to make amends. Just this year, he started reaching out to his son, but Matt refused to take his calls, let alone see him.

Libby approached Matt, who was standing near a painting of Indian ponies dancing in the dust. He adjusted his hat, fitting it lower on his head.

"Do you have a minute?" she asked.

He turned more fully toward her, the make-believe horses prancing at his shoulder. "For one of my guests? Always."

"Is it okay if we take a walk?" She didn't want anyone to overhear their conversation. Some of the others were still milling around the lodge.

"Sure." He gestured to a side door leading to a rustic garden, where flowers sprouted amid wagon wheels, old water pumps and wrought iron benches. Once they were outside, he asked, "Is everything all right? Are you enjoying your stay so far?"

She fell into step with him. "It's a wonderful ranch, and I'm looking forward to the activities. I missed your

Independence Day celebration." The ranch was famous for hosting a huge fireworks display, drawing crowds from neighboring communities. "You were booked solid then." She'd arrived just after July Fourth and would be staying until the beginning of August. "This is so different from where I live, so vast and rural." Libby was from Southern California, where she'd been born and raised. Kirby, however, resided in Nashville, on an enormous compound he'd built. She'd already been there several times. "My son will be joining me in a few weeks. My mother is going to bring him. She's going to stay with us, too."

"How old is your son?"

"Six. This place is going to thrill him. He wants to be a cowboy when he grows up."

He smiled a little crookedly. "I'll be sure to give him the grand tour."

"His daddy passed away. It'll be three years this fall." She wasn't sure why she felt inclined to tell Matt that, especially with how weirdly attracted to him she was. Then again, he'd been married to a widow, so maybe he would understand more than most people would?

By now, he was frowning, hard and deep. "I'm sorry for your loss."

"Thank you. His name was Becker." Kirby Talbot had been his idol, too. She'd met Becker at one of Kirby's concerts. "He got sick. But it happened really quickly. A bacterial infection that…" She let her words drift. Becker wouldn't want her talking about the way he died. He was a vibrant person, filled with hope and joy. "But this isn't what I intended to discuss with you." She managed a smile, knowing Becker would be encouraging her to move forward, especially with her career. Then, suddenly, she hesitated, fully aware that Matt wasn't going to be pleased with her news. Finally, she slapped the smile back on her face and went for it. "I'm doing a book about your father. He hired me to write his biography, and—"

"Kirby sent you here?" Matt flinched, his amber eyes flashing beneath the brim of his straw Stetson.

She nodded. "He asked me to come. He wants to reveal your parentage in the book and wants to give you the opportunity to tell your side of the story."

Anger edged his voice. "So you're here to interview me?"

She nodded again, maintaining a professional air. Libby wasn't going to let Matt's frustration affect her. She had a job to do, a biography to write, possibly even bringing him and his father together. "I'd like the chance to get to know you, to spend as much time with you as I can. Kirby told me—"

"He told you what?" Those eyes flashed again. "That his bastard son wants nothing to do with him?"

"He didn't word it like that, but yes, he said that you were estranged from him. But he also admitted how he'd done you wrong. How he was never really there for you when you were growing up. He wants to atone for his mistakes."

A cynical smile thinned Matt's lips. "So it'll make him look good in the book you're writing? So his fans can worship him more than they already do?" Tall and handsome and lethal, he took a step closer to her. "You can tell my arrogant, womanizing daddy to go straight to hell. That I'm not impressed with him or his half-assed biography."

*Half-assed?* Libby set her chin. "I'm going to write a true account of his life, his loves, his mistakes, his music. His children," she added. Kirby had two other

sons, legitimate heirs with his former wife, the woman
to whom he'd been married when Matt's mother had
tumbled into an affair with him. "From my understanding, you've never even met your brothers."

"My *half* brothers," he reminded her. "And I'm not
any more interested in them than I am in Kirby."

"They're interested in you."

He shifted his booted feet. "They told you that?"

"Yes, they did." They were willing participants in the
book. "I haven't interviewed them yet, not extensively,
but we've had a couple of nice talks where they ex-
pressed their desire to meet you." He was the lone-wolf
brother they couldn't help but wonder about. "Brandon
is an entertainment lawyer who represents the family,
and Tommy..." She paused. "Well, he's a lot like Kirby."

Matt raised his eyebrows. "You think I don't know
that? I'm familiar with Tommy Talbot's music. I know
how he followed in our old man's footsteps."

Yes, she thought. Tommy was as wild as their father.
Or wilder, if that was possible. Whereas Kirby had been
dubbed the bad boy of country, Tommy was now known
as the *baddest* boy of country, surpassing his father.

She said, "If you agree to do this, I promise that I'll
quote you accurately, that I'll present you in a deep and
honest light. Your words matter. Your thoughts, your
feelings. I'm hoping to interview your mother, as well."
Libby knew that his mom lived on the ranch. "She just
got married, didn't she? To a man who works for you?"

"Yes, but they're out of town right now." He moved
even closer to her, so close their boot tips were almost
touching. "So you can't go chasing after her for an interview."

"That's okay. I can wait." He towered over her and
Libby lifted her head to get a better look at him. This

close, he was even more appealing, his features etched in masculine lines and candid emotion. He smelled good, too, his cologne a tantalizing blend of woods and musk.

"Has he hit on you yet?"

She started. "I'm sorry. What?"

"Kirby. Has he tried to get you into bed?"

"Oh, my goodness, no." Discomfort blasted through her blood. It was the son who stirred her, not the father. "He's been nothing but respectful to me."

"Are you sure?" he asked, his voice going a tad too soft. In it, she heard a gentle concern, a protective tone.

"I'm positive." She knew that Kirby wasn't interested in her. If anything, he'd been paternal toward her. But she decided not to mention that to Matt, given how easily Kirby had once walked away from him.

He went silent, and his gaze locked onto hers. Then, as if suddenly realizing how close he was standing to her, he stepped back.

"Sorry," he said.

"You don't have to apologize. I rather liked it." She tried for a goofy smile. "This noble side of you."

He remained serious. "If my dad got a hold of you, he would destroy your soul. You and your naive ways."

And what would Matt do if he got a hold of her? "There's nothing going on with your father and me. I don't feel that way about him." She closed the gap between them, wanting to be near him again. "And I'm not as naive as I look."

"Oh, yeah. So what are you going to do, little girl? Seduce me for the sake of your book?"

Mercy, she thought. Were they actually having this conversation? Was it really going in this direction? Struggling to breathe, to keep the air in her lungs from rushing out, she said, "If I seduced you, it wouldn't be for the sake of the book." She quickly clarified, "But I'm not here to seduce anyone. And for the record, I'm not a little girl. I'm twenty-nine."

His gaze didn't falter, not one whiskey inch. "I'll keep that in mind."

He would keep what in mind? Her self-proclaimed maturity? Or her unwillingness to seduce anyone? Either way, she was still feeling a bit too breathless. "Are you going to grant me an interview? Are you going to agree to spend some time with me? Or am I going to have to keep trying to convince you to be part of my project?"

"You'll have to keep trying. For all the good it will do you."

"It'll do me plenty of good." This was her first book, and she intended to do it right.

"Then I guess I'll see you around." He sent her a pulse-jarring look, right before he walked away, leaving her staring after him.

Like a fresh-faced schoolgirl with a crush.

Matt cursed the situation he was in. Of all the beautiful blondes who could have shown up at his ranch, did it have to be someone who was working for his dad? Someone who was prying into the past? Who was writing a book that was going to unmask the chaos in his life? The last thing Matt wanted was to be publically identified as Kirby Talbot's son. Damn his dad all to hell.

And damn Libby, too.

Yesterday when she arrived, Matt had gotten a hot, sexy, zipper-tightening reaction to her. So much so, he'd given her the cabin next to his. Normally he didn't work the front desk or place his guests. But he'd just happened to be there when she'd come in, so he'd handled the transaction.

Honestly, though, he didn't know what he was trying to accomplish by putting her next to him. For all he knew, she could have been in a relationship. Sure, she seemed single from the way she'd been checking him out, but he knew better than to lust after one of his guests.

Cripes, he thought. Besides being his father's biographer, she was widowed with a kid. This was the nightmare of nightmares. He'd gotten his heart broken by the last widow, the last blonde, who caught his eye. He missed Sandy. He missed her children, too. Two adorable little twins girls.

Matt had wanted so desperately to be a father—a good, kind, caring dad to Sandy's girls. He wanted to give them what his old man had never given him.

Love. Affection. Attention.

But after the divorce, she'd taken the twins and moved out of the area. She didn't think it would be healthy for her or the girls to keep seeing him. Sandy had only married him to soothe the loss of the man she really loved. The guy she'd buried.

How was he supposed to compete with that? Sandy's memories of her other husband had always been there, floating like a ghost between them. Matt's mixed-up marriage, which lasted all of six months, had been a crushing failure. He thought that he could help Sandy through her grief, that he would become her hero and the new husband she couldn't live without.

A year had passed since the divorce, and just as he was starting to lick to his wounds and move on, in walked another young widow, except she was working for his dad.

Oh, yeah. This was a nightmare, all right. Was he supposed to avoid Libby while she was here, to walk away from her at every turn? Considering how long she would be hanging around, that wasn't going to be an easy feat.

He could ask her to leave. This was his ranch, after all—he'd started the business from a trust account Kirby had set up for him. Of course, it wasn't as cut-and-dried as that. After Matt got the ranch established, making it a tremendous success, he returned the money to the trust, making sure his dad knew that he no longer needed or wanted it. By now, Matt was wealthy in his own right.

Initially, he'd acquired a lump sum on his twenty-first birthday, based on a deal that had been negotiated when he was a baby, as part of a child-support settlement. His mom had agreed to the terms, which required her to keep Matt's paternity a secret.

Disturbing as it was, the contract had never restricted Kirby from speaking out. Only Matt's mother had been silenced, and she'd taught Matt to stay silent, as well, to never tell anyone who his father was. And now, all these years later, Kirby wanted to blow all that out of the water.

Matt headed to his private barn, preparing to saddle one of his horses and ride into the hills, taking a trail that was unavailable to his guests. He often carved out time for himself, and today in particular he wasn't in the mood to socialize, not with what Libby had sprung on him.

Unfortunately, when his mom returned from her trip, she would probably support this damned book. She'd already been encouraging Matt to make peace with his father, to accept the olive branches Kirby had been offering.

He kept walking, and just as he entered his barn, he turned and saw Libby strolling up behind him.

Holy hell.

Half annoyed, half intrigued and a whole lot confused, he let his gaze roam over her. She'd actually followed him out here, and without him even knowing it. "When I said that I would see you around, I didn't mean this soon."

"Really, you didn't? Oh, silly me." She grinned, two perfect dimples lighting up her face.

He wanted to grab her by that fringy top of hers and shake her till those dimples rattled. But he wanted to kiss her, too, as roughly as he could, curious to know if she tasted as feisty as she looked.

"Yeah, silly you," he shot back.

She was still grinning, still being cute and clever. "I'm prone to getting the last word, and you left me standing there like a dolt."

He had no idea what that meant. "A dolt?"

"A stupid person."

Matt was the stupid one, wishing he could kiss her. "Working for Kirby doesn't exactly make you the brightest bulb in the chandelier."

"Funny, I'm wearing chandelier earrings, and they're pretty bright." She tapped the crystal jewels at her ears. "I made them myself."

Way to change the subject, he thought, enticed by how sparkly she was. "Okay, so you got the last word. Will you leave me alone now?"

"Nope." She spun around in a pretty little pirouette, making her fringe fly. "I think you should dance with me."

He blinked at her. "You want me to two-step with you? Here? Now?"

"No. Tomorrow night." She glanced down at her feet. Her silver glitter boots were as flashy as her earrings. "At the hoedown."

Right. The weekly barn dance at the ranch. "I don't always go to those." Sometimes he preferred to stay home, letting his guests kick up their heels without him. "And dancing with you sounds like a dolt of a thing to do."

"Come on. Take a chance."

He wasn't making any promises, especially to her. "I might show up, and I might not. But just so you know, the house band isn't allowed to play Kirby's music. Or Tommy's, either. So don't get smart and make any requests."

"I won't. But doesn't the band wonder why the Talbots are off-limits? Or why they have to turn down requests for their songs?"

"My ranch. My rules. And there are plenty of other artists they cover. Traditional, bluegrass, honky-tonk, alternative, outlaw. They play it all." Except for the badass Talbots. Their brand of outlaw twisted Matt's gut.

She bounced in her boots. "Dancing with you is going to be fun. Think how easily we're going to become friends." She teased him, "Or frenemies, if you prefer."

"I just told you that I might not be there."

"Personally, I don't think you're going to be able to resist. I'm the most persuasive cowgirl you're ever going to meet."

"You're not a cowgirl. You're a chick from Hermosa Beach who wears fancy Western clothes and dotes on my ass-hat of a father."

She laughed, obviously amused by his assessment of her. He knew where she was from because when he'd checked her into the ranch, he'd seen her driver's license, with her name, her address, her birth date. He already knew she was twenty-nine, even before she told him how old she was.

"You have a wicked sense of humor, Matt."

"I wasn't trying to be funny."

"That's just my point."

He squared his shoulders. "I'm going riding now, and you're not coming with me. So whatever you do, don't follow me into the hills."

Her dimples twitched. "We'll save that for another time. Only I won't be following you. You're going to like me enough that you'll be inviting me to join you."

"Gee, humble much?" This wannabe cowgirl was hell on wheels. And the crazy part was, he already liked her, even if he didn't want to.

She laughed again. "See, there you go. Funny, but not trying to be. Enjoy your ride, and I'll see you tomorrow night."

One last smile, and she exited the barn, taking her last words with her. And damn if he wasn't tempted to teach her a lesson. And leave her dancing all by her beautiful self.

# Two

Libby stood in front of the mirror, putting the final touches on her outfit. Soon she would be leaving for the dance. She planned to walk to the barn where the soiree was being held. From her cabin, the path was well lit and paved with stones. She could have called ahead and gotten a ride from a lodge attendant. The ranch offered a shuttle service, taking guests to and from activities. But she intended to bask in the night air, enjoying the sights and scents along the way.

She returned her gaze to the mirror. She was wearing a short, sassy skirt and the same boots and earrings Matt had already seen before.

What he'd said about her was true. She wasn't a cowgirl, at least not in the literal sense of the word. She didn't herd cattle or compete in rodeos. But she loved all things country, especially the music.

She didn't mind being a chick from Hermosa Beach

who wore fancy Western clothes. She was proud to own that identity. But had she gone too far, baiting Matt to dance with her? At the time it had seemed like a good way to create a friendly rapport between them. Only now, as the opportunity drew near, she was nervous about seeing him.

Nervous about how he made her feel.

Granted, Libby kept telling herself that she wasn't ready for a lover, but the thought of being with him kept crossing her mind, making her warm all over.

She'd never slept with anyone except Becker, so the idea of seducing Matt seemed almost laughable. But it seemed hot and wild and exciting, too. Too wild? Too exciting? Even if she had the guts to do it, being with Matt would complicate an already complicated situation, jumbling her plans to interview him. Then why did she keep thinking about him in sexual ways? Why did sleeping with him keep invading her thoughts?

Maybe it would be better if he ditched her tonight, if he didn't show up. Or maybe she should bail out.

Oh, right. Like that wouldn't make her look like an idiot, after the overly confident way she'd presented herself. No. Libby was going to see this through. She was going to march into that place with a big, bright smile on her face.

She ventured onto her porch and glanced over at Matt's cabin. She assumed he wasn't home because his truck wasn't parked in the gravel driveway. Was he at the hoedown already? Or had he gone somewhere else instead?

She took a second glance at his cabin. It appeared to be the same two-bedroom model as hers. Was that where he'd always lived, even during his short-lived marriage? Or had he been planning to build a bigger place on his property? It struck her odd that he chose to live in a modest cabin when he could have a mansion if he wanted one. There was no way to know why he did what he did, except to ask him. Kirby certainly wasn't privy to that information. What he knew about his son could fill a thimble.

Libby locked her cabin and left for the dance. By the time she arrived, the big wooden building was filled with people—adults and children—eating and drinking and being merry.

The decor was charmingly Western, with twinkling lights streaming from the rafters, red-and-white table-cloths and folding chairs upholstered in cowhide.

The band hadn't taken the stage yet, but they would probably appear soon enough.

She looked around for Matt. He was nowhere to be seen. Keeping herself busy, she wandered over to the buffet and filled her plate. She took a seat at one of the tables, chatted with other guests and dived into her meal.

The fried chicken was to die for and the mashed potatoes were even better. She didn't go back for dessert. She was already getting full.

An hour passed. By then the band was playing, and people were line dancing, laughing, clapping and missing steps. Of course some of them were right on the money. Libby was a good dancer, too. But at this point she was standing in a corner like a wallflower, watching the festivities.

Okay, so maybe Matt wasn't coming. Maybe he didn't find her, or her spunky personality, as irresistible as she assumed he would.

Served her right, she supposed. But suddenly something inside her felt far too alone, far too widowed. She didn't like being here without a partner.

She toyed with her empty ring finger. She'd removed her wedding band about a year after Becker passed, but now she wished she'd kept it on.

Still, she knew better than to wallow in sadness. She'd worked hard to overcome her grief.

Should she get out there and dance? Should she join the party on her own? Or should she give Matt a little more time, in case he decided to materialize?

"Have you been waiting for me?" a raspy voice whispered in her ear from behind her.

*Matt.* It was him. Talk about materializing, and at the perfect moment, too. But she was reluctant to turn around, afraid that he would disappear as mysteriously as he'd arrived.

"I knew you'd come," she said, lying through her teeth.

"Oh, yeah?" Still standing behind her, he gripped her waist. "Then let's dance." As quick as could be, he spun her around to face him.

Making her heart spin, too.

Matt and Libby danced for hours. They did fancy two-steps and three-steps. They country waltzed, line danced and did the push, the Cotton Eye Joe and the schottische.

The fast dances were easy for Matt. The slow ones, not so much. He had to hold Libby closer for those.

Like now. The band was doing a cover of Lady Antebellum's "Can't Take My Eyes Off You," with lyrics about a woman's devotion to her partner.

"I love this song," Libby said, sounding a little dreamy.

Matt didn't comment on the music. He was doing his damnedest not to press his body even closer to hers.

This wasn't a sexy setting, and he couldn't misbehave, not here, not like this. Not at all, he warned himself.

Her hair, he noticed, smelled like lemons, and her cheeks were flushed with a healthy glow. Did she surf and swim and do all those California-girl-type things? Did she go to beach parties with her friends or walk barefoot through the sand at night? He was as curious about her as she was about him.

But he wasn't writing a book that would damage her. He wasn't doing anything except getting distracted by her nearness, lowering his guard with a woman who wanted to invade his privacy.

She looked up at him. "Things are starting to wind down."

He slid his hand a bit lower on her back. "The parents usually take their little ones back to their cabins or rooms by now. But not everyone has kids. Some of the couples who come to the ranch are honeymooners. Some are long-married seniors, too." He stopped and adjusted his hand, returning it to a more proper position. But it didn't help. He was still struggling with her proximity. "We don't get many single folks."

"Like me?"

"You're not a regular guest."

She followed his lead, moving in sync with him. "No, but I'm still a real person."

Too real, he thought, too warm and pliable in his arms. Now all he wanted was for the song to end. Finally, it did, leaving him with a knot in his chest. The last time he'd danced this close to a woman was with Sandy, when he'd still believed he could make his marriage work.

He hastily asked, "Do you want to go outside and catch a breath of air?"

"Why? Do you think it's getting warm in here?"

"Warm enough." He needed to stop holding Libby, to stop swaying to romantic songs. But more ballads were on the way. He knew the band's set.

He escorted her onto the patio, where hay bales draped in blue gingham served as seats. They sat next to each other in a secluded spot. He glanced up at the starry sky, then shifted his gaze back to her. She was as bright as the night, with her silver boots and shimmery earrings.

As she settled onto the hay bale she adjusted the hem of her skirt, keeping it from riding farther up her thighs. It made Matt wonder what she had going on under that flouncy garment. Cute little bikini panties? A seductive thong? Whatever her undies were, they were none of his business.

None whatsoever.

"I almost stood you up," he said. "I went to the local watering hole before I came here, and that's where I was going to stay. But I changed my mind." He hadn't even finished his beer. He'd just tipped the gnarly old bartender and left. "I guess I wanted to see if you'd be waiting for me."

"Truthfully?" She tugged at her hem again. "I started to worry that you might leave me hanging."

"So you're not as self-assured as you claim to be?" To him, she still seemed like a force to be reckoned with.

"Mostly I am. Only with you, I wasn't sure what to expect. But it worked out nicely, I think."

"What did? Us dancing together?"

"Yep." She smiled, disarming him with her dimples.

He turned away, staring into the distance, the darkness. Sandy's smile wasn't as girlish as Libby's. She didn't have blue eyes, either. Hers were a brownish hazel. Aside from being blondes, they didn't look that much alike. But they had other things in common, like the way they made him feel. That, and the fact that they were both widows.

He returned his gaze to hers. "You should have never come to my ranch, sneaking in, pretending to be a guest."

"How else was I supposed to get to know you? If I would have called ahead and told you who I was and what my agenda was, you wouldn't have agreed to see me."

"You're right. I wouldn't have." He paused, then asked, "Have you been to Kirby's place? Or Kirbyville, as everyone calls it."

"Yes. It's a spectacular compound. That's where I'll be going when I leave here. He wants you to visit him there, too."

"So he keeps saying." Matt couldn't stand the thought of her going back to his dad. "Now that you're here, I'm not going to send you away. I considered it, but it didn't seem right, somehow."

"Thank you. You're a fascinating man. You intrigued me from the start."

"You wouldn't be saying that if I wasn't Kirby's bastard."

She frowned. "Why do you keep calling yourself that?"

"Because that's what I am. And it's how Kirby always made me feel, sweeping me under the carpet when I was a kid. He never even—" Matt hesitated, stopping himself from opening up more than he already had. "I shouldn't be talking to you about this, giving you material for your book."

"I can't just take our conversations and use them,

not without getting a signed release from you. The publisher is being very strict about that. I need to interview you properly, to record you and quote you accurately."

She expected to record him? Fat chance of that. "So anything we say without the release is off the record?"

"Yes. But if you don't let me interview you, everything in the book that pertains to you will come from Kirby or your brothers or whoever else mentions you. That's all I'll be able to write about you."

"I don't want you writing about me at all." How many times did he have to tell her that? "I just want to be left alone."

She replied in a gentle tone, "This book is an amazing opportunity for me, and I'm going to write it, no matter what. But my heart is in the right place. I'm not trying to hurt or sensationalize you."

"It sure seems that way to me. The sensationalize part, anyway." He didn't think that she'd set out to hurt him, even if her actions would be doing just that. "Do you know the mess Kirby's biography is going to make of my life? I won't have any privacy after my paternity is revealed."

"It'll cause some attention at first, but Kirby said he'll hire a PR team to help you manage it. He doesn't expect you to weather it by yourself."

"Gee, how gracious of him."

"I understand that you're angry about the way he treated you. But your paternity shouldn't have been kept a secret to begin with. If Kirby had acknowledged you from the beginning, you would already be known as his son."

"That's a moot point all these years later. If he wanted to be my father, he should have manned up back then."

Matt didn't have any patience for his dad's newfound interest in him. His old man should have forewarned him about the book, too, instead of sending a pretty little writer to do it.

She went silent, letting him brood. A moment later, she said, "I was thinking of taking a shuttle into town tomorrow, then renting a car while I'm there. Unless you'd be willing to drive me. You could be my guide."

"Sorry, but I'm going to pass." He didn't want to show her around his hometown. He figured that she just wanted to go there to try to learn more about where he'd grown up. "But I'd be glad to escort you back to your cabin now."

"The dance isn't even over yet."

"It's getting close. This is the last song." He could hear the music drifting outside. "They always end with a Texas waltz."

"It sure is pretty."

As pretty as it got, he supposed. Just like her. "So, do you want me to give you a ride back to your cabin?"

She tucked a strand of her lemony hair behind her ear. "Sure, I'll go with you." She lifted her feet off the ground, tipping her toes to the sky. "It'll make me feel like a rodeo queen, riding beside the handsomest cowboy in the land."

"You wish." He stood and extended a hand. "And calling me handsome isn't going to boost your cause."

She accepted his hand and let him help her up. "Are you sure about that?"

"Yeah." Nothing was going to take the sting out of her writing Kirby's biography. Except maybe sweeping her into a mindless kiss that would make him forget his worries. Or reaching his hand under her skirt. Or hauling her off, like a caveman, to his bed. But he wasn't going to do any of those things.

No matter how good they would make him feel.

When Matt pulled into his driveway and parked, Libby was still thinking about the book and how she was going to get him to agree to be part of it. But as they turned toward each other, a strange sensation came over her—almost as if they were on a date and she was going home with him for the very first time.

He frowned, and she suspected the same awkward notion had come over him. The porch light from his cabin created a misty glow, intensifying the ambience.

Neither of them spoke. Not a word. Until he said, "Don't worry. I'll walk you to your door."

"That isn't necessary." She'd walked to the dance by herself. So why would she need an escort now? "My cabin is just right over there."

"Yes, but sometimes the coyotes come down from the hills at this hour. We've got lots of them around here."

"But they wouldn't approach me, would they?" She couldn't imagine it.

"They might." He spoke in a serious tone. "I've heard they're partial to blondes in short skirts and fancy boots."

She broke into a smile, grateful for his offbeat sense of humor. She knew now that he was kidding. "I can fend them off. I'm tougher than I look."

"That's good." He chuckled. "Because you look like a sugar cookie dipped in silver sprinkles."

She feigned offense. "You don't like sugar cookies? What kind of crazy person are you?"

"I never said I didn't like them." His humor faded. "I can eat dozens of them." His amber eyes turned hungry. "I could even devour one whole."

Libby fidgeted in her seat. If she were smart, she would make an off-the-cuff remark. She would crack a joke. But she didn't do anything except sit there like the cookie in question.

She finally drummed up the courage to say, "You're making me nervous, Matt." She didn't usually admit defeat, but her defensive mechanism was on the blink, screws and bolts coming loose.

He stared at her mouth. A second later, he lifted his gaze back to her face, snaring her in his trap.

"I've been thinking about kissing you," he said. "I'm not going to do it, but I keep thinking about it."

"You probably shouldn't be telling me this." Just as she shouldn't be imagining how his kiss would feel—hot and wild, with his hands tangled in her hair, his tongue slipping past her lips.

"I even wondered about what kind of panties you have on."

Embarrassed by his admission, by the shameful thrill it gave her, she pressed her knees together. "I'm not going to tell you."

"I'm not asking you to. But I'm not taking it back, either. I admitted how I feel, and it's over and done with now."

It wasn't over for her. She wanted to know more about him, so much more. "Have you been playing around since your divorce?" she asked, curious about his habits, his primal needs. "Do you go to the bar to meet women?"

He scowled at her. "You have no right to ask me that."

"After the things you said to me, I think I'm entitled to a little payback." She was still pinning her knees together, still feeling the discomfort of being the cookie he wanted to devour.

He cursed quietly.

She went flippant. "Is that a yes or a no? I couldn't quite tell."

He almost laughed. But he almost snarled, too. The sound that erupted from him was as unhinged as their attraction.

"If I'd been getting laid," he said, "would I be acting like a rutting bull around you?"

"I don't know," she challenged him, determined to get a straight answer. "Would you?"

He shook his head. "You're something else, Libby."

She was just trying to make being the object of his desire more bearable, even if meant getting him to admit that he'd been alone since his divorce. "Maybe I better go home now."

"Back to California?"

*Big, handsome jerk.* "Back to my cabin."

"Damn. I should have known you wouldn't cut bait and run."

"You don't have to walk me to my door." Now that she knew there weren't any coyotes out to get her. "You don't have to play the gentleman."

"I wasn't playing at anything. But it's probably better if I keep my distance. I'd just want to kiss you, and that'll only make things worse."

She wasn't sure if they could get any worse. He was already making her far too weak. If he kissed her at her door, she would probably melt at his feet.

He said, "You should go home for real."

She refused to concede, to get any weaker than she already was. "Sorry, cowboy, but you're stuck with me."

He leaned back against the seat, as if he were weary. Or lonely. Or something along those lines.

He sat forward again. "Maybe I will take you into town tomorrow."

Her pulse bumped a beat. "Really?"

"Sure. Why not? There's a bakery where we can get some cookies."

She laughed even if she shouldn't have. "You've got a hankering, do you?"

"Hell, yes. Don't you?"

More than he could possibly know. "Will you show me the house where you grew up?" It was at the top of her list of places to see. She had the address, but she hadn't run a map on it yet.

"I suppose I could take you. It's better than you poking around out there alone."

She eagerly asked, "Is this the start of us being friends?"

"I think it's more like the other thing you said we could become."

"Frenemies?"

"That's it. I'll pick you up tomorrow around two. I have some work to do on the ranch before then. But for now, we both need to get some sleep."

Yes, they did, she thought, each of them in his or her own bed. "I'll see you." Libby bid him a hasty goodbye, opened the passenger's-side door and darted off, clinging to the shadows, trying to be less visible. She sensed that he was watching every move she made.

Was he still thinking sexy thoughts? Did he wish that he'd kissed her? That he'd pulled her body close to his? That he'd put his mouth all over hers?

She ascended her porch steps without glancing back. Self-conscious, she fumbled putting the key in the lock. She went inside, and as soon as she closed the door, she crept over to the living room window and peered through the blinds.

Matt remained in his truck, a lone figure behind the wheel.

She kept spying on him, holding her breath, anxious to see him walk to his door. He finally got out of the vehicle, taking long determined strides. She watched, absorbed by his rugged movements, breathless for every dizzying moment until he entered his cabin and turned on his lights.

Leaving her alone in the dark.

The next afternoon, Libby waited on her porch for Matt. She'd dressed down a bit, wearing a plaid shirt, blue jeans and a pair of traditional brown boots. Of course, her belt buckle was shiny and so was her jewelry. She never left the house without a touch of glamour.

She removed her phone from her purse and checked the time. Matt wasn't late, but he was cutting it close. And now, in the light of day, with nothing between them except last night's convoluted hunger, she was concerned that he might cancel their outing.

She frowned at her phone. They hadn't even exchanged numbers. She couldn't text him to see if he was on his way.

He hadn't told her what type of work he had to do on the ranch today, and when she'd awakened this morning his truck was already gone. She hadn't seen him at the lodge during breakfast or lunch, either.

Funny how she missed him already. She'd known him all of three days, and her interactions with him were shaky, at best. There was no logic in missing him.

Missing Becker made sense.

She kept tons of pictures of her late husband on her phone. Her son loved looking at them. He adored chatting about his daddy and asking Libby questions about him. Chance was three when Becker died. He didn't have many memories to rely on.

She plopped down on a barrel chair to wait for Matt. She hadn't mentioned her son's name to him. Maybe she would do that today. Of course, she doubted that Matt was going to like that she'd named her son Chance Mitchell after a fictitious character, a legendary outlaw, in one of Kirby's most famous songs.

She looked up and saw Matt's truck. It appeared out of a cloud of dust, and she popped up from her seat. The man certainly knew how to make an entrance.

She glanced at her phone before she put it away. He was right on time. Not a minute late, not a second early. Somehow he managed to get there at 2:00 p.m. on the dot.

He pulled into her driveway and kept the engine running. She raced down the porch steps, her hair flying. She'd washed it this morning with her latest favorite shampoo. She changed her toiletries nearly as often as she changed her clothes. She liked trying new products. She wasn't nearly as adventurous about trying new men. Yet here she was, getting swept away by Matt.

She climbed into his truck, and he said, "Hey, Libby."

"Hey, yourself." She noticed that his hat was sitting in the back seat, as it were along for the ride.

Off they went, with the sun shining in the Texas sky. She gazed out the window, watching the landscape go by. The drive was long and scenic, with roads that wound through the hills.

"This is the back way," he said.

"I gathered as much." They weren't on the main highway that led to and from the ranch.

In the next bout of silence, she studied Matt's appearance. His hair looked mussed, spiky in spots from where he'd probably dragged his hands through it. He seemed dangerous, forbidden. But why wouldn't he, with the way he made her feel? Last night she'd slept with her bedroom window open, letting the breeze drift over her half-clothed body. She'd gone to bed wearing the panties he'd wondered about. She'd even touched herself, sliding her fingers past the waistband and down into the fabric, fantasizing that he was doing it.

Matt shot her a quick glance, and her cheeks went horribly hot. He couldn't know what she'd been thinking, but she reacted as if he did.

"You okay?" he asked.

Not in the least, she thought. "I'm fine."

"You're usually more talkative."

She adjusted the air-conditioning vent on her side, angling it to get a stronger flow. "You don't know me well enough to say what I usually do."

"All right, then. Based on my experiences with you, you're usually more talkative."

"I'm just enjoying the ride."

"You don't seem like you are. What are you thinking about?"

She couldn't stand the tension that was building inside her. And now she wanted him to suffer, too. He was being too danged casual. "That they were pink."

"What?"

"My panties. They were pink, low-rise hipsters, silk, with a see-through lace panel in front."

He nearly lost his grip on the wheel, and she felt a

whole lot better. She even managed to toss a "got ya" grin at him.

"Don't you flash your dimples at me, woman. You could have gotten us killed."

"Over an itty-bitty pair of panties? You're a better driver than that."

He focused on looking out the windshield.

She tortured him some more. "I have a similar pair on now. Only they're blue."

His breath went choppy. "I'm going to strangle you. I swear I am."

"I'm just getting you in the mood for the cookie you were hankering for."

"Knock it off." He took a bend in the road. "Just stop yapping about it."

She sat smugly in her seat, grateful her tactic had worked. She needed to take charge, to feel strong and powerful in his presence. "You wanted me to be more talkative."

"You think I'm kidding about strangling you?" His tone turned feral. "Or maybe I ought to kiss you instead."

*Oh, my God.* Now she'd gone and done it. She'd awakened the predator in him. His lips, she noticed, were twisted into a snarl. "You look more like you're going to bite me."

"That'll work, too. But I'm not going to do either."

Libby didn't know whether to be relieved or disappointed. Her heart was practically leaping out of her chest.

"We're almost there," he said, changing the subject.

"Almost where?"

"At my old house. You asked to see it."

"It's way out here?" She'd assumed it was on the

outskirts of town, but she hadn't expected it to be this far out.

He veered onto a dirt road, and she craned her neck to get a better look. A lovely stone house, a miniranch of sorts, sat in a canyon all by itself.

He stopped at the top of the road, where a private gate blocked them from going any farther.

"Who lives there now?" she asked.

"The people Mom rents it to. They raise paint horses. We had a little breeding farm, too. Mom called it Canyon Farms then."

"It's so isolated."

"Kirby built it for Mom when I was a baby." His tone turned pensive. "Mom was originally from Austin, and her parents had passed away about three years before, so she was alone, except for me. She liked this area. Her folks used to bring her here on camping trips. It held nice memories for her. So when Kirby offered to buy her a place, she asked him if it could be in Creek Hill."

"Did she want to be this far from town?" Libby glanced around again. "Just the two of you, in the middle of a canyon?"

"Not necessarily. It was Kirby who chose this location, so he could visit without anyone seeing him coming and going. It was mostly at night since that's the schedule he was used to keeping. It continued on that way, even as I got older. I remember how Mom would fuss over him on the nights he came by, as if he was royalty." Matt made a disgusted sound. "What did he tell you about his relationship with my mother?"

"He said that she's the longest mistress he ever had. That it ended when you were around twelve." A clandestine affair for over a decade, she thought. Libby couldn't fathom subjecting herself to something like that. But it wasn't her place to judge Kirby or Matt's mother or anyone else.

"She was foolish enough to remain faithful to him, even when she knew that he had other mistresses or girl-friends or whatever. And then there was his wife and other children. The family he was protecting." Matt's expression went taut. "In the beginning I didn't know he was my father. Mom just told me that he was her friend. I was too young to recognize him or know that he was famous." He roughly added, "I'm not telling you this so you can feel bad for me. I'm telling you because I want you to know the kind of man Kirby really is, to get a better idea of who you're working for."

"I know who he is." She wasn't going to hold Kir-by's mistakes against him, not when he was trying, with all of his heart, to repair the damage he'd done. "And I know how badly he wants to make amends with you."

Matt squinted at her. "I started to suspect that he was my dad even before Mom told me that he was. This tall, bearded man in a long black duster, this larger-than-life guy. He never got up before noon, but Mom would still cook him breakfast food, treating the afternoons as if they were mornings. Sometimes he would even sit at the table with his sunglasses on. I'd never seen anyone do that indoors before. I knew he was different from other people. I just didn't know how different. But ei-ther way, he was just too important to my mother, too revered, I figured, for him to be someone other than my father. Once I learned the truth, I accepted it as the status quo."

"You must have been a highly observant child."

"Yes, but I was ridiculously impressionable, too. Kirby told me once that I looked like I was part wolf, and I figured my eyes were this color because I was supposed to be nocturnal, the way he was. But I'd get so sleepy when he first arrived at night and I was waiting up to see him. I didn't understand how I could be part wolf if I couldn't stay up at night."

"Your eyes are beautiful." Mesmerizing, she thought. Hypnotizing. She could stare at them for hours.

He scoffed at her compliment. "They're weird, and you're missing my point."

"No, I'm not." She understood what he was trying to convey. How lonely Kirby had made him feel. How he needed to be part of the daylight, where fathers took their sons out in public, where there were no secrets, where normalcy existed. "It was wrong, what he did to you. I'm not denying that." And neither was Kirby. He knew, better than anyone, how terribly he'd hurt Matt.

"I was taught to tell people that my daddy was a cowboy drifter and that my mom never even knew his real name." A sharp laugh rattled from his throat. "Even now, if someone asks about my father, I still recount that same fake story."

"Does your mother's husband know the truth?"

"She couldn't bear to keep lying to him, so she told him right before they got married. Of course, it's only been a few months, so they're still in the honeymoon stages. But he would never betray her trust. Or mine. He stays out of our personal business."

"What about your ex?" Libby thought about his marriage and how quickly it had ended. "Did you ever tell her?"

"No."

"Did you ever want to tell her?"

"No."

"Why not?"

"Because being Kirby's son doesn't matter to me,

and I didn't want it to matter to her, either. Besides, we had other things to contend with." He searched Libby's gaze, as if he were searching for someone's grave. "Did you know that she was a widow? Like you?"

"It came up in my research." But Libby hadn't expected him to make a comparison in such a disturbing way. "According to what I uncovered, her name is Sandra Molloy, and she and her first husband had two kids and owned the dry cleaner's in town." It wasn't much to go on, but it was the only information she had.

"She went by Sandy, and she sold that business when she married me. She cried about her husband nearly every day. Do you still think about your husband?"

"Of course I do." Libby glanced away, wishing that Matt would stop staring at her. "But I've come to terms with my grief." With the tears and pain, with waking up alone. "I'm not letting it rule my life."

"Then why can I see him, like a ghost inside you?"

"You don't even know what he looks like."

"I didn't mean it literally."

She thought about the images of Becker on her phone. The happy, smiling, easygoing father of her child. He was so different from Matt. "You're just seeing what you want to see."

"Why would I want to see something like that when I look at you? When I'm this close—" he created a tiny space between his thumb and forefinger "—to giving up the fight and kissing you?"

"Then do it, damn you. Just do it." She didn't want to keep fantasizing about being kissed by him. She just wanted to lose herself in the feeling, no matter how wrong it was.

He leaned into her, his gaze challenging hers. Was he baiting her stop him, to push him away?

Libby challenged him right back, staring him down, daring him to go through with it.

Heaven help them.

He kept coming toward her, until his hands were tangled in her hair and his mouth was fused passionately to hers.

Just the way she'd imagined it.

# Three

Matt cursed in his mind. He was getting consumed with this woman in ways that were driving him mad.

He undid his seat belt and so did she. The straps were too confining, and they both needed to be free.

With his eyes tightly closed, he deepened the kiss, craving the taste of her. He pushed his tongue into her mouth. She reacted just as uncontrollably, pressing closer to him, her hunger equal to his.

Hellfire, he thought. He was getting hard beneath his jeans. From a kiss. From one soft, slick, wet…

She wrapped her arms around his neck, and he pulled her, like a rag doll, right over the center console and onto his lap.

He envisioned how they must look, parked on the road that overlooked his old place, with her straddling him in the driver's seat, the steering wheel butting against her back.

Matt felt like a teenager, making out in the middle of the day, his hormones jerking and jumping.

He wound his hands more fully in her hair. He liked how wild and wavy it was. She rocked forward, rubbing him where it hurt, where it felt good, where his zipper made friction with hers.

They kept kissing, mindless and carnal. She mewled, then moaned, hot and sweet, and he suspected that she would make those same fevered sounds if he was deep inside her.

When they came up for air, she asked, "Is the truck still running? Is that the vibration I feel?"

"I think it's us." He'd shut the engine off earlier. Hadn't he? Just to be sure, he double-checked. "It's not running."

"It's not? Are you sure?"

"I'm positive. But we should stop now."

"You first."

"You want me to end it?" He didn't appreciate her leaving it up to him. "You're the one who's sitting on my lap."

"And you're the one who put me there."

Touché, he thought. "Yeah, but you can climb off me and get back in your own seat." His frustration was building, at himself, at her. He wanted to strip her naked, right here, right now.

"I could." Her eyes were glazed over and her hair was totally mussed, maybe even knotted in spots. Her frustration was mounting, too. "Or you could make me."

"Screw that." He kissed her again, harder this time, making good on his threat to bite her.

"Ouch." She flinched, then kissed him right back.

A heartbeat later, he said, "It was only a nibble."

"Says you. My lips are going to be swollen."

"They already are." And she wore it insanely well. "Now get off me before I do something I'll regret."

"You're already regretting this, and so am I."

"So go back on your own side of the truck."

She didn't budge. She stayed there, desire bristling from her pores. She snared his gaze, her eyelashes long and fluttery. "You owe me a cookie."

Seriously? She was going to hold him to that? "Fine. As soon as I can take the wheel, we'll go to the bakery."

"I want coffee, too." She crawled over the console and nearly kneed him in the nuts, missing him by mere inches. But she didn't even notice that she'd almost done it.

Matt snarled to himself. He deserved a swift kick, but the entire situation still made him angry. Everything about it ticked him off. Especially what he couldn't have—like Libby sprawled out beneath him.

He wanted to take her home and make hot-blooded love to her, to be rough and animalistic, to bite her again a hundred more times.

She settled onto her seat, lowered the visor and gawked at herself in the mirror. "Oh, my goodness. What did you do to my hair? I look like a blowfish."

Since when did fish have hair? Spiny things coming out of their heads, maybe. "You liked it when I was doing it."

She finger-combed her way through the mess. "We're never kissing again. Not ever."

"I know." He tugged at his jeans, trying to make his bulge less noticeable. "It was awful of us." Awfully hot, awfully barbaric, awfully amazing. He could think of a hundred mixed-up ways to describe what they'd done.

She kept fussing with her hair, struggling to tame it.

"You're making it worse," he said.

"What?" she asked. "Your hard-on or my hair?"

"Your hair, smarty."

She glanced at his lap. "Not from where I'm sitting."

"Don't start." But it was too late. They both burst into a quick, crazy laugh. The situation was too disturbing to keep it bottled up.

She raised the visor, giving up on her hair. He gave up on adjusting his jeans, too. Then he went serious and asked, "Are you going to tell Kirby that we kissed?"

"I would never do that. This was a private moment between you and me. It's no one else's business."

"So what happens between you and me is private, but the rest of my life isn't?"

"Your relationship with Kirby is the only part of your life that I'll be writing about." She glanced down at the canyon house. "Yours and your mother's. And that's why it's so important for me to get your input, and hers, too. I have lots of interview questions, for both of you."

"No doubt you do. But I'm not signing a release or answering them. If I tell you anything, it's going to be the way we've been doing it, off the record." He followed her line of sight to the house. He remembered his mom crying on the night Kirby had ended their affair. How she'd sat outside and bawled in the moonlight. Matt had been old enough then to understand what was going on. He'd sensed it was over for him, too, that his dad's sporadic visits would become even less frequent. He'd even worried that Kirby would eventually stop coming around at all. And he'd been right on both counts. So painfully right.

"Please, just think about it," Libby implored him.

He blew out a breath. "I can't willingly be part of your book." He didn't want to bleed all over the pages of his old man's self-serving biography. "I just can't do it."

"If you were involved in the book, I would get to know you, better than I am now."

He laughed, as foolishly as before. "You're getting to know me just fine."

"That's not funny." She rolled her big blue eyes, frowned, smiled, shook her messy-haired head. "Well, maybe it is."

He noticed that her lips were still sexily swollen. "Buckle up." He reached over and pulled the strap across her body, doing it for her. "I've got to back out of here."

And try to forget that he'd ever kissed her.

Libby couldn't believe that she'd taunted Matt to kiss her. That she wouldn't get off his lap. That she let it go that far.

She needed to be flogged, tortured for her idiotic behavior. What part of professionalism had escaped her? She'd been acting up since the moment she'd met him, being so coy and cute, pushing her attraction to him in directions it wasn't supposed to go.

When they arrived at the bakery, he parked directly in front of the small, pastel-colored building. The town itself was quaint, with its Main Street simplicity and homespun vibe.

"Maybe I should order a tart," she said.

"Those fruit-filled things?"

"Yes, but that was a joke." She pointed to herself. "A *tart*, get it?"

He didn't laugh. "Don't call yourself names, Libby. I'm just as responsible as you are. We're just lucky that we stopped when we did."

"It wasn't luck. It was restraint."

"You know what I mean."

She most certainly did. She'd never kissed anyone that ferociously before, not even Becker.

They got out of the truck, and she glanced at the bakery window. A big, frothy, three-tiered wedding cake was showcased. The bride and groom on top looked a bit like her and Matt. It was their coloring, the bride being blonde and the groom having black hair. She doubted that Matt noticed the cake, let alone the topper. He headed straight for the front door.

"Let's go get those cookies," he said.

She nodded, and they went inside. A middle-aged woman in blue jeans and a crisp white apron greeted them. She smiled and acknowledged Matt by name. The bakery lady knew him? This piqued Libby's curiosity.

But soon she discovered that he'd gone to high school with the woman's son. In a town this size, Libby shouldn't have been surprised. Most of the locals probably knew each other. It did make her wonder about Matt's experiences in high school and if he was as much a loner then as he seemed to be now.

He chose the cookies randomly, four dozen of them, in every shape, size and color they had.

"What are we supposed to do with all of those?" Libby asked as they left the bakery and set out on foot, heading for the little coffee joint across the street.

"You can take them back to your cabin later."

"Chance would love them if he were here."

He stopped midstride. "Chance?"

"Chance Mitchell Penn. My son." She watched the troubled emotion that crossed Matt's face. She hadn't meant to blurt out Chance's name, but at least she'd gone ahead and said it.

"You named him after Kirby's song?"

"Initially, it was Becker's idea. But I thought it was a brilliant choice." She was going to stand by her child's name, no matter how uncomfortable it made Matt. "If we had a girl, we were going to call her Lilly Fay, after the saloon girl in the song. The one Chance Mitchell loves and leaves."

"I don't like any of Kirby's songs, least of all that one. It came out when…"

"When what?" she asked. They stood on the sidewalk, with Matt clutching the pink bakery box.

"When I fell off the roof of our house and broke my arm. It was just after my ninth birthday, and I was pretending to be Chance Mitchell. I was crawling around up there with a toy gun, a six-shooter, strapped to my hip. I was hiding from the law."

Libby reached up and skimmed his jaw. She knew she shouldn't be touching him, but she wanted to comfort him somehow. "You must have liked the song then, or else why would you be pretending to be Chance?"

He took a step back, forcing her to lower her hand. "Sure. I liked his music when I was a kid. But it started to grate on me later."

She tried to draw more of the story out of him. "Did they put your broken arm in a cast?"

He nodded. "Kirby never saw it, though. He was on his *Outlaw at Large* tour, promoting the Chance Mitchell album, and my arm healed before he stopped back to see us."

"I'm sorry he didn't make more time for you then."

"I don't care anymore."

That was a lie, she thought. He cared far too much. "Kirby told me that he was impressed with your junior rodeo accomplishments. That you were just a little tyke, riding and roping like the devil was inside you."

"What does he know about it? He never attended any of my events. All he saw were the videos Mom showed him."

"He remembers those videos. He thinks about them when he's feeling guilty and blue. He wrote a song about you, too, but he hasn't recorded it yet."

"Holy crap." Matt tightened his grip on the box. "That's all I need, to be immortalized in one of his frigging songs."

"He's not going to record it until the two of you become father and son."

"Then he's never going to put it out there." Matt approached the crosswalk and stepped off the curb.

She followed him. "The song is called 'The Boy I Left Behind.' He played it for me. It's beautiful, raw and touching."

"That's a low blow."

"What is? Me telling you how good it is?"

"No. Him playing it for you. He's using you, Libby. He's pushing you around like a pawn."

"He's sharing his life with me. That's my role in all of this, to document his life, to write about his feelings." After they made it to the other side of the street, she said, "I know you don't believe that he ever loved you, but in his own tortured way, he did. You were the part of himself that he couldn't control. He promised his wife that he would never father a child from any of his affairs, and then you came along. The baby that wasn't supposed to exist. His secret. A sweet little boy who needed more than his daddy knew how to give."

"I'm well aware of what he promised his wife. It's the reason I had to stay in the shadows, the excuse that was drilled into my head. My famous father had another family, and it would hurt them if they knew about me. But his wife found out and divorced him, anyway."

"She's over it now. She and Kirby are friends again. I haven't met her yet, but I'll be interviewing her for the book." Her name was Melinda, and she was a former fashion model who used her celebrity to create a cosmetics and skin care line. Her face, her brand, were featured in TV infomercials. "She agrees with Kirby that everything should be out in the open now."

"Of course she does. He always gets women to forgive him. And can we please talk about something else? I'm sick of my dad."

"Okay. We'll work on other topics." She sent him her best smile, even if he was still scowling, much too fiercely, at her.

Matt and Libby sat outside at a café table. He drank his coffee black. She put sugar *and* an artificial sweetener in hers, along with cream and milk. He'd never seen anyone mix so much stuff together in one cup.

She opened the cookies. "Look how cute they are." She lifted a smiley face from the bunch. "This one looks like me."

He took it from her and held it upside down. "And now it looks like me."

Her eyes twinkled. "At least you have a sense of humor about that disposition of yours." She removed a flower-shaped cookie from the box and nibbled on it, leaving the happy face for him.

He broke off a piece of its smile. "I'm sorry if I've been such lousy company since you met me. I'm not always this difficult to get along with."

She ate more of the flower, dropping crumbs onto the

table. "I expected you to react to me with resistance. I just didn't expect for us to…"

Fall into lust with each other? "We already agreed to put that to rest, so there's no point in rehashing it."

"You're right. I shouldn't have brought it up."

Yeah, he thought, but were they fooling themselves in believing that they would never do it again? Even now, as she made a pretty little mess out of her cookie, he was fixated on her mouth. Forgetting that he'd kissed her was proving to be impossible.

"Where did you get married?" she asked suddenly. "Was it on your ranch?"

The hits just kept on coming with this girl. Sucker punches to the gut. "Why are you asking me about my wedding?"

"Because I'm curious about you, and the couple on top on the wedding cake at the bakery sort of looked like us."

"I didn't see a cake like that."

"You weren't paying attention." She gestured to the other side of the street. "It's in the window."

He didn't turn to look, not from this distance. "If I tell you about my wedding, then you have to tell me about yours, too." He wasn't going to stab himself in the heart without making her do the same. "Turnabout is fair play, or however that saying goes."

"All right. But I asked you first."

"Then no, I didn't get married on the ranch."

"Why not?" She gazed at him from across the table. "It seems like the perfect place for it."

"Sandy didn't want to get married in this area. She wanted to go away, to elope. So she left her kids with her parents and we flew to Las Vegas. She didn't tell her folks or anyone else what we were doing until we got back. I kept quiet, too." He'd respected Sandy's wishes. "She wanted it to be different from her first wedding. No prepping or planning, no guests, no fuss, no muss, no hoopla."

Libby angled her head. "Did any of that matter to you?"

"Not really. I just wanted to have a family—her and the kids. But I should have sensed that she was trying too hard to make it different from her first wedding, with us going to Vegas and whatnot."

Her eyes grew wider. "You didn't get married by an Elvis impersonator, did you?"

He stifled a laugh. Trust Libby to say something funny. "It was just a normal minister in a quiet little chapel. They provided the witnesses, but none of them looked like Elvis, either."

"Did you get a honeymoon suite at your hotel?"

"No. We just stayed in a regular room."

"Was that Sandy's idea, too?"

He nodded. "She didn't want the hotel making a fuss over us. At the time, it seemed okay. But if I ever got married again, I would have the wedding right here in my hometown and make it a celebratory occasion."

She removed another cookie—a frosted cowboy boot—from the box. "So you're planning on having another wife?"

"Someday, maybe. But she's not going to be someone who's hurting over another man. I'm never going to put myself through that again." He leaned back in his chair, playing it cool, hating how exposed he felt. "So I guess that leaves you out, huh?"

She wagged the boot at him. "Is that supposed to be a joke? I told you I was doing fine in that regard."

He didn't believe her bravado. He was certain that

she cried when no one was there to see her do it. "You have to admit that we would make a terrible match." Great kisses. Horrendous fights. "We don't get along worth a lick."

"True." She flicked a crumb at him. "But it's your pissy personality that would be the problem."

"Right. Because you're such a gem." He came forward in his seat. "So what's the deal with your wedding? You owe me the details."

"First off, I was pregnant when I got married." She pulled her blouse out in front of her, stretching the fabric. "Almost seven months."

"Oh, my." He exaggerated his drawl. "Do tell."

"Don't mock me. I was a lovely bride."

"I'm sure you were." He pictured her glowing like a pregnant lady should. "But why did you wait so long to seal the deal?"

"We couldn't decide if we should get married before or after the baby was born. We thought it would be cute to wait until he or she could be part of the ceremony. But our families convinced us to do it before."

"I agree. I think it's better for kids to have married parents." Matt sure as hell wished that he'd come into this world legitimately. "When did you know you were having a boy?"

"On the day Chance was born. We could have found out sooner, but we wanted to be surprised. That's part of the beauty of having children. To let them surprise you."

He drank his coffee. "I bet you wore a sparkly dress."

She toyed with the rim of her cup. "At the wedding? Yes, it was quite glittery. We got married on the beach, in our cowboy boots. Mine were white and decorated with rhinestones." She gazed at her half-eaten cookie. "I still have them."

And her dress, too, no doubt, preserved for all time. Sandy had kept her first gown. Matt didn't have a clue what happened to the dress she'd worn when she'd married him. "That doesn't sound like a typical beach wedding."

"It wasn't. We created a country theme. We put up a rustic wooden arch decorated with horseshoes and flowers, and I walked down the aisle to 'Chantilly Heart.'"

Well, of course she did, he thought. That was right up her alley. "I should have known that you would pick one of Kirby's songs."

"It's such a gorgeous ballad. It's a favorite at Western-themed weddings."

Matt turned droll. "I'd rather have an Elvis impersonator." He would've welcomed a guy in a white jumpsuit over a Kirby Talbot tune any day. It was beyond him how his dad could write such compelling love songs, when you took into account what a womanizer he was. "Maybe I'll do the Elvis thing next time."

Her laughter rang rich and true. "I really like you, Matt, even if we don't get along worth a lick."

A lick of sugar, he thought, as she polished off the cowboy boot cookie. "I begrudgingly liked you from the start."

"Glad to hear it. Well, not the begrudgingly part." She quickly asked, "Will you take me to see your old high school?"

There she went again, throwing him off-kilter. "What for?"

"I got curious after the bakery lady mentioned it."

"It's just a typical small-town high school." He didn't see the point in dredging up yet another aspect of his youth. "It's nothing special."

"I'd still like to see it."

"It's a Sunday in July. It'll be closed."

"Is it fenced, locked and gated?"

"No. They don't have those types of security issues around here."

"Then why can't we walk around the grounds?"

He shook his head. "You sure are pesky."

"I already warned you that I was. Don't you remember? The most persuasive cowgirl you'll ever meet."

He corrected her. "Yeah, and besides the fact that I told you you're not a cowgirl, *pesky* and *persuasive* don't mean the same thing."

She dusted the sprinkles from her fingertips. "In my case they do. So, what were you like in school?"

He shrugged. "I wasn't one of the popular kids, but I wasn't a social outcast, either. Believe it or not, I had friends." He still did, even if he rarely saw them anymore. His closest buddies were happily married, making him feel even more miserably divorced.

Libby asked, "What about the secret you were keeping about who your father was? Didn't that bother you when you were in high school?"

"By then, I was used to the lie, and Kirby wasn't coming around anymore, anyway. The toughest part, I guess, was that I was the only Native American kid at my school. This town doesn't have much of a Native population." He finished his coffee, pushed his cup aside. "I'm registered with the Cherokee Nation, but I also have a teeny bit of Tonkawa blood. I'm not an enrolled member of the Tonkawa tribe. But I heard they were originally from this area, and they claimed to have descended from a mystical wolf."

Libby stared at him. "Like the wolf Kirby said you were? You and your gold eyes?"

"Not all wolves' eyes are yellow. Some are brown or

gray or green. I read somewhere that cubs are born with blue eyes, but they fade within six to ten weeks, changing into the adult color."

"Were you born with blue eyes?"

"No." His were always this shade. "Yours are certainly blue." They were especially bright in the sunlight.

"Could it be that I'm part wolf, too, but mine never changed?"

"Nope." He came up with an animal identity that suited her far better. "You're part badger, that's what you are."

"Oh, that's a good one." She grinned, dimples and all. "And badger that I am, I still want to see your high school. I'm not letting up about that."

"All right. That'll be our next stop." Another trip down memory lane. Call him crazy. But he wanted to spend more time with her, even if he had to give up bits and pieces of himself to do it.

# Four

As Matt and Libby walked around Creek Hill High, he felt like a warped tour guide. He wasn't an outcast in school, but the shell he'd built around himself when he was a kid was still there. He was certain that Libby had built a shell around herself, too. Maybe not when she was a child, but later, after her husband died. He didn't believe for a city slicker minute that she was handling her loss as well as she claimed to be.

"I told you this place was nothing special," he said. They continued to stroll along the grass-flanked pathways.

"I think it's nice, cozy." She glanced around. "It's definitely a lot smaller than the school I attended. I was the editor of our newspaper. I worked on the yearbook, too. We had a journalism club. That's where I spent most of my time."

"I should have guessed as much. The little writer."

He looked into those blue eyes of hers. "Did you listen to country music and wear Western clothes back then?" He wanted to get a complete picture of her. He was just as curious about her youth as she was about his.

"Yes, I was into it then. But it wasn't just the clothes and the music that fascinated me. I used to watch rodeos on TV, and I would get these dreamy, sexy crushes on the cowboys. Sort of like I have on you." She winced. "Sorry. I shouldn't have said that."

His body reacted, his pulse galloping from his head to his toes. "At least now I know why you kissed me the way you did."

"Right. My latent cowboy fantasies." She swept her hand through the air, as if she were trying to wave those fantasies away. "I got interested in horses, too, and asked my parents if I could take riding lessons, so they took me to the local equestrian center. I wanted my own horse, but we couldn't afford it. My parents are just working folk. Mom was a supermarket checker, and Dad sells cars. She's retired now and has a small pension. He still works for a dealer. They've been married for thirty-five years. They wanted more kids, but Mom kept losing babies. I was the only one she carried full-term."

"I'll bet they're wonderful grandparents." He imagined them doting on Libby's son.

"They're the best. They adore Chance. So do Becker's parents. I'm still really close to them, too. Becker was from a big family, brothers and sisters and aunts and uncles and cousins. Chance loves hanging out with all of them."

Matt escorted her to the back of the campus, where the football field was. "Where did you meet Becker?"

She made a beeline for the bleachers. But it took her a moment to say, "It was at one of your dad's concerts.

I sat next to him at the show. I was with some friends from the equestrian center, and he was with two of his brothers."

Matt frowned. Of all the places she could've met her husband, did it have to be connected to Kirby? "How old were you?"

"Nineteen, and Becker was twenty. He wasn't the type I dreamed about. He wasn't a cowboy or a rough-and-tumble guy. It was his heart I saw, his openness, his kindness. But he shared my love of country, and that mattered, too, of course." She climbed onto the first set of bleachers. "He was my first. Not my first boyfriend, but the first man I..."

"Slept with?" Matt stepped up onto the bleachers, too.

She nodded. "It was gentle and romantic, the way it should be for a girl's first time. But it was always like that when we were together."

An immediate urge to apologize came over him. "I didn't mean to hurt you when we kissed, Libby."

She blinked, teetered on her feet. They had yet to sit down. "You didn't hurt me. It felt good." She sucked her bottom lip between her teeth. "A good kind of pain."

He knew precisely what she meant. "I'm not normally that aggressive."

"I just bring it out in you?"

"So it seems." And if he had it to do over, he would probably behave just as roughly. But he would try to be romantic somehow, too.

She finally sat, and so did he. Silent, they stared out at the empty field. He was tempted to hold her hand, like a high school boy might do, but he kept his calloused paws to himself. They weren't teenagers, and he wasn't dating her.

"When did you quit competing in junior rodeos?" she asked.

He turned to look at her. Her hair was still messy from earlier, tangled beautifully around her face. "When I was thirteen."

"The year after Kirby ended his relationship with your mom? Is that significant as to why you quit?"

"Overall, it was a challenging time in my life, with me being a teenager, and their breakup only made it more difficult. I didn't understand why Mom was still defending Kirby, especially since they weren't together anymore. I was starting to hate him, to hold him accountable for his actions, but she was asking me to be patient, saying that he was going through a bad time and needed help."

"With what? The drinking? The drugs?"

Matt nodded. "He was partying really heavily then. By that time I hardly ever saw him. Not that he was a constant in my life, anyway. But he was coming by even less and less, and on the rare occasions that he did show up, he was either high or hungover." Soon after that, Kirby stopped visiting him at all.

"I'm so sorry that he put you through that. Even your brothers mentioned how difficult his addictions were for them to tolerate. But he's completely clean and sober now."

"Did they help him with his recovery? Were they part of it?"

"Yes, they were."

A stream of anger, of envy, of everything being the odd kid out had made him feel, shot through his veins. He hadn't been allowed to help, even if he'd wanted to. Which he didn't, he told himself. Kirby didn't deserve his empathy. "What about Tommy and that supposedly wild streak of his?"

"Tommy doesn't drink or do drugs. Most of his wildness is in the form of his music, his rebellious lyrics and his antics on stage. The reckless stunts he pulls. He takes risks that he shouldn't, climbing up riggings and swinging from ropes that weren't designed to hold him, jumping off platforms without warning. He drives his road crew crazy with worry."

Matt scoffed. Tommy sounded like an idiot to him.

Libby continued, "Kirby says that Tommy has always been a daredevil, even when he was a kid. I heard that Tommy is supposed to be wild in bed, too. Or that's the reputation he has, with lots of groupies hanging around."

Matt didn't give two figs about Tommy's conquests. But he cared about how it affected Libby. "Are you attracted to him?"

"Who? Tommy?" She shook her head. "I haven't been attracted to anyone since Becker passed." She paused, bit her lip, then said, "Except for you."

Matt wanted to kiss her again. He wanted it so badly, he ached from the need. "I wish you weren't writing my dad's book." He hated how closely tied she was to his father and Tommy and the rest of the Talbots.

"I would have never even met you if I wasn't."

The urge to kiss her got stronger, more painful. But he kept his distance. "Maybe it would be better if we'd never met."

"We can't go back in time and erase it."

"I'm never going to sign a release or let you interview me."

"I think eventually you will. You need to get Kirby off your chest. Look at all of the things you've told me so far."

"But you can't use any of it in the book, so it doesn't matter what I say or how much I reveal. I could tell you every agonizing thing that's in my heart and you still couldn't write about it."

"Are you going to do that, Matt?"

"Do what?"

"Tell me every agonizing thing in your heart?"

"I might. If you tell me what's in yours."

"I don't have as much to tell as you do."

He called her bluff. "You're twenty-nine with a six-year-old son and a husband who died. You've got plenty of agony."

She sighed. "I'm not Sandy. You can't keep looking at me as if I'm her."

"I see what I see. A woman who lost her mate."

"Yes, but everyone mourns differently. And I already told you that I've accepted being a widow. I have a support group in my family and in Becker's. I got professional counseling, too, and that was a big step for me. It helped me understand the stages of grief and move toward a place of hope."

"And yet three years later you're at my ranch, having mixed-up feelings for me. The ex-husband of another widow. That's got to mean something, Libby."

She shook her head. "I'm not getting attached to you because you had a wife whose husband died. That's not why you make me feel the way you do."

"Not consciously, maybe. But it has to be part of it. You knew I was married to a widow when you met me. You researched my background."

"That wasn't the reason I felt something for you when I first met you. It was just our chemistry. The instant heat." She glanced away, as if she were feeling it now. Or fighting it. Or whatever it was she was doing.

He said, "In the beginning what Sandy felt for me was sexual, too, all tied up with her grief."

Libby returned her gaze to his. "That still doesn't give you the right to say that my attraction to you is associated with grief."

Based on his experiences, he believed otherwise. But for now, he went quiet, waiting for her to resume their dialogue.

A moment later, she asked, "How did you and Sandy meet?"

"She was at the bar with some of her girlfriends, drinking a little, playing songs on the jukebox. I'd seen Sandy and her husband around town before, but I'd never officially met either of them. Sandy is older than me by about six years, and so was he." Matt gestured to their surroundings. "They both went to school here, just not at the same time as I did."

"But you still knew who Sandy was when you saw her at the bar?"

"Yes. I also knew that she'd lost her husband. That he passed away a year or so before. His name was Greg Molloy." But maybe Libby knew that already? Maybe his name had come up in her research? Matt couldn't tell by her reaction.

Either way, she went silent for a second. Then she asked, "What happened to him? How did he die?"

Matt relayed the details, tragic as they were. "He was in a plane crash. An out-of-town relative of his owned one of those little two-seater aircrafts, and there was a malfunction that sent them spinning to the ground."

"How awful." Libby pressed both hands to her chest. "Just the way you described it makes me hurt for Sandy."

"It gave her nightmares." Matt couldn't begin to count the number of times she'd awakened next to him, crying out from a bad dream. "But she still managed to get on a plane afterward. Or commercial flights, anyway." Like the one that had taken them to Vegas to be married. But maybe that was a bit of a death wish on her part—the flight, the wedding, the whole damned thing.

"So tell me more about how you met. And what happened at the bar."

"I was waiting for a buddy of mine, but he called and said he couldn't make it. I stayed there by myself, watching everyone in the place and giving myself something to do. I've never been much of a barfly, even if I still go there now and then." To escape, he thought, to be alone in a crowd. "I noticed Sandy and her friends. There was a guy who kept bothering Sandy, who was getting too rowdy, and she kept trying to push him away. So I stepped in and took over, telling him to beat it. After that, I hung out with Sandy and her girlfriends. It was their idea to take her out to begin with. She hadn't gone anywhere since Greg died." The more memories he conjured up, the more vivid they became. "As the evening wore on, her friends wanted to leave and Sandy wanted to stay there with me. So I promised her friends that I would get her home safely."

"And they were okay with that?"

"They trusted me, so it wasn't an issue. I'd actually met some of them before, and they knew I owned the Flying Creek Ranch and had a decent reputation. I doubt they would have left her alone with me if they thought I was going to sleep with her that night. But that wasn't my intention." He preferred to date the usual way, getting to know someone first. "I never even kissed her at the bar."

"When did you kiss her?" Libby quietly asked.

"At her front door, after I drove her home. And that's

how I was going to leave it, with a chaste kiss. I figured I would get her phone number and we would go from there. But it got hot and heavy. Only I didn't start it, the way I did with you in the truck. She initiated the sexual stuff." His memories went raw. "It didn't dawn on me that she was transposing her loneliness into lust." He hadn't expected to fall in love with her, either, or to marry her later, or to try to heal her broken heart. None of that had crossed his mind on that fateful night. "She cried about Greg afterward. Deep, soul-wrenching tears. So I held her until morning. I whispered in her ear, I stroked my hand down her hair, I told her everything would be all right."

"That was wonderful of you to console her, Matt, even if sleeping with her so soon wasn't a good idea."

Even now, with as messed up as everything was, he wanted to touch Libby, to skim her cheek, to feel her skin beneath his fingertips. He couldn't seem to get this woman out of his blood. "If you and I had gone too far today—"

She shook her head. "We shouldn't even be talking about this. We're not going to be together like that."

"You're right. We're not." But he still wasn't convinced that they weren't headed for trouble. As overpowering as their chemistry was, anything could happen.

Libby stood in front of the mirror, her hair damp from the shower and a towel wrapped snugly around her body. She couldn't stop thinking about the things Matt had said to her yesterday.

He was wrong about her. Her attraction to him didn't put her in the same category as his former wife. Libby wasn't following in Sandy's shaky footsteps. She wasn't getting close to Matt to fill a void being widowed had left behind.

As much as Libby missed Becker, she wasn't trapped in the same kind of grief as Sandy's. If by some crazy, hungry, uncontrollable chance she decided to make love with Matt, she wouldn't break down in his arms. She would simply appreciate Matt for who he was.

Her living, breathing fantasy.

She dropped her towel and gazed at herself in the mirror. She was young and single, free and alone. So maybe she should just cave into those urges and sleep with Matt.

She squeezed her eyes shut, warning herself to back off. She was here to do a job, to gather research, to convince Matt to be interviewed. Having an affair with him wasn't part of the deal.

Opening her eyes, she picked up her towel and hung it back on the rack. She planned on going to the lodge for breakfast. After that, she wasn't sure what she was going to do. She intended to see Matt, of course. The more time she spent with him, the more likely she was to convince him to be part of the book. Because, really, that was all that mattered.

Right? *Right.*

Libby scrunched her hair, working a hair-polishing serum through it to make it shine. She put on her makeup, adding a dollop of gloss to her lips, making them shine, too. Next, she got dressed, shrugging into skinny jeans. The blouse she chose left her midriff bare.

She rummaged through her jewelry and accessorized her outfit with silver hoop earrings and a rhinestone-studded skull-and-crossbones pendant. She yanked on a pair of tall black cowboy boots, tucking her skin-tight jeans into them. Finally, she plopped a black Stetson on her head.

It certainly wasn't her typical morning attire. "But what the heck?" she said aloud. At least she wasn't cowering from her libido. She needed to look rebellious, to feel sexy, even if she wasn't going to act on her feelings.

She returned to her makeup case and dug around for her liquid eyeliner. With precision, she created cat eyes, making them dark and bold. Last, she spritzed a spicy perfume into the air and walked through the mist, letting it settle around her. Now she was ready, totally ready, to present herself as the strong and steady widow that she was.

She poked her head out the door to see if Matt's truck was in his driveway. Sure enough, it was.

With her chin held high and her boot heels kicking up dirt, she strode over to his cabin and rapped on the door.

He answered her summons, his gaze roaming the length of her. "Damn, Libby. What poor sap did you just consume for breakfast?"

Was that his way of saying that she looked like a man-eater? "Breakfast is precisely why I'm here. I was hoping you'd join me at the lodge. They put on a darned fine spread, in case you haven't heard."

He was still eyeballing her. "Come to think of it, I have heard. But I already had a bowl of cereal."

She poked at the flatness of his stomach. He was wearing a plain gray T-shirt tucked into his jeans. "Surely you have room in there for eggs and potatoes. Or gravy and biscuits. Mmm," she said for effect. "That's my favorite."

He glanced at her pendant, then shifted his attention to her feline-inspired eye makeup. "I think you need a guy with a big flashy motorcycle to take you."

She fingered the skull. She liked that he was being glib. She was in that kind of mood, too. "I'd rather have a guy with a big, flashy stallion." She batted her lashes. She had on two coats of mascara today. "Oh, wait. You have one of those, don't you?"

"Indeed I do." He played along with her. "But I think you'd be safer in my truck. The stallion would probably get one whiff of you and fall head over heels."

"Promising Spirit." She remembered seeing the horse's name in the ranch brochure. She'd also gotten a gander at his picture, and he was quite the buckskin beauty. "I'll take my chances." Suddenly she was no longer flirting. She was just being her regular self again. "Do you have any new foals?"

Matt went back to normal, too. "We've got three on the way. One of them should arrive in about ten days or so."

"Just around the time Chance is coming." Her son would be here by then, along with Libby's mother.

"I'd be glad to show him the foal when it's born."

"That would be great." She suspected that Matt had been a good caregiver to Sandy's children. "He's going to love your ranch. He's going to be enthralled with you, too. The man in charge."

"I like kids." He ducked his head and stepped away from the door. "Come in and I'll get my boots on."

She entered his home. It appeared to be professionally decorated, similar to her accommodations, with rough-hewn furnishings and Old West artifacts on the walls. But she didn't catch sight of anything that defined him in a personal way, no photographs or items that spoke his name. This could have been just another rental cabin. "So you're going to accompany me to breakfast?"

"I might as well. But I have to work afterward." He

paused, as if he were debating something. He finally said, "There's a hayride and marshmallow roast tonight." Another long, drawn-out pause, then, "We can get together later for that, if you want to."

"Thanks. That sounds fun." She appreciated the invitation, even as hesitantly as he'd extended it.

She watched him walk to the master bedroom to get his boots. The door was open, a portion of his bed visible. His covers were turned down and rumpled from where he'd slept.

He returned with his socks and boots and sat on the sofa to put them on. She perched on the edge of a leather chair, but she could still see the corner of his unmade bed.

Blocking it out of her mind, she asked, "Did Sandy and the kids live here with you?" She'd been wondering about that, and now she had the opportunity to find out.

He looked up from his task. "I have a house on the other side of the ranch."

"You do? I thought maybe you were going to build a house for you and Sandy and the kids, but things ended before you got the chance to do it."

"It was my house before I got married, before Sandy came into my life. I built it at the same time as the ranch. I just haven't felt like living there since the divorce, so I moved into this cabin." He angled his head. "And how is it that we're back to talking about my ex?"

"I'm not going to avoid the subject just because you compared me to her." She refused to fall prey to that. "I already told you that I'm not Sandy, and it isn't right for you to lump us together."

"Yes, you told me. But what are we doing, Libby?"

Her response was quick. "We're going to breakfast."

He furrowed his brow. "That's not what I meant."

She knew what he meant: What were they doing, steeped in uncomfortable feelings for each other? But that was a question she couldn't quite answer. "I'm just trying to convince you to participate in Kirby's book."

"Showing up at my door in that getup? You look like you're going to ride me hard and fast and put me away wet."

Her mouth went dry. Suddenly she was thirsty as sin, in more ways than one. But she didn't hide the truth. She said, "I considered it."

He stared at her, and she noticed how he hadn't yet pulled one of his pant legs down to his boot.

"You did?" he asked. "When?"

"This morning, after my shower, I contemplated having an affair with you."

He rolled his pant leg down. "And?"

"And I reminded myself that it wouldn't be right. That I didn't come to your ranch to sleep with you. But that doesn't mean I'm going to stop fantasizing about it." Hot and dizzy, she headed for his kitchen. "Is it okay if I get a glass of water?"

He was still staring at her. "Help yourself."

Help herself to what? Anything she wanted, or just the water? She went for the H2O. She located a plastic tumbler and poured a drink from the tap.

Once she was steadier on her feet, she said, "We better go before everyone else beats us to the buffet."

"That's a good idea." He didn't return to the topic of their nonexistent affair. He didn't say another word about it.

They went to breakfast, both of them behaving, at least outwardly, as though it had never been mentioned at all.

# Five

Matt and Libby rode in the back of a straw-filled, horse-drawn wagon that they had all to themselves, not counting the driver. The shiny red cart had high rails for a certain amount of privacy, with plenty of comfort for two.

The rest of the people were ahead of them in big noisy groups, making Matt and Libby's the last wagon trailing quietly behind. But he preferred it that way. On this moonlit evening, his mind was elsewhere. He was still trying to absorb the sexy little things Libby had told him earlier.

"It's beautiful out here," she said. "All the twinkling lights and night-blooming flowers." She peered over the side. "Oh, and look at the colorful bottles hanging from the trees."

Matt merely nodded. He'd seen all of this a zillion times before. He'd even decorated some of it himself.

At this point, he just wanted to get Libby out of his

system. To make long, hard love to her. To fulfill their mutual screwed-up fantasies, no matter what the consequences. But he knew better than to act on impulse. Apparently Libby knew better, too. What a responsible pair they were, he thought. Torturing themselves.

"What's the significance of the bottles?" she asked.

He frowned. "I'm sorry. What?"

"The bottles. What's the purpose of hanging them like that?"

He snapped into owner-of-the-ranch mode, doing his best to be her hayride host. "Mostly they're just garden ornaments. Or that's what they've become in this day and age. A bit of folk art." He sat forward, keeping himself more alert. He couldn't dwell on his dilemma with Libby the whole blasted night, not if he expected to stay sane. "Historically, it's an old tradition brought to the States by African slaves. They believed that the bottles could capture roving or evil spirits. It's a common practice in the South now, especially in the Appalachians. That's where my Cherokee ancestors were from, so I adopted the tradition, too."

"It certainly makes this trail more scenic." Soft and pale, her hair blew around her face and shoulders. "Do you believe they can capture roving spirits?"

"I don't know." He'd never had any experience in that realm. "But a lot of people in the Appalachians still do. In hoodoo folklore, blue creates a crossroads between heaven and earth, with the elements of water and sky being blue."

"So that's why most of the bottles out here are blue?"

Matt nodded. "Blue feels right to me, too, because I'm from the Blue Clan. There are seven clans in Cherokee society."

"Are the other clans named after colors, too?"

"No. Some are animals and other things. There's a Wolf Clan. It's the largest one, but my family isn't in it. Clanship comes from one's mother. If you don't have a Cherokee mother, then you don't have a clan. But no one keeps formal or written records of clanships. You just have the knowledge of what you've been told."

"Kirby has a song called 'Cherokee Tears.' As I'm sure you know, it was written before he met your mother. So it wasn't inspired by her. But he told me that it's her favorite song of his."

Matt blew out his breath. There was no escaping Kirby, not where Libby was concerned. With that damned book of hers, she mentioned him every day.

"What do you think of 'Cherokee Tears'?" she asked.

He wanted to say that he hated it, but when he was a kid, it had been one of his favorites, too. "It's a powerful song, with it being about the Trail of Tears." How could Matt dislike a song that paid tribute to the Cherokee who'd been forced to leave their homeland and migrate to Indian Territory, dying from hunger, exposure and disease along the way?

"You just said something nice about your dad."

"No, I didn't." He shrugged it off. "I said something nice about one of his songs."

"His music is what makes him who he is."

"What? A prick?"

She almost laughed. He could see her holding back. "You have his sense of humor, you know. He's prone to saying things like that, too."

"Oh, lucky me. A chip off the old smart-ass block."

She reached for his hand and took it in hers. "Lie down with me, Matt. Let's look at the stars from here."

"I don't know much about the constellations." He

sank onto the straw beside her, letting himself enjoy the feeling of being near her, of holding hands. "Do you?"

She lifted her chin to the sky. "Not enough to point them out or recognize them."

"Maybe we can make up our own." He pointed to a grouping of stars, using their joined hands. "That looks like an X." He made the symbol in the air. "And those look like an O."

"So we can call them tic-tac-toe?"

"Or hugs and kisses." He turned his face toward hers. "It would be so easy to kiss you again." He paused for an excruciating second. "So damned easy."

She made a breathy sound. "We can't do it, Matt. We shouldn't."

"I know." Because easy would turn to difficult, and they would struggle with it later. He lowered their hands, and their interlocked fingers drifted apart.

Silent, she sat upright, no longer looking at the stars.

He sat up, too, and with the banned kiss still on his mind, he said, "For the sake of us imagining how it would be, I'd be really gentle this time."

"You'd make me want more than a kiss." Her voice hitched on her words. "So much more."

His pulse jumped. "In the wagon? Like this?"

"It's a romantic setting."

"Not if we got caught. It wouldn't take much for our driver to notice the boss making out with one of the guests on the way to the marshmallow roast."

"I probably already look like we've been messing around. I've got straw in my hair." She blew a piece of it away from her face.

"Everyone has it all over them by the time these things are over." He threw a handful of it at her, showing her how it was done.

"Ooh, you." She grabbed a bunch and tossed it at him.

They laughed like a couple of kids having a pillow fight. Or what he assumed that would be like. He'd never actually been involved in a pillow fight before.

When they settled down, she asked, "What prompted you to build a recreational ranch?"

"I thought it would be a good investment, owning this much land and doing something with it. Of course, no one knows the truth about where I originally got the money. I told everyone that it came from my grandparents' life insurance policy and that my mother had put it in trust for me. I had to explain it somehow. Otherwise people would've wondered how I afforded all of this."

"So it was strictly an investment for you?"

"No. I liked the idea of creating a place for families to come, to have fun together. In the beginning, it gave me a sense of family, too."

"But it doesn't anymore?"

"Sometimes it does. But I've had the ranch for almost ten years now, so mostly it just makes me aware that I don't have a family of my own, other than when I was a stepfather to Sandy's kids."

"You miss them, don't you?"

"The kids? Yes, I do." Even if he hadn't been their dad for very long. "They're identical twins named Cassie and Kelly. They were seven when I married their mom."

She drew her knees up to her chest. The wagon was still rolling along. "Were you able to tell them apart?"

"Yes, but there were times they would try to trick me and insist that I was calling them by the wrong name. They thought it was funny to pretend they were the other sister." He smiled from the happy memory. "They already had that twin thing going on, with their own language and all of that."

She smiled, too. "Oh, that's cute. My maternal grand-mother is a twin. She and her sister are fraternal, not identical, though."

"I always wished that I had a brother or sister. Kirby's other sons didn't count." He clarified the difference. "I wanted a sibling who belonged to my mom, who lived with us, who was the same as me. Not some faraway strangers who belonged to my dad."

"Just remember that they're interested in you now."

"So you keep saying." But he wasn't going to sub-ject himself to meeting them. He couldn't handle being around anyone who was close to his dad. Except for Libby, and that wasn't going in his favor, either. Not with how much he wanted her. "Was it tough for you being an only child?"

She nodded. "It was lonely sometimes."

He knew the isolated feeling. "Does Chance get lonely?" He was curious about her son.

"He has cousins on his dad's side who are around his age, so he has plenty of companionship. Mostly he gets lonely about not having a father."

Matt glanced out the wagon. They were nearing the spot where they would be having the marshmallow roast. "Maybe you'll get remarried someday."

"It's tough to think about that right now, especially when I haven't even dated anyone." She pressed a fin-ger to her lips. "And the only man I've kissed so far is you."

"At least it's a start. At least you know what it's like to be attracted to someone again." He studied her in the moonlight. It was especially bright, and the stars they'd pointed out made it even brighter. "I haven't dated or been with anyone since my divorce. You probably al-ready figured that out with the way I've been behaving around you. But you asked about it before and I never gave you a straight answer, so I'm telling you now."

"Thank you for opening up to me."

"I've been doing that a lot since I met you."

She put her hand on his knee, quickly, lightly, before she removed it. "We're becoming friends, Matt. Real friends."

"I think so, too. But that doesn't really help with the other stuff." The unfulfilled need, he thought, the fantasies, the desperation of wanting each other.

"I have to keep pretending when we're around other people that I don't have a crush on you. I'm going to have to do that when my mom gets here, too."

"Does your mom know that I'm Kirby's son? Have you told her?"

"Yes, she knows. My dad does, too. This was too big of a project for me to leave my parents out of it. I didn't want to have to lie about why I was spending time at a recreational ranch in Texas. I wanted the comfort of having my son here, too, along with my mom. I assured Kirby that my parents could be trusted to keep the information private. They would never leak anything to the press or try to sabotage the book."

"So how do they feel about all of this? Do they think Kirby is doing the right thing? Are they siding with him?"

"They aren't siding with anyone. It isn't their place to do that."

"Have they met Kirby?"

"No. But when I leave here and go to Kirby's place, my mom and Chance are going with me, so Mom will get to meet him then. And so will Chance, of course. Chance knows he was named after one of Kirby's songs."

"Has he heard the song?"

"Oh, yes. He loves it. He listens to it all the time. But it will be great when he meets Kirby, because Kirby promised that he would serenade Chance with it."

Matt couldn't stand the thought of Libby returning to his dad's house. And now it bugged him that her mother and son would be going there, too, with Kirby playing the gracious host. But he wasn't going to let it ruin his night.

He was enjoying Libby's company far too much.

The marshmallow roast was warm and cozy with guests gathered around multiple fire pits. Everyone was making s'mores, squishing their toasted marshmallows between layers of chocolate and graham crackers. And there were campfire songs, particularly for the kids.

Libby sat next to Matt with a group of other people, all devouring their treats. One of the moms kept wiping her son's face and hands every few seconds. Libby wasn't that type of parent. She would simply let her son enjoy the goo.

She leaned over and said to Matt, "I wish Chance was here."

He replied, "Don't worry. We have these every week. You can do this again with him."

"Will you join us?" She wanted Matt to be there.

"Sure. I can do that."

"Thanks." She was eager for Chance and Matt to meet. As close as she was getting to Matt, she couldn't help feeling that way. Of course, it only heightened the complexity of her attraction to him, adding a gentler layer to it. But out here by the fire with other people around, they had to refrain from saying sensual things.

She noticed that Matt was on his second s'more, lick-ing the messiness off his fingers. She smiled at him, doing her best to keep her thoughts clean. "You're enjoying that."

"Yes, ma'am, I am."

Libby managed another smile. He sounded like a full-blown Texan. He looked like one, too, his Western attire still covered with scattered blades of straw from the wagon. He hadn't bothered to dust himself off. The environment suited him, and so did the firelight, casting a glow on his already bronzed skin.

"Have you ever celebrated National S'mores Day?" he asked.

"I didn't even know there was such a thing."

"It's observed every August tenth. We have a big bash that day, with all sorts of fun and games. We even serve s'mores spaghetti."

She made a face. "Sorry, but that sounds awful."

"It's chocolate spaghetti, not real pasta."

She softened her expression, laughed a little. "You had me worried there for a second."

"Yeah, I'll bet." He laughed, too. "In the evening we have a cocktail party of sorts, with s'mores martinis for the adults and s'mores milkshakes for the kids."

"Oh, wow." Now he was talking her language. "I'd love to try one of those martinis. I like experimenting with different drinks."

"I can make you one sometime. I have the recipe down pat." He finished his treat. "Or maybe you can stay a bit longer and join in on the S'mores Day celebration."

"I can't do that. Not with my work schedule. I have to be in Nashville by then."

"Can't you at least try? I'm sure Chance would enjoy the celebration."

"Yes, I'm sure he would." But was there more to Matt's suggestion? Was he trying to keep her and Chance away from Kirby? She looked into his eyes. They were a deeper shade of amber, enhanced by the flames. He returned her gaze, and her pulse fluttered at her neck.

By now, one of the ranch attendants was leading everyone in another song, a silly tune that her son was sure to like. But Chance wasn't here right now, and Libby wasn't in the mood to sing. Not while she was looking at Matt.

She asked him, "Will you go for a walk with me?" She needed to talk to him in private.

He got to his feet and accompanied her.

Once they were a safe distance from the activity, she unloaded the question that was on her mind. "Do you want me to stay because you're trying to keep me away from Kirby for as long as you can?"

"That's part of it. But I like having you around, even as difficult as it can be."

She fanned her face, feeling a heat that had nothing to do with the fire they'd walked away from. If anything, she should be cold, being so far away from it. "I like being around you, too. But I can't stay longer." She couldn't prolong her trip, even if she wanted to.

Matt blew out a breath. "Then I guess we'll just keep seeing each other and hanging out as friends while you're here."

"And suffer through the rest of it?"

"We don't have much of a choice in that regard, do we?"

"No, we don't." Just talking about it was bad enough. "I think we should invite some of the other guests to ride in our wagon on the way back."

"For appearance's sake? Or because you can't cope with being alone with me for the duration of the evening?"

"Both." If she climbed back into that straw-filled wagon with him, it would spark more of the feelings she was trying to avoid. And Libby was doing everything in her power to control her urges for Matt, and help him control his, too.

Nearly a week later, Libby sat alone on her porch, resting her weary bones. While hiking earlier, she'd taken a tumble and skinned her knee. It was a superficial injury, but it still hurt like the dickens.

Or maybe she was just missing Matt. He was out of town at a horse auction. He'd been gone since yesterday. She wasn't sure when he was coming back—tonight or maybe tomorrow. It depended on how his trip went.

Although their friendship was growing by leaps and bounds, forbidden urges continued to plague them. Since neither of them expected that to improve, they had learned to deal with it. Another thing that hadn't changed was Matt's unwillingness to participate in the book. He was still as reluctant as ever.

Eager to clear her mind, Libby adjusted the wooden chaise to a reclining position. Maybe she should take a nap and forget everything that was in her head.

She often dozed off at the beach, sinking into the sand on a towel. So why not sleep here on this late afternoon, surrounded by the Texas landscape? Besides, the chaise was padded with a nice, thick cushion.

Getting comfortable, she removed her lace-up boots and tucked her socks inside.

She closed her eyes, snuggled up and let herself drift.

The next thing she knew she was awakening from a floaty-feeling dream, with a make-believe Matt stroking her cheek. She murmured his name while he whispered hers.

"Libby. Are you okay?"

Suddenly he seemed too real to be coming from her subconscious, his hand much too solid against her skin. In her haze, she forced her eyes open and squinted at the shadow in front of her, wondering if Matt was truly there.

"Is that you?" she asked.

"Yes, it's me," he answered. "What are you doing out here in the dark?"

"I was taking a nap." She sat up and blinked, trying to gauge how long she'd been out. She looked past him and noticed that the sky was riddled with stars. "What time is it?"

"It's just after nine."

She'd slept for hours. "I was really tired. I had an eventful afternoon. I scraped my knee when I was on a hike today."

"Were you with a group?"

"I was alone, but it was only a short hike." She knew better than to go deep into the hills by herself. She didn't know the area well enough.

"Come on." He sounded concerned. "I'll take you inside."

He lifted her up, cradling her in his arms before she could stop him. Not that she wanted to, but still…

"I can walk, Matt."

"Too late. I've already got you." He opened the front door of her cabin and flipped on the wall switch with his elbow, illuminating the living room.

As the light shone on his face, she noticed how tired

he was. But he'd been on a road trip, a long drive from the ranch.

"You have beard stubble," she said. She'd only seen him clean-shaven. "It makes you look even more like a cowboy."

"I forgot my razor. But I don't like stubble. It itches."

She thought it was sexy, but she didn't say so. "You can put me down now."

He glanced at the sofa, but he bypassed it and headed for her room. Good heavens, she thought. He was taking her to bed. Not in a romantic sense, but it still made her feel that way.

He was good at maneuvering her in his arms. Too good, she decided. Her heart thumped, being this close to him.

He plopped her down on the unmade bed. She'd left a few clothes strewn about, too. She hadn't tidied up this morning. She'd also left her bedroom light on.

"Let me take a look at your knee." Instead of covering her with a blanket, he sat on the edge of the bed, leaving her exposed to his view.

"It's just a scrape." She was wearing shorts, the same pair she'd worn on the hike. "See? No big deal."

"You should have bandaged it."

"It's not that bad." She wiggled her toes, even if her feet had nothing to do with her injury.

"Even small cuts can get infected. Did you use an antibacterial on it?"

"No, but I poured water over it when it first happened."

He shook his head. "Let me take care of it properly for you."

"That isn't necessary."

His handsome features hardened. "Yes, it is."

With how persistent he was being, she quit her meager protests and let him take over.

He went into the bathroom and returned with a first-aid kit the ranch provided. She'd seen it under the sink, but hadn't thought to use it.

"You need to be more careful," he scolded. "The least you could have done was brought medical supplies with you."

"I didn't expect to fall."

He dabbed a liquid antiseptic on her knee, cleaning it his way. "You're not going hiking again by yourself."

"Wow. Listen to you." She smiled, hoping to defuse the situation. "Being the boss of me."

"That's right, I am. Next time you want to go on a hike, I'll go with you." He finished with her knee, placing a bandage on it. "You're not riding alone, either. You'll be going out with me, like we've been doing."

They'd been riding nearly every day this week, packing picnic lunches and eating by the creek. "You're just trying to hoard my time."

"So what if I am?" He closed the first-aid kit, snapping down on the plastic hinges a bit too noisily, and placed it on the nightstand.

She looked into his eyes, and he smoothed her hair away from her forehead. But he took his hand back soon enough. He seemed cautious about touching her in a way that hadn't been part of his doctoring.

"My mom and Lester are home," he said. "They just got back today. She called me while I was on the road."

Libby assumed that Lester was his mother's husband. Matt hadn't mentioned him by name until now. "Did you tell her about me?"

"Yes, I did, and she's interested in meeting you and discussing the book."

Her excitement mounted. "When do you think I'll get to talk to her?"

"Soon, I suspect. She seemed eager to meet you. I gave her your number."

"That was nice of you."

He frowned and pulled up the blanket, tucking it around her. "She asked for your number. I didn't offer it."

"I'm sorry if me meeting your mom causes you distress. But it's part of my job."

"Just keep me out of it, okay? I don't want to know what she tells you about my dad. Not unless she admits that she secretly hates him. But I doubt that's the direction it's going to take."

She fingered the blanket, the barrier he'd put between them. "You're the only one who hates him."

"Maybe I'm the only one with an ounce of brains around here." He cupped her chin, his expression softening. "You're a pretty little thorn in my side. You know that?"

Yes, she knew how she affected him. She leaned forward, put her arms around his neck and whispered, "Thanks for taking care of my knee."

"You're welcome." He nuzzled her cheek, his beard stubble rough against her skin. "I have to go. It's been a long night and I need to get some sleep."

She breathed him in, all the way to her soul. "I'd invite you to sleep here, but we both know the trouble that would get us into."

"The kind we can't undo once it's done. I'm going home like I'm supposed to." He moved away from her. "Do you want me to turn out the light?"

"I'm not ready for bed. I still have to change." She wasn't going to sleep in her clothes any more than he was likely to sleep in his. "Good night, Matt."

"Night." Before he left her room, he paused in the doorway and glanced back at her. One last time.

And then he was gone.

# Six

The following morning, Libby got a call from Julie Clark-Simpson, Matt's mother, asking if they could meet that day.

She accepted the invitation, of course. She didn't tell Matt because he'd already left for work; his truck was gone from his driveway. But he was expecting his mother to contact her, so it wouldn't have come as a surprise to him, anyway. She just wished that he was as interested in the book as his mom was. That would certainly make things easier.

She headed over to the lodge, where Julie and her husband had their own suite of rooms in a quiet section of the east wing. Her anxiety mounting, she knocked on their door. A moment later, a tall, lanky man with weathered skin and thinning gray hair answered it. When he smiled, the crow's feet around his pale blue eyes crinkled. He was probably around Kirby's age, maybe sixty or so. But other than that, they weren't anything alike. This old cowboy had an unassuming disposition, whereas Kirby took center stage, even when he was trying to be humble.

"I'm Lester," he said. "Come on in. Julie will be with you shortly."

"Thank you." Libby entered the main room and glanced around. Amid the woodsy decor were magazines spread out on tabletops and plaid pillows tossed on the beige-and-brown sofa. Family photos decorated the fireplace mantel. Unable to help herself, she wandered over to them. Some were of Matt when he was a kid. A handsome boy, she thought, with familiar eyes.

"I didn't know him back then," Lester said, joining her at the mantel.

"But you know him now."

"Yes, I do. He's a good man, strong and kind and generous. He gave me a job when I needed one, and now I'm married to his mama." He gestured to a picture of an older couple. "Those are his grandparents. Julie's folks."

They looked happy, smiling in front of a Christmas tree, with opened gifts strewn on the floor at their feet. "It's too bad Matt never got to meet them. He told me that they died before he was born."

"A month apart. Can you imagine? Julie still misses them. It's a shame that they aren't here."

"How did they pass, so soon apart?"

"He was sick with cancer, and she had heart failure."

Libby studied the photo. Then she glanced at one of Matt's childhood pictures, where he sat outside on a fence rail, his boots layered with dust. She guessed him to be about seven, eight at the most. He was wearing a cowboy hat that was far too big for him. She realized it was the same hat his grandfather was wearing in the

Christmas picture. She quickly surmised that his mother had probably given it to him as a keepsake.

Lester interrupted the quiet. "Can I offer you a snack? I've got a pot of coffee ready to go, and Julie made some bean bread this morning. That's why she's running late. She was bustling around the kitchen after she called you. She wanted to have something special for you to nibble on. It's a modern recipe based on an old Cherokee dish."

"That sounds great." Libby hadn't eaten breakfast. She'd been in too much of a hurry to come here. "I appreciate her thinking of me."

He led her to the kitchen. "Have a seat, and I'll get it for you."

She scooted onto one of the dining chairs. The table was round, scratched up a bit, with sturdy legs and a traditional Western star inlay pattern in the center. A matching hutch stood nearby.

"How do you take your coffee?" Lester asked.

"Truthfully, with anything you've got. Milk, cream, sugar, the fake sweeteners. I mix it altogether."

He chuckled and loaded up the table with her request. "Julie likes those flavored creamers. Hazelnut is her favorite." He set that out, as well.

"Thanks." Libby added a dollop to her cup, along with everything else. "When I first started drinking coffee, I couldn't decide how I liked it best, so I just went for it all."

"You sound like an adventurous gal." He placed a hearty piece of the bread in front of her, along with a napkin and a fork. "This is mostly made from corn, but you can see some of the pinto beans in there. We slather ours with butter," he said, offering it to her. "Some folks put sugar or syrup on theirs. It can also be eaten with meat and gravy."

She spread the butter and took a bite. "It's wonderful." The bread was thick and filling, with a homemade flavor. "I could make a meal out of this."

"Glad you like it. Julie is all aflutter about making a good impression on you. The book you're writing has got her coming and going. She barely slept a wink last night, and this morning she was rushing around like a headless chicken. She really wants Matt and his daddy to reconcile."

"Me, too." Libby continued eating. "I keep hoping he'll come around to the idea. But he hasn't yet."

"I'll leave that up to you and his mama." He patted the back of her chair. "I need to head off to work. But first, I'll check on Julie and let her know you're enjoying her bread."

"Boy, am I ever." By now, her plate was down to crumbs.

"If you're hankering for more, just help yourself." He gestured to the pan on the stove. "Eat as much as you want."

"Thanks. I will."

After he left the room, she went ahead and took another piece, then resumed her seat and glanced out the window. She liked the ambience at Matt's mother's suite.

When Julie dashed into the kitchen, Libby snapped to attention. She was a striking woman with straight, shoulder-length black hair and elegant bone structure. She wore a red blouse tucked into a pair of boot-cut jeans. Her only jewelry was her wedding band. Her makeup was minimal, mostly just a splash of cherry lip gloss that accentuated her blouse. She was in her early fifties, but looked much younger.

"I'm so sorry I'm late," she said. "But Lester already told you how scattered I've been since I found out about

Kirby's biography." She paused as if to compose herself. "It really is a pleasure to meet you."

"It's wonderful to meet you, too." Libby stood to shake her hand. "The bread you made for me is delicious. I'm on my second helping."

"It's one of Matt's favorites. I was hoping you would like it, too."

"I definitely do." Libby sat down again. "I've become friends with your son, even if he doesn't approve of the book."

"Matt is touchy when it comes to his father. But it's been a long, hard road for him, having Kirby as his dad." Julie gestured to her coffee. "Would you like a refill?"

"Thanks, but I'm good. Your husband is quite the host."

"Lester is a sweetheart." Julie poured herself a cup and joined Libby at the table. "I'm lucky to have him." She added the hazelnut creamer and stirred it. "Before we get started, I want to clarify that I'm not ready to be interviewed. This is just an informal talk."

"Don't worry. I'm not going to rush you into anything." Libby understood that Matt's mother probably needed time to work through the past and consider the things she was willing to share. "I already explained over the phone that you'll have to sign a release for our conversations to be official and for me to record you. So for now you can just say whatever you want, and we can start over on another day when you're ready to do a formal interview. I want this to be a comfortable experience for you."

"Maybe I should start at the beginning, with how Kirby and I met and why I allowed myself to become his mistress." She glanced up from her cup. "If I tell you all of this now, I think it will be easier for me to repeat it later for the book."

"I agree." Libby wanted to hear as much as Matt's mother was willing to tell her, on and off the record.

"Okay, let's get started then," Julie said, nervously clasping her hands in her lap. "I met Kirby when I was twenty. It was a difficult time in my life. I'd already lost my parents and was feeling terribly alone. After they passed, I moved in with my best friend and her boyfriend, but we had a falling out because I didn't get along with her boyfriend. So they asked me to leave their apartment."

Julie blew out an audible breath, as if the memory still pained her. "At the time I was in Austin, working at a horse boarding facility. I was also taking animal husbandry classes at a community college. I checked the bulletin boards at school and found a new roommate. After I moved in, she invited me to attend Kirby's concert with her. She'd won two free tickets from a local radio station and didn't have anyone to go with. She was new to the area and hadn't really made any friends."

Libby curiously asked, "Were you a fan of Kirby's?"

"I didn't know anything about him as a person, but I loved his music. It was especially exciting because the tickets included backstage passes, and it was the first time either of us had ever been backstage at a show."

Intrigued, Libby imagined the scenario in her mind, picturing Julia as a younger woman, en route to a concert that would ultimately change her life.

"After the show, we went to this area where there was food and drinks with some folding tables and chairs set up for the guests. Our passes weren't the all-access kind, where we could go back to the dressing rooms or anything like that. We were disappointed at first. We envisioned something grander."

Libby understood. She knew how the levels of backstage access worked and that it wasn't nearly as glamorous as people thought. "Did Kirby come out to where you were?"

"It took a while, but he finally did. And then he kept looking over and smiling at us, flirting, if you will. But he didn't approach us, and we were too shy to go over to him. He was surrounded by other people."

"So how did you meet him?"

"After he went back to his dressing room, his manager came over to us and said that Kirby was having a party the following night at his hotel and that we were invited. But my roommate couldn't go. She was going out of town for a family wedding that weekend. I debated what to do, and if I was brave enough to attend Kirby's party by myself."

"I assume that you were."

Julie nodded. "It was the scariest thing I'd ever done. Kirby had a suite that overlooked the city, and I went traipsing up there, this little nobody, totally out of my element. I was too nervous to mingle. All I wanted was to get out of there. And just as I was planning on leaving, Kirby came up to me. He told me that he'd been looking for me and my friend, hoping that we came. But mostly it was me he wanted to see. I was the reason he invited us."

Here was where the plot thickened, Libby thought.

A range of emotions crossed Julie's face. She sat quietly for a moment before she said, "He was the most compelling man I'd ever met, so rough and wild and charming. He wasn't partial to groupies or women who threw themselves at him. He liked that I was a regular girl." A frown creased her brow. "He told me that he was married, but that he and his wife had an understanding. I should have walked away then. Being with a married man, under any circumstances, wasn't within my moral compass. But God forgive me, I got swept up in it."

"How often did you see him after that?"

"Just here and there. He would send me airline tickets so I could meet him on the road. I kept it from my roommate. I didn't want her to know I was sleeping with a married man. In fact, I lied and told her that I never went to the party. She had no idea that I'd even met Kirby. I pretended that I had out-of-town jobs on the weekends I was gone. After a while, it didn't matter because she went back to the little farm town in Iowa where she was from, and I moved into a big fancy apartment that Kirby paid for. He pretty much paid for everything, so I quit my job and went to school full-time. But I had to be available whenever he needed me. I kept telling myself that it didn't matter that he was married or that he had two small boys. According to my newfound rationale, I wasn't a home wrecker. He'd told me that his wife's only stipulation in their arrangement was that he didn't have any kids with anyone except her, so I wasn't breaking any of their rules." Julie sighed. "About a year later, I got pregnant."

Silent, Libby nodded.

Julie shifted in her seat. "I was on the Pill, and I was diligent about taking it. I never missed a dose. So the best I can figure is that I threw it up on one of the nights when I had too much wine with Kirby. I've never been much of a drinker, and I don't handle alcohol very well."

"How did Kirby react when you told him about the baby?" About Matt, Libby thought.

"He went nuts, freaking out about what to do. He

didn't ask me to terminate the pregnancy because he knew that wasn't an option for me, not with my spiritual beliefs. Finally, he said that we would just have to keep it a secret so his wife never found out. And that's what we did, for many, many years." Tension edged Julie's voice. "I wasn't Kirby's only mistress. But eventually, I was the one who ended his marriage. Melinda divorced him when she discovered Matt's existence."

"I know, but she's friends with Kirby again. In fact, she wants to meet Matt. She's interested in knowing him. So are his brothers."

"Really? Oh, thank goodness." Julie relaxed a bit. "My guilt has been eating away at me all these years, with the way I hurt her and her children. I realize it was Kirby who kept the truth from them, but I was still part of the lie."

"Matt told me how faithful you were to Kirby. The years you spent being loyal to him, staying up at night, waiting for him to visit."

"It sounds crazy when I look back on it. But he was the father of my child, and I loved him as much as a woman can love a man who's sharing himself with other women. I think he loved me, too, in his own needy way. But he was as guilty as I was, so our relationship never really made much sense. Plus there were his drug and alcohol problems. He had all sorts of demons."

"He's conquered most of them, except for the way he abandoned Matt. Aside from this book, Kirby doesn't know what else to do to get Matt's attention."

"Matt has other issues. Not only what he suffered from Kirby."

"I'm aware of his divorce and how it affected him." Libby knew he was more than just Kirby's secret son.

Julie seemed surprised, her cup coming to a halt midway to her mouth. "He told you about Sandy and her children?"

"Yes, and I've been telling him about my deceased husband and my son. I'm a widow, too."

"Oh, my." Julie was still holding her cup in the same position, without drinking, without moving. "I'm so sorry you lost someone you loved." Her gaze turned soft and searching. "I'm glad you're friends with my son. That you're confiding in each other."

"I'm glad, too." But there was more to Libby's feelings for Matt than she was letting on: the ever-raging battle of their attraction. She couldn't say that to his mother.

"I'm convinced that Matt reconciling with his father is the right thing to do. I think it'll help Matt move on with his life."

"I agree. But so far I haven't been able to bring him around to my way of thinking."

"You must be more influential than you're giving yourself credit for or Matt wouldn't have told you so many personal things about himself. He doesn't do that with just anyone."

"We've established a deep rapport." But a confusing one, too. Nothing in her research had prepared her for being as attached to Matt as she was. But again, she didn't reveal that to his mother. Libby was being cautious, keeping her romantic notions to herself.

At ten o'clock that night, Libby climbed out of a long, warm bath and put on a pair of blue silk pajamas. Her hair was pinned up, with damp tendrils curling around her face.

A knock sounded on her door, and she assumed it was Matt. She hadn't seen him all day. Besides, who else would show up at her cabin like this?

Sure enough, when she opened the door, there he was, standing under the porch light, his T-shirt stretched across his shoulders and his jeans fitting in all the right places.

He gazed at her pajamas. "Oh, I'm sorry. Were you on your way to bed?"

"Not yet. I just was going to make a cup of herb tea. But now that you're here, why don't you come and join me?" She couldn't very well send him away.

"Okay." He crossed the threshold. "I just got off work. I was swamped this evening, but I wanted to see how your knee was doing."

"It's fine. Hardly noticeable anymore." Unlike the pounding of her heart. Last night he'd carried her to bed to doctor her knee, and tonight he was here again, checking up on her.

He followed her into the kitchen, and she put the water on to boil. While they waited, he said, "Those match your eyes."

"What does?"

"Your pj's."

Her breath lodged in her throat. She wasn't wearing a bra, and now her nipples were getting hard—a reaction to being around him. She wished the water would hurry up and boil.

He shifted his stance. "That color looks pretty on you."

"Thank you." She reached up to remove the pins from her hair and let it fall. "I forgot to take my hair down after I got out of the bath." She pulled some long strands forward, trying to camouflage the outline of her nipples.

Her hair wasn't covering her all the way, but he didn't appear to notice her dilemma. Or he was pretending not to. She could have kissed him for that. Well, maybe not kissed him, exactly. Not for real, anyway.

He said, "I don't drink tea very often."

She removed two plain white cups from the cabinet, glad that he'd said something mundane. She could handle normal, everyday conversation. "I prefer coffee, but herb tea is nice at night."

"I think the water is ready."

Libby glanced at the pot. It was just starting to bubble. "You're right." She put the tea bags in their cups and poured the water. "Do you want sugar or anything?"

"No, thanks. It'll be fine the way it is."

"For me, too."

"You don't put all sorts of junk in your tea?"

"I just do that to my coffee." She dunked her tea bag, making the liquid stronger and darker.

Matt did the same thing. Then they both removed the bags and set them in the sink.

He sipped his tea first. "This tastes pretty good. It smells good, too." In a quiet voice, he added, "So do you, Libby. Like flowers or something."

Heat rose in her cheeks, and it wasn't just from her teacup. Damn him for putting her in this predicament. He was back to saying things she wished he wouldn't say.

He continued, "On the first night we danced together, you smelled lemony. And on the day you came to my place dressed in that motorcycle-type gear, you smelled spicy."

"I like to change up my fragrances." Tonight she'd used rose-scented bath salts.

"It all works on you." He glanced toward the living room. "Should we sit a spell?"

She nodded. Standing in the kitchen talking about how good she smelled certainly wasn't helping the situation.

They went over to the sofa and sat down. Before he

said something else that disturbed her, she asked, "Did your mother tell you that I met with her this morning?"

"No, she didn't." He put his cup on the end table next to him. "I haven't seen her today." Frowning, he asked, "How did it go?"

"It was an informal discussion. Not an interview."

"Is she going to let you interview her?"

"Yes. She just needs a bit of time to think about how much information she's willing to share."

"What did she share with you today?"

Libby cocked her head. "I thought you didn't want me to tell you."

"You're right, I don't. I just got curious for a second. But forget I asked." He waved away his interest. "I don't want to hear about my mom's relationship with Kirby. I lived through enough of it already. It'll just bug me all over again."

Libby agreed that this wasn't the time to discuss it. But since neither of them could think of anything else to say, they slipped into a bout of painfully awkward silence.

He looked into her eyes, capturing her gaze with his, and that was all it took for the sexual awareness to come back.

Her pulse ticked like a time bomb. His was probably doing the same. Now what were they supposed to do? Stare at each other half the night, with heat zigzagging between them?

She'd never been so frazzled in all her life.

# Seven

When Libby finally summoned the strength to break eye contact, the only thing she managed to do was glance down at Matt's jeans. She noticed how the denim was worn and faded at the seams, with tiny gold threads coming loose. It seemed symbolic, somehow. She was unraveling, too.

He breathed roughly, heavily. "I should probably go home."

He definitely should. But she didn't want him to leave. As overwhelming as it was, she longed to keep him as close as she could, for as long as she could. Clearly, she was losing her mind, going time-bomb crazy. Her pulse was still ticking away.

She forced herself to say, "You can stay awhile. We'll get through it."

"Will we really?" he asked.

She lifted her gaze to his face, to his black hair. He

was as dark and thrilling as a man could be. If she inhaled deeply enough she could even smell the ranch, the hay and horses, on his skin. She imagined it mingling with the rose-soft scent of her bath salts.

He cleared his throat. Or tried to. "If I stay, I'm just going to sit here and fantasize about putting my hands all over you."

She fidgeted with her top, where her nipples were still pressing against the fabric. "That's what I do, especially when I'm in bed. I think about you touching me."

He scooted closer to her, his leg nearly bumping hers. "You're tempting me to make our fantasies come true, but I know I'm not supposed to."

She should end this now and tell him to go home. Tell him that he was right about leaving. But it wouldn't change anything. She would just wake up tomorrow feeling the same way.

"Maybe we should stop fighting it," she said. Maybe it was insane to think they could keep drowning in desire and not do anything about it. "Maybe you should just stay the night."

*There.* She'd made the decision.

He seemed ready to pounce, his reflexes on carnal alert. But he hesitated and asked, "Are you sure?"

"I'm positive." Or as positive as she could be with the desire that was spiraling through her veins and clouding her judgment. "Except that we need to use protection, and I certainly don't have any."

"I have some. But they're—"

"You don't have to explain." She didn't need to know why he was carrying condoms around, if they were tucked away in his wallet from when he was married or placed there after the divorce. His celibacy was about to be broken, either way.

She reached for him, and he reacted quickly. He pushed her down on the couch, climbed on top of her and kissed her.

Hotly. Roughly. Passionately.

He undid her top, opening the first three buttons and slipping his hands inside the material to cup her breasts. He thumbed her nipples, and she lifted her hips and rubbed against his fly, wanting to feel the hardness beneath his zipper.

He kissed his way to her neck and scraped her with his teeth. He went lower, nibbling at her collarbone.

When he undid the rest of her buttons and opened her top all the way, she caught her breath. He took one of her nipples straight into his mouth.

Libby thrust her hands into his hair, tugging on the short, choppy strands. He lowered a roving hand into her pajama bottoms, pushed past her panties and touched her in the most intimate of places. He used his fingers, toying with her senses.

She blinked through the haze and focused on the beamed ceiling dappled in light. Was she actually sprawled out on the sofa, with Matt doing wicked things to her? "If you keep doing that, I'm going to come."

"That's the idea." He moved his mouth to her other nipple, his hand still wedged in her panties.

She wanted to feel him up, too, but she couldn't. She was pinned beneath him, his weight holding her in place. Was this how women felt in bondage situations? Was this why they enjoyed it, giving themselves over to the men who dominated them?

Libby was giving herself over to Matt. He could do whatever he wanted, and she would let him. Every pull of his mouth, every slick rub of his hand, every hot, erotic sensation made her wonderfully weak. Or maybe they were making her sinfully strong.

Whatever it was, he commanded her to his will. He tugged her pajama bottoms past her hips, along with her panties, removing them and leaving her bare to his touch. In the next wild-hearted instant, he went down on her, burying his face between her legs.

She gazed up at the ceiling again, afraid the roof was going to crash and tumble down on her. It was like being in the middle of an earthquake. Or maybe it was more like a tornado, with the way she was twisting and turning and rocking against Matt. Had she ever been this wet, this warm or this eager to be pleasured? She couldn't have stopped him if she tried. His tongue was on her trigger.

Libby convulsed when she came, every nerve ending in her body fusing in fire. She curled her toes into the couch; she dragged oxygen into her lungs; she did whatever she could to survive it.

After the climax ended, she lay there, dazed from the feeling. She meant to smile at Matt, but then he sat up and said, "Now I really do have to go home."

"You're leaving?" After what he'd just done to her? She reached for her panties and put them back on, trapped in a sudden wave of self-consciousness. "Why?"

"To get the protection. It's at my cabin." He shook his head, as if he was confused. "And why are you covering yourself up?"

She let out the breath she'd been holding. "I felt weird sitting here with no underwear on."

"But why?"

"I didn't understand why you were going home. I assumed you had the protection on you." A mistake, obviously, since she hadn't let him explain earlier.

A muscle twitched in his jaw. "Did you think I was going home for good?"

"I wasn't sure."

"I would never leave in the middle of us being together. I want to make love with you so damned bad."

Excited by his admission, she squeezed her thighs together. "Then hurry back and take me to bed."

"I will. But are you sure you're going to be okay with this?"

"I'm going to be fine, Matt."

"Okay, but you seem sort of vulnerable, even now."

"That's because of us getting our wires crossed." She leaned forward, kissing him, showing him that she wasn't a damsel in distress. She wasn't sure how convincing she was, because he was very gentle as he returned her affection.

She refused to swoon, to get all girlie and such. Instead, she pushed him away and said, "Go. Before I start biting you."

"Oh, yeah?" He grabbed her and set her on her feet. "Just wait here for me, exactly as you are."

"Hot and ready for you?" She would wait the entire night if she had to. "That's not a problem." Not as much as she wanted him.

Matt dashed over to his cabin, went into his bedroom, grabbed a handful of condoms and stuffed them in his pocket.

Was he doing the right thing? Was Libby really going to be okay? She insisted that having sex with him wasn't going to mess with her emotions, and he hoped that was true. He knew how quickly a woman could cry. Or curl into a ball. Or stare into space, wishing her husband was still alive, the way Sandy had.

He went outside and stood on his porch, breathing in the night air. If only Libby didn't have the pain of being a widow. But he couldn't change who she was, any more than he could change who he was.

He returned to her cabin and opened her door. She stood in the same spot, waiting for him, just as he'd asked her to.

"I'm ready," he said.

"Then let's do this." She went over to him, took his hand and led him to her bedroom, where a night-light was already burning, soft and low.

He wondered what her bedroom was like at her house in California. But he knew he was never going to find out. His affair with Libby would be limited to Texas, to the remaining time she was here.

He removed the condoms from his pocket and tossed them onto the nightstand. The packets glittered as they scattered on the wood surface. "I figured it wouldn't hurt to have extras."

"It won't hurt at all." She gazed at him from beneath her lashes. "Is your heart beating as fast as mine?"

"It depends on how fast yours is going." His was thumping like a monster rattling its cage. He removed his boots then peeled off his T-shirt, pulling it over his head and tossing it aside. He undid the top button on his jeans, too, relieving the pressure. He was getting hard just standing here, thinking about being with her.

She moved closer, running her hand down his stomach, then past his navel, heading farther and farther south. A sound of pleasure erupted from his throat and escaped his lips. He loved being steeped in her foreplay.

She unzipped his jeans, reached into his pants and stroked him. He could have come on the spot. But he didn't, of course. He wasn't a kid and this wasn't his first rodeo. He was a grown man with plenty of control.

"I could get on my knees for you," she said.

Holy hell. He jerked forward. "Let's save that for another time." Control aside, he wanted this to last as long as it possibly could.

"But you already did it to me."

"That's different."

"It's a double standard, that's what it is."

He kissed her, just to shut her up. Or maybe he did it because he was desperate to put his tongue in her mouth.

Yeah, he thought. It was as primal and basic as that.

In a sensual blur, they got into bed, tousling the covers and kissing some more. Somehow, he managed to shed the rest of his clothes. She got rid of what was left of hers, too.

Finally, they were naked together, with lust curling low in his belly. She was wet and ready and grinding against him.

Matt took a condom off the nightstand and tore into the package. She watched as he put on the protection.

Then all at once, he pushed himself inside her, air hissing between his teeth. She wrapped her legs around him, and he began to thrust with a strong rocking motion.

He didn't stay on top for long. He shifted to another position, rolling her over so she was straddling him.

"Now you can show me what kind of cowgirl you are," he said, poking fun at all of the times he'd treated her like a city girl.

She tossed her head and smiled. "I'll just go for a nice, long, hard ride."

"Damn right, you will." Encouraging her to do just that, he circled his hands around her waist.

She impaled herself, taking him deep. Matt's eyes nearly rolled to the back of his head. She moved up and down, her skin glowing in the light.

She was the most provocative cowgirl he'd ever seen, and for now she was his. He liked being in possession of her. It almost made him feel married again.

Almost, he told himself. There was more to marriage than hot-blooded, hip-thrusting sex. If it had been that easy, he would still have a wife.

"Kiss me," he said, giving her a passionate order.

She leaned forward and bit him, making good on her threat from earlier. He growled and nipped her right back. But they kissed, too, as roughly as they could.

He tightened his grip on her. A few bewitching minutes later, he shifted their positions again. He wanted to finish while he was on top.

He practically pounded her into the bed, moving fast and hard. It was dangerously wild. He twined her hair around his fingers, tugging on the wavy blond strands.

Her big blue eyes bored into his. She looked beautifully, savagely ravished, her skin flushed with animalistic fever. Her appetite was as feral as his.

"I'll hold you when it's over," he said.

She dug her nails into his shoulders, leaving halfmoon marks on his skin. "I'm not concerned about that."

"I am." He wanted the afterglow to mean something, not be mired in regret. But for now he just needed to come. And make her come, too. Matt was determined for it all to happen at the same time.

And it did. So help him, it did.

He used his fingers to guide her to her climax. He didn't need any more coaxing. He closed his eyes and let himself explode into a thousand jagged pieces.

With Libby shattering beneath him.

* * *

Libby sank into the bed, her limbs wobbly, her body spent.

Matt got up to discard the condom, and when he returned, he took her in his arms. Holding her, as he'd told her he would.

"You don't have to baby me," she said.

"I'm not babying you. I'm treating you like I'm supposed to."

"I'm not going to break." She didn't need as much attention as he was giving her. She'd already told him, countless times, that she wasn't going to get emotional over sleeping with him. So why did he have to keep pushing the issue? "I'm not the type you have to fuss over."

"So Becker never held you after sex?"

"Of course he did." And now the memory was jabbing her straight in the heart. But so was Matt's concern for her. She couldn't bear the cautious way he was looking at her. "But not every time. Sometimes we just rolled over and went to sleep."

He frowned. "So that's what you want me to do? To roll over and let you sleep?"

She sighed, realizing that she didn't actually know what she wanted. This was strangely new to her. As amazing as it was, there was no familiarity in being with Matt. He wasn't her boyfriend or her husband or the father of her child. There was no commitment between them.

"You can hold me," she said, doing her darnedest to figure it out, to let it flow, to make it as natural as it could be. "But not because I'm going to fall apart or because you think it's your obligation. Just do it because it feels nice."

"It does feel nice." He tucked her in the crook of his arm. "Everything with you does."

Libby snuggled closer to him, and suddenly this mattered far more than she could say. The warmth and kindness he was offering, the romantic way in which he wrapped her in his embrace. She put her head against his chest and listened to the beat of his heart. Being naked with him, warm and toasty in her bed, was heaven on earth.

But was that a good thing? she asked herself. Or would it only serve to make her more attached to him than she should be?

"I'm going to take the day off tomorrow," he said.

Fascinated with his body, with how big and strong it was against hers, she skimmed her fingers along his abs. "To hang out with me?"

"Absolutely. I won't be able to work with you on my mind. It'll drive me batty."

She stopped just shy of moving her hand lower, of making him hard, of arousing him again, even though she wanted to. "How long are we going to do this?"

"Do what? Have sex?" He nuzzled her cheek. "For as long as you're at the ranch." He nipped her earlobe, his voice sending chills up her spine. "I'm game if you are."

She shivered from his touch, his playfulness, his sexiness. "My mother and Chance will be here soon. It'll be difficult for us to be together then."

"We'll just do the best we can." He covered her hand with his and nudged it between his legs, encouraging her to stroke him, just the way she wanted to.

She rubbed her thumb over the tip, memorizing the shape of him, creating familiarity. "Are we making up for lost time already?"

"Yes, ma'am." He shifted onto his side. "I'm going to be ready to go again."

"I can tell." His erection was growing, popping up and pressing between them. "And just so you know, I like it when you call me ma'am. It's so country boy of you."

"That's what I am. A guy who owns a ranch."

He was also the abandoned son of a celebrity and the former husband of a lost and lonely widow. Those were major facets of Matt's personality. But Libby didn't say that out loud. They both already knew the effect Kirby's betrayal and Sandy's grief had on him.

"What are you thinking about?" he asked, watching her through curious eyes.

"Nothing," she lied. "I just want you inside me again."

"I'm here for whatever you want." He kissed her, long and sweet and slow.

Libby sighed. Maybe it wasn't so bad being with a man who understood the emotional needs of a woman, who cared so deeply about giving his partner comfort. Even if Libby wasn't broken inside, she still had moments of feeling lost and lonely, too. If she didn't, she wouldn't be human.

"You're going to have to hold me again afterward," she said. "I want to sleep in your arms."

"I can make that happen." He climbed on top of her, and they kissed some more.

His lips were utterly delicious. She couldn't get enough of him. He removed a condom from the night-stand. But she took it from him and opened the packet, fitting him with the protection. She wanted any and every excuse to touch him.

This time when they made love, it was soft and dreamy. He caressed her, and she smiled at him. They whispered words of encouragement, of tenderness, of togetherness.

It wasn't going to last forever. But for now, it was what Libby needed.

Matt had been awake for hours, watching Libby sleep.

Her face, her features fascinated him. She could look innocent or sultry, depending on how she presented herself. At the moment, she struck him as both. A naughty angel, he thought, with her night-tousled hair strewn across a pillow and the covers bunched around her naked body.

He opened the blinds a crack, letting in more light and giving him a sunnier view of her.

Itching to touch her, he leaned over and skimmed his knuckles, ever so softly, along her jaw.

A second later, he took his hand away and glanced at the clock. It was early, but he was accustomed to ranch hours.

Eventually, Matt got out of bed. He grabbed his jeans off the floor and put them on. Libby's pajama top and panties were on the floor, too.

He went into the bathroom, put some toothpaste on his finger and rubbed it over his teeth. He rinsed and spit. It was the best he could do under the circumstances.

He also needed a shower, but he would rather take one with Libby, so he decided to wait until she was up. He intended to make the most of the time they had left, starting with today.

Matt headed for the kitchen to make a pot of coffee. He brewed it strong and dark and poured himself a cup.

Curious about Libby's domestic habits, he opened the fridge, taking inventory of its contents. Although the ranch offered meals at the lodge, guests could order groceries from the local market and have them delivered. Of course, they could go into town for their own supplies, too. But Libby didn't do that. The only time she'd been to town, as far as he knew, was when he'd taken her there.

Did she like to cook? he wondered. For now, she had mostly fruits, salad stuff and sandwich fixings on hand. But she was by herself. It might be different once her mother and son arrived.

"Good morning," Libby said from behind him.

He closed the fridge. Apparently she was up and about now. He turned around. She was delightfully disheveled, wrapped in a terry-cloth robe embroidered with the Flying Creek Ranch logo.

"Are you hungry?" she asked.

"I wasn't looking for anything to eat."

"Then what were you doing?"

"Truthfully, I was just snooping around."

She cocked her head. "To see what my food preferences are? That's not very exciting."

To him, it was. He figured it was the closest he was going to get to seeing how she lived, short of going to California.

He gestured to her robe. "What have you got on under that thing?"

Her lips curved into a siren's smile. "Nothing."

"Oh, yeah. Would you care to show me?"

"I could, I suppose."

With a flirty air, she flashed him, opening and closing the robe too damned quickly. He barely got to see a smidgen of skin.

He reached for his coffee. "That's not fair."

"It's what you get, cowboy, at this time of the morning." She came closer and peered into his cup. "That looks like motor oil."

"Want to be daring and try it?" He held it under her nose. "Without any of the sweet and creamy junk you put in yours?"

"I'll pass." She glanced down, past his cup. "You forgot to button your jeans."

He glanced down, too. "At least I zipped them. Do you want to go to my house?"

"To your cabin?"

"To the house I built." He wanted Libby to see it for what it was—the big, sprawling place that used to be his home. As close as they'd become, it seemed like the thing to do.

Her eyes turned bright. "I'd love to go there with you. Should we go now? I can hurry and get dressed."

He figured she would jump at the chance. She was always eager to learn more about him. She'd come to the ranch to meet him, after all, and try to interview him for Kirby's biography.

He put his coffee on the counter. Taking her to his house had nothing to do with the book. Nothing about them becoming lovers did.

"Here's the deal," he said. "We're not getting dressed or going anywhere. Not until we get naked again."

She pulled a cute face. "Is that so?"

"Yes, *ma'am*." He put a sexy emphasis on the last part because she'd told him that she liked him calling her that, and he wanted to please her and tease her and make her smile. "You and I are going to get squeaky clean together."

She laughed. "Is that an invitation to shower with you?"

"You bet it is." He kissed her, tasting a fresh burst of

mint on her lips. Apparently she'd brushed her teeth before she came stumbling in here. She might have combed her hair, too. With that long, tumbling mane of hers, it was hard to tell.

Either way, he could have kissed her to the sun and back. Or to the moon. Or the stars. Wherever it took him.

After they separated, she said, "You'll have to use the soap the ranch gives its guests. If you use mine, you'll smell like a girl."

"Yeah, you and all those fancy scents of yours. Come on." He tugged on the belt of her robe, using it as leverage before he hauled her off to the shower.

And stripped her bare.

# Eight

Libby and Matt took turns beneath the spray of water. She went first, using the citrus body wash and shampoo she'd brought from home. By the time she was done, she would probably smell like lemon meringue pie. Somehow she doubted that Matt would mind. He enjoyed her fragrances.

He stood back and watched. In the oversize bathtub doubling as a shower stall, he had plenty of room to observe, to be a tall, dark, silent voyeur. He had a condom handy, but for now they didn't need it. That would come later, Libby thought.

She felt downright scandalous, running her hands over her own body while Matt pierced her with his gaze. Clearly, he was gaining gratification from watching her. He was already half aroused, his erection jutting against his stomach. Every so often, he took a deep and ragged breath, inhaling the scented steam that rose in the air.

Libby took special care washing her breasts, over and around her nipples. Matt kept watching. With deliberate slowness, she moved lower, using the liquid soap between her thighs.

"Tease," he said.

"My, my." She checked out his muscle-roped body. He was nearly fully aroused now. "Look at the state you're in."

"Yeah, and who made me this way?"

She fluttered her lashes. "Was it little ole me?" She stepped out from under the showerhead, making room for him. "I'm done. You can take your turn now."

He switched places with her. But he didn't put on a show the way she did. He moved at a quick and efficient pace, lathering with the plain white bar of soap that was compliments of his ranch. Just as she'd suggested.

"I think you need to slow down a bit." She took the soap from him. "Why don't you let me help?" She focused mostly on his erection, using her hands, making him bigger and harder.

"Is that the only part of me you're going to touch?" he asked in a gruff voice.

"It is for now." She dropped to her knees. Heart skipping a beat, she looked up at him, waiting to see how he would react.

"Libby." His voice turned even huskier. "What am I going to do with you?"

"You're going to enjoy having me around."

His fingertips skimmed her cheek. "I should stop you."

"You already stopped me last night. You have to be good today."

"I think it's more like being bad."

Good. Bad. It was all the same to her. She took him in

her mouth, causing his entire body to shiver. He latched onto her wet hair, twining it around his fingers.

When he rocked his hips, he created a motion that drove her forward, inspiring her to take him deeper.

All the way to the back of her throat.

He gripped her scalp, his hands tight upon her head. He was definitely being good. Or bad. Or whatever either of them chose to call it. He'd fallen under the spell she'd hoped to cast.

Steam continued to rise. The water was still running, too. It splashed from the showerhead, bouncing off Libby's breasts, running down her stomach and pooling around her knees. She imagined how erotic she must look to Matt, doing what she was doing to him. Excitement mounted between them. Giving him pleasure was turning her on, too.

He moved in and out of her mouth, encouraging her to keep going, but when he reached a point where he could no longer endure it, he insisted that she stop. That he needed her. That he wanted her. That he couldn't wait.

Empowered by his urgency, Libby smiled and climbed to her feet. In a matter of seconds, he put on the protection and entered her so hard, she almost banged her head.

So much for being smug.

She flung her arms around his neck, but they struggled to find their rhythm. He was too tall for her to meet his thrusts and for him to stay inside.

Finally, he turned her around and positioned her in front of him. She bent forward and put her palms flat against the wall, using it to brace herself. She also lifted one of her legs onto the side of the tub. It was just what they needed to get around their height difference.

He grabbed her hips and went to town. She moaned,

and he growled in her ear. She loved the sounds he made during sex. She loved how he held her afterward, too—making her feel safe, as if nothing tragic would ever happen to her again.

She gulped a breath of steam. The tub was ridiculously foggy now. And so was her brain. Deep down, she knew that Matt didn't have the power to shelter her from the world. It just seemed as if he did.

This kind, beautiful man. This fantasy cowboy of hers.

He was pushing her toward an orgasm. Already he knew what to do to make her come, as their bodies slapped together with such heat that it made her head swim. She pitched forward, giving in to the passion.

After it was over, after he came, too, she turned around and sagged against him, falling into his arms and letting him be her protector. Or at least the warm, sweet illusion of one.

After Matt and Libby got dressed and made instant oatmeal for breakfast, he took her to the house he'd built. But as soon as they arrived, he questioned his reasoning for bringing her here. This house wasn't just the place where he'd lived with Sandy and the twins. It held a frustrating connection to Kirby, too.

"The architecture is beautiful," Libby said as they exited his truck and stood in the yard.

"I wanted it to be rustic, but modern, too, to fit with the rest of the ranch." The grounds were elegantly landscaped, with acres of grass and towering trees.

"It looks like a country mansion."

He shrugged, making light of its size. "When I built it, I was planning on having a family someday." He unlocked the door, and they entered the living room. Everything was still fully furnished, exactly the same as when he'd lived here. "When I moved into the cabin where I am now, all I took were a few suitcases."

She glanced around. "You have impeccable taste."

"I didn't do this myself. I used a decorator, the same one who decorated the lodge and the cabins. But I wanted it to have a homey feeling, with the brick walls and limestone floors. Or my kind of homey, I guess. Even with how big it is."

They wandered into the kitchen, and she said, "It would be fun to cook in here. You've got a wonderful setup."

"I've got a great patio out back for barbecuing, too." He leaned against the counter, giving her the full story. "I did have a family in mind when I built this place, but there was a part of me that was trying to compete with Kirby, too. I knew that he had a compound in Nashville, and I wanted to have something grand, too. I realize this is nowhere near what he has, but it made me feel better to spoil myself." He made a tight face. "And then later, it didn't matter. A house is just a house. It's people who make it a home."

"Some guys would have blown their trust fund on frivolous things. You built a recreational ranch, along with a home for yourself. There's nothing wrong with that."

"At first I wanted to throw the money back in Kirby's face. Or do something frivolous with it, as you said. But then I decided that after I got the ranch going, after it was a success, I would return the money to the trust. I wanted Kirby to know that I was making it on my own and I was never going to touch his money again." He paused and added, "I also wanted to work toward having a wife and kids someday. Needless to say, my divorce hit me hard. But I'm trying to get over it."

Libby stood near a window, where sunlight danced through the glass. "By having an affair with me?"

"It is a damn fine affair." He admired the way the sun highlighted the whiteness of her hair, giving her a snow-in-the-summer quality. "We should have given in sooner than we did."

"At least we're doing something about it now."

He thought about what she'd done to him in the shower. "I'll say." A second later, he got a brainstorm. "We should sleep here tonight."

She gaped at him. "Does that mean that you're moving back in? Making this your home again?"

"I don't know. Maybe." He didn't want to make a snap decision about that. "But for now, it's better than us bed-hopping between our cabins."

"It would definitely be more convenient."

"Then why don't you stay here for the duration of your trip? We can both move our stuff in today. Your mom and Chance can stay here, too. I've got plenty of room for all of you."

She gaped at him again. "I can't share a room with you while they're here."

"That wasn't what I was suggesting." He would never put her in that position. "You'd be sleeping in one of the guest rooms by then."

"I don't know if me staying here with my family is a good idea. It might be better for me to keep my cabin."

Frustrated by her reluctance, he scowled. "After you leave here, you're taking them with you to Kirby's. So why does he get to be their host, but you won't let me do it?"

"You're right. It isn't fair. But I still don't think it's a good idea."

"Come on, Libby. I want to get to know your son and make a nice impression on your mom. Even if I haven't agreed to participate in the book, I want to show your family that I can be as hospitable as my dad."

"And us staying with you is the only way you can do that?"

"No, but it would make it easier."

"What if my mom figures out that you and I…"

"Is that what you're worried about?" He tried to reassure her. "We'll be as careful as possible. I promise that we won't take any chances that we shouldn't take."

"Okay." She came over to him. "I'll accept your invitation. And I'll tell my mom that you want the opportunity to entertain her and Chance the way Kirby will be entertaining them at his house."

"Thanks. That'd be great." A new idea sprang into his head. "You know what I should do to get the hospitality ball rolling? Get everyone together for a barbecue. I can invite my mom and Lester over when your mom and Chance are here."

"I like that," she readily replied. "It would be nice for our families to get acquainted."

"I think so, too." He reached for her, taking her in his arms. "We're not going to let anyone know that we're sleeping together, but we can certainly show them what good friends we are." He nuzzled her hair. "Exactly how long do we have until your mom and Chance get here?"

She looked up at him. "Three days."

"Then let's get our stuff moved in as soon as we can." He thought about how he'd poked around in her kitchen earlier. "We'll have to empty out your fridge and bring your food here, too. But we can also go into town for groceries."

"How about if I make dinner for you tonight?"

"That sounds great." He would never turn down a home-cooked meal. "You can fix anything you want."

"Spaghetti and meatballs is my specialty, but you have to help."

"I'd be glad to." He wanted to spend as much time with her as possible, in whatever ways he could.

Libby inhaled the aroma of spices. She'd already made a big batch of meatballs that were simmering in a pot of dark, rich sauce.

She put the water on to boil for the pasta and sprinkled in a generous helping of salt. She didn't add oil because all it did was make the noodles greasy, preventing the sauce from sticking to them later. She'd learned that from Becker's grandma. Nonna, as he called her.

She glanced at Matt. She'd put him in charge of the salad, and just for the fun of it she'd taught him how to curl cucumbers and make radishes look like roses. That was more know-how she'd learned from Nonna.

"I miss doing things like this," she said.

He glanced up at her from where he stood at the center island, creating his masterpiece. "Things like what?" He smiled, then winked. "Having affairs? And here I thought I was your first."

"Ha ha." She rolled her eyes. "I was talking about cooking with—" *Oh, my God*, she thought. She'd almost said *my husband*. She recovered quickly and said, "My man."

But that didn't sound much better. The only man she'd ever had besides Matt *was* her husband.

He stilled his knife, gazing at the vegetables in front

of him. "Did you and Becker make this exact meal together?"

"Sometimes we did." By now, her hands were shaking. She couldn't believe she'd nearly referred to Matt as her husband. What part of her brain had conjured up that crazy notion? "Becker was part Italian. This is his maternal grandma's recipe."

Matt's shoulders tensed. "So you chose the same dish for me?"

"I wasn't thinking of how it would affect you." Or how it would affect her, either. "It's just something I wanted to make for you."

"I'm sorry. I didn't mean to cause a fuss. Maybe it's just that Becker is still a bit of a mystery to me."

Her hands hadn't quit shaking. She brushed them against her skirt, using the fabric like an apron. "I've told you lots of things about him."

"You never said what he did for a living. You never said where he's buried, either."

"Becker doesn't have a grave." Her heart squeezed inside her chest. Deciding what to do with his remains had been a painful experience. "He was cremated."

"Did you sprinkle his ashes somewhere special?"

"No." She doubted that anyone other than Matt would be asking her these types of questions. But given his history with Sandy, he probably couldn't help himself. "Becker's ashes are in a gold-and-green urn at my apartment. I chose gold because of the plain gold wedding band I gave him and green because of how environmentally conscious he was. He worked for a company that produced wind turbines and solar panels. He thought of it as an earth-friendly job."

"That's nice that he respected Mother Earth. That he was such a caring guy."

"In the beginning, I thought about getting a permit to sprinkle his ashes at the beach or in the mountains. But I changed my mind. Once I brought his remains home, I took comfort in having them there." She'd realized that she needed a connection to Becker. And so did Chance. Her son had his own sweet and loving concept of death.

Matt watched her, as intense as ever. "I knew you were still grieving."

"Not in the way you think I am."

"But you're still hurting, Libby."

"Of course I am. I lost the man I loved, the father of my child. But I don't need to dwell on it every moment of the day." To stop herself from crying, she took a long, grueling breath, letting it rattle her lungs. "I'm still here, and he isn't. I have to go on with my life, wherever that life takes me."

"For now, it brought you to me."

*For now.* The temporary sound of those words delivered another threat of tears to her eyes. And the last thing she wanted was to bawl in front of Matt.

Anxious, she returned to cooking. It was time to put the spaghetti in the pot. Time to focus. To have a normal affair.

"I'd like to make a deal with you," she said.

He remained at the center island, the salad half made. "What kind of deal?"

"That neither of us falls in love."

He flinched, looking uncomfortably confused. Then he asked, "In the future, like with other people? Or did you mean with each other?"

"With each other." She couldn't handle falling in love with him, and then being in California while he was in Texas and longing for the comfort of his big, strong body next to hers. Nor could she bear to mistake him for her husband, tripping up like that again, putting him in Becker's place. "I just want it to be free and easy."

"That's what I want, too. Loving you would hurt too much, Libby. It would be too much like what happened with Sandy. I've already been stressing about you being a widow."

"Then we're in agreement. We're not going to get more attached than we should."

"Absolutely." He waggled his eyebrows. "We'll just be friends with benefits."

He sauntered over to her and fed her a slice of red bell pepper he'd chopped. She chewed and swallowed, and he said, "I should do you right here."

"Against the stove? With the spaghetti boiling and the meatballs simmering? We'd burn our butts off."

He grinned. "You're right. There's already plenty of steam in here. I'll have to get you after dinner."

"And I'll have to hold you to it."

He angled his head. "Did we just make another deal?"

"So it seems." A sex deal. A no-love deal. They were on a roll. She quickly kissed him and went back to fixing the meal, content with both of the deals they'd made.

Matt sat across from Libby at the dining room table, twining spaghetti around his fork. She sipped her wine, and he watched the ladylike way she curled her fingers around the stem of the glass. He didn't want to fall in love with Libby any more than she wanted to fall for him. And now that she'd brought it up, he felt an overwhelming sense of relief.

He had to give her credit for getting it out in the open. Maybe if he'd done that with Sandy up front, he would have been more cautious about getting involved with her. Maybe he wouldn't have even married her at all. But he didn't have to worry about developing something with Libby that was going to blow up in his face. She'd eliminated the prospect of getting too attached.

So far, he and Libby had only known each other for two weeks. And in another two weeks, she would be leaving for good. To most people, that would seem like nothing. But he'd fallen for Sandy within that amount of time. Things sometimes happened fast. Apparently Libby knew that, too, taking into account how quickly she and Becker had gotten together.

"I'm glad we figured things out," he said.

"So am I. And look at this fabulous dinner we created."

"I didn't do all that much."

"Are you kidding?" She skewered a radish and held it up in the light from the chandelier. "Look at this work of art."

"Me and my trusty knife. Who knew I could do something like that?" He lingered over his spaghetti, pondering his affection for her. He thought about their friendship. Their sexual chemistry. He liked knowing their affair was going to end without hurting more than it should.

She ate the radish. "You know what I just realized? We forgot about dessert for tonight."

"No, we didn't. Or I didn't, anyway. I got a carton of spumoni when we were at the store. You must have been in another aisle when I tossed it into the cart."

"Thanks for thinking of it. Italian ice cream is just what we need to go with this."

"I'm good at remembering the sweet stuff." He flirted with her. "I like sweet women, too."

She flicked a drop of her wine at him, missing him by a mile. "I hope I'm sweet enough for you."

"You definitely are. But you have terrible aim." He flicked his wine at her, hitting his mark.

She laughed, and they finished their main course. When it was time for dessert, they cleared their plates and went into the kitchen together. He took the spumoni out of the freezer and tasted it directly from the carton.

*"Matt,"* she scolded him. "Don't I get some?"

"Of course you do." He gave her the next bite, feeding it to her. "What do you think?"

She sucked it off the spoon. "It's yummy."

He agreed. But not as yummy as what he intended to do to her. He dropped a dollop of the ice cream down the front of her blouse.

"Oh, my God!" She jumped and shivered. "That's cold."

"Sorry. My bad. You better take off your top and let me clean you up."

"You did that on purpose." She removed her blouse, slanting him a wanton look. The spumoni was now dripping into her bra. "Maybe I should take this off, too?"

"Yeah, I think you should. Or maybe you should let me do it." He unfastened the hooks, and without the slightest delay, he licked the dessert off her breasts. He swirled his tongue back and forth, over each pert pink nipple.

She moaned and pulled him closer. "You really are going to do me in the kitchen."

"Damn right, I am." He had a condom in his pocket; he'd put it there earlier for just such an occasion. He was going to carry one everywhere. Or everywhere that Libby would be.

They slid to the floor, and he reached under her skirt and pulled off her panties. But he didn't remove her skirt. He merely bunched it around her hips.

She opened her legs, and he slid between them and

yanked his jeans down. He left the spumoni on the counter. But he wasn't worried about it melting. He intended for this to happen fast. Hard and fast, he thought.

He sheathed himself with the condom and slammed into her, making her gasp from the quick, rough invasion. While he moved deep inside, she fisted his T-shirt, clawing at the material as if it was his skin.

She muttered something deliciously dirty in his ear, and he turned his head and captured her mouth. They mated like animals, rolling all over the floor, the limestone cool against their bodies. Hot sex on a cold surface. It didn't get any freer than that.

He aroused every warm, wet part of her, and she begged him for more. And he gave her everything he could. Libby with the stunning blue eyes, he thought, with the tangled blond hair.

He kissed her again, and she came in a flurry of gyrating thrusts and shaky moans, dragging him into a nail-biting, pelvis-rocking, brain-numbing climax of his own.

Minutes ticked by when neither them could find the strength to move. Finally, he got up, ditched the condom and zipped his pants. When he returned, she was still sprawled out on the floor, topless, with her skirt askew.

"Let me help you." He offered a hand, and she smiled and latched onto him.

Matt grabbed the spumoni and two spoons, and she fished around for her blouse. Locating it near the dishwasher, she put it on, leaving it unbuttoned. Her bra was forgotten.

From there, he took her to his room, where they sat on the bed and dug into the ice cream, enjoying the nighttime coziness of being lovers.

# Nine

After three wondrous days, Libby's sexy stint of sleeping in the master suite with Matt was over. Her mom and Chance would be here this afternoon.

She turned toward Matt. He stood beside an oak armoire, looking as solid and rugged as the furniture. They were in the guest room where she would be staying.

"You seem nervous," he said.

"I'm starting to get worried again that my mom might figure us out."

"We're going to be careful, Libby."

"I know." She glanced at the bed and its sunburst-patterned quilt. It was a lovely room, with all sorts of creature comforts. But she was going to miss sleeping with Matt. She gestured to the adjoining bath. "I staged the bathroom so it looks like I got ready there this morning. I left my toothbrush and toothpaste out. I lined up my fragrances on the counter, too, and left the cap off the perfume I used today."

He came toward her and sniffed her skin. "Do you really think your mom is going to notice something like that?"

"I'm just trying to be thorough."

He jumped onto the bed and pulled her down with him. "I think you're being paranoid."

She squealed when he yanked up her T-shirt and tickled her ribs. She laughed and tried to push him away. "We're making a disaster out of this bed."

"So it'll look like you did a crappy job of making it this morning."

"Are you sure it's not going to look like some big, sexy cowboy ravished me on it?"

"I'm not ravishing you. But I can if you want me to."

"You need to behave." He'd already done a bang-up job of ravishing her every night since she'd moved in with him. He'd had his way with her this morning, too, hauling her into the shower with him. Shower sex had become their thing. Along with kitchen floor sex. And every other kind of sex they could think of.

To keep the tickling at bay, she whopped him with a pillow. He wrestled the pillow away, set it aside and kissed her, soft and slow, his lips tender against hers. But that was as far as it went: a warm, romantic kiss.

She got up and righted her T-shirt. He was still reclining on the bed. She wanted to slip back into his arms, but she refrained. She needed to control her urges for him.

"I'm really glad I'm going to meet your son," he said.

His interest in Chance made her heart beat faster. She had a soft spot when it came to her child. "He's a chatterbox, so don't be surprised if he talks your ear off."

"That's okay." He smiled at her for a breathless moment and climbed off the bed. "His mama talks my ear off sometimes, too."

"I do not." She fluffed the pillow that she'd used to smack him, and together they smoothed the quilt, him on one side, her on the other.

"I'm just trying to lighten your mood."

"I know." Her nerves remained on edge. Libby wasn't used to hiding things from her family. She'd dated Becker openly before she married him. But that was different than what she was doing with Matt. "I just have a lot on my mind."

Matt went quiet. Then he said, "I hope Chance likes the room I chose for him. When the twins were here, I offered each of them their own room, but they wanted to stay together. They were inseparable that way. They brought their bunk beds with them. But all of that is gone now."

"Chance has bunk beds in his room, for when a friend or cousin spends the night. Children that age enjoy pairing up."

"What's your apartment like?" Curiosity colored his voice. There was a searching look in his eyes, too.

"We're on the first floor of a triplex. It's not walkable to the beach, but there's a bus we can take."

"Can't you drive to the beach?"

"Yes, but parking is a nightmare." She thought about how modest her place was. "Becker and I were hoping to buy a house someday, but it wasn't in our budget."

"What about the book advance? Can you use it as a down payment on a condo or something?"

"I wish I could, but property is ridiculously expensive in my area, and I need to live on the advance. For now, that's my only income. I used to supplement my writing with temp jobs. Hopefully I'll get more book deals in the future and won't have to do that again."

"I'm sure you will. You're one of the most ambitious women I've ever known. But you're sweet and homey, too."

"Thank you." That meant a lot coming from him. "I'm doing what I can to be a single mom and have a successful career, too."

"I hope you're able to have your own house someday. At the beach or wherever you want it to be."

For a heart-jarring second, she envisioned living here with him. Clearly, she was losing her marbles; those little suckers were rolling right out of her head. The other day she'd laid down the law about not falling in love, and today she was having cozy thoughts about moving in with him?

Libby needed to get a hold of her emotions, a tight, tight hold on them, especially before Chance and her mom got here.

Chance Mitchell Penn was a whirlwind, a fast-talking, toy-slinging tyke with bright blue eyes. It was only the first day, and he was following Matt all over the house, yapping up a storm. Right off the bat, Matt learned that Chance hated shampooing his hair. In fact, he wore it in a buzz cut to make washing it easier. He didn't like taking baths, either, or going to bed early.

Libby's son had an opinion on everything: steamed vegetables were gross, but raw ones were fun and snappy; girls acted silly when they giggled with their friends, and boys acted stupid when they got into fights. Matt had never been so amused. He adored this kid already. Of course he was trying to keep it in perspective and not get too attached, the way he'd done with the twins when he'd first met them. But damn, Chance was tough to resist.

Libby's mother, Debra, was far more reserved. She

didn't run off at the mouth like Chance. Nor did she dress in flashy clothes like Libby. Although her hair was blond, she sported a short, simple, conservative do. But in spite of their differences, the love between mother and daughter was apparent. He suspected that Libby's father was a decent guy, too. She'd been raised in a normal household. No country star dad or mistress mom.

Not that Matt was blaming his mother. He loved her as much as Libby obviously loved her mom. But he'd always longed for the kind of family Libby had.

"Can I see my room again?" Chance asked Matt.

"If you want to." Matt had already showed it to him twice, but maybe three times would be the charm.

The boy bounced on his heels. "You come, too, Mom." He grabbed Libby's hand, then glanced over at his grandmother, who was seated in a living room recliner, reading the ranch brochure. "You can stay there, Nana."

Debra glanced up. "Why, thanks for that."

"No prob'em," Chance said.

Matt caught Debra's eye, and she sent him a vacation-weary smile. She looked ready for a nap. Traveling with a rambunctious six-year-old had obviously worn her out. But at least Chance was astute enough to know when his grandmother was tired and needed a break.

Chance's room offered a queen-size bed and a picture window with a view of the hills. It also had a big flat-screen TV. All the guest rooms did. Earlier Libby had set the parental controls, which had given Matt a familiar feeling. When the twins first moved in, Sandy had done that, as well.

"This is cool," Chance said. "Can I jump on the bed?"

Matt started to say *why not?* but Libby cut him off and said, "Get real," to her son. That obviously meant no.

The boy shrugged and shifted his feet, rocking back and forth. He'd yet to be still. He gazed up at the ceiling. A second later, he asked Matt, "Did you know my dad is in heaven?"

More déjà vu. The twins used to talk about how their daddy was in heaven, too. "Yes, your mother told me."

Chance kept rocking. "He's in an angel pot at our house."

Matt assumed he was referring to the urn that contained Becker's ashes. He dared a glance at Libby. But she was looking at her son.

"He flies around at night and watches over us," Chance said. "That's what angels who live in pots do. They're sort of like genies, only they don't give you wishes. But if they did, I would wish for my dad to be here with me."

Matt nodded as if he understood. And in his own mixed-up way, he did. He'd lived through something like this before. But as similar as it seemed, it wasn't exactly the same. He wasn't repeating the mistakes he'd made with Sandy. He wasn't going to fall in love with Libby or marry her or compete with her late husband's memory.

"Wanna see some pictures of my dad?" Chance asked.

"Sure. I'd like to see your father." Matt wasn't going to deny the boy.

"Okay, but he wasn't an angel back then. He was just a person. People don't become angels till they go to heaven." Chance nudged Libby. "Go get your phone so I can show him the pictures."

She put a hand on her son's shoulder, but her gaze was on Matt. She smiled, oh so softly, at him. A thank-you, he thought, for indulging her child.

She left the room, and Chance glanced at the bed, as

if he was considering jumping on it while she was gone. Or maybe he was just planning on doing that later, when no one was around.

Libby returned, and the three of them sat on the edge of the bed, with Chance in the middle. As he scrolled through the photographs, he narrated each one. He moved quickly; it was clear that he had them memorized.

Becker was smiling in every picture. He had a happy, relaxed air about him, with a tanned complexion, a neatly trimmed goatee and hair that was long on top and clipped close on the sides, the same medium-brown shade as his son's.

"You look like your dad," Matt said to Chance. They had comparable features, except for the eyes. Those had definitely come from Libby.

"Check this out." Chance stopped at a wedding photo of his parents. "See how big my mom's belly is? That's me in there."

Matt studied the picture. Libby looked young and beautiful, a pregnant bride in her sparkling white gown and spiffy white boots.

He leaned over and said to her, "That's how I imagined you when you described your wedding to me."

"It was the happiest day of my life." She put her arm around Chance. "Along with the day he was born."

Chance scrolled to another photo, an image of his father holding him on his lap. Becker was grinning like a loon.

Libby said, "That's the last picture that was taken of them together."

Matt didn't know how to respond. Even chatty Chance had gone quiet. By now, he could feel the boy staring at him.

Then the kid asked, "Are you a real cowboy?"

The change of topic threw Matt off-kilter. He was still looking at the last-ever picture of Chance and his dad.

"I told you he was," Libby said, chiming in with an answer.

"Yeah, but is he a *real* one?"

"Darned right, I am," Matt said. "When I was your age, I was competing in junior rodeos."

Chance's mouth dropped open. "You were doing that when you were small, like me?"

"I used to ride and rope my little butt off." Matt remembered the joy it gave him in those early years. Without it, he would have been lost. "My mom took me to my events."

Chance was still slack-jawed in wonder. "She must be a great mom."

"Yeah, she is." Not a conventional one, but a great one. "She lives here on the ranch with her husband. They're going to come by later in the week for a barbecue."

The kid looked over at Libby. "Can I learn to become a rodeo cowboy?"

She ran her hand over his buzz cut. "How about if you just pretend to be one for now?"

"That's not the same as doing it." He frowned at the phone in his hand. Somewhere in the midst of their conversation, the screen had gone black. He touched it, bringing the picture of him and Becker back up. "I bet my dad would let me do it if he was here."

Libby sighed. She seemed sad and alone, as widowed as a woman could be. Particularly when she said, "I take you on pony rides at the big park in LA."

Chance pouted. "That's baby stuff."

Matt wondered if he should come to the rescue. Not as a father figure, he warned himself, but as a cowboy.

When he thought Chance might cry, he stepped in and said, "Sometimes I give roping lessons on the ranch. And if it's okay with your mom, I can teach you a few pointers. But we'd be doing it on the ground, not on horseback. That's how everyone learns at first."

"That would be so much fun." Libby's son danced in his seat. "Is it okay, Mom? Is it?"

She nodded, and Chance leaped into her arms and hugged her. After they separated, he grinned at Matt and handed him the phone, tearing off out of the room to tell his grandmother the good news.

Matt and Libby both fell silent. During the gentle pause, Matt returned the phone to her, and she pressed it against her chest. The picture of Becker and Chance was still on the screen.

"I wish I could kiss you for what you did for my son," she said in a whisper.

He wanted to kiss her, too. But he couldn't. Not here. Not like this. He spoke as softly as she did. "Was it your idea to tell him that his dad lived in an angel pot?"

"I told him that the urn was connected to his father and his dad was in heaven, but he came up with the rest of it. I never said that Becker was an angel flying around our house at night. Nor did I mention genies or wishes that couldn't be granted. Becker's family didn't encourage those stories, either." She lowered the phone to her lap. "It's just Chance's way of comforting himself, of rationalizing why his dad can't come back to us."

"I'm sorry he doesn't have a father anymore." Matt couldn't think of anything else to say, except to give his condolences. No child should lose his or her parent.

"He doesn't have many memories of Becker, but he tries to create them. He loves showing off those pictures. But it doesn't always help." Libby tucked a strand of hair behind her ear, where it curled toward her cheek. "I can't thank you enough for offering to teach him to rope. You're already becoming his hero."

A lump formed in his throat. "He's a nice kid."

"And you're a really nice man."

"I just did what I thought was right." He tried to play it down, but with the tender way she was looking at him, he was actually starting to feel like her son's hero.

If only for a little while.

On the day of the family barbecue, Libby analyzed the people gathered around the table. You'd think that Julie and her mom had known each other for years. They hit it off beautifully. Lester was his usual kind self, and Chance was chomping on his burger and smiling at Matt. Chance had loved every moment of his first week on the ranch, and most of his joy had come from spending time with Matt.

As promised, Matt had been teaching him how to rope. The dummy they used—a plastic steer head attached to a bale of straw—was out on the grass. By now, Libby had gotten used to seeing it. Chance had even named it Stanley, short for Stanley the Steer. As for the rest of Chance's gear, Matt had provided him with an extrasoft, kid-sized rope and one cotton glove.

Libby was downright crazy about Matt, especially after seeing how amazing he was with her son, but she was being careful not to let her attraction to him show. So far she'd lucked out with her mom. They'd been keeping Chance and her so busy attending group activities on the ranch, she didn't have time to notice the heat between Libby and Matt.

Matt's mom didn't seem to be aware of it, either. Just yesterday, Libby had interviewed Julie for the book. So in that regard, Libby's work on the ranch was done. Unless Matt miraculously changed his mind and agreed to be interviewed. But that wasn't very likely.

Chance wiggled in his seat, drawing Libby's attention to him. After swallowing the big, messy bite in his mouth, he said to her, "You should have Matt teach you to rope. You'd be good at it. Not as good as I am," he added, being young and boastful, "but still good."

"That's okay. I'd rather watch you." She'd seen how close Matt got to Chance during their lessons. She didn't need Matt getting that close to her, at least not in public. Unfortunately, they weren't doing it in private, either. It wasn't easy to slip off together. In fact, it was proving impossible. They hadn't kissed or touched or done anything even remotely romantic the entire week.

"Come on, Mom. Just try it."

Libby blew out her breath. Chance could be a pest when he wanted something, and at the moment he wanted her to be a roper. She decided that her best line of defense was to change the subject. "How about if you just finish your burger, and let me eat mine?"

Chance rolled his eyes. Just then, Matt turned his gaze on Libby. Apparently he'd been listening to the exchange.

"Don't you want to be a cowgirl?" he asked.

She almost kicked him under the table. He knew darned well that she'd already ridden him like a cowgirl, buck naked on his lap. Surely that counted for something.

"She's probably just scared of Stanley," Chance said.

Great. Her son was back in the game, baiting her.

"That steer head is pretty scary." This came from Libby's mother. *Her mother.* Good grief. So now she was joining in on it, too?

The conversation sparked Julie's interest, as well. She said, "I always thought the ones with the red eyes were a little creepy. But Matt liked them when he was a kid. He thought they looked more menacing."

Libby gazed across the grass at Stanley. Its plastic eyes glowed in the sunlight, glaring at her like balls of fire. Its horns were rather demonic, too. "I'm not scared of the stupid steer head."

Matt's tone was blasé. "It sort of sounds as if you are."

Lester chuckled under his breath before stuffing his face with another spoonful of potato salad.

"This is a conspiracy," Libby said.

"It's just a roping lesson." Matt took a slice of watermelon and put it on his plate. He'd already eaten two burgers and a bacon-wrapped hot dog smothered in cheese. Sometimes that man had an enormous appetite. And not just for food. She knew his hunger all too well.

"Just do it, Mom." Chance refused to let up. "I'll even help you."

"All right. Fine." She gave in. The bigger the stink she made, the worse it was going to get. "When we're done eating, you and Matt can teach me to become a cowgirl." She shot a glance at Matt, and he smiled a bit too triumphantly.

When everyone finished their food, Julie helped Libby's mom clear the table, leaving Libby and Matt free for the lesson. Lester wandered off to have a smoke, and Chance hopped along with Libby and Matt, bouncing like a kangaroo.

"First things first." Matt gave Chance his hat. "Will you hold on to this for me?"

"Sure." The boy plopped it on his own head.

It was too big for him, but he wore it proudly, reminding Libby of the oversize hat Matt had worn in the childhood picture she'd seen of him at his mom's house.

"I'll be back." Matt went into a shed and came back with an adult-sized rope and a glove.

He gave Libby the glove. "This should fit you."

She put it on her right hand.

Her son piped up. "In team roping, the first guy ropes the horns, and he's called a header. The other guy ropes the heels, and he's called a heeler."

Libby knew all of that. Her obsession with cowboys had come from watching rodeos on TV.

Chance adjusted the hat, which kept falling forward on his head. "Matt is a header. That's what he's teaching me to be, too. It's okay for women to be team ropers and to play against the men."

Libby knew that, too. But at the moment, she was more concerned about swooning over her lover than competing with him.

Matt said, "First, I'm going to show you how to a coil a rope." He tossed the rope and demonstrated, explaining each step.

She watched him, listening to him the best she could.

He stood next to her and threw the rope again. "Now you try."

She did her best. But it wasn't quite right. Matt covered her hand with his and showed her again. "See?" he said. "Like this."

Yes, she saw. She felt the warmth of his touch, too.

If he turned her face toward his, she could kiss him, which was the worst thought she could've had. Chance was watching.

"You're doing good, Mom," he said.

No, she wasn't. But she thanked her son, anyway. She certainly wouldn't be roping a steer anytime soon, not even Stanley, with its red, raging eyes. Libby could barely breathe, let alone coil the rope. How in the world was she going to graduate to the next step?

But somehow, she did. Matt moved her along, giving her an accelerated lesson. By then, Julie, Lester and her mom were back on the patio. Libby felt like an animal in a zoo, with everyone watching. Matt was showing her how to build a loop with the rope.

"I did great at this part," Chance said.

Libby sucked at it. "I can't learn this in a day."

Matt brushed up against her, as if it was part of the lesson. Or maybe it was. She couldn't tell anymore.

"We're just doing this for fun," he said.

Her idea of fun would be slipping into his room tonight. Not standing here with an audience, getting weak in the knees.

"Let me take over," Chance said, eager to show off what he knew. He returned Matt's hat, then put on his glove and picked up his rope.

Libby stood back, but not far enough, apparently. Matt reached for her hand and tugged her farther back, making sure that Chance didn't accidentally hit her with the rope. But Libby already felt as if she'd been struck upside the head, wishing she really could slip into Matt's room tonight.

And let him lasso her to the bed.

# Ten

At 1:00 a.m. Libby was awake, thinking about Matt. But she wasn't going to go sneaking into his room. She wouldn't dare risk something like that, not while she was under the same roof as Chance and her mother.

Nonetheless, she switched on the lamp next to her bed. Being in the dark, fretting under the covers, certainly wasn't helping. She could turn on the TV, she supposed. Since sleep eluded her, she needed something to keep her mind occupied.

Just as she reached for the remote, a knock sounded on her door. She jumped out of bed. Was it Chance? No, that didn't make sense. What would he be doing up at this hour? Besides, he wouldn't knock. If he needed her for some reason, he would march right in, bellowing, "Mom!"

Her mother, then? She had no idea why her mom would be awake, either, and coming to see her.

A sudden panic set in. Was it Matt? Was he—

"Libby?" he said from the other side.

Okay, so it was Matt. But dang it, he should know better than to come to her room at this hour. Already the thought of being with him was making her heart pound.

She went to the door, opened it a crack and gazed out at him. He looked as if he'd gotten dressed in a hurry, with no belt, no hat and a T-shirt hanging loose. His midnight-black hair was barely combed.

"What's going on?" she asked.

"My birthing attendant just called. We've got a mare that's getting ready to foal."

"Right now?"

He nodded. "They tend to foal in the middle of the night. Anyway, I noticed that your light was on and I wondered if you wanted to go to the broodmare barn with me." He smiled like a nervous new dad. "I always assist with the births."

She opened the door wider. "I'd love to go with you. I've never seen a mare foal." Human babies tended to arrive in the middle of the night, too. Or Chance did, anyway.

"The labor comes in stages. She's already in the first stage. Once her water breaks, it'll be the second stage and that's when the foal will emerge. The third one is the expulsion of the placenta. But her water is probably going to break anytime now."

"I'll throw myself together and meet you in the living room. I need to write a note, too, to my mom, in case she or Chance wakes up and I'm not here. I doubt they will, but it will make me feel better to do it." She hurriedly asked, "How long do you think we'll be gone?"

"I don't know. It could last until daylight. But more than likely, we'll be back before then."

"I'll tell her it could take all night. Then if she's up before we get back, she won't worry."

"Okay. I'll see you in a few."

He turned and walked away, leaving her with an excited feeling. She rushed to peel off her nightgown and climb into a pair of jeans and an oversize blouse. She didn't have time to fuss with a bra, so she skipped it. No makeup and tousled hair would also have to do. This wasn't a glamour gig.

She dug around in the closet and reached for the nearest boots. She grabbed a jacket and her phone, too.

Next, she scribbled out the note to her mom and headed for the living room. On the way, she put the note on the kitchen table, where it would be most visible.

"Ready?" Matt asked as she approached him.

She nodded. She was good to go.

They climbed in his truck, and he started the engine. He backed out of the driveway and tore off down the private road that led to and from his house.

"Earlier, when I knocked on your door, I noticed your light was already on," he said, repeating what he'd told her when he'd first come to her room. "So what kept you up tonight?" he asked.

"You," she answered honestly. "We haven't been together at all this week."

"I know." He adjusted his hands on the wheel. "It's been making me crazy. I've spent some sleepless nights, too, wondering how we can be alone."

She sent him a goofy grin. "We're alone now."

"Yeah, on our way to birthing a foal." He rewarded her with a foolish grin in return. "If you want, I can send the attendant home after the foal arrives, and if there's time left over, you and I can stay there by ourselves until the sun comes up."

Her pulse spiked. "There won't be any ranch hands around between now and then?"

"No. It'll be just us."

This outing was starting to sound beautifully romantic. So much so, she got a dreamy pang in the center of her stomach. "I hope there's time left over."

"Me, too. We can celebrate with some sparkling cider. When I was a kid, my mom and I did that whenever we had a new foal. I always keep a supply on hand now."

"That's a nice tradition." She was eager to have this experience with him. "We'll have to bring Chance and my mom back later to see the foal."

"Definitely. My mom and Lester, too. They're always happy to have new life around here."

"Who wouldn't be?" She remembered the joy of seeing Chance for the first time. She recalled the long and grueling labor, too. "Why do mares typically foal at night?" she asked.

"They like to feel secure, when there's less activity around them. They can even prolong their labor if they aren't comfortable in their surroundings."

When Libby and Matt arrived at the broodmare barn, it was quiet, giving the mare the security she needed. The attendant, Hector Ramirez, was an older man with lots of experience. The mare, a lovely sorrel quarter horse with a flaxen mane, was known as Annie Oakley.

Annie's timing was spot on. Her water broke soon after Matt and Libby got there. Fascinated, Libby stood on the other side of the stall and watched.

An amniotic sac appeared with the foal inside it. Matt checked to make sure the foal was in the correct position. Apparently it was, with its front feet first and its soles pointing down.

The foal's nose and knees came next. Or that was

how it looked to Libby; she couldn't quite tell because of how it was curled up. Annie rested before the shoulders appeared. Then she finished pushing, until the whole body was free of the birth canal.

The damp foal broke through the water bag and was as adorable as could be. Matt cleared the membrane from its nostrils. Libby smiled. Annie was the proud parent of a perfect little filly.

The passing of the placenta took about an hour. Hector checked to make sure there were no pieces missing, except for the hole where the foal had been.

Neither Matt nor Hector cut the umbilical cord. It happened naturally, when the mare stood to examine her baby. The tenderness between Annie and the foal gave Libby the sweet and unsettling urge to have another child. She glanced over at Matt and imagined having her next baby with him.

*Seriously?*

She squeezed her eyes shut, trying to block the insanity spiraling through her mind. But it wasn't helping. The thought of having a baby with him wouldn't go away.

Matt and Hector exited the stall and headed to the restroom to clean up. Libby stayed where she was, panicking inside.

The men returned, and Matt dismissed Hector. The entire process had gone quickly and efficiently, with plenty of time to spare for Matt and Libby to be alone. After Hector left the barn, Matt came up behind Libby.

"Look," he said. "The foal is standing. She should start nursing soon, too. We need to stay nearby to make sure she eats. Then we can take a break and spend some time together."

She gazed at the little beauty, wobbling on its spindly

legs. Having a baby with Matt was out of the question. Yet the thought kept invading her mind.

Matt slipped his arms around Libby's waist, bringing the back of her body closer to his front. She was glad that he was behind her, giving her time to compose herself. By now, her legs were starting to wobble, worse than the foal's.

Once the filly began taking her first meal, Matt quietly asked, "Did you nurse Chance or was he bottle-fed?"

"I nursed him." But this wasn't a topic she wanted to discuss. It just made her want another baby even more. With Matt, she thought. With a man she vowed *not* to love.

"It's cute how the foal is getting the milk on her whiskers," he said. "I really love being part of this."

"You're going to make a great dad someday." It was a stupid thing to say, especially with the way she was feeling.

"I hope so." He released his hold on her. "We can have the cider now, if you want."

"I'd like that." Her mouth had gone terribly dry.

"Then I'll go get it." He gestured to another section of the barn. "There's an empty stall with fresh straw. You can wait over there. I'll get a blanket for us, too."

While he headed to a supply room, she entered the stall and prayed that her knees wouldn't buckle. Was it possible that she was falling in love with Matt, doing exactly what she wasn't supposed to do? Of course it was possible, she told herself.

Why else would she be feeling this way? She wanted to roll up and die over the ache she knew it was going to cause. How was she going to leave the ranch, loving him, longing for him, missing him beyond reason?

He returned with a big plaid blanket, a bottle of cider and two plastic champagne flutes. He spread the blanket on the straw, and Libby sat down and removed her jacket. She wasn't the least bit relaxed, but she pretended to be.

He joined her on the blanket, opened the bottle and poured their drinks. He tapped his glass to hers and said, "Here's to the new filly on the Flying Creek Ranch."

"What are you going to name her?"

"I don't know. Maybe Chance can help me come up with something."

"That will thrill him, I'm sure." She sipped the cider, grateful for its crisp apple flavor. The carbonation was helping a bit, too. She needed it to settle the jumpiness in her stomach. "He's been having the time of his life here." Not only was Matt teaching her son to rope, they'd been taking Chance out on trail rides with a gentle old mare that Matt had chosen for him to ride. Was it any wonder she was falling in love with Matt? Her son adored him, too.

He drained his glass and refilled it. "I'm impressed with what a fine cowboy Chance is turning out to be. If you're able to keep the riding and roping lessons up, he's really going to improve."

"I'll look into a trainer in my area." She wanted to give Chance the opportunity to grow into whatever he wanted to be. But it pained her to think that Matt wasn't going to part of his future. Or hers. Libby's life was going to seem empty without Matt. So horribly empty. If she could make her feelings for him go away, she would. But it was too late for that. The damage had already been done.

"I can ask around for recommendations for trainers.

Offhand, I don't know anyone in Los Angeles, but I'd be glad to check into it."

"Thank you. That would be helpful." She drank more of her cider and commented on their surroundings. "It's so quiet here now, with just the two of us."

He moved closer. "It's nice. This affair of ours."

Their free-and-easy affair, she thought, mocking herself for coming up with that. She'd already lost her husband, and now she was falling for someone who didn't belong to her. It didn't get more complicated than that.

When he leaned into her, she reached for him, desperate for a kiss. Even as emotionally tormented as she was, she couldn't deny the need to be with him.

Their mouths came together, the sensation passionately familiar. In between kisses, he unbuttoned her blouse, and she lifted his T-shirt over his head.

They stood and undressed all the way, draping their clothes over the stall door, making it seem like a bedroom. The nighttime lights in the barn enhanced the ambience.

He lowered her to the blanket, using it as a bed. The straw beneath it was bumpy, but somehow warm and inviting, too. Everything seemed right yet wrong. Good yet bad. Libby wished that she'd never fallen in love with him. It would be so much easier if she could have left things the way they were. But to him, nothing had changed. He didn't know how she was feeling, and she wasn't going to tell him.

She noticed that her glass had tipped over, her cider spilling onto a corner of the blanket. Matt's glass was still upright.

"What are you looking at?" he asked.

"How my glass fell over but yours didn't."

"Maybe I'm just more careful than you are."

He definitely was, she thought. Not just with his cider, but with his heart. "I'd rather see yours spilled, too. I don't want you to be the only careful one."

"Whatever you say." He flung out his arm and knocked over his flute, sending cider pouring out of it. "Is that better?"

She nodded and pulled him down on top of her, biting and kissing and clawing, making marks on his skin. She wanted to brand him, to make him hers, if only for tonight.

"This might be our last time together," she said, trying to explain her frantic behavior. "We might not find the time to be alone again."

"I know." He pushed back against the pressure. "I'll do whatever you want, however you want it."

"Then do it fast." She wanted it quick and hard, to crash and burn, to shatter from the ache of loving him.

He used his fingers to stimulate her. He put his mouth on her, too, inciting slick, wet heat. She reacted to every sexy thing he did, arching her body, mewling and moaning.

When he put on protection and entered her, she knew there was no way out. No matter what pace he set, her heart spun like a battered pinwheel.

His stomach muscles tensed with every thrust. Immersed in the motion, she skimmed a hand down his abs. She lowered her fingers, dangerously close to where they were joined.

She kissed him, savoring the taste of his lips. He took her arms and lifted them above her head, pinning her in place. Libby gulped her next breath. She always got excited when he did that.

"Are you close?" he asked, his penetration strong and deep.

"Yes." She needed a release, to let it rush through her body.

Sweat beaded on his forehead. He was close, too. She knew he liked for them to come at the same time. She wanted to give him what he wanted. She longed to give him everything, even what he didn't want. Love, she thought.

Damnable love.

If only he could see the secret in her eyes. But he probably couldn't see anything through the blur of good, hard sex. Lust was written all over his deliciously handsome face.

He increased the rhythm, pulling her into the orgasm they both craved. When it happened, she shook and shivered, tumbling into a hopeless abyss.

In the moments that followed, he released her arms, but he didn't lift his body from hers. He breathed heavily against her ear, his chest rising and falling against hers.

Libby feared that she might cry, like the grieving widow he kept accusing her of being. Now that the sex was over, she needed to untangle her limbs from his, to free herself from the beautiful weight of him. Trying to break the connection, she said, "You're getting heavy."

He raised his head and rolled off her. "Sorry about that." He sat up. "I have to take care of the condom, anyway. Messy things."

She nodded, needing the reprieve. "We should probably get dressed, before the sun comes up."

"We've still got time. But I suppose you're right." He grabbed his clothes off the stall door and left her alone.

Libby got up and put her clothes on. Matt was gone a bit longer than she expected, but he was probably checking on the mare and her foal.

He returned, and she asked, "Are Annie and the baby all right?"

"They're fine." He angled his head. "Are you all right? You seem sort of anxious."

If he only knew. "I just want to get the stall cleaned up before any of your ranch hands get here." She gestured to the blanket, the cider bottle, the plastic glasses.

"That'll only take a minute."

"It's better to be safe than sorry."

"Sure. Okay." He balled up the blanket. "Are you going to take a nap after we get back to the house?"

"No. I'm going to stay up." She didn't see how she would be able to sleep.

"I'm staying up, too. I can't wait until everyone sees the foal."

She nodded, as if that was her first priority, too. But for now, all she wanted was to protect her heart from the ache that was tearing her apart. Nothing was ever going to be right in Libby's world again, not if she couldn't find a way to stop loving Matt.

After breakfast, Matt and Libby took Chance to see the foal. Debra decided to stay behind. She was going to meet them there later, with Matt's mom and Lester. Matt didn't mind. He was enjoying it either way.

He hoisted Chance up so he could see the foal over the stall door. Chance was being his usual wiggle-worm self, twisting and turning in Matt's arms.

Matt smiled and said, "You can help me name her."

The boy craned his neck. "Really? Truly? I can?"

"Absolutely. But since she's going to be registered with a quarter horse association, there are some guidelines we have to follow. We can only use a name that has a maximum of twenty characters. That includes letters, numbers and blank spaces. We can't use punctuation marks, either. Once we choose a name, I'll have to submit it to be sure there aren't any other horses with that exact name. If there are, then I'll have to change it up a bit."

Chance made a perplexed face. "That's a lot to think about."

"I know, but that's how it's done. Some people prefer to name their foal something that's composed of the sire's and dam's names. And some prefer to come up with something different, a name that sets the foal apart."

Chance looked even more perplexed. "I don't get it. What's a dam and a sire?"

"Oh, sorry." Matt had forgotten to define the lingo ahead of time. As easily as Chance had adapted to the ranch, he was still a city kid. "The sire is the father, and the dam is the mother."

Chance flashed a mischief-making grin. "Does that mean I can call my mom a dam, too?"

Matt couldn't help but laugh. Even Libby chuckled a little, before she shook her head and said, "Sorry, no. You can't call me that."

Matt was glad to see Libby smile. But she seemed distant. Ever since they'd made love earlier, she'd been behaving oddly. Even now, there was a glimmer of something unsettling in her eyes. Of course, he could be reading too much into it. They'd both been up all night, and sleep deprivation could do strange things to people. But he'd never been good at figuring women out, so he couldn't be sure.

"Who's the sire?" Chance asked, using the new term he'd learned. "Who's the foal's daddy?"

Matt replied, "His name is Promising Spirit. He's the stud that services my mares. Sometimes other people breed their mares to him, too."

"Why are you calling him a stud?" Chance scratched his head, punctuating his confusion. "I thought he was a sire."

"It's sort of the same thing, except that he's a sire after the foals are born and a stud before. He's also called a stallion. Male horses that aren't used for breeding are called geldings. Also, boy horses are known as colts and girls as fillies, but that's only when they're young. Baby horses in general are referred to as foals. When they're between one and two years old, they're called yearlings."

"Wow. That's a lot to remember."

"It's easy once you get used to it. It's also something every cowboy should know."

"Then I'm gonna learn it, for sure." Chance puffed up his chest. Pinned to his shirt was a tin star, a toy sheriff's badge that had come from the ranch's gift store. "I'm gonna be the best cowboy ever."

Matt smiled and glanced over at Libby to get her reaction, but she wasn't looking at him or listening to Chance. She was watching the mare and the foal. When she turned and caught Matt eyeing her, she returned his gaze with an uncomfortable start. She was definitely acting strange. He couldn't question her about it, at least not in front of her son. But she was confusing the hell out of Matt.

"Can we start working on names now?" Chance asked.

Matt redirected his focus. "Absolutely. I was thinking that we could give her something associated with both the sire's and dam's names."

The boy made one of his puzzled faces. "How come the dam is called Annie Oakley? That sounds like a person's name."

Matt explained, "Annie Oakley was a real person, and the horse was named after her. Annie was a sharpshooter in the Old West. She performed with Buffalo Bill's Wild West. It was a show that traveled around, sort of like a circus. She was married to a guy named Frank E. Butler, and he was a marksman, too. There was also a famous Indian who appeared in the show. His name was Sitting Bull. He was a great warrior in his day, and he and Annie became friends. He nicknamed her Little Sure Shot."

Chance appeared to be taking it all in, listening intently to Matt's tale. After a minute of silence, he asked, "Are you from the same tribe as Sitting Bull?"

"No. He was Lakota Sioux, and I'm Cherokee. But I've always admired him."

"What did you say his nickname for Annie was?"

"Little Sure Shot."

"Can we name the foal something like that, except add something from the sire's name, too?"

Matt grinned. This kid was a natural. "What a great idea." He tossed out some combinations. "How about Little Spirit Shot? Or we could shorten it to Lil Spirit Shot? Or even Lil Shot of Spirit?"

"I like Lil Spirit Shot." Chance beamed, as bright and shiny as the badge he wore. "That's my favorite."

"Then that'll be our first choice. I'll check the registry and see if it's available, and we'll go from there."

"Okay." Chance turned toward Libby. "I just helped name the foal, Mom. Do you like what I picked?"

"It's wonderful. You're good with horses, in all sorts of ways." She smiled proudly at her son.

But Matt noticed that she still seemed out of sorts. He could see the faraway look that remained in her eyes, leaving him as confused as ever.

# Eleven

Libby couldn't handle being around Matt, especially when he kept asking her if something was wrong. Her only solution was to say that she didn't feel well. So over the next few days, she faked being sick. Fatigue, chills, body aches: whatever she could drum up.

Her mom had been entertaining Chance, allowing Libby to rest. But she wasn't resting. Mostly she just stayed in her room, steeped in anxiety and hiding from Matt. The only time she emerged was when he was at work.

Today, Mom brought her breakfast, entering her room with a food tray. There was even a little daisy on it.

"The orange juice is fresh," her mother said. "Matt thought the vitamin C might help. Oh, and the flower is from Chance. He picked it from the yard."

Feeling horribly guilty, Libby glanced at the meal. There were poached eggs and whole wheat toast, too. "That was sweet of them."

Mom placed the tray on the nightstand. "Are you feeling any better?"

"Not really." Libby was in bed, with the covers pulled up to her neck. She didn't know how she was ever going to feel normal again.

Her mom sat on the edge of the mattress. "You need to eat."

"I'm not very hungry." At least she wasn't faking that. She didn't have much of an appetite.

"Maybe just try the toast." Her mom handed her a slice.

Libby sat up and nibbled on it. She sipped the juice, too.

Her mom wasn't dressed. She still had on her pajamas. But unlike Libby, her hair was neatly combed, and she'd put on a smidgen of lipstick.

"Matt is taking care of Chance today," she said.

"Really? Matt's not working?" Libby assumed he would be leaving soon.

"He took the day off to spend it with Chance. They're going to a children's storytelling event on the ranch, where actors are portraying characters from the Old West. Chance is excited about it. There's going to be a woman dressed as Annie Oakley, and he wants to get her autograph."

"Oh, that's so cute." But it heightened Libby's guilt. Cheating the way she was, lying about having flu symptoms. She should be attending the event, too.

"Matt actually plans to take the rest of the week off. He wants to spend as much time with Chance as he can before we leave. I think he wants to keep an eye on you, too, and make sure you recover." Her mom's gaze bore into hers. "But you're not really sick, are you?"

Stunned by the accurate accusation, Libby tightened her hold on her glass. "Why would you say that?"

"Because you did this when you were little. Just once, when you were in kindergarten. Don't you remember?"

"No. What exactly did I do?"

"You pretended to be sick so you didn't have to go to school. There was a boy you liked, but he didn't like you back, and you were too upset to see him."

Suddenly Libby had a vague recollection of having a crush on a kid who made stupid faces at her. "Was his name Paul?"

"I don't know. It could have been. But the important part is that I convinced you to go to school the next day, to be brave and challenge your fears. And you did. You paraded into that classroom with your head held high, and you never backed away from anyone or anything again."

"This is different."

"No, it isn't. Whatever is wrong between you and Matt, you have to confront it. I can tell that you have feelings for him. I suspected it all along. I just didn't think it was my place to say anything until now."

So she hadn't fooled her mother, not one little bit. "Does Julie know, too?"

"She didn't notice it right away, but the more time she spent around you and Matt, the more she thought that something might be going on. That you two were romantically involved."

"I'm in love with him, Mom."

"Have you told him how you feel?"

"No." She put her juice aside. Her fingers were going numb from the iron grip she had on holding it. "But what's the point? He's not going to be able to cope with it, and he's not going to love me back."

"How do you know what he can or can't or will or won't do?"

"We made a deal not to fall in love."

Her mother furrowed her brow. "Was that his idea?"

"It was mine. But he readily agreed to it. He wants to get married again someday, but not to a widow. He thinks I'm too much like his ex-wife."

"Are you?"

"No. She wasn't ready to love again. She only married Matt for comfort. But I love him as much as I loved Becker."

"Then stand up for yourself and prove it."

"I don't know if I can."

"So you're not even going to try? That's not like you, Libby. You've always gone after what you wanted."

"Yes, and look at what I've lost in my life. How much more pain am I supposed to bear?"

"I'm so sorry." Her mom reached for her hand and held it. "But you're already hurting over Matt. Not telling him that you love him isn't taking the pain away, either. So just think about talking to him."

"I'll consider it. But I'm not making any promises." She wasn't a kindergartener being prodded to go back to school. And Matt wasn't a boy who'd been making stupid faces at her. He was the man she loved, on the heels of losing the husband she loved.

"I'm going to leave you alone now." Her mom stood and smoothed her pajamas. "But how about if I open the blinds? You shouldn't be sitting here in the dark."

Libby wanted to be immersed in darkness, to wallow in her pain, but she let her mother open the blinds anyway, allowing the sun to come spilling into the room.

Drenching her in light.

The following day, Libby decided to do it. To talk to Matt. To be brave. Her mom was right about confronting her feelings for him. Hiding out in bed wasn't helping.

Since he was at work, she texted him. She kept it short and simple, telling him that she was no longer ill and needed to see him. She suggested meeting at his cabin later. She chose that location because his house was too crowded, with her mom and Chance being there. She wanted as much privacy as possible.

He replied that he could be there at six and that he was looking forward to seeing her. He even included a happy face emoji in his text. He obviously thought this was going to be a nice get-together.

She took a long, hot shower and fixed herself up. Attired in a summer blouse and slim-fitting jeans, with her hair decorated with two shiny jeweled barrettes, she tried to look bright and breezy and confident. Like the happy face he'd sent.

But deep down, where it hurt, she was prepared for an emotional disaster. She didn't expect Matt to take her news lightly. If anything, he would probably panic and pull away from her. But at least he would know that she loved him. At this point, she just wanted him to know the truth.

She arrived at the cabin at a quarter to six. She didn't have a key, so she sat on the porch and waited.

Time passed slowly...one minute ticking into the next. When Matt's truck appeared, gravel crunching beneath its tires, her pulse jumped like a scared rabbit.

Could she do this? Could she say what she'd come here to say? Yes, she told herself. No matter how difficult it was, she could do it. She stood, determined to follow through.

Matt parked and climbed out of his truck. She admired the denim-clad, dusty-booted way in which he moved. The ultimate rancher, she thought. The long, tall country boy.

"Hey, Libby." He adjusted the brim of his hat. "You sure look pretty."

"Thank you." She reminded herself to breathe. He was nearing the porch steps.

When he reached the top, he said, "I'm so glad you're feeling better. I've been worried about you."

"I have a confession to make," she said, wanting to get it over with quickly. "I didn't have the flu. Or anything else anyone could catch." If her lovesick condition had been contagious, she would've infected him purposely, making him love her, making him want her for the rest of his life.

"So what was wrong with you?"

"I was just run-down." That was the easiest and fastest way for her to explain it until she gave him the full story. "But I'm stronger now." Or as strong as the moment would allow.

He jangled his keys and flashed what could only be described as a kissable smile. If only she could grab him and kiss him.

"Is this some sort of secret date?" he asked. "Are you going to take me inside and do wild things to me?"

"That's not why I'm here." But it was tempting, so darned tempting. "I need to tell you something."

His smile faded. "Is it about the book?"

"What? No." Kirby's biography was the last thing on her mind. And that troubled her, too. She'd lost sight of her goals, of convincing Matt to participate in the book. Yet that was the reason she'd come to the ranch, and now she'd gotten sidetracked by her feelings for him. "This isn't about your dad." She shifted her stance, her boots sounding on the wooden planks beneath her feet. "Can we go inside? I just want to say what I have to say before I lose my nerve, and I don't want to talk out here."

He unlocked the door. "You're starting to freak me out, Libby."

And it was only going to get worse, she thought.

They went into the cabin, and she made a beeline for the sofa, needing to sit. He took a chair across from her, as if he was leery of sitting next to her. He was already pulling away, and she hadn't even told him what was going on yet.

She took a big, noisy breath, and he watched her with a taut expression.

She said, "I broke our deal, Matt. I know we agreed not to fall in love, but I'm in love with you. Irrecoverably, frighteningly in love with you."

He just stared at her, as if she was speaking a foreign language he didn't understand.

Libby glanced up at the ceiling, praying for divine intervention. But she didn't get any.

Matt finally spoke, his voice rattled and gruff. "I can't believe you…"

She couldn't fault him for his disbelief, for not being able to form the rest of his words. She said, "I didn't mean to blindside you. I blindsided myself, too. I stayed in bed, pretending to be sick, not knowing how to face this. But I couldn't hide from you anymore. I had to tell you."

"What do you want from me?" He tensed as if he'd been sucker punched. "What is it that I'm supposed to do?"

"I'm not asking you to do anything."

He gave her a bewildered look. "You love me, but you don't want to be with me?"

"No, I do. I mean, I…" Now she was struggling to find her words. She took a second to compose her next sentence. "I would spend the rest of my life with you if

I could." She wasn't going to lie about that. She had to express how she felt, to let honesty be her guide.

"So in your estimation, how would that work?" His voice was still rattled, still wrecked with emotion. "Chance is still so hung up on his father. If I married you, I couldn't replace Becker for you or your son." He stood and moved away from his chair. "Would you expect me to exist in Becker's shadow, like I did with Greg?"

"It wouldn't be like that." She remained seated, watching him pace. "It wouldn't be a competition between you and Becker. You'd be my husband, the man I'd be devoting my heart to. And you'd be Chance's father in every way."

"But Becker's memory would still be there. I don't think I can do it, Libby. I can't go down that road again. If I let myself love you, it would tear me apart."

"If you *let* yourself love me?" She leaned forward, her heart teetering on the edge of pain, of hope, of determination. "That sounds like you're capable of falling in love with me, too."

He stopped pacing, stalled in the middle of the room, staring at her, as if the walls were threatening to close in on him. "What difference does it make? It would never work between us."

"Maybe it could, if you let it." She ached for him, for herself, for Chance, for the life they could have together. "I understand what you went through with Sandy and the twins, but it wouldn't be the same." She softly added, "I love you the way a wife should love a husband. And Becker would be happy for me if I married you. He would want me to have a full and joyous life, and he would want you to become Chance's father. Becker wouldn't overshadow you—"

"I'm sorry," he interrupted. "If we tried it and it didn't

work out, it would be devastating for all of us." He didn't move from the spot where he stood. He seemed riveted to the floor, waiting for the walls to crush him, to break him in two. "I can't put myself in a position like that. Or you or Chance."

And she couldn't sit here and beg him to love her, if Matt loving her was even possible. "You're right. If you can't love me back, it won't work between us. I need to go on with my life, and you go on with yours."

"That's what we agreed on when we started our affair."

"I know." That was the bargain they'd struck, the deal she'd broken. Her eyes turned watery. "But when the foal was born, I imagined having my next child with you. And it scared me. It scared me so much. But I still wanted it."

"Don't cry." He took a cautious step toward her. "Please, don't cry."

She stood, warding him off, trying to keep him away from her. "I need to get some air."

She turned and headed for the door, rushing onto the porch and bursting into the tears he'd asked her not to cry.

Matt's head was reeling. How was he supposed to think clearly, knowing that Libby loved him; that she wanted to marry him; that she longed to have his babies and give Chance little brothers or sisters?

And now she was outside, probably bawling her eyes out. Deep, sobbing tears, he thought, like the kind Sandy used to cry.

Matt couldn't leave her out there alone. He couldn't bear to see her hurting more than she already was. He was hurting, too, picturing the life she'd described. But it was a false dream, a fairy tale that couldn't possibly come true.

He grabbed a box of tissues from the bathroom and went onto the patio. She sat on the porch steps, with her head in her hands. He sat next to her, and she lifted her head. Her face was covered in tears.

He handed her the tissues. "I thought you might need these."

"Thank you." She dabbed at her eyes. "I haven't cried like this since Becker died." She sniffed through her tears. "I feel like someone is dying all over again."

So did Matt. The death of the kind of man he wished he could be. "You deserve someone who can make you happy, who can give you what you need, who doesn't have my hang-ups."

She sniffed again, her voice soft, sad. "You're encouraging me to find someone else someday?"

"Yes." But when he envisioned her with another man, he got a knot in the center of his chest, clawing its way to his heart. It was torture because the fear of keeping her, of making her his bride, incited the same tangled feeling. "I'm going to go away for the rest of the week." He couldn't stay at the ranch. He needed to escape.

"Where will you go?"

Anywhere, nowhere. "I'll do a road trip." He would simply drive to wherever his aimlessness took him. "You can keep staying at my house while I'm gone."

She clutched the tissue box to her chest. "That isn't necessary."

"It is to me. I want you to stay there." He waited an agonizing beat before he said, "When I go back to the house to grab some things, I'll tell Chance and your mom that I have to go away on business."

"There's no point in creating a story for my mother. I already told her that I love you."

He winced. "Does my mother know?"

"Not the whole story. Not yet. But she suspected that something was going on between us, so I'm sure my mom will tell her."

"They're going to think I'm an idiot." And he was, no doubt, for letting Libby and her son go. But he'd already tried creating that type of family with Sandy and the twins, and he'd failed miserably at it. So how would it be any different this time?

"No one is going to think badly of you." She blew out a sigh. "And you don't have to leave town, either. I can pack up and go to Kirby's early."

"No." He couldn't stand the thought of her spending extra time at his father's. He already hated that she was going there. "Just stay at my house, please. Let Chance enjoy the ranch for a few more days."

"He's going to miss you."

"I'll miss him, too." Suddenly he felt as if he was abandoning Libby and Chance in the way Kirby had abandoned him. But he couldn't blame his dad. Matt was destroying his relationship with Libby on his own. "I really suck at this."

Her breaths came out choppy. "I obviously do, too."

"No, you don't." He wanted to reach for her, to hold her, to soothe her. But he didn't have the right to take her in his arms. Still, he moved a bit closer, trying to inhale the scent of her skin.

She reacted by scooting farther away from him. But he understood that she was only trying to protect herself from the guy who was breaking her heart.

She said, "We need to go back to the house and get the rest of this over with."

"Yes, we do." There was nothing else left to do, except separate from each other for good.

* * *

It was over.

Matt had left hours ago, and now Libby was suffering through self-imposed bouts of romantic torture, the pain of wandering through his house, of touching everything he'd touched.

She gazed out the living room window, wishing he would come back. But his truck didn't reappear out of the blue. The driveway was as empty as her soul.

"Are you sure you're not sick no more?" Chance asked.

She turned and looked at her son. He was playing a video game that Matt had given him, where the players participated in rodeo events. At the moment, it was bull riding.

"I'm doing okay," she said.

"You don't seem better." He leaned into the game, his gaze fixed on the giant TV screen. "Are you sad 'cause Matt had to go away?"

Her heart clenched. Her six-year-old was far more observant than she'd expected him to be. Everyone was, it seemed, when it came to her and Matt. "Yes."

"Me, too. I wish he was still here." The virtual cowboy Chance was maneuvering fell off the bull and scrambled to his feet. He put the machine on pause. "Wanna play? I can teach you the way Matt taught me. It might make you feel better."

"Thanks, honey. But I'll just watch you." She sat beside him. "You know I'm not a gamer."

He didn't restart it. "Matt's one of my all-time favorite people."

"Mine, too." She wanted to stay in Texas forever, on this ranch, in this house, with Matt by her side.

"He said I can call him if I ever need anything."

"He did?" Her heart clenched again. "That was nice of him." Matt hadn't made the same offer to her. But his relationship with her was far more complex than the one he'd built with Chance.

"I'd have to use your phone if I ever called him. Or Nana's or somebody else's. Unless you want to buy me one."

She shook her head, being the responsible parent she was supposed to be. "Nice try. But you're not getting a smartphone, at least not for a while."

He made a face. Then he asked, "Are we still going to Kirby Talbot's house after we leave here?"

"Yes, we're still going. He's going to sing you the song you're named after, remember?"

"Oh, yeah." Chance grinned. "That'll be fun. Do you like having him as your book boss?"

"I absolutely do. He's nice to work for. But I also have an editor who's involved in it. So I guess you could say that I have two book bosses." Of course, she couldn't tell Chance that Kirby was Matt's father or how pivotal their past was to the project. Her son was too young to be dragged into something like that.

Libby reflected on her job and the decision she'd made. Considering everything else that had happened, she'd given up on trying to interview Matt. She couldn't force him to be part of his father's biography any more than she could force him to love her.

"Are there going to be any kids at Kirby's for me to play with?" Chance asked.

"Not that I know of." Kirby didn't have any grand-children. None of his sons, including Matt, had fathered any children. "But you and Nana are going to go sight-seeing in Nashville while Kirby and I work on the book. Nana is going to take you to Memphis, too, on a big fancy bus." Her mother had already booked the tour. "She wants to see Graceland. That's where Elvis Presley used to live."

"I wish Matt was going to do all of that stuff with us."

So did Libby. But again, that wasn't something she could discuss with her son. She quickly asked, "Are you hungry? I can fix you some lunch."

"Okay." He restarted the game.

Libby went into the kitchen and opened the fridge. She removed the sandwich fixings, trying to keep her restless mind off Matt. But it wasn't working. He was all she could think about.

She fumbled with the food, struggling to make a simple sandwich. This wasn't the time to dwell on unrequited love. But she couldn't seem to shake it from her shattered heart.

Libby was lost without Matt.

# Twelve

When Matt returned to his house, Libby and her family were long gone. There was nothing from Libby. No notes. No mementos. But he hadn't expected as much. Chance, however, had left him a brightly colored crayon drawing on the fridge. It depicted a stick figure of Chance roping red-eyed Stanley with a much taller stick figure of Matt standing nearby. The kid had captured them with happy expressions on their faces.

Matt was anything but happy. Being on the road, driving into an endless horizon, sleeping in off-the-beaten-path motels had been lonely as hell. But this was worse. His house felt like a big, empty echo. But that was the reason he'd stopped living here before. After Sandy and the girls had left, he couldn't stand being here alone.

And now he was alone again. But it wasn't Sandy and the twins he was missing. It was Libby and Chance.

He went into his bedroom and tossed his overnight

bag on the bed. Going back to the cabin wouldn't do him any good. That location would only remind him of Libby, too.

She was everywhere: in the air, in the flowers, in the trees, in the hills that surrounded the ranch, in the sparkle of sunlight that seeped through his windows. But mostly, she was inside him.

Sweet, beautiful Libby.

He'd rejected her out of fear. Afraid that if he married her, their union would fail. That he would be reliving the turmoil with Sandy. But Libby had kept telling him that she wasn't Sandy.

And she was right. They were two completely different women, with separate feelings, with opposite needs. Libby loved him, truly loved him, in a way that Sandy never could have.

Libby longed to be the girl of his dreams, to become his forever wife, to share her son with him, to have more children together. Yet Matt had been so fixated on his fears, he'd walked away from the best thing that had ever happened to him.

Suddenly, it was so damned clear. And so were his feelings. He loved Libby, too. He absolutely loved her.

Libby had already explained how she felt. She even told him that Becker would be happy for her if she and Matt became a couple. That he would want them to be together.

Clearly, Becker had been a kind and caring man, deserving of the family he had. And now Matt wanted to follow in his footsteps. If he married Libby, he wouldn't be competing with Becker. He would be taking over where Becker left off. It was a blessing that was being given to him.

Matt hadn't been able to soothe Sandy's soul because

they didn't belong together. But Matt and Libby clicked. She was right for him. Someday, maybe, Sandy would find someone who was right for her, too, who could help her make peace with losing Greg. Or maybe she would have to travel that road alone, as Libby had done before she'd met Matt. But one thing Matt knew for certain was that he loved Libby as much as she loved him.

He closed his eyes, feeling free and strong. But when he reopened them and caught his reflection in a mirror from across the room, he still saw a troubled version of himself.

Because there was another obstacle, he thought, one that had been there all along. Matt's father.

How was he going to start over with Libby if he didn't start over with Kirby, if he didn't give his old man a chance?

Matt cursed to himself. Could he do it? Could he let bygones be bygones? Could he give his father an open invitation into his life?

Libby believed that he needed to make peace with his dad. She saw Kirby as a man who deserved to be forgiven, who wanted to make up for the past.

But Matt still hated him. He still wanted to rage at his dad for the pain he caused. But was that the example he wanted to set for Chance? Or the future children he and Libby could have? Did he want to deliver a message of anger and hate?

No, he thought. He didn't. If he was going to create a strong, solid family of his own, then he had to let Kirby be part of it, too. No matter how difficult it was, Matt didn't have a choice, not if he intended to be with Libby.

No doubt about it, Matt was going to have to book a trip to Nashville to see Libby, to tell her how he felt, to open himself up to her. He was going to have to see his father, too, and dig down deep to forgive him.

But first he needed to take some time to shop for an engagement ring. When he proposed to Libby, he wanted to do it with the biggest, fanciest, shiniest diamond he could find.

Something as dazzling as the woman he loved.

Libby stared at the mind-blowing text she'd just received from Matt. He was in Nashville, and he wanted to know if she would come to his hotel room. So they could talk privately. So he could say something extremely important to her. But it had to be in person. He couldn't do it over the phone.

She agreed to see him. But while she was getting ready, she worried herself sick. Why had he traveled all this way? And why was it so imperative that it be in person? Was it about the book? Or was it much more personal?

Was it possible that he loved her, too, that those were the words he was going to say? She hoped and prayed they were. But was she being unrealistic? Longing for something that wasn't going to happen? The last time she saw Matt, he insisted that it would never work between them.

She couldn't talk to anyone else about it. She wouldn't dare say something to Kirby. He didn't even know that she and Matt had been lovers, and this certainly wasn't the time to tell him. Libby couldn't talk to her mom, either. She and Chance were on their overnight trip to Memphis, getting their Elvis on. No way was she going to disturb them with a high-anxiety phone call.

Alone in her thoughts, she glanced around the luxurious guesthouse where she was staying. Kirby's enormous compound offered a parklike setting with a stream that ran through the middle. He lived in the main house, a mansion he'd renovated to fit his needs. He'd also built extra houses for family and friends, along with a recording studio. Kirby had everything he wanted, except a relationship with Matt.

Once again, Libby fretted about seeing Matt and what he was going to say. If she pinned her hopes on him loving her and she was wrong, she would fall apart all over again.

She finished getting dressed in a lacy sundress and gold sandals and climbed into her rental car. Matt's hotel was actually quite close. She assumed he'd chosen it because of its location, making it more convenient for them to meet. It was a newly renovated resort, and he was staying in room 614.

Once Libby arrived, she took the elevator to the sixth floor. It felt like the longest ride of her life, with other people stopping on other floors. Her stomach was overrun with butterflies.

When she exited the elevator, she followed the room number signs. Matt's room was near the end of the hallway. She took a deep breath and knocked on his door.

He answered with an anxious smile, looking as nervous as she felt. But he looked stylish, too. He wore a swanky Western shirt, crisply laundered jeans and freshly polished boots.

"Come in." He stepped back.

She crossed the threshold, and he closed the door. They stood a bit awkwardly, with neither of them moving forward to initiate a hug. But they hadn't hugged goodbye the last time they'd seen each other, either. They hadn't touched since the night they'd made love in the barn, and that seemed like an eternity ago.

"This is a nice place," she said, trying to break the ice. His suite was artfully designed, with a sitting room, kitchen, dining cove, bathroom and bedroom. The balcony overlooked a big, flourishing garden.

"Do you want to go out there?" He gestured to the balcony.

Libby nodded, and they proceeded outside. She was grateful for the fresh air. She was having trouble catching her breath.

They sat at a mosaic-topped table, and she said, "The garden is beautiful."

"You're the one who's beautiful." He traced the pattern on the table with restless hands. "I'm so sorry that I hurt you. That I turned you away. I missed you so badly when we were apart. I came home to an empty house and knew what a mistake I'd made."

She perched on the edge of her chair. Was he heading toward the admission of love she'd been hoping and praying to hear? And if he was, could she be certain that he meant it? That he wasn't going to hurt her again? Or reject her if things got too difficult?

He continued, his voice deep and clear, "I don't want to live the rest of my life without you. I love you, Libby."

*There it was. He'd said it.* But she hesitated to respond.

He nervously asked, "Did I do something wrong? Have your feelings for me changed? Please, Libby, tell me what you're thinking."

"I'm just a little scared. Worried about all of the stuff you said before."

"I was scared, too, when I said those things. But once I came home to an empty house, I searched my soul and worked through my fears. I love you. I honestly do. And I don't want anything to ever keep us apart again."

She blinked back tears and reached across the table for his hand. "I love you, too. You're all I've been thinking about."

His fingertips connected with hers. "I should have listened to you from the start. You were right about everything, about how different you are from Sandy, about how I needed to stop comparing you to her."

She searched his gaze, losing herself in those whiskey eyes. Just holding his hand was electrifying. "So you're never going to compare me to her again?"

"No. And I'm not going to punish you for staying close to Becker's memory. I want Chance to grow up with happy thoughts about his father. But I want to become Chance's daddy, too."

Matt stood and came around to her chair. He got down on bended knee, and the tears she'd been banking began to fall.

He removed a small jewelry box from his pocket. Inside was a halo ring, a gold band encrusted with multicolored stones and set with a big, bright, round-cut diamond, surrounded by even more diamonds.

He softly asked, "Will you marry me?"

She nodded, her voice cracking when she replied, "Yes. A thousand times, yes."

He put the ring on her finger, and it fit perfectly. Everything was perfect, she thought, so much more than she could have imagined.

"It's absolutely gorgeous," she said. "How did you know my size?"

"I didn't. I guessed what it was."

"You guessed right."

He came to his feet. "Because I've been memorizing you, so I have a detailed picture in my mind."

She stood and kissed him. His mouth was warm

against hers. So was his body. Those big strong arms held her tenderly close. She'd been memorizing him, too.

Once the kiss ended, he said, "I'm going to take this as far as I can go. I'm going to participate in the book, and I'm going to do my damnedest to make to peace with Kirby, to find the power to forgive him."

She started. "Oh, my God. You are?"

"I can't keep letting the pain from my childhood fester. Not if I want to be the kind of man our kids can be proud of."

He couldn't have said anything more right, more perfect. "Our kids? As in plural?"

"You said that you wanted to have a baby with me." He nuzzled her cheek. "But I want to wait until after we're married. I want to do this the traditional way."

She nuzzled him right back. "That works for me. We can plan everything just right. We can have the ceremony on your ranch."

"With everyone we love there. You can invite Becker's family, if you want to. That would be nice for Chance, wouldn't it?"

This proposal kept getting better and better. "It would be amazing for him to have all of us together in one place. Thank you so much for thinking of him."

"He's going to be my son. I want what's best for him."

"You're just what he needs, Matt." She couldn't have asked for a better father for her child. "You're what I need, too."

"We're going to be a family, Libby, for the rest of our lives. And if you need to spend more time at Kirby's to finish the book, that's okay, too. I'm not going to stand in your way." He swept her up and carried her inside.

She wrapped her arms around his neck. Matt's support meant everything to her.

He hauled her straight to the bedroom, deposited her on the bed and removed her sandals. "Stay here. I'm going to fix us a special drink."

She felt giddy. She even wiggled her toes. "I'm not going anywhere."

He left, and she waited for him, with the diamonds he'd given her glittering on her finger. To Libby, the ring was a symbol of her future, of her shiny new life with Matt. She was glad that he'd chosen something so bright and colorful.

He returned in his bare feet, with two cocktail glasses rimmed with marshmallow fluff and crushed-up pieces of graham crackers. The drinks themselves were a creamy mocha color. He got into bed and handed her one.

She smiled. "A s'mores martini, I presume?"

"Yes, ma'am. Today is August tenth. National S'mores Day. I figured it would be a great day to get engaged."

He'd obviously skipped the celebration on the ranch to come here and be with her. "Maybe we can choose this as our wedding date, too, for next summer. We can combine it with the party you always have at the ranch."

"A chocolate-themed wedding?" He clinked his glass with hers. "It doesn't get any sweeter than that."

She sipped her martini and moaned. The flavor was rich and smooth and sexy. "What's in this?"

"Marshmallow vodka and chocolate liqueur. It's as fun to make as it is to drink."

"Do you have to shake it in one of those glamorous cocktail shakers?"

"Yep." He waggled his eyebrows. "It's very James Bond."

After they consumed every delicious drop, they rolled over the bed, kissing and touching and peeling off each other's clothes. They both had marshmallow fluff all over their lips. She wasn't sure what Bond would think of that.

But Libby loved it. She was naked with the cowboy of her dreams, and they had the sweetest, most romantic, most erotic sex possible. For now nothing mattered but being together. Just the two of them, making up for lost time with a lifetime of commitment between them.

# Thirteen

Matt entered his father's mansion with Libby by his side. It was surreal, being in the house where Kirby lived, where Matt's brothers had grown up. The entire compound was as spectacular as he always imagined it would be. As a kid, he used to fantasize about coming here.

There was a sweeping staircase, hardwood floors and windows at every turn. It was an old plantation-style house with gold records lining the walls. Matt wasn't surprised that Kirby had them prominently displayed or that they were one of the first things you saw when you went inside.

His dad was expecting him. Matt had called Kirby from the hotel, giving him a condensed version of what was going on. That Libby and Matt were a couple. That Matt was going to participate in the book. That he was accepting Kirby's offer to get to know each other again.

Kirby's maid, who introduced herself as June, escorted Matt and Libby to the parlor. They waited for Kirby there. Libby sat on a velvet settee, but Matt was too anxious to sit. He stood tall and straight, his gaze fixed on the double doors. They were open, with an extravagant view of the foyer.

Someone soon appeared, but it wasn't Kirby. It was June again, bringing in a pitcher of sweet tea and three tall glasses.

After June left, Matt turned to look at Libby. She sent him a reassuring smile. But Matt was still anxious.

He said, "You'd think my dad would have already been here, waiting for us, instead of us waiting for him."

"He's probably as nervous as you are."

"Either that or he just wants to make a grand entrance."

Libby poured herself a glass of tea. "He is a showman. But this is a big day for the two of you. Are you sure you don't want to meet with him alone? I can go to the guesthouse where I've been staying and you can text me when the meeting is over."

"No way. I want you here." She was his inspiration, his lover, his friend, his fiancée—the person who'd helped him reach this point in his life. "I couldn't do this without you."

She nodded, and they both went silent.

Kirby finally came through the doorway, with his signature black clothes and country-star swagger. But he didn't speak. He just stared at Matt.

Matt stared back. He'd seen recent photos and videos of his dad on TV, in magazines and on the internet. He knew Kirby had aged and that his hair and beard were now threaded with gray. But seeing him in person created a gut-wrenching feeling. Matt wanted to turn and walk away. But he squared his shoulders and said, "Hey, Dad," instead.

Kirby moved closer to him. "Damn. Look at you. It's been so long since I've seen you. I might not even recognize you if it wasn't for your eyes."

Nearly two decades had passed since their last encounter. Matt was bound to change after all of that time. "I grew up."

"I'll say." There was an expression of awe on Kirby's face. "You're as tall as me."

"And just as ornery," Matt said. He couldn't help but throw that out there.

His old man smiled and reached out to hug him. Matt tensed for a moment, but he thought about the future, about his life with Libby, and he relaxed. He'd promised himself he was going to make this work with his dad. No more hatred. No more anger.

"I'm so sorry for what I did to you," Kirby said. "You deserved so much better. Please forgive me."

"I do forgive you." Matt was ready to move forward, to be Kirby Talbot's son. The hug ended, and Matt stepped back, needing to catch his breath. "But I'm going to be honest in the book. If I tell my side of the story, then I need to tell it truthfully."

"That's what I want you to do. I wouldn't expect any less from you."

Matt could feel Libby watching them. He glanced her way, and she smiled at him. She'd been smiling at him all day, making him feel strong and secure.

Nonetheless, Matt said to Kirby, "I'm not thrilled about how the press is going to hound me once they find out I'm your son."

His dad nodded. "I understand. It's not easy being in the public eye. Maybe we can do some interviews together. That will take some of the pressure off you. We might even want to consider making the announcement before the book is released. I can talk to the publisher about it, and they can work with my publicist on scheduling the interviews."

"Sure. We can do it that way. Promoting the book ahead of time will probably get people more interested in reading it." For Libby's sake, Matt wanted his father's biography to be a success.

Kirby shifted his feet. His boots were adorned with sterling silver tips. He'd always worn fancy garb, on and off stage. Matt was just glad that he wasn't hiding behind a pair of sunglasses, the way he used to do when Matt was a kid.

"We're going to have to arrange a meeting between you and your brothers," Kirby said. "Neither of them is in town right now. Tommy is on tour, and Brandon is away on business. But they both want to meet you."

"I know. Libby told me. She's been championing all of this since the beginning."

Kirby shot Libby a superstar grin. "And now you're together." He turned his attention back to Matt. "I'm happy you found each other, and that I could be part of it. Without the book, you two wouldn't have met."

*Really?* Matt thought. His old man was taking credit for being their matchmaker? "That's quite an ego you got there, Dad."

Kirby chuckled. "That's what everyone who knows me says about me. That I'm the most egotistical guy around. But I'll work on being more humble."

"That's going to be difficult for you." Matt's father wouldn't know humble if bit him in the balls. But Matt was going to accept his arrogant old man, faults and all. "I appreciate the effort, though."

Kirby went serious. "I want you to be proud of me, son."

Matt responded with affection. "I'm proud of this moment, of what we've accomplished so far. I can tell how much this reunion matters to you. It's important to me, too."

"Thank you. Having you become part of my family means everything to me. We have so much catching up to do, so many gaps to fill. I hope you'll be inviting me to your wedding."

"I definitely will." He wasn't going to leave his dad or his brothers or anyone else out of it. "But you'll have to come to Texas, to my ranch, because that where it's going to be."

"I'll be there with bells on." Kirby waved Libby over, bringing her into the fold. "Come show me the ring this boy put on your finger. It's already blinding me from here."

She hopped off the settee and dashed over to them. When she held out her hand, Kirby whistled. "That's some rock." He smiled at Matt. "You did a wonderful job, with the ring, with the woman. You're going to be a hell of a husband, and a damned fine father to her son, too." Kirby rocked on his heels. "And how amazing is it that he was named after one of my songs?"

Matt nearly laughed. There went his dad's ego again. But it did seem to make a poetic kind of sense. "Especially since Chance is going to become your grandson."

"I know, right? And what a great kid he is."

"He's the best." Matt couldn't wait to tell Chance that he and Libby were getting married. Chance would also have to be told that Kirby was Matt's father. But for now, Matt wanted to take it one day at a time.

Libby leaned into him, and he put his arm around her,

holding her close. Kirby smiled at them in a paternal way, and Matt thanked the Creator for bringing peace to his life. And love, he thought, so much love and support from Libby. Matt continued to hold her, grateful for the journey that had just begun.

\* \* \* \* \*